PRAISE FOR LESLIE ARCHER

"Defies and exceeds expectations."

—Lisa Scottoline, *New York Times* bestselling author

"The expression *page-turner* was coined to describe exactly what Archer offers."

—Bookreporter

"Leslie Archer is a born storyteller."

—Jill Dawson, author of *The Great Lover*

"Fascinating and unexpected. Current, smart, and completely involving."

—Gregg Olsen, #1 *New York Times* bestselling author

"An author with a distinct voice."

—Robert Dugoni, *New York Times* bestselling author

UNTIL
WE ARE
LOST

ALSO BY LESLIE ARCHER

The Girl at the Border

UNTIL WE ARE

A NOVEL

LOST

LESLIE ARCHER

AUTHOR OF *THE GIRL AT THE BORDER*

LAKE UNION
PUBLISHING

Text copyright © 2021 by Six String Theory Inc.
All rights reserved.

Published by Lake Union Publishing, Seattle
www.apub.com

Amazon, the Amazon logo, and Lake Union Publishing are trademarks of Amazon.com, Inc., or its affiliates.

ISBN-13: 9781542019439 (hardcover)
ISBN-10: 1542019435 (hardcover)

ISBN-13: 9781542017909 (paperback)
ISBN-10: 1542017904 (paperback)

Cover design by Kimberly Glyder

Printed in the United States of America

First edition

Not until we are lost do we begin
to understand ourselves.
—Henry David Thoreau

PART 1
THE CURTAIN

I have lost confidence in myself.

—Robert Louis Stevenson,
The Strange Case of Dr. Jekyll and Mr. Hyde

1

New York City—Present Day

I t started the night Hickory was shot to death. Hickory, my dog."
Tara looks forlornly at Dr. Christie Lind. "Like a, I don't know, a
premonition of doom."

Dr. Lind watches her, silently, patiently. As is her therapeutic wont
in difficult situations, when a client appears stuck, a smile appears
on her face—soft, warm, comforting. Impossible to misconstrue.
"Premonition of what? Can you say precisely?"

Tara nods. "A week after I found Hickory, my mother died. Three
weeks after that, our house burned down with my father in it."

If it shocks Lind, she doesn't show it. After the merest hesitation,
she says only, "I'm curious as to why you waited until now to tell me
about the untimely deaths of your parents."

I'll tell you why, Tara thinks. Because I can't remember anything
for the six months after they died.

Tara shrugs, her mind shying away from the unknown. Her gaze
holds steady on the painting of the swimmer on the wall over Dr. Lind's
head. Nothing, she thinks. That time evaporated like mist in sunlight
as if it never happened.

Lind waits, relaxed in her sand-colored chair. She crosses her legs.
She wears wide-legged trousers and a short-sleeve cotton sweater and

has what look like elegant slippers on her feet. She reaches for the small black notebook on the table next to her chair, snaps off the bit of blue elastic that binds it. She opens the notebook, smooths the pages down, takes up her silver pen. When she twists the barrel, the nib emerges, but the pen itself hangs, unmoving, a cue for Tara to get back on track. With her blue eyes, porcelain skin, and pale-gold hair, Lind projects an air of quiet authority and a certain kindness—an unusual combination, at least in Tara's experience.

Tara finds Lind's neutral tone soothing. She has been perched on the edge of a matching sand-colored love seat, but now she allows herself to sit back. These two pieces of furniture, the wooden table by her chair, a small lacquered escritoire with a carved wooden chair, and a black metal wastebasket exist in an ocean of blue and green: cerulean blue walls, aquamarine carpet, a sea-green coffee table between chair and love seat with a blue-and-green box of tissues resting on it. The painting behind Lind, of a body of water—a pool, the sea?—is calming, with its swimmer in midstroke, part of her face showing her complete dedication to her desire.

At their first session, Lind told Tara that she disliked being called Doctor, despite having both a PhD and an MD. The formality did not fit her modality of therapy, she explained to her new clients—another term she insisted on, rather than *patient* or the clinical *analysand*. Both, she explained, tended to erect an artificial barrier between the two people in the room. "Keeping you at what other therapists refer to as a 'strict remove' does not engender either trust or the foundation for a safe place, both of which I will strive to provide you."

This session is Tara's fifth. The morning sun, so bright and optimistic, is now overrun by pewter clouds thick enough to be armor plating. Outside the window Tara can see the leaves on the plane trees rustling in a rising wind. She can almost feel the dampness sweeping in off the Hudson River, foretelling imminent rain.

The swimmer won't mind the rain, she thinks. As long as there is no lightning.

"Tara?"

She lowers her gaze from the swimmer to Lind.

"I suppose I didn't want to think about it. I never talk about it . . . with anyone."

"Not even your previous therapists?"

Tara shakes her head. "Nope."

The ghost of a smile on Lind's lips, quickly gone. "Can you be more specific?"

"They didn't . . . ," Tara begins. "It was kinda like . . . I dunno, I didn't trust them."

There is silence for a time. Is Lind digesting the implications of what Tara has just said, or is she waiting for more explication? Since Tara is unwilling to fill in details she no longer cares to think about, she says nothing.

At last, Lind says: "Can you tell me about how you felt after your parents' deaths?"

Clearly, she is willing to move on. But for Tara this topic is even more of a minefield. Or mind field. Fear strikes her, like an arrow through her soul.

"Tara, you understand that anything you say in this room is sacro-sanct. It will never be repeated to anyone, ever." Lind's smile is warm, inviting. "It seems clear to me that your trust issues are central to why you came to see me."

Tara keeps her gaze on Lind. "I come by my trust issues honestly."

"I don't doubt it," Lind says. "In here, with me, you need trust. It's one of the most powerful tools you have at your disposal." When Tara makes no reply, Lind goes on. Perhaps she doesn't expect Tara to answer right away. "If you are to succeed, we need to trust each other, trust the process, difficult as it will be at times." She pauses. "Does this make sense to you?"

Tara says nothing, but after a moment she exhales and sinks back into the love seat's soft cushion.

Taking that as a yes, Lind continues. "So. About your father."

"My father. Jamison Montgomery Peary. J. M., my mother called him. Never 'dear' or 'darling.'"

"You're deflecting, Tara," Lind comments lightly.

She's right, of course. And, anyway, Tara thinks, what am I here for but to finally trust someone enough to tell the truth. "He was famous," she begins. "Not nationally famous but tabloid famous. In certain circles, anyway." She makes a face. "In other circles, he was known as a fraud, a charlatan, by the so-called scientists who came to see his act. They considered him dangerous."

"Dangerous? To his audience?"

"No, to them." A wry look on Tara's face. "Because they couldn't figure out how he did what he did. They were sure he used plants in the audience, the way other hypnotists did, but they never could prove that."

"But you didn't find him dangerous."

Tara shakes her head. "And neither did Sophie."

"What *did* you think of him?"

"I loved him," Tara says immediately, because it's the truth. "More than that, I adored him. He took me under his wing and taught me things I'd never learn in school, or even in the library, where I went almost every day after the nuns let us out."

"Such as?"

"Practical things."

"Like hypnosis?"

"Well, I'm not sure how practical hypnosis is. But yes, he'd put me under. I performed with him. I knew he wasn't a fake, a charlatan. He had a gift, kind of amazing." She bites her lower lip, remembering. "But also I mean he taught me about the real world, things my mother had no interest in—her focus was solely on God.

"My father taught me how to see a snake at twenty yards and catch it. How to break a horse and ride it. How to train Hickory."

"And your mother? What did she think of him?"

"She was Norma Jean Lockhart; my mother never took my father's name. That should tell you all you need to know about how she felt about him," she says.

Lind does not respond, which, to Tara, who knows the psychoanalytic drill by now, means that isn't all the doctor needs to know.

"To be honest, I think they also recognized in each other a kind of outsider who could get their odd lifestyles."

"Are you speaking of a marriage of convenience?"

Tara considers this for a moment. "In a way, maybe, but my father was totally under my mother's spell. They were both crooks, in their own way, but who was the bigger crook depended on which one of them you asked." She glances down at the back of her hand, a habit she hates but seems incapable of breaking. "Their stories kept changing, like sunlight on water."

"So it was impossible for you to distinguish lies from the truth."

"Just like real life," Tara says in a surge of self-loathing.

"I'm not sure that's entirely true."

"By the time Sophie and I entered the picture, we were already settled in rural Georgia, where both my parents set up their respective tents. Jamison Montgomery Peary should have been a bigger name. But it was my mother who attracted more and more worshippers. Her ministry was electric, and anyway, in those parts God always beat out science."

"And how did you and your sister react to these crowds your mother attracted?" Lind asks.

"What do you mean?"

Lind watches her for a moment. "Your mother was in high demand. Did you feel that she had enough time for you and Sophie?"

"There was always my father," she says. "He was always around when we needed him."

"What about his own . . . shows?"

"Oh, he took me with him. When I was old enough. He made me part of his act."

"He hypnotized you."

"Uh-huh."

"Do you remember anything from when you were under?"

"That's not how it works." Tara cocks her head, tries to fathom the meaning behind these questions. "You don't believe in hypnotism, do you?"

Lind appears unperturbed. "What I think isn't important, Tara. I'd like you to tell me why you believe your mother felt his hypnotism was an act, that he was a fake."

"Like I said, my mother's business was God. Jesus the Savior. But it wasn't only her business. It was her innate belief. It was here, through and through: a true believer." Tara shrugs. "So of course she was sure my father was a fake. She needed to believe that. Because what my father did—what he was—went against everything she believed."

"Did she ever ask you your opinion as to your father's hypnotism?"

"My mother never asked my opinion about anything."

"Why was that, do you think?"

"I came to believe that she was always afraid my father was turning me against her."

"Was there any truth to that?"

Tara doesn't know how to answer that; her thoughts are too tangled with emotion. "There's lots of things about them I never understood."

"I think that's true of all of us when it comes to our parents." Lind offers another gentle smile even as she plows on. "Was their antagonism mutual?"

"My father's anger was more secretive. He wasn't vocal about it like my mother was."

Lind considers for a moment. "Their love for each other—or whatever the bond between them was—must have been very powerful to overcome such a disparity."

Tara smiles thinly. "In my mother's own words, it was a miracle."

"Did your sister, Sophie, share your outlook on your parents' relationship?"

Tara frowns. "Why shouldn't she?"

"Well, it would be perfectly understandable if sisters—even twins—didn't see eye to eye, especially when it comes to their parents."

Now this is interesting, Tara thinks. Lind hasn't made that a question, and she is waiting to hear what Tara will do with it. She's smart—and clever. But is she trustworthy? The jury is still out.

"No, we were on the same wavelength, always," Tara says.

"About God, as well?" Lind asks in a carefully neutral tone.

"Especially about God. Sophie was about as irreligious as you could get."

"How did your mother react to Sophie's apostasy?"

"Her what?" she asks.

Lind appears unfazed. "The fact that she didn't believe in God."

Ahh, Tara thinks. Okay, then. "Sophie was a terrific liar. When she was with Mother, she was as pious as any of the nuns that taught us." She pauses long enough for Lind to prompt her.

"What are you thinking, Tara?"

"My sister was everything I wanted to be," she says with a smile. "She was beautiful, confident, and clever."

"Are you sure you're not also describing yourself?"

Something clenches in Tara's gut. This is an unexpected curveball, and for just an instant her fear at being outmaneuvered rises up. She shakes her head. "I wouldn't say that I'm any of those things."

In not responding, Lind is urging a further response. Good shrinks know how to do that. She says: "Something happened to me when my sister took me in her arms. We couldn't have been more than five years old, but I remember that moment so very vividly. Inside me, something cracked open. I felt safe."

"Safe?" Lind doesn't move a muscle; she appears as relaxed as a sunbather in Ibiza. "In what way?"

"I felt I had an ally."

This response seems to give Lind pause. Tara has surprised her. "Why did you feel you needed an ally? Was there an antagonist?"

"There was; there is," Tara says. "Life."

Lind's pen hovers over her pad. "Tell me."

Tara looks down at her left hand again—scaled, scarred as if with a second set of veins, vine-like, twisted, pink, white, one the color of dried blood. In her first session she sat on her hands, not wanting her left hand to be a topic of discussion. But when, at the second session, she reached for the glass of water Lind had offered her, the therapist did nothing more than glance at it briefly. She hasn't, so far, asked Tara what happened. Possibly she senses that Tara will tell her in her own time, and not before. But perhaps this is an outward manifestation of trust: she has been silently asking Tara to trust her.

In a strange way that both terrifies and fascinates her, Tara realizes that Lind's acceptance of her deformity is causing a subtle change to take up residence between them, that there is trust between them, hesitant as a fawn in a forest glade, ephemeral as moonlight on a cloud.

2

In Seventh Haven, every moment is controlled; an emergency intake is no exception. The precise orchestration of duties that stems from perfectly coordinated teamwork is as good as any at top-flight metropolitan hospitals. It is, however, far more private.

As soon as Tara pushes through the doors, she rushes to help the intake crew, which includes M, Tara's friend and a key member of Richard Burnside's admin team, overseen by Constant Horizons LLC, the nonprofit in charge of funding for Seventh Haven. M has a PhD in psychology, which she uses to good advantage in her counseling of the troubled teens—marginalized LGBTs, drug addicted, physically and emotionally abused—who walk or are brought by stretcher through the door. Because Seventh Haven is always cash strapped, despite the periodic donations of its benefactors, she also doubles as the HR person, in charge of hiring and firing.

A young trans teen of about fourteen, Tara judges, has been brought in. OD'ing, like a lot of the kids who have been thrown out of their families for being "abominations against God and man." Out on the street, they are easy prey for the sharks eternally swimming in the shadows at the edges of civilization. Sad, lonely, disenfranchised, enisled. Which is why Seventh Haven came into being six years ago. Financed by a mixed bag of philanthropists, artists, actors, and digital businesses, it has quickly attracted medical, psychological, and counseling personnel of a high order, who volunteer their time and expertise to giving back life to people who have lost sight of it.

The teen is nonresponsive, and the team is into rescue breathing. M directs the team in clear, crisp commands. Tara cradles his head, locking it in a tilted position, while Suzanna keeps his chin lifted. Carlos pinches his nose, forces two quick puffs of air through his opened lips, then administers one long breath, counting off five seconds between each exhale.

At the same time, Danielle, Seventh Haven's head physician's assistant, injects the patient with one cc of naloxone into his shoulder muscle. Meanwhile, Carlos keeps up the rescue breathing procedure, counting out loud between breathing into the teen's mouth. Danielle is standing by with another syringe of naloxone, if needed.

Happily, this time it isn't. Tara and M have seen too many ODs never come back from the abyss, despite the team's best efforts. The teen stirs and begins breathing on his own, and Carlos takes his fingers off the patient's nose. The kid looks like he is sleeping, like he doesn't have a care in the world, but oh, what a hurricane of woe has snowed him under, Tara thinks. And for the single blink of an eye, the double thump of a single heartbeat, the kid is Sophie, lying on some ER gurney. Tara blinks again; a tear pearls off her lower lid.

Suzanna and M trundle the gurney he is on from the triage bay into the small but well-equipped OR, where Danielle will pump his stomach. Tara waits in triage to see if anyone else is going to be brought in. She is still waiting, trembling over Sophie's unknown fate, when M reappears.

"The patient's name is Sam," M says. "I'll be counseling him as soon as he's up and compos mentis." Seventh Haven is acutely aware that naloxone, while the drug of choice for the first acute stages of OD, can, without proper psychological counseling, become a crutch for serial ODs, knowing the drug can always bring them back for more of what they crave most.

M eyes Tara. "You hungry?"

Tara nods. "Always."

———

M and Tara met seven weeks earlier, when Tara walked in to Seventh Haven in response to an old-school job posting for assistant counselor ("No advanced degree necessary—learn on the job!") on the bulletin board at the East Village coffee shop around the corner from Tara's apartment. Tara had been in New York a week and was in there every morning for café au lait and a chocolate croissant. Because of a staff member being out sick, M was working intake that evening.

"You should know I have no formal training as a counselor," Tara said as M presented her with a one-page form.

"No worries," M replied. "We're looking for aptitude and instinct, not degrees, and anyway this is a part-time gig." Then she shrugged. "Plus which, we can't afford to hire a PhD." She watched Tara as she began to fill out the form. "Doesn't mean, though, we'll hire just anyone. We're extremely serious about aptitude and instinct."

Finishing up the form, part safe truth, part careful lie, using as her last name Gemini, Tara said, "In a place like this with the lives of troubled kids at stake, I should hope so."

M nodded, seemingly satisfied with Tara's response. She looked briefly over the filled-in application. "Hmm . . . you have some good experience, I see: an orderly at a South Side hospital in Chicago. I'm sure you saw it all there." One of the safe truths. "Okay." M lifted her head. "There's something else," she said. "M stands for Margo. But everyone calls me M."

M was second generation; she had family in Veracruz, near the Gulf of Mexico. Dusky skinned, solidly built, she was a hard body who must have hit the gym at least three or four times a week; Tara wouldn't have relished confronting her in a boxing ring. Her broad Olmec face was beautiful, her dark eyes, upturned at the outer corners, quite arresting. She wore her dark-brown hair short and punky. Something about her—possibly her fluidity—attracted Tara.

She gave Tara a level stare. "All this cool with you, you being from Texas and all?"

Tara grew up in southwest Georgia, but she wasn't about to tell anyone that. Just like she wasn't about to tell anyone she was twenty. Twenty-six was what she put down on paper, every time, which was her age on her fake ID. "Your business," she said. "Not mine."

M made a sound, seeming pleased. "Okay, let's get the ball rolling."

"Does that mean I'm hired?"

"You'll know in about an hour." M led her down the hall, past several closed doors on either side. The walls were hung with artwork— paintings and drawings—done by the kids who were in residence or had passed through on their way to a better life. They might have been in a middle school.

"It's interesting. You don't sound like a Texan," M said after she'd explained the origins of the artwork.

Tara, of course, didn't. But neither did she sound like she was from Georgia. Neither of her parents was from the South; they assiduously kept their accents nonregional to help ensure their privacy. Tara and Sophie naturally followed their lead. Sophie especially despised the southern drawl; she made fun of it early and often.

"My time in Chicago," she said, which was true, after a fashion. "I wanted to fit in."

"Huh! You don't seem like the fitting-in type to me." M threw a look back over her shoulder. "Otherwise you wouldn't be here."

M stopped them in front of a closed door on their right. "We're going in to counsel Angelo. He's a repeat offender. Believe it or not, he just turned twelve. Not trans—I don't think he knows quite what he is. He's been on practically every drug known to humans, but his drug of choice is Special K." She meant ketamine, the fast-acting anesthetic and hypnotic, sometimes used for date rape. It was a highly dangerous and addictive recreational drug. With her hand on the doorknob, she turned back to Tara. "Just follow my lead. You can observe for a bit, but you're here to interact with Angelo."

"Throwing me to the lion." Tara nodded. "Got it."

The room was square, windowless, lit by standing lamps in three corners. A small sofa, a pair of upholstered chairs, and a wooden table comprised the furnishings. On the left-hand wall someone had painted a window that looked out on a tropical island landscape, complete with palm trees, breakers rolling into a wide crescent beach. In the distance, a surfer rode a cresting wave. The work was very good, far more accomplished than the childlike art in the hallway.

Angelo was seated on one of the chairs. Suzanne stood behind him, hands placed loosely on the chairback. Was she guardian or guard? Tara wondered. Suzanne, a young, petite brunette with a pale face and a starburst of freckles across the bridge of her nose, smiled at Tara when M introduced her. She seemed relieved to have them in the room and left as soon as M gave her a small nod.

Angelo was slim but tall for his age. He could have been either male or female. He wore his hair pulled back into a ponytail, long, dark, and thick. Angelo's skin was the color of café au lait, his eyes black. He wore a pair of two-sizes-too-large jeans, filthy high-top kicks, a ratty jacket over what looked like a wife-beater undershirt.

M sat down in the chair opposite the boy. "Hey, Angelo," she said.

Angelo answered in a grunt that somehow managed to convey sullenness. He startled Tara by giving her the once-over of an adult, then turned his attention to the wall over M's right shoulder. Tara couldn't tell if he was strung out or just a nasty piece of work. Either way, this wasn't going to be a walk along the seashore; M had thrown her into the deep water with an adolescent shark.

"How are you feeling, Angelo?" As she spoke, M indicated that Tara could park herself on the sofa, but for the moment Tara stayed where she was.

"Like I look," the kid said. "Like I look."

"And how d'you think you look?"

Angelo stared up at the ceiling, into the corner, where one of the lamps stood, at the shadows on the floor, and finally at the space between his kicks.

"Not going well" would be an upgrade from what is happening now, Tara thought. Or, more accurately, what wasn't happening. Well, she told herself, it's now or never.

Pushing the wooden table away, she made a place for herself and sat cross-legged on the floor next to the kid. "Hey there, A, my name's Tara," she said conversationally, as if they were at a party. "I'll tell you frankly how you look: like shit, that's what."

M seemed to twitch in her chair, as if stuck with a pin in her backside, but the kid turned his head, eyed her, said, "Right, huh?" He shrugged. "I've looked better."

"Have you looked worse?" Tara asked.

He gave her the ghost of a crooked smile, gone almost before it began. "Yeah, huh. But I dunno, maybe not."

"So what's up with you, anyway?" M was caught in the corner of her eye. That is a definite twitch, she thought.

"Same old shit," the kid said morbidly.

"Ah, no." Tara kept her gaze firmly on Angelo's face, as if he were the most important person in the world, so that he knew that he was seen and acknowledged. "You haven't looked worse than this, so I'm not buying what you're selling."

Now she was gifted with a bit more of a smile. "Yeah, well . . ."

Could she push him? She decided to try. "Yeah, well, what like?" When he made no reply, she said, "I could tell you that coming clean is good for the soul."

"Hah! Is that what *you're* selling?"

"God, no. I had a mother who was a Holy Roller. Can you believe that? She had a tent, lots of followers. When she opened her mouth, fire and brimstone would come out."

"Burning in hell."

"You got that right." He had gotten with the program. Whatever else he is, the kid is no fool, Tara thought. "And, according to her, I was going to be the first one into the fire." Tara shuddered inwardly. Just saying the word *fire* had become a trigger for her. How she hated that! Weakness, that's what triggers were. Holes in your soul.

Angelo turned in his chair to face her fully. "That's fucking bullshit."

"I know, right? But we've all gotta put up with bullshit sometimes. No way around it."

The kid puffed out his lips. "It is what it is, yah?"

"Yup." She grinned. "So now . . ." She deliberately let the question hang in the air. He knew where she was going, and now she knew that was where he wanted to go too. But maybe not quite yet. He sat very still, seeming hardly to breathe. His gaze was fixed inward. What is he thinking about? she wondered. What horrors is he reliving?

Maybe one more nudge was all he needed.

Reaching up, she put her left hand atop his on the arm of the chair. He flinched, was about to jerk his own hand away, when he glanced down. For several seconds he did nothing. Then he said, in a wholly different tone of voice, "What are those?"

"I think you know, Angelo."

"Scars."

They seemed to fascinate him. Well, why not, she thought.

Scars of any sort were things a kid like him could relate to in an immediate and visceral way.

He blinked, as if he'd just awoken from a dream. "Was that you that did that?"

She took a ragged breath. Her stomach was roiling; she could taste bile in her mouth. "No. There was a fire."

Angelo's eyes were wide and staring. "Oh, wow."

Tara bit her lower lip. "The truth is . . ." She glanced over at M, who was sitting on the edge of her chair, her hands clasped together, as if in prayer. Tara had never revealed a word of this tragedy. Her eyes reengaged with the kid's. "For years all I could think about are these scars. That is a stupid thing to do. Worse, it's selfish."

Angelo's brows knit together. "Selfish?"

Tara nodded. "I made the fire about me," she said softly, "when it is about something else altogether."

"What?" Angelo asked. The one word propelled out of him.

"The death of my family."

———

"You're hired," M said later. "That was fantastic! Scary good." They were in the admin office. "I wish to God I could offer you more money." She gave Tara a rueful grin. "But on the bright side, I'm going to screw around with the paperwork so all your medical is free. I mean, after what I just saw, you sure as shit deserve it."

And later, after she had introduced Tara around to the staff, she said, "Listen, is everything you said to Angelo the emmis?"

Tara blinked. "The what?"

"The straight scoop. You know, the truth."

Tara mimicked Angelo's ghost of a smile, but she didn't think M noticed. "More or less." The truth was a lost soul, wandering, long gone from her sight.

———

M became Tara's gateway into the caring world of Seventh Haven, from its revolving staff of nurse practitioners, ER doctors, and psychologists to its outreach personnel. From that first moment, as improbable as it was inevitable, Tara, a person from the American South, for whom lying had become a way of life, and M, a person born and bred in the multicultural crucible of Jackson Heights, Queens, found their way to a friendship. Undoubtedly, perhaps unconsciously, they sensed in each other a kindred spirit. But then friendship—true friendship—is a lot like love: its nature is mysterious, its bonds invisible, all the stronger for that. Over the next several weeks, the friendship grew quickly. They saw a lot of each other; Tara had no friends in New York, and from what she'd gathered, M's medium-term relationship with someone named Stevie seemed to be headed for a dirt nap. Their inner loneliness drew them to one another immediately, but it was a mutual recognition that they were both fleeing former lives, former selves, trying to navigate the unknown, that cemented their bond. And for Tara, M's handling of herself was a source of admiration. She seemed to know precisely what she wanted and to be on the way to getting it, whereas Tara had already screwed up the handling of herself.

After walking for five or six minutes, they settle at a table along one exposed brick wall of their favorite vegetarian spot near the sprawling NYU campus, not much more than a hole-in-the-wall: a polished wooden counter and a half dozen bistro-size tables and bentwood chairs. The Israeli food is superb. At noon the line for takeout would have snaked out the door, but after three the place is comparatively quiet, less than half the tables occupied.

Tara and M order falafel sandwiches and bottles of Dos Equis Ambar. Briefly, they thought about going to Japonica, their usual sushi restaurant, but after the emergency at Seventh Haven, neither of them has the appetite for raw fish.

"Your timing was impeccable today," M says, then takes a swig of the beer. "Thanks, as always, for your help."

"Anytime," Tara says.

The falafel sandwiches are set in front of them.

"You know, and being frank, I never would have pegged you as someone who'd respond to our ad for Seventh Haven," M says.

"You can't judge a girl by her farm roots."

"Ha, no. Right." M laughs. "What I meant is we don't pay enough. In Podunk, Iowa, maybe, but not here."

"You work at Seventh Haven."

"I also work at Forest."

"Weekend nights, I know." Tara turns her beer bottle around and around. "But what exactly do you do?"

"Forest is a high-end bottle club. No bridge-and-tunnel riff-raff allowed. But guys with money who want to show it off get full of themselves, usually at others' expense. I train the bouncers how to deal with these young hedgies without letting situations get out of hand." She gives Tara a smirk. "And, yes, for this I get the big bucks."

Tara starts to peel off the label. "Sounds like an easy gig."

"Huh." M puts her elbows on the table. "It's dangerous, is what it is." She pulls beer into her mouth, swallows. "These little shits with money—they're so young they don't know what to do with it except spend it. And you can't just throw them out on their butts if they're causing a scene—and believe me, they cause some scenes."

"All around women, I'll bet," Tara says.

"Oh, dear God, yes."

"If it's so dangerous, why don't you quit?"

"I, too, have been corrupted by money." M grins. "Besides, these people fascinate me."

"And how does Stevie feel about you never being home? Is that the problem between you?"

"Ah, Stevie." All at once her expression changes. "Well, let's just say our rough patch isn't getting any smoother."

"I'm sorry to hear that. Do you think you and she will work it out?"

"Your guess is as good as mine." M takes a bite of falafel, chews thoughtfully. "But enough about me." She gives Tara a significant look. "If it's okay to ask, I'm wondering why you never talk about Sophie?"

Tara moves her food around the plate, giving herself breathing room to figure out what to say. "My sister vanished twenty months ago, more or less. I've been trying to find her ever since. Little bits and pieces from people who had caught a glimpse of her when she left—or thought they had anyway—led me to Tucumcari."

M frowns. "Where the hell is Tucumcari?"

"New Mexico." Eliding over the six months of her own life she can't account for, waking up in a roadside motel, disoriented and alone. "But she left a trail of clues only I would understand, on social media accounts and elsewhere online. The trail took me to Kansas City, Springfield, Bloomington—always heading east by northeast, until I fetched up in Chicago, where the clues gave out. Assuming she'd settled there, I spent more than a year searching for her at places where I thought she might hang out—bars, clubs. She's a night owl. I was sure I had spotted her any number of times, but no go."

"But you haven't found any clues yet?"

Tara shakes her head. "Not for lack of trying." It hurts to talk about Sophie. Literally. A burning pain in her chest spreads outward, as if a stiletto is being twisted inside her.

"But after all this time," M says soberly, "maybe she really doesn't want to be found or changed her mind. Have you considered that?"

"Honestly, no. I . . . Sophie and I are twins—identical twins. We're extremely close." To keep feigning indifference is exhausting. That is all she is prepared to say on the subject, and she can sense from M's expression that she understands. Plus, lying to M about the hole in her own life is becoming more and more difficult.

Nevertheless, she feels she needs to say: "I think it's a game—an adult hide-and-seek. Sophie loved that game; she was far better at it than I was." But that is a lie, or at least, Tara thinks, it might be a lie. Because there might be another reason Sophie doesn't want to be found, by her or by anyone else. Tara cannot imagine what that reason might be, but she knows that the possibility exists, and it makes her very afraid.

"But I have a feeling it'll end here," she continues, mostly to hold back this black thought, this terrible possibility. "This is the best place for both of us."

"Why is that?"

"Because, if you don't have a passport, New York is the ultimate arena to play hide-and-seek in."

When M shoots her a curious look, Tara adds, "Like Sophie, I'm running away."

M, face darkening, puts down her fork. "From what?"

Tara gazes at her levelly. "Myself."

And that, at least, is the truth.

3

Tara has waited patiently for Christie Lind to finish the last hour of her working day. She has been standing in the shadows of a brownstone, five steps above the sidewalk, across West Tenth Street from the townhouse that includes Lind's ground floor office suite. Outside in the long spring twilight, amid the nesting birds and the gathering Greenwich Village crowds accessorized with ZOE XL2 strollers or Babybjörns, Tara has become completely absorbed in her surroundings—light failing, manhole covers drooling noxious odors from underground, cabs honking at Ubers, Lyfts honking at bicyclists, the laughter of children, the mumblings of crazies and people on their cell phones—sinking into them like ink on paper.

Now, safely invisible from the entrance to the therapist's West Tenth Street townhouse, Tara sees Christie emerge and head east. Tara finds it quite pleasing to overlook her like a god or an angel, in just the way Christie Lind metaphorically overlooks her during their sessions.

Thirty-five minutes later, she returns, loaded down with shopping bags full of premium food at premium prices, and walks up the steps to her home.

She isn't a therapist now. She is Christie, married to Marwyn Rusk.

As is her wont, Tara has done a Google search on them: Christie got five stars across the board, mother to Charlotte, a girl of fourteen, who was easy to find on Instagram, Snapchat, and Twitter. Marwyn is a big kahuna, the managing partner of Millbank Partners LLP, a private equity firm in Westport, Connecticut. Tara has seen photos of Marwyn online, not only on the impressive Millbank website but also at financial and political functions, with the mayor and councilmen, in Washington at a dinner with any number of political and financial bigwigs. Tellingly, though, no women. After that, she had no interest in further web searches. She simply wanted to get a grip on Christie's rep, to feel reassured she made the right choice.

Now Christie is home. Tara sits down on the brownstone's stoop and watches the darkened windows glow bright lemon. Downstairs and upstairs both. Christie and Marwyn own the whole building. Nice, Tara thinks. No tenants. Probably a garden out back, as well. She closes her eyes, picturing it: a fistful of scraggly grass eternally yearning for sun, a tree that needs pruning and is never going to get it, maybe some geraniums and tulips in cut-off wine-barrel containers bought at Pier 1. An old-fashioned iron bench and some metal chairs like they have in the Tuileries. That would be wonderful. But not as wonderful as a Lab mix named Hickory.

With a rumbling down the street, a giant moving van heaves into view like a battleship. With a squeal of brakes it comes to a stop. It is black and gold, with the words **MASTERPIECE LLC, WE MOVE TREASURES RIGHT** painted on its massive side. Moments later a couple of burly men emerge from the cab, begin to slowly make their way to the rear. It looks like a family is moving into the brownstone just east of Christie's.

The noise and exhaust intrude on Tara's thoughts, and the huge van blocks her perfect view of Christie's brownstone. The hour is growing late anyway. She rises and heads east, intending to go straight home to her fifth-floor walkup in Alphabet City. But on the way she feels the need to stop at Seventh Haven to see how Angelo is doing—he has returned for the third time. The kid has gotten under her skin.

The moment she comes through the door, she knows something bad has happened, and Suzanne's face, pale as a midwinter's morning as she comes toward her, tells her all she needs to know.

"When?" she says.

"About an hour ago." Suzanne shakes her head. "We tried, but you know, if they want to die, they'll find a way to do it."

"Is he still here?"

She nods unhappily. "This time there was no saving him. The cops have been called, but naturally they have more important things to do, so who knows when they'll show."

"I want to see him."

Suzanne nods. "Sure."

They proceed down the central corridor, past intake, triage, and the OR. Suzanne lifts an arm. "He's in here." She opens a door on their left, stands back to allow Tara to step inside.

And there is Angelo, his face a blotchy red black, the tip of his tongue protruding from between bloodless lips. The ligature marks around his neck are raw and livid. A jolt lances through her like an ice pick. What if this were Sophie? What if this is how her sister ended up? She shivers, trying to breathe, but the air seems caught in the back of her throat.

"What did he use?" Tara asks thickly, coming closer.

Suzanne sighs. "His belt." This is far from her first suicide rodeo.

Tara reaches out, places her hand on the side of Angelo's cheek, cool, dry, like a fallen leaf trod under bare feet.

"Goddammit," she says.

Behind her, Suzanne stands with her fingers clasped in front of her. "I called M. She should be here soon. Perhaps you want to wait for her."

But Tara doesn't. She turns and, without a word, steps out of the room, back down the corridor, and out into the street. Night has fallen: time to hurry home. As usual, her building's cramped entryway and narrow stairwell reek of pot and the well-entrenched sweat of desperation. And, it being Friday, the stench of fried cod radiates from old Mrs. Lombardi's ground floor apartment. Tonight it makes Tara's eyes water, sticks in her throat like the spine of a bony fish.

Home. A downtrodden apartment she has sublet—she doesn't want her name on the lease—from a grad student spending a year at architectural school in Milan. The place is grimy and homey at the same time. It is in back, the windows overlooking a single plane tree, dusty, scabrous, and forlorn. Dying from pollution and lack of light. A silver Mylar balloon, almost completely deflated now, is caught in its arthritic fingers. The view, as well as the one-bedroom apartment itself, suits her needs. It is cheap and as anonymous as anything in New York can be. She has a little money but has no place to spend it anyway.

Taking a Dos Equis Ambar from the minifridge, she stares into the fridge's chilly depths at just about nothing—a half-eaten container of yogurt; a paper box with a red Chinese pagoda stamped on the side, full of desiccated brown rice; a single sour pickle in a jar, floating like a dead body. And in the tiny freezer? Nothing but ice turned a vague yellow from disuse. She isn't hungry anyway.

She throws herself on the broken-backed sofa and tries to block out Angelo's face, black and bloated. The beer bottle sits on the steamer trunk table. A last droplet of cold water slides down one side. Inescapable sounds of the tenement wash over her, but they mean nothing to her, like static on a radio tuned to a station too far away to hear clearly.

She is detached, an electric cord that hasn't been plugged in. And she thinks of the swimmer on the wall in Christie's office. She feels more connected to her than she does to the people around her.

She starts to get up, to get herself another beer, but her throat constricts painfully. Ever since the fire, ever since she awakened in a shabby motel room in Tucumcari, New Mexico, her memory of the previous six months has been as blurred as a windshield in a rainstorm.

I should have waited for M, she thinks. M, who at lunch said, "You and I have a lot in common. You're running away from yourself; I'm running away from my family. I guess that's why I trust you." Her smile had struck Tara like a backhand blow. "I do trust you, Tara."

After I've lied and lied to you, Tara thinks. What kind of friend am I? Unbidden, almost against her will, an answer rises up like a goblin in the night . . .

———

"The wages of sin is death."

Nine-year-old Tara stood in the wings of the great stage beneath the pure-white tent, the air foaming with the religious zeal her mother had whipped up, heard her mother's striking oratorical voice. The tone she summoned from deep inside her, used only at her revival performances. "The wages of sin is lawlessness." Her mother's arms opened wide, embracing her audience, rapt, febrile. Hanging on every word as they clutched the crosses hanging around their necks, sold at a rich profit before the beginning and after the end of each performance. "And the wages of lawlessness is corruption of the soul, the sure and ever-present terror of hell—the eternal damnation of the soul." She grasped the air in front of her, as if beseeching the congregation. "Death leads to eternal life, with the help and grace of our savior, Jesus Christ. But sin brings annihilation—the end of all things."

———

Is that where I am now? Tara asks herself now, trembling. At the end of all things?

Sometime during the night, a punishing sleep arrives, like a car crash. Within its depths the nightmare arises and once again ensnares her in its dreadful tentacles.

Her eyes open. Early-morning light flutters past the curtains. Still enwebbed in the sticky strands of her recurring dream of being pursued through the forest on fire, she lies on her back, paralyzed. Fear strikes her like a physical blow. She tries to move her arms, her legs, tries to turn her head from side to side. Nothing. She cannot budge even a millimeter. She knows from experience that the best thing to do is to allow herself to sink into the paralysis. Fighting it is futile, but her mind is as frantic as a bird trapped in a cottage.

Finally, her body is released from its prison, and she weeps.

4

"So last night I had this dream," Tara says. "Again."

"Can you describe the dream?" Lind asks.

"More or less. I mean I woke up gripped by the same panic."

"Tell me."

"I'm running through the forest with Hickory," Tara says, looking up, putting thoughts of her scarred hand away. "We are two hearts beating as one. We are alive and free."

Tara stops there, surprised at what she has said, what she has let slip out. She meant to tell Lind just the gist of the dream, while artfully avoiding the crux of the matter. Whatever; now her words are hanging out there for Lind.

"'Alive and free.'" And there it is, Lind never missing a single thing, no matter how small. First stage of this test passed. Tara feels a fleeting elation. "You've never used those words before."

Tara turns her head for a moment. The afternoon light, softened by the wooden blinds that divide the window into horizontal segments, falls across Lind's face. Her short hair glimmers like gold as the light moves between the swaying branches of the plane tree. From somewhere in its embrace, a bird can be heard singing to its children or calling to its mate. It is important for Tara to remind herself that this isn't, after all, the end of all things, that there is life outside, vital and strong, that somewhere a snug harbor exists for her. She finds herself briefly fantasizing that this might be it.

Turning back to Lind, she says, "Hickory was a Lab mix—big, even for a male. We hunted together. Anyway, in the dream, Hickory and I are running through the woods. In this world we're alive and free. There's a kind of giddiness, a sense of flying, almost."

With an involuntary shiver, she says: "But then something changes. At first it's subtle—the trees are thicker and taller. They're massed closer together. And the light is different, and it's harder and harder to run. And then the change really comes—something is coming up fast, right on our heels—something dark and big and evil. Very, very evil."

"Can you see or sense what it is?" Lind asks.

Tara shakes her head. "I try to look over my shoulder, but I can't."

"Go back to the beginning of the dream." Lind's voice takes on a soft violet color, like the magic time just after the sun sets, before night comes down. It's a beautiful tone. "Your sense of freedom." It is also a beguiling tone.

"Yes." Tara is abruptly wary. "Why?" Her defenses come up with hair-trigger swiftness.

"I'm wondering at the origin of your freedom." Lind looks encouragingly at Tara. "Is it the forest? Being away from your parents?"

"It's Hickory: lovely, protective Hickory." But Hickory is dead . . . all of a sudden she doesn't want to go on. She doesn't want to be here in this room with Lind. The blue-green space has shrunk; the atmosphere is hot as the forest on fire, deep in the realm of monsters. Flaming and shifting, and the twisting shape like a whirlwind coming ever closer.

"Tara?" Lind prompts.

She recalls the feeling of abject terror when she woke up in a strange room, in a strange city, without Hickory, without Sophie; turned on the TV; and saw that it was six months since the fire.

"Tara, you're safe," Lind says softly. "You are protected here." She bends forward, elbows on knees. "Nothing can harm you." Gesturing, she says, "Please sit down again."

Tara hesitates only a moment. She sits, first on the edge of the sofa, then—as if assuring herself that she is, indeed, safe—scooting back, sitting fully, if still not entirely relaxed.

Lind allows a silence to settle around them before she says, "What just happened, Tara? Can you tell me?"

Tara licks her lips. Her tongue feels thick, her mouth intolerably dry. As if sensing this, Lind fills a blue glass with water from a pitcher, hands it to her. Tara gulps it down in one go.

"Thanks," she says. She does not want to let the glass go, as if its blueness is a talisman that might protect her against the resurrection of the flames.

Lind lifts the pitcher. "More?"

Tara nods gratefully, drinks greedily. She rubs her sweating palms on her jeans, her gaze zeroing in on the back of her left hand. She has the terrible urge to pour water over it, to beat back the flames . . .

"So . . ." Lind's tiny nudge off the plank.

"So," Tara says after a moment's reflection. "I was thinking of Hickory, how devastated I was when he died." She stops, puts her palms together as if she is at prayer. They are moist again.

"Do you think that's what the dream is about?" Lind asks. "Hickory's death?"

"I . . . I don't know. I look down, and Hickory is gone. Gone, as if he never existed. And I'm alone and the thing is coming for me and Hickory can't save me. I realize that the forest behind me is on fire—great flames crackling, shooting up, blotting out the stars and the moon. Somehow, I think of the fire as a kind of blessing. That it will consume whatever it is that's after me, but the thing is . . ."

She trails off.

Across from her, Lind waits patiently, watchful and kind.

And right then and there Tara feels the quickening of the connection she has been seeking, a kind of warmth long ached for, a line. She reaches out, terrified that it will flicker away. Or reveal itself as a mirage.

"The thing, whatever it is, burns up in the fire. I can see it blackening, turning to a crisp, smell its nauseating stench. But then I see that something of it still remains—the heart of it, and this essence emerges from the flames, unscathed, unhurt. The fire can't kill it." She looks up into Lind's face. "And then I wake up. I can't move. I mean I'm awake, but I'm paralyzed, like I've, I don't know, taken a date rape drug."

"How long has this been going on?"

Tara shrugs, but Lind will not be denied.

"Weeks, months?"

"Twenty," Tara says. "Months." She has whispered it, yet the two separate words seem to fill the space between her and Lind, echoing on and on, as if they are in a vast cathedral.

Lind says, "Tara, listen to me: sleep paralysis is not that uncommon. When you're in REM sleep—dreaming, that is—your brain relaxes your muscles, and your body enters into a state we call atonia. Atonia is an autonomous response that ensures your body won't react to whatever is happening in your dream. It's a kind of protection."

Lind puts aside her pen and notebook. "On rare occasions your mind stays in REM sleep while your body starts to wake up. Your eyes open, you become conscious, but because you're still in atonia, you can't move. Sleep paralysis usually abates within a minute or two. But during that time, which can seem much longer, it's not uncommon to feel anxiety, even panic."

"So there's nothing wrong with me?"

Lind's smile is reassuring. "No."

"But it's not normal."

"Personally, I don't care for that word." Lind takes up the implements of her profession again. "There's a very wide spectrum of responses that—how shall I put it—are most common. Think of the spectrum as a bell curve. Percentages rise and fall depending on where a particular response appears on the curve. So I'd say sleep paralysis is unusual but not abnormal."

Tara bites her lip. "Why does it happen?"

"There are many theories, but the truth of the matter is we simply don't know."

"Theories like what?" Abruptly, Tara is desperate to understand.

"Well, let's see . . . a side effect of drugs is a possible cause, or it might be a symptom of narcolepsy—you know what that is."

Tara nods. "What else?"

"In certain circumstances stress can trigger it."

Tara feels compelled to persist. "What's your theory?"

"I'll share something with you that may relieve some of your anxiety," Lind says. "When I was about eleven years old, I was out on a camping trip with my parents and some friends of theirs and mine. One morning, I woke up very early. I don't know what time exactly, but it was just getting light. I vividly remember seeing the dew shining on the grass through an opening in the tent flap. I wanted to get up and run through that grass, feel the wetness on the soles of my feet and between my toes. But I couldn't move."

"Sleep paralysis," Tara says.

Lind nods. "Precisely."

Tara thinks for a moment. "Did it ever happen again?"

"Just that one time."

"What caused it?"

"It's a mystery." Lind taps her pen against the open page on which she has been taking notes. "Tara, you told me this has been going on for nearly two years."

"Yes, since the night Sophie left."

"Do you think the two are linked in some way?"

It seems a question with a built-in answer so obvious a three-year-old would see it. Still, being of two minds, Tara doesn't immediately respond. But she has decided on a particular path, and she is nothing if not faithful to the paths she chooses.

"Without Sophie there is only death and annihilation," she says.

5

The Masterpiece moving van is there again, but a little farther up the street, not blocking her view. Four men are unloading crates, boxes, furniture into the townhouse next door to Christie Lind's. Tara pays them no attention. She is the close observer, watching the brownstone and wondering where Marwyn Rusk, Lind's husband, is. She has never seen him in the flesh. Does he never come home at the dinner hour—even a late dinner, say, 8:30 or 9:00 p.m.? Does he come home at all? What sort of homelife does their daughter, Charlotte, have? Her attention is abruptly diverted from these vexing questions. Someone has plopped himself down beside her. He smells of aftershave and clove cigarettes. When Tara turns to look at him, he smiles.

"Okay if I sit here?"

"Of all the stone stoops, in all the cities, in all the world, you sit down on mine."

"Nice." His laugh is easy, warm as buttered toast. He is handsome, though actually *handsome* scarcely covers his great good looks. With his dark burnished skin, he seems exotic as a tamarind. "Is it yours, this stoop?" He hooks his thumb over his shoulder. "This fancy townhouse." A deadpan look. "Do I have to pay rent to sit here?"

Tara eyes him warily, as she does with all strangers.

He extends his hand. "Figgy's a nickname from childhood. I loved figs."

"Tara." His hand is dry and smooth. But there is something about it, the electricity of the artist. So not a workman, then, but a finishing carpenter, a sculptor? He wears black narrow-legged jeans, a blue-and-purple-checked shirt, a pair of no-name red high-tops.

"From the South, like me?" he asks. "Anderson, South Carolina." When she gives no response, he adds: "I mean your name." Spreads his hands. "You know, plantations, the Civil War . . ."

A ghostly hand grips the back of her neck. "I'm from here, there, and everywhere," she says, as if she hasn't heard his attempt at a joke.

"Again! Nice!"

Which means he caught the Beatles reference, just like he has for *Gone with the Wind* and *Casablanca*. Smart and with a head for history beyond last week. With each checked box an alarm bell clangs in the recesses of Tara's mind.

His head dips slightly, then rises. "So, like me, you come from many lands." His voice is smooth and clear, maybe professionally trained.

Many lands. Yes, in a way that's true, she thinks. "Are you a singer?"

"I wish." His eyes twinkle as they catch the streetlights that have just come on. He is not too young, not too old either. In the far reaches of her mind are more warning bells. Hardly a surprise, but still . . .

"I do a fair karaoke. Does that count?"

"I hate karaoke," she retorts. "Every time I see that part in *Lost in Translation* where—what's his name?"

"Bill Murray."

She nods. "Right. I cringe every time Bill Murray croaks out 'More Than This.'"

"Good song, though."

"*Great* song, just not when anyone other than Bryan Ferry sings it."

His half smile is boyish, which has the effect of making him seem even more appealing. "Do you always have to have the last word?" He says it seriously, without a hint of snark.

At that moment, a gleaming black Lincoln Navigator pulls up to the curb in front of Christie Lind's brownstone, so close behind the Masterpiece truck the movers can't maneuver their cargo of furniture out. A discussion ensues between the Navigator's driver and the head mover. All too soon the Navigator's driver emerges, and the discussion becomes an argument. Voices are raised; threats are tossed around like so many Frisbees. Tara can feel the tension from where she and Figgy sit, feels it escalate rapidly when the mover's assistant raises his fists.

"New York, right?" Figgy says. "Here comes the street brawl."

But before that can happen, a slim, very handsome man in an expensive suit unfolds out of the Navigator's back seat, steps briskly along the sidewalk, and gets between his driver and the movers. The online photos don't do Marwyn Rusk justice. In person, bursting with life, he is graced with the kind of aura that Don Draper had in *Mad Men*. He has charisma, and plenty of it.

The front door of the brownstone opens. The heated altercation has drawn Lind. Christie stands in the doorway, a concerned expression on her face. Tara can see Charlotte peeking out from behind her left shoulder.

"Marwyn," Lind calls. "Is everything all right?"

Marwyn Rusk either doesn't hear her or chooses not to answer. His attention is on the two men whose fists are clenched and who are just about to come to blows. Tara can hear his well-modulated voice—not the words, just the tone, which is enough. In less than a minute, he's talked both men off the ledge neither of them really wanted to be on. He indicates his driver should back the car up and, while that is happening, spends a couple more moments mollifying the mover. Maybe some bills crossed palms, maybe not; Tara can't tell. In any event, the mover nods and motions for his pal not to get involved, and it's all over.

His hero's work done, Marwyn fairly skips up the stairs to the townhouse. But Charlotte has already turned away, disappeared into the interior, and Lind just stands there, staring blankly at the van, as Marwyn brushes past her.

Not a good look for a family portrait, Tara thinks with some alarm.

"So." Figgy wraps his arms around his shins. "What are you doing here?" His interest has swiftly returned to her. "Waiting for your man—or woman?"

"Very subtle." She contrives to ignore the wariness that clenches her shoulder and arm muscles. "If you must know, I'm waiting for no one." Her voice is edgier than she intends.

The front door closes behind the troubled family, and the Navigator pulls out, disappears down the street. Tara wonders what the happy family is doing. *Happy* and *family* are two words she has never put together in her life.

"That being the case . . ." Figgy glances up into the trees, takes a deep breath, lets it go. "If I'm you, I'm wondering whether this good-looking fella is going to take me out for a prime rib dinner."

"I don't like fellas, and I hate the smell of cooked meat."

"Ah."

"No. Don't like gals either." She gives him a sideways glance. "I'm just not in the market at the moment."

"That's cool." A vertical line appears between his eyes. "What do you like then—at the moment?" He laughs loopily. "Dogs?"

"Only if they're named Hickory."

"Hickory," he muses. "Puts me in mind of a chocolate Lab."

"He was just that," Tara says. "Or a part of him anyway." Her head comes down. "He was a good boy, my best friend to the very end."

"Ah, I'm sorry. It's like losing a member of the family, isn't it?" When she looks at him questioningly, he goes on. "We had a dog named

Bear. A pug—you know, one of those little dogs that snuffles all the time 'cause they're inbred to within an inch of their lives. Anyway, Bear was my mom's dog, but he'd follow me all around, being an annoying little bugger until I played with him. Like a younger brother, you know?"

His eyes crinkle suddenly, his teeth white and even. "What he loved best . . . I used to take him to parties. I'd wrap him up, swaddle him like a baby, sort of hide him so you couldn't see him until you got very close. Then whenever anyone bent over to get a good look, he'd snuffle at them, and they'd rear back shrieking." He can't stop laughing. "It was hilarious. Then I'd let him run around, give him a mouthful of cake or a cookie, and amid the forest of legs he'd be in heaven."

She stares down. Her hands are locked together, ropy scars on her left hand white as bone. She is smiling—a secret smile—but she should be laughing. She wants to; the story is indeed funny. A pug named Bear. That, in itself, is hilarious. But bringing up Hickory always sends a spear of anguish through her system.

Truth be told, she's let her mind drift from being with Figgy to the inside of Christie's brownstone, wondering what is going on, the conversation between Christie and Marwyn, what Charlotte thinks of the friction between her parents.

She feels divided, tidal pulls in both directions—here, where she is; there, where she has no business being. Does she feel connected to either?

"I should go," she says, starting to rise.

"Will I see you again?"

Tara smiles; he deserves at least that much. "Maybe."

"How about we exchange numbers?" he asks hopefully.

"I don't think so."

They are both standing now, facing each other.

"Can I at least give you mine?"

She hesitates. "Sure." What harm will it do?

Tara leaves him on the stoop. She feels his light eyes following her, and even though it draws her away from Christie and Charlotte, it doesn't feel bad. In fact, his voice is running through her head like a song, and it doesn't feel bad at all.

6

I met someone," Tara says. "Yesterday."
M stops in her tracks. They have been heading west on Seventeenth Street, toward the venue where one of M's favorite groups is about to perform. She bought tickets for both of them. Beyond the hectic life of the West Side Highway, the reflections of the lights of New Jersey splay their fingers, dancing across the blackened keyboard of the Hudson River.

"Who?"

Tara tells her how Figgy sat down on the stoop beside her.

"Talk about meet-cute."

"Oh, come on."

A group of seven or eight postteens, obviously high, pushes their way past them, voices loud; they show their tickets and are admitted to the theater.

M's eyes twinkle. "Well, like him, don't like him, too soon to tell? Pick one."

"Too soon." Tara's laugh carries a note of uncertainty.

"What's up with you, girl? You've been fidgety ever since we met tonight."

Tara sighs. She is tired of lying—to M, at least. She likes M. Further, she feels close to her, which is a first. "I had a dream last night that unsettled me." Then she tells M about it, feeling the onrush of fear grip her. "It was just a dream," she concludes. "But still."

"It's that damn drug-ridden neighborhood you live in. I mean, I'd have nightmares if I lived there. You've got to get the hell out."

"If I could afford it, I would, believe me." She gestures. "Now let's get going. We'll be late."

M shakes her head. "No one's ever late to these things." Nevertheless, she ushers Tara through the entrance.

Inside, the venue is dim, cold as a meat locker. They can see the little clouds of their exhalations. Tara expects them to form icicles in the frigid air. Apart from the stage and the light bars overhead, the place is completely bereft of either character or adornment. She has the sense that they have stepped into an abandoned barn. She imagines the stalls against the right-hand wall, sees Miss Molly's head sticking out of the half door, craning her gleaming roan neck, looking for her.

Everyone is standing. There are no seats. Neither is there any pushing or shoving; everyone is chill. The heavy atmosphere reeks of pot. As they squirm their way toward the front, Tara can see that the stage is dominated by twin sets of amps on their side of the band's setup, monstrously huge, hulking like giant guardians. No wonder the temperature is set so low; when the band gets going, their massive equipment will radiate heat like a dying sun.

A shock wave shoots through the audience as the band comes out onstage, cantering from the wings: two women and two men, all rail thin, their high-as-a-kite grins and avid eyes aimed at the first couple of rows.

"Hello, New York!" the lead singer shouts into the mic, in the same voice Tara's mother used onstage. But then she says something her mother never would have conceived of, let alone uttered: "Hella great to see you all!"

Another shock wave of sound, arms raised, mobile cameras flashing. With a crash like a tsunami hitting the shore, the music starts up.

Individuals and groups within the audience begin to dance, which, because of the press of bodies, means hardly more than jumping up and down.

Then the entire band joins the drummer, and the wall of sound strikes Tara's chest like a hammerblow. Again and again to the song's beat. The low-frequency vibrations are a physical assault, causing her heartbeat to race wildly. She presses her hands to her chest as if to ward off the assault. Her lungs are being squeezed by a giant fist. She takes an involuntary step back, but M, clearly sensing her distress, puts her arm around her waist, holds on to her through the rest of the concert. Tara imagines the beat is the sound of Miss Molly's hooves as she rides her horse along country lanes and into a thick copse, beyond which the river pulses silver and black in the moonlight.

———

For several moments, until they cross Tenth Avenue, they are pushed along West Seventeenth Street by a tidal wave of people still buzzing about the concert. Some of them clutch T-shirts or other merch being sold just inside the front door to the venue. Tara's ears are still ringing from the cranked volume that never seemed to let up. Her brain is awash in the blinding colors of the spotlights, which for the finale strobed at seizure-inducing speed.

"Listen, you're welcome to stay with me," M says, when the sounds of the city have returned to normal. "Temporarily, or for as long as you want."

"Wow. M. Well, but there's the not-inconsiderable matter of rent. I'm where I am now because my therapy costs a fortune. That rathole is all I can afford."

"Don't give the rent another thought," M says. "I don't need it; I simply want you to be safe."

"I'm . . . wow again," Tara stammers. A frown darkens her face. "But still I don't know."

"Hey, I wouldn't have offered if I didn't think it was a good idea."

"I don't want you to think . . . I mean, I'm not a charity case."

"Hey, whoa there, girl. Charity doesn't enter into it," M assures her. "Friendship does. I mean, what are friends for?"

Tara wishes she knew.

M grins. "Come on. It'll be good for both of us."

Tara's eyes cloud over. "What about Stevie? I can't imagine she'd be too thrilled."

"Stevie has decamped to the Wrong Coast—LA." M can't keep the sourness out of her voice. "And to rub salt in the wound, she left me for a guy—a guy who claims he's a film director." She snorts. "Every guy in LA claims he's a director or a producer. Or both."

"You're better off," Tara says, then immediately regrets it. Is the wound too raw? She puts out a hand. "Sorry, M. Really. But you know, the one time I met her, there was something off, something—I don't know—phony about her." She grins. "She'll fit right into the LA scene." They come to a corner. This time of night there is hardly any traffic on Eighth Avenue. They cross on the red, like good New Yorkers. The rank, bracing scent of the river is gone now, subsumed by the smells of soot, tires, rusted metal, dark streams of urine on the sidewalk.

M says, "I used to think if I gave up fear, I'd find love. But that's just bullshit. Real life is something different altogether."

"Isn't it always?"

They come to a corner, cross against the light, hurrying and laughing like schoolgirls.

"Tell me more about Figgy," M says.

Tara shrugs, already embarrassed. "Not much to tell yet. We talked for a bit; he seemed nice—and smart. But I don't know what he does for a living, or . . ."

"Hey, why don't you just take it as it comes for once." M grins. "You'll have more fun that way." She squeezes Tara's arm. "Speaking of which, I'm going to Forest. I know the club scene isn't your thing, but a night out may be just what you need."

It is and it isn't, Tara thinks. But it seems that M is an old soul; her heart is in the right place. She hugs her friend. "Thanks, but no thanks. I'm already way over my limit for noise and crowds."

"I hear you," M says in her no-nonsense manner. "Forest is kind of over the top, but I thought you might want to have people around, just for tonight."

Tara feels M's desire to protect her, and this makes her happy. She hugs her friend tighter. "Be safe in Forest's neverland."

"And you, in your own neverland." M gives her a wink and quick kiss on the cheek. "And have a serious think about staying with me, yeah?"

7

Maybe I should've stayed with M, Tara thinks as she makes her way east. She feels alone in the city, usually a good thing for her, the night wrapped around her, securing her anonymity. Not this night, though. Tonight she feels naked, vulnerable. She stops at a street corner, watches couples piling into a small, cozy-looking restaurant. Reluctantly, she realizes that meeting Figgy has changed the way she feels about her current life. She is abruptly aware of how alone she is. Previously, she hasn't thought much about it, or if she did, she just dismissed it. But now the loneliness seems to seep into her, sending a shiver down her spine. Just past the restaurant, its beckoning warmth, its repellent din, she pauses under a bird-shit-stained awning, takes out her cell phone, scrolls through until she finds his number. Her thumb hovers over the call button. Racked with indecision, she curses, thrusts the phone back in the pocket of her coat.

A terrible sorrow grips her, squeezing whatever is left of her heart so hard she gasps for breath. More than once she is forced to stop, grabbing onto the base of a streetlight for support.

And what awaits her in Alphabet City? Her empty refrigerator, her coven of cockroaches, her cold bed.

And a wintry sleep.

8

Running through the dense woods with Hickory. Her hand reaches out to stroke his back, encounters fingers: Sophie's hand. With a ragged indrawn breath, she grips it hard. Stars and moon hidden from them. Only the dream night. And the terrifying thing chasing them. She is white with dread. Her heart is pounding so hard she can feel her rib cage expanding and contracting with each beat. *Thump-thub, thump-thub*, the very specific beat of a metronome. Through the woods they run, snaking around trees, faces whipped by low branches, leaping over fallen logs, moss covered, rotting, crawling with carapaced insects.

And then, in the way of dreams, it's through a house they're running—a house so vast there seems no beginning, no end to it. Running through rooms, shadowed and dark. In each room, illumination—a bare bulb—throws a circle of light onto the bare floor. The floor is cold as ice; it numbs her bare feet. Sophie is immune to cold, of course, and to heat. From room to room they flee until their pace falters, the way ahead blocked by a wall. And behind them the dreadful thing is gaining, gaining. The magnetic draw of it makes her skin crawl, her mouth go dry. Now here comes that thing, striding inexorably toward them, a hunter stalking its prey.

Her skin feels as if a thousand ants are crawling over it. It's the hunter or oblivion. Sophie, she calls. Sophie! But Sophie is nowhere to be seen; Sophie is gone. Falling to her knees, or pushed, there's nowhere to hide from the dreadful thing. She feels the hands on her, searching, probing, and there's nothing, nothing she can do. It's happening again. Again . . .

And Tara wakes, paralyzed, as usual, her pulse beating a frenzied tattoo in her ears. She stares at the cracks in the ceiling; tonight they look like tiny demons, dancing, capering, grinning down at her. The nightmare is still paralyzing her limbs.

And then, all at once released, she sits up, bedcovers sliding down her torso to pool at her waist. She is soaked in sweat, her hair hanging lankly on either side of her damp, bone-white face.

She heaves a deep breath, gasps, and weeps, great heaving sobs spilling out of her like blood.

9

I 'd like to begin where we left off the last time," Lind says. "You told me that without your sister there's only death and annihilation. Can you elaborate on that?"

Tara frowns. "I don't know what you want me to say."

"I simply want to understand."

"Understand what?"

Lind peers at her with a certain intent. "Have you ever tried to take your own life?"

"God, no," Tara answers truthfully. "Suicide isn't a viable path. I have proof of that every shift I work at Seventh Haven."

"Okay then. Please tell me what you meant."

"I just . . ." For a moment, Tara's gaze strays above Lind's head. "You know that swimmer on your wall."

Lind nods.

"Well, I feel like that's me. I mean, she's swimming, on and on, endlessly."

"Yes."

"Well, she never gets anywhere, does she?"

"She never gets tired either," Lind says. "It depends on your point of view."

Tara stares at the swimmer. "I'm trying to find Sophie. She left, and I don't know why. No goodbye, no note, nothing. As if I didn't exist."

"That's quite an extreme statement." Lind is writing now. "Have you always felt that you don't exist when your sister doesn't acknowledge you?"

"Please."

For a moment Lind seems about to ask another question, but at the last minute she changes her mind. "Making light of what you just said is a way of hiding from pain."

Tara stares at the swimmer above Lind's head. "And sometimes *hello* is just *hello*."

Lind appears unfazed by her difficult client. "Death and annihilation, you said, in the last session."

"Did I?" Something unspeakable crawls up Tara's spine, on its way to her brain, an insect unknown, yet disturbingly familiar. Many legs like delicate pistons on her skin, antennae questing. For what? The truth or . . . how long can she keep lying to Lind?

"You said that your anxiety dream—your sleep paralysis—started after Sophie vanished. I think it would be helpful to explore this further."

Tara feels as if she is dying inside, shriveling up and blowing away on the slightest breath of air.

"Are you all right?" Lind asks. "You look quite pale." She pours out some water, slides it over.

Tara stares at it for a moment, as if she has lost the ability to recognize even the simplest object. Then she takes up the glass. Her hand shakes. Leaning forward, Lind takes the glass out of Tara's hand.

"Put your head between your knees," she says softly.

Tara does as she is bidden. She feels unspeakably cold, her fingers stiff as if she has aged fifty years in fifty seconds. Her head feels both heavy and weightless, shadows and light vying for control. Whichever wins will matter a great deal.

"Now sit up slowly," Lind says. "Deep breaths from your core."

Presently, Tara feels a sense of normality returning.

Lind hands her back the glass, waits until she's drained the cold water. "Can you tell me what just happened?"

Tara shakes her head. "I don't know."

"Your defenses went up again. I mentioned your sister, Sophie, in the context of your recurring dream, and you retreated behind a wall, as you did the last time."

Tara says nothing, but the brief calm she felt is gone as if it has never existed. Her chest is congested, in turmoil.

Lind sets down her pen and notebook. "I have an alternate scenario to present to you."

Tara crosses her arms over her chest, then, at once, unfolds them, knowing the posture is defensive. "I'm listening." But she rises, steps to the window, stares out, sees nothing.

"I wonder if your dream isn't about you and Hickory at all," Lind says. "But rather about you and Sophie." She pauses for a moment, as if to take the measurement of Tara's chimerical moods. "Does that strike a chord?"

"I don't . . ." Tara has broken out into a cold sweat. She cannot summon the right words to deflect Lind's probing. And, she reminds herself, isn't this what she wanted? Really?

"Tara, please turn to me," Lind says. And when Tara does, she says, "Isn't it possible the main reason you came here was to talk about your sister? To talk about Sophie?"

Tara is back to staring at the ragged terrain of her hand. "I don't know." Why don't you tell her? Because I don't yet trust her. So goes her internal dialogue. Again. And again. It never changes, never stops. How can she make it stop? How can she ever learn how or whom to trust?

10

Figgy, smoking one of his clove cigarettes, is already sitting on the stoop she chose to overlook Christie's townhouse when Tara arrives. It is late; dusk is getting ready to settle, blue shadows stretching their legs along the street. He gives her a sideways glance as she sits down beside him. The Masterpiece truck is back yet again, the men now unloading crates that, according to the labels, contain paintings and various pieces of artwork. Whoever is taking possession of the townhouse adjacent to Lind's must be worth boocoodles, Tara thinks.

"Don't say it," Tara says.

"What? You mean of all the stone stoops—"

"Stop."

With that, he turns to look at her. "What's your problem, anyway?"

"Me?" Her eyebrows arch. "I don't have a problem."

"*Pardonnez-moi*, but you do." He takes a long toke on his cigarette, lets the aromatic smoke out slowly. "In fact, if all we had was one problem, everything would be dope."

"Speak for yourself." She eyes Christie's brownstone across the street and wonders why she is being so hostile. She hates when she gets this way. But of course she knows. Lind frightened her at the end of the last session. She morphed the fright into anger, which is easier to handle.

Figgy returns to the state of seeming contemplation of nothing he was in until she showed up.

"So," Tara begins, struggling to find a way to start over, "I guess I shouldn't have walked away so abruptly the other day."

Figgy shrugs. "Your prerogative."

"I'm just saying . . ."

He is smiling. "It's okay." The smile thaws something between them. "I mean, you let me give you my number. We're cool."

"It's just that I can be a dick sometimes."

"Yes." With a grin. "Yes you can."

She shakes her head. "Why are you being so nice to me?"

"I don't have time for being a dick. I'm just saying . . ."

They both laugh, and it is a nice thing for Tara to feel a kind of tentative kinship she hasn't experienced with a man in what seems forever.

He looks away for a moment, down the street where a mom is pushing her baby in one of those super-expensive strollers that, improbably or maybe inevitably, has become a status symbol. Everything is a status symbol these days. When he turns back, he says, "So I'm here because of you." A wry grin. "What's your excuse?"

She has a reason all right, but she isn't about to tell him. Anyway, he'd only misunderstand: chances are he'd think she was a creep or a stalker when she is neither. She just wants to be near Lind outside of their twice-weekly fifty minutes together to be sure she can trust her. "Maybe my reason involves you." This admission surprises her so much that she blurts out, "Does that invitation for dinner still stand?" before her inner checks have a chance to grab hold of her words and stuff them back down her throat.

Figgy finishes his clove cigarette, and she notes that after he grinds out the butt on the stone step, he drops it into the pocket of his jacket rather than flicking it into the street like a thousand out of a thousand other smokers would. A little thing, but sometimes, Tara thinks, little things mean a lot.

He rises and, turning to her, offers his hand, as if for a dance. "It would be my pleasure."

After a moment's hesitation, she takes his hand and stands. "Where to?"

He gives her a look of mock bewilderment. "You mean you're letting me choose?"

———

He takes her to a popular noodle shop. It is hot, packed, the noise so dense it seems possible they will need a machete to cut through it, but even if the atmosphere had been serene, Tara would still have been in something of a daze. When is the last time she has been out on a date— a real date—with anyone appropriate to her age?

The interior is all blond wood and bamboo and endless chatter. Figgy must know someone high up in the restaurant, because they cut the line, which is out the door, and wind up perched on wooden stools. The kitchen is open plan. Steam billows out of enormous tureens, and heady smoke swirls up from gigantic woks.

"What d'you think?" Figgy says after their first course has been wolfed down.

"Wow, I never dreamed of eating a meal in a place like this," she says. "Nevertheless, firsts on every level."

The second course arrives in a piping-hot bowl bigger than her head. He picks up one of those porcelain spoons they give you in Chinatowns all over the world.

They both taste the contents of the pot: slippery noodles, about a dozen kinds of vegetables. For a time, they eat in silence.

Afterward, she puts down her spoon, folds her arms, resting them on the tabletop. "So I work at Seventh Haven, helping kids who've lost themselves." She gestures. "What is it you do?"

"Ah, well, that's a long and winding road." They both grin at the Beatles reference. "By the time I was in my third year at Stanford, I'd decided I'd rather make money than get a degree. I mean, what would I do with a degree? So I quit and thereby pissed off my father royally. He's never really gotten over it, not even when I got a job at Intel in Silicon Valley, right away. Or when I graduated to a number of start-ups, all of which crashed and burned. Then, others that didn't."

"Then what are you doing here?"

"Start-ups in the gig economy are cesspits. It's like the Wild West, and God forbid you're a female. They get belittled; harassed; do great work, for which their bosses invariably take credit; and then are passed over for promotions."

Tara's brow furrows. "Even now, in this MeToo era?"

Figgy nods. "I saw it happen time and again, but the last straw came when I asked my boss at the last job out there to promote my assistant, Grace, to manager. She is a great talent, destined, I thought, for great things.

"My boss looked at me as if I'd grown another head. 'She looks good, nice piece of ass, Figgy,' he says. 'Are you fucking her, is that it?' 'No,' I tell him, 'I'm not.' He gives me the stink eye, like he doesn't believe me." Figgy mimics the look in exaggerated fashion, at which Tara would have guffawed, except that the story isn't funny—it isn't funny at all. Figgy continues: "He says, 'Then why the fuck're you being disruptive?' I tell him I'm not, but when I press Grace's case with details of her most recent work, he gets red in the face and says, 'She sits in on meetings and keeps her mouth shut. That's all that's required of her.' And turns on his heel. I packed up my things that afternoon, took them and Grace, and got the hell out of there.

"Now I've got other things to occupy my time."

"You mean Grace?" Tara says coyly, disconcerting herself by flirting.

Figgy's laugh is easy and free, like a kid's. "Well, tonight that would be you. So . . . then I took part of the booty I had amassed in Silicon Valley and founded a little start-up with Grace and a partner."

"What's your 'little start-up' do exactly?"

"The software algorithm scours the internet, finding people who are embezzling money from their companies."

A slight catch in the pit of her stomach is all that is left of that particular slice of her parents' past. "I think that's great," she says. "Good for you."

"Well, we'll see," he says, downplaying her enthusiasm. "We're still working out the bugs, trying to perfect the algorithm."

"But still . . ."

"Indeed."

She looks him up and down. Impossibly handsome, smart, empathetic, funny, and most surprisingly of all, hasn't yet turned into an octopus, hands all over her. Experience has taught her when something seems too good to be true, it usually is. Keep those quills up, she thinks.

"You know, you're kind of intimidating," he says in all seriousness.

"What? I don't mean to be."

"Oh, come on."

"I am who I am."

"Me too. That's why we're getting along so well."

"Are we?" Then she purses her lips. "Yes, I guess we are at that."

———

The light-spangled night is cool, a relief from the heat and humidity and constant din of the restaurant. They stroll back crosstown, entering Washington Square Park through the marble triumphal arch.

As they approach the large circular fountain through whose rainbow spray kids run during the heat of high summer days, Tara says, "Tell me something more about yourself. About your parents, maybe."

"Mm, my father's now married to a woman half his age. My mom moved to Geneva. Lucky for her France is just a couple of minutes away. She goes to see my sister and brother-in-law all the time. They live in Annecy, a beautiful town with a rather grim history during the German occupation."

"What does your father do?"

"He's a professor of philosophy, a doctor, really," he says.

"No wonder he was pissed when you dropped out of Stanford."

"You said it."

As they strolled around the circumference of the fountain, an itinerant singer with the smudge of a soul patch and a porkpie hat is strumming his acoustic guitar, singing "Precious," a Depeche Mode song much beloved by her. *What have we done to you?*

They stop to listen.

Precious and fragile things.

Stepping forward, Tara gives the singer five dollars. He tips his hat as he thanks her. He starts playing "In Your Room." *Where souls disappear.*

They drift away toward the dog run. Barking and high-pitched yips come to them on a cooling breeze.

"What about your parents?" Figgy asks.

"Dead."

"I'm sorry. Sore spot?"

"No . . . yes." I'll always be with you, her mother said. Truer words have never been spoken, her Jesus heart inflamed like a fiery furnace in the center of Tara's chest.

"Sorry. As I told you, with mine too."

She looks away. Behind them, on Fourth Street, a young couple strolls by, holding hands. "My mother went first. Suddenly. The county coroner said she had a massive coronary. My father died in a fire three weeks later." No mention of Sophie tonight, maybe never, Tara thinks, still wary that this connection will inevitably end in tears.

There is silence for a time, just the dogs barking and yipping at each other as they lope playfully around the pen. They lean on the railing, close together.

"Tell me about Bear," Tara says. "Your pug."

"Bear, well, Bear was lovable if you were my mother but a swift pain in the backside if you were my father. He hated the creature."

Tara swipes several stray strands of hair off her face, tucks them behind her ear. "But you liked Bear."

"Of course. I loved Bear; he and I were buddies. We'd do things together.

"We had a small wood out behind the house. I'd take him in there—you can imagine my mother had a stroke every time I did. Bear loved it, loved the fallen leaves, the small branches storms had broken off the trees. He'd gnaw on them, making the most god-awful snuffling noises." Figgy's eyes have clouded over with memories. "Then we'd play fetch. Do pugs do that? I don't know, but Bear did."

"Hickory was my buddy too." Should I tell him that we hunted together? I dunno. Maybe not. "He was my father's dog, but my father lost interest in him, so he became mine. I had to keep him away from my mother; she hated him and never wasted a moment without telling him so."

They laugh in unison, their shoulders pressed together. Neither pulls away.

"Can I ask your father's profession?" Figgy asks after a time.

"Promise not to laugh?"

"You ask too much of me, woman."

Tara smiles; she can't help herself. "He was a hypnotist."

Figgy's expression turns serious. "You mean a psychologist who used hypnotism?"

"Good God, no." The idea of her father listening to other people's neuroses and helping them through them is absurd. "He was a stage hypnotist."

Figgy's eyebrows arch. "No kidding."

"And I was a central figure in it."

"You mean he hypnotized you onstage, as part of his act."

"Yup."

Figgy laughs. "My dear Tara, you've suddenly become even more fascinating."

Then he kisses her square on the lips.

11

A bout Sophie," Lind begins.
"Actually, I think my father knew Sophie best," Tara says at last. The best compromise she can come up with. Besides, it has the advantage of being the truth, more or less.

"You're deflecting again."

Yes, of course she is. "The truth is . . ." And this is the truth. "The truth is Sophie and I had a love-hate relationship."

"That isn't all that unusual between siblings," Lind says. "Why do you think the relationship is so fraught for you?"

"I don't . . ." A certain darkness is stealing over Tara. In the silence of the room, an awful roaring in her mind.

"Where did you go?" Lind's silver pen is poised above her open notebook. "Just now, where did you go?"

"I'm right here." But she isn't; her mind messages to her in a kind of Morse code that contains too many blanks she fails to fill. Yet even without comprehension, she feels the heavy burden of guilt, hammered into her time and again by her mother, fierce messenger of God.

Lind remains preternaturally still. "I'd like you to think about why you won't talk about Sophie."

Silence winds around them like a cocoon.

Lind, attuned to Tara's vibrations, reacts. "Are you all right?"

"I'm fine." But she says it too fast, too sharply, and she knows Lind must suspect the opposite.

"I'd like to return to my previous question."

"What was that?" Tara's voice is thick, her thoughts muddy, shrinking into shadow. Another shiver capers down her spine. What is happening to her?

"Why you have difficulty articulating your relationship with your sister."

Tara, feeling abruptly chilled, says, "It has to do with my parents."

"Can you say more about that?"

"My parents—" Tara momentarily loses her voice, starts over: "My parents always hid things from us."

Lind remains silent. By which Tara infers that she hasn't given Lind the answer she is looking for, even though it is the truth, as far as it goes.

The silence gathers like shadows at dusk. At last, Tara says compulsively, "I think my mother didn't understand us at all. She was too busy with her ministry, too busy communicating with God."

"Does that mean your father took care of you two?"

"Yes."

"Did he want to or did he have to?"

"I think both."

"So there was a kind of dissonance there, a shift in the family structure."

Tara knows, but she shrugs anyway.

Lind seems to change direction. "Did your parents argue?"

"Yeah."

"A lot?"

"Enough."

"Was that resolved in any way?"

"My father took me to his study, where he'd hypnotize me. That's where he told me not to be upset if he and my mother had arguments, that all married couples argued from time to time."

"That's true enough," Lind says. "But it's often a matter of what the people are arguing about rather than if they do or not."

Tara stares at the back of her left hand.

"Do you know what your parents were fighting about?"

The scars seem livid to her, pulsing, as if they have a life of their own. "No," she lies. Enough of the truth has already leaked out.

"We can end the session here," Lind says now. She has an uncanny ability to measure the passage of time without consulting either her watch or a clock. At least within these four walls. "Or—I have a few more minutes—we could go on." She has set down her pen. It lies diagonally across her open notebook. "Your choice."

Silence, while a metronome tick-tocks inexorably in Tara's mind.

"Sometimes it was my mother accusing my father of whoring, and him denying it," Tara says. "But mostly it was about me." Tara's consciousness is drifting closer and closer to the swimmer above Lind's head, with whom she has come to identify strongly. "My mother was incensed by my father using me in his act. My father insisted it was the main draw. 'Without her the money will dry up,' he'd say. 'Is that what you want?'" She touches her scars, tracing them like a road map. "It was a kind of power play."

"A power play." Lind seems to be testing the words in her mouth, as if they have a particular flavor. And perhaps, Tara thinks, they do: roasted meat. "Can you say more about that?"

"Sure, sure." Tara's barking laugh cuts like a knife. "Whoever won me over to their side would claim victory."

12

Party time. Happy/sad, approach/avoidance. Me all over, Tara thinks. In a little black dress she has bought at Forever 21 for almost no money, she accompanies Figgy to what she assumes is an artist's loft in Tribeca. There is plenty of art on the decorator-white walls, all of it postmodern, all of it offensively expensive, all of it hideous to her eye. The loft, as it turns out, is owned by a guy named Stephen Ripley, who, fifteen years ago, started a hedge fund now worth more than the GDP of a quarter of the countries in the world. The place is huge, as postmodern as the art—a kind of cubist nightmare with no exit, except for french doors out to a long terrace. To gain entrance to the loft, Figgy had to show some form of ID to the two immense guards flanking the front door. Already, Tara is feeling weird, as if she has dropped acid.

The vast space is furnished solely in black or white. Chairs look like lamps, lamps look like chairs. Sofas look like a crazy person's take on Louis XVI furniture: all stubby legs and tufted ultra-high backs. None of it looks comfortable. Then again, no one is seated. Alice down the rabbit hole, Tara thinks, as she half jokingly looks around for a stoppered flask marked "Drink Me."

There is a weird mixture of older artists, middle-aged suits, and young men in black turtlenecks, jeans, sandaled or loafered—tech types: blockchain innovators, start-up entrepreneurs, algorithm geniuses, she gathers from the snatched bits of conversations she manages to overhear. Figgy intros her to a couple of them. The men assess her coolly with their entitled male gaze—entitled because, after all, they are men of wealth and fame. Circling in the outer orbits are a number of women: young, slim, bored, in tight skirts, low-cut tops, and super-high heels. If they aren't high-level escorts, they sure are trying to look the part. It is the women who notice Tara's scars, eyes staring and then quickly looking away as if they've been seared. As for the men, they are too busy checking out her legs and breasts to notice her hand.

A Spotify playlist of '70s and '80s rock wafts through the loft. Uniformed waiters glide through the crowd with trays laden with champagne and tapas. A bar has been set up, where the guests can take their pick of any or all high-end brands of liquor. Every now and again, she catches a glimpse of glass finger bowls filled with what look like after-dinner mints but are clearly nothing of the sort.

Figgy, glass of champagne in one hand, is asking what she thinks of the crew, and she is wondering what he is doing at a party like this, a place full of lily-white high technocrats full of booze and pills. She even has the fleeting thought that Figgy has brought her here for her own lily whiteness, as a kind of shield or trophy, but almost immediately she feels ashamed of the thought. Because now she is trying to see the party through his eyes: as the only person of color in the apartment. As a female, her marginalized-persons ticket is always punched, but at least she has some company. Figgy, however, is all alone in a sea of white faces, green money, and cryptocurrency. Tara slips an arm through his, a gesture of friendship and solidarity.

Seeing her pale, pinched face, Figgy, as sensitive to her as she is to him, asks her if she is all right. "Fine," she replies. What else can she say? But her tone sounds faint and false. Craven, even, as if she has abruptly lost the ability to be herself, as if she is turning into a creature that is a complete stranger to herself.

An overheard snatch of conversation catches her attention, and she holds up her forefinger to Figgy. He nods and drifts away to engage with someone else. A small circle of men stands off to Tara's left, deep into what sounds like serious conversation, the subject of which is neither the international transfer of money nor the results of Sotheby's latest auction. The phrase she has overheard that intrigues her so much is *tribal epistemology*.

You can't get any more pretentious than that, she thinks as she joins the loose circle of five men. The one who used the phrase is an older man, with wings of silver hair swept back from a wide, intelligent forehead. His piercing blue eyes and animated mouth single him out from among the self-important financial suits he is addressing. She is immediately assaulted by a fistful of designer colognes—moss and fig and leather, manly notes for the postmodern major mogul. One of them also smells of tobacco and must have come in from the long terrace, where he smoked a cigarette or two before returning to the fray.

"To reiterate," the older man says, "this country has gone to the dogs. And by dogs I mean it's gripped by a tribal epistemology."

"Who cares?" the man in a tan suit across from him replies. "We're getting just what we want." That brings a round of laughs. "The market's upward trajectory can't be stopped now," he continues. "We're making more money than we have in a decade."

"And I think it's longer," another financial wizard in chalk stripes chimes in.

"But at what cost?" Blue Eyes queries.

"I don't give a fuck," Tan Suit retorts.

"Of course you don't," Blue Eyes says.

"None of us does," Chalk Stripe says, as the hedgies close ranks against this interloper.

"The only question is why you do," Tan Suit says with his nose figuratively in the air.

"You know, boys, I'm beginning to smell a rotten odor coming off all of you. Do you even know what tribal epistemology is?"

"It's what's happening now, all across the country," Tara breaks in.

"Who the hell are you?" Tan Suit snaps. "And what do you know about any of this?"

"This has already gotten too emotional," Chalk Stripe adds.

Tara is being subjected not only to the male gaze but also to the male mindset. She is a woman—a young woman, at that.

"Hold on," Blue Eyes says. "Clearly the young lady has something on her mind. Why don't we hear what it is?"

Chalk Stripe leaves off ogling Tara's boobs long enough to chuckle. "Sure. Let's give her all the rope she needs to hang herself." He laughs. "Figuratively speaking, that is."

They all laugh—all except Blue Eyes. He is watching her like a professor who believes he's prepared a great big surprise for his class. Smiling at her, he says, "May I ask your name, Mademoiselle?"

Very old world. Any one of the other women here would have laughed in his face, but not Tara. She likes it. "Tara Fischer." By this time she has become inured to not using either of her parents' family names: Peary, Lockhart.

"Brandon Fiske." He offers his hand, and she takes it briefly. Something passes between them, a kind of recognition maybe, but she thinks of this only later. "Now let's hear what you have to say about tribal epistemology."

"You're absolutely right, Brandon," Tara begins, as if she and Brandon Fiske are old friends. "Many people in America—the religious right, the poorly educated, evangelicals, especially—are in its grip."

"Which means?" Tan Suit says, baring teeth that could use a good cleaning. Tara wants to tell him to shut his mouth.

"For them, there are no facts; there is no objective truth. Tribal epistemology means that they believe what the tribe believes: the tribe lays down the laws, and they follow them willingly, blindly, trusting in the tribe to take care of them, to keep them safe from all outsiders hostile to the tribe's aims and intents."

Chalk Stripe sneers at her. "Do you mean they've all swallowed the Kool-Aid?"

"Tara is absolutely correct," Brandon says. "Fox News, Breitbart, Infowars, Reddit, *Der Stürmer*, the flat-earthers—they're all tribes."

Tan Suit shifts from one foot to the other. He looks terribly discommoded. "I don't believe in conspiracy theories. And anyway, all the news media these days are biased. They all have a point of view to hawk."

"That only strengthens my contention that the tribal warfare is being fought online," Brandon says. "How else can you explain the proliferation of what's called 'fake news'? Millions of Americans believe CNN, the *New York Times*, the *Washington Post*, NPR are all purveyors of 'fake news.'"

"Some of them are," Tan Suit says.

"Quite right." Brandon nods. "This frenzied atmosphere is making the job of the real news people, both conservative and liberal, almost impossible because virtually no one is listening to them."

"But that right there is the real news," Tan Suit exclaims. "I mean, it's factual. Irrefutable. We all know that."

"Not if the tribe says it's fake," Tara says. "For them, there is no objective truth. And as you should know by now, the uninformed are being led around by the nose by troll bots pumping out crap faster than you can find them."

"No, what I mean is the market. The economy is good, unemployment is down, we've all got tax breaks, and stocks keep making all-time highs."

"What about human rights?" Tara says. "What about women's rights? What about voters' rights? What about the rights of people of color? Lives are being trampled."

"'People of color,'" Chalk Stripe scoffs. "Listen to the feminazi."

"That's enough, Scott," Brandon admonishes.

"To say nothing of the environmental atrocities, the cynical global warming denials while towns in the—"

"Jesus, what am I doing listening to this drivel?" Chalk Stripe says. "I came here to have a good time, not to listen to a hysterical lecture by a—" Whatever he is going to call her, he bites it off, and without another word he stalks away. The others follow, leaving only Brandon standing with Tara.

"Lovely fellow," Tara says.

Brandon snorts. "Don't mind him. Once a putz, always a putz."

Tara has never heard that word before; nevertheless, she gets the gist and laughs.

Brandon snatches two flutes of champagne from a waiter floating by, hands her one. They clink rims and drink. "You have a very sharp mind," he says. "Quick. Intelligent."

"For a woman."

"I didn't say that."

"But you were thinking it."

Brandon laughs. "What I am thinking is that you scared the bejesus out of those schmucks."

Another word she hasn't heard; again she gets the meaning. She makes a mental note to check the Urban Dictionary site when she gets home.

"And to be honest, you're an interloper in their stadium." One corner of his mouth gives a quick flicker upward. "What is it you do currently?"

"I work at Seventh Haven. Counseling kids who are in desperate need of being heard and acknowledged."

"Do you like your work?"

"Very much, even though it can be emotionally hammering at times."

His eyebrows arch up. "Have you ever worked for anyone?"

"I'm not so good at that. I don't seem to work and play well with others. Stupidity gets on my nerves."

His chuckle deepens. "Birds of a feather." He hands Tara his card. "I'd be pleased if you'd come in and talk with me."

"About what?"

"Oh, I don't know. A job, maybe."

"After what I just said?"

"*Because* of what you've said."

CONSTANT HORIZONS LLC, she reads. The address is somewhere way downtown. "You're founder and chairman of the board."

"I am," he says matter-of-factly.

She likes that. Her eyes rise to meet his. "The company that funds Seventh Haven, the clinic where I work."

"We solicit funds for Seventh Haven," he corrects. "As we do for about a dozen nonprofits."

"Then what are you doing here? Slumming?"

His laugh is deep, genuine. "Now you *must* come see me, Tara." He shakes his head.

"Why?"

"I invest in the future. The future interests me."

"The future of what?"

"People," he says. "And I get the feeling that interests you too." When she makes no reply, he continues: "What Constant Horizons does—what *I* do—is get these guys here and others like them to fork over millions to help the needy. We're also working on creating our own charity network." He inclines his head toward her. "Which is where I have a feeling you might fit in. Interested?"

"Maybe."

He laughs again. "Okay, then. Give me a buzz in the next day or so." Regarding her over the rim of his glass. "If you've a mind to."

Tara is beginning to take a real shine to ole Brandon, someone who strikes her as different from other men she has encountered, including Figgy. She is about to thank him, but right then Marwyn Rusk, managing partner of Millbank Partners, bounces through the front door.

Lind's Marwyn, with the long working hours in Westport, Connecticut. The only thing he is working right now is a pneumatic blonde in a skintight wrap dress, scarlet choker, and five-inch-heel pumps that show off her porno boobs and an ass you could bounce a quarter off to perfection. The polar opposite of his wife. All the breath goes out of her, and she almost stumbles. A shiver runs down her spine, and she grows cold inside. He is holding the porno blonde tight, cooing into her ear, doing everything but taking a piss around her to mark out his territory. Hands off, boys, she's mine!

Not that he has cause for worry. All the financial partygoers recognize Marwyn as one of their own. More than one of their own. Hell, they hail him like a conquering hero. And who can blame them, with his built-in charisma and wide-screen smile. And now, through the fog of bitter disillusion, she sees the flip side of that charisma and wide-screen smile, the Viking, the Vandal, the Hun. A throbbing starts up behind her eyes, as if she literally doesn't want to see this betrayal, wants to wake up from this nightmare and find herself comfortably in bed. Find that it has never happened. That she has dreamed it. That Christie hasn't been pissed on. That Christie and Charlotte will be able to navigate through his betrayal.

Spinning the blonde around, Marwyn kisses her on the lips while his roving hand squeezes her butt.

An image of the strangled family scene she and Figgy witnessed floats into her mind. She sensed a breach then. Now she thinks she knows why. Christie and Charlotte won't be all right. Not now, not ever.

At that moment Figgy returns from the back of beyond.

"So, I see you recognize that guy," he says, indicating Marwyn with his head. He smells of clove smoke; he must have been outside on the terrace.

"Sure. The peacemaker between his driver and those movers." She tries for a casual tone, fails miserably. Tries again. "I was actually wondering which pornos the blonde starred in."

He laughs. "Yeah, right. Name's Marwyn, remember? Marwyn Rusk. He runs a successful financial firm up in Westport."

"Hedgie territory."

"Uh-huh."

"You know him?"

"Everybody here knows Marwyn."

"And does everybody know he's got a wife and kid on West Tenth Street?"

"Honey, no one in this room cares."

I care. "You haven't earned the right to call me *honey*." The last thing she needs is someone she barely knows calling her *honey*. Here, in this milieu, he seems to be a different person altogether. It doesn't suit him.

"Maybe I misjudged you. Maybe it *is* women you prefer."

"Oh, wow," she says. "This now? Really?" She turns her back to him. "I've had enough of this place, these people. Honestly, I don't know why you dragged me here. Showing me off, are you?"

"Jesus, is that who you are now?" Clearly stung.

She might have said something really cutting, but seeing Marwyn out on the town has taken a lot out of her. "I'm going for a pee, and then I'm out of here. Whether you stay or go with me is strictly up to you."

She leaves him standing there, his mouth still half-open. She is as hot as an overrevved engine as she threads her way through the crowd, whose drinking, snorting, flirting, sweating turns the atmosphere in the loft toxic. She finds the bathroom free and steps inside, closes and locks the door, and gratefully empties her bladder.

Afterward, she stands in front of the mirror, staring at her face: heart shaped, high cheekbones. Her lips, colorless as her cheeks, her upper lids. And her eyes, wide apart, green as Emerald City, hold an expression as unforgiving as a repo man's. Running her fingers through her combed-back hair, she considers herself. She doesn't think herself beautiful, or even pretty, but she knows others do. Including Sophie. *Face it*, Sophie once said. *You're one hot kitten.* Maybe that's why she doesn't wear makeup.

Staring at herself, she wonders what the hell she is doing. She isn't Sophie; she doesn't belong here, in the company of shallow men giving vent to their venality, lack of empathy, feelings of superiority, their enraging sense of entitlement; and hollow women, eager to do anything asked of them, eerily similar to the women who worshipped in her mother's revival tent. She feels sick, feverish. With an almost physical ache, she longs to be back in her apartment.

Tears sting her eyes, blurring her vision. Blindly, she unlocks the door, pulls it open, and promptly collides with Marwyn. She immediately takes an unsteady step back. They stand facing each other, no more than a handbreadth apart.

"Sorry," they say at the same time, and he laughs an easy laugh.

Stunned to be this close to Christie's husband, Tara makes no move either forward or back. He smells strongly of cognac. And it isn't until later that night that she realizes that he took her inaction as an invitation. Before she can make a move, he shuts the bathroom door and is drunkenly pushing against her, his thigh between her legs, rubbing against her pubic mound.

"Nice, isn't it?" he whispers into her ear, and she freezes as if he has plunged an ice pick into her belly. "There's more where that came from." A low sound, like the snap of a trap closing, freezing her in place. "A whole lot more."

This can't be happening! Does she say that or think it? The agitated confusion of the party beyond the bathroom door vanishes. She is thrust into a limbo where time stands still and all she can hear is a voice crying, "No, no, no!" But that voice, mouselike, seems far away, spoken by another person, in another time, another place.

"Oh, come on. No is yes with you girls, isn't it?" Before she has a chance to answer, he unbuttons the collar of his shirt. She sees a slim gold chain. He brings out what is hanging from it: a large gold coke spoon. Well, that figures.

"How about a taste?" he whispers. "Choice-quality stuff, I assure you."

She shakes her head. Her tongue feels glued to the roof of her mouth. Words are stuck inside her frozen mind.

"This then," he says. "Better than . . ." He tries to push his tongue past her teeth, but she clamps her jaws shut tight. "Ah," he says, as if he is a dentist and she his patient. He grabs the hinges of her jaw between his thumb and middle finger, pressing inward so hard that in reflex her mouth gapes open to relieve the pain. Immediately, like an adder, his tongue slithers in, invading the interior.

When the tip touches her tongue, it is as if a galvanic shock rockets through her system. It reaches her brain, and time comes unstuck, accelerating at a hideous pace. Paralysis vanishes. Thought cedes to instinct. She slaps his ear with the flat of her hand and shoves hard, and while he is off balance, she slams him against the doorframe.

"Oh, yeah." Still he holds on, clawing at her, grinning. "I like it a little rough too."

"No, no, no!"

"Uh. Can't change your mind now." Reaching out for her.

She lets him get close again, then slips her leg between his. As his eyes open wide in delight, she slams the crown of her knee into his balls.

"Cunt!" Snatching his hand away, eyes bloodred as he almost doubles over. He is deflating as rapidly as a pricked balloon.

"Explain that to your wife, motherfucker."

"Whore," he spits, cradling his groin. "You're nothing but a filthy whore. Do you know who I am? I'll ruin you!" But she is already away, striding back into the crowd, where she almost runs headlong into Brandon Fiske.

"Whoa," he says. "Was that Rusk? That guy is such a prick." His eyes search her face. "Are you okay? Do you need help?"

She hardly registers a word he says, just pushes past him, almost running now toward the door.

13

She reaches her apartment, hardly knowing how she got there. She might have gone to M's, but she can't bear the thought of sleeping in Stevie's bed, not tonight. The instinct of the wounded animal brings her back to her own lair, miserable though it may be.

Her head is exploding, and she feels like weeping. She doesn't, though, but can't tell whether that is a good thing. Running the water, she sheds her sweaty clothes, which she feels like hurling onto Marwyn's funeral pyre. Not only Marwyn, no, but she won't allow herself to go there. She steps into the shower, turns the hot on full, and begins to scrub herself inside and out. Even so, she remains chilled to the bone. Her skin crawls at the memory of his leg between hers, his tongue flicking against her teeth, probing the inside of her mouth . . . and then the tears come, overflowing her eyes, mixing with the cascading water as she sobs, shoulder jammed against the tiles. She puts her hand out, pressing it against the warm tiles, sinking into the solidity of the wall. Shelter from the storm. But there is no shelter, not really, not now. Not then.

She turns off the water, stumbles out of the shower, and curls into a ball, shivering, on the cloth bathmat on the floor. She folds her hands over her head, as if she can cover her mind, hold back the horror her unconscious has walled away to protect herself, to keep herself sane. But Marwyn's assault has not been only on her person but on that wall inside herself, and now it is slowly crumbling, the poison of her child-hood flooding out.

"No," she murmurs, speaking to the damp cotton against which her cheek is pressed, speaking to the walls beyond the bathroom, the cracked ceiling of her bedroom, the cockroaches that are somewhere about, hiding from her in terror. Contrary to what she so bravely, and perhaps foolishly, told Lind, she wants the world to stop; she wants to get off the ride.

She thinks of the knife on the kitchen cutting board, the cleaning fluid in the rickety vanity under the bathroom sink, the pain pills in the medicine cabinet mere feet away. She thinks of a leaky living room window, the city howling in her ears, stygian nighttime coming. The end.

From the depths of Tara's despair surfaces the image of the swimmer in the painting in Lind's office. It's curious how the swimmer at first seemed to be swimming to nowhere. Now Tara experiences her in an altogether different light. Tara wishes she were there now, curled on Christie's love seat, listening to her voice warming her, washing away the seeping poison. Rising unsteadily, she stuffs her party clothes into the hamper. As she does so, the card Brandon Fiske gave her flutters to the floor. She picks it up and throws it into the trash can. Like a child with a fever, she crawls into bed. Head spinning, all cried out, she closes her eyes. Breathe, she tells herself. Breathe. It will be over soon. Which is what she told herself, over and over, when she was young.

At length, she relaxes, her mind freed from her body's bondage. She falls asleep. She dreams of Sophie, and in her dream, as she wanders in a wilderness of pine trees, she keeps repeating, "Sophie, where are you? Sophie, I need you. Help me, Sophie." Her whisper is lost in the clamor of the evil memories inside her head.

On waking, Tara realizes her pleas have gone unanswered. She rises, dresses quickly, and flees into the night.

Perched on the stoop across the street from Christie's brownstone, she feels somehow calmer. Lights burn in only one window on the third floor, probably Christie's bedroom. Does she know what Marwyn gets up to when he is "working"? The sick feeling in the pit of her stomach returns, and she tries to ease her breathing. A tricked-out SUV drives by, and a snatch of the Weeknd's "I Feel It Coming" rises from the street, then sweeps away. After that, the street is quiet. A couple of pedestrians, one with a schnauzer on a leash, walking quickly, heads down.

Staring at the lighted window, she sees Christie pass by briefly. Arms wound tightly around herself, Tara rocks back and forth, longing so hard to be inside, to be part of that life, a life that would value her, that would cherish her, that she feels sick. Lips and fingertips trembling, she wills herself inside the brownstone, imagines herself in Christie's company, hearing her compassionate voice. How comforting it would be to be with her and Charlotte, to feel their closeness. To experience their love. Briefly, she even entertains the insane idea of crossing the street, ringing the doorbell. And seeing her framed in the buttery light of the entryway, would say—what? "I saw your husband tonight. He's cheating on you. Oh, and by the way, the shitbird sexually assaulted me."

No. No, no, no.

That isn't going to happen. If not never, then certainly not tonight. And yet, Tara thinks, I need an ally. And she thinks, Tonight M is working; she won't answer—she won't even hear her phone. She calls Figgy. But Figgy doesn't answer; she leaves a voicemail. A moment later she can't remember what she's said.

She rises and calls for an Uber to take her to Forest. Twelve minutes later, she spills out of the car onto Vesey Street. Forest is accessed through a velvet curtain at the rear of the Black Rabbit Bar and Lounge. The Black Rabbit is the kind of place you go to if you want thirty-dollar cocktails and selfie ops and if you are networking with denizens of Manhattan's artistic demimonde. The lighting is low, the seating plush;

the music, if you can call it that, is like the frothy burbles out of an infant's mouth. The various cliques—writers, artists, so forth—all turn their backs on newcomers after giving them the stink eye. Tara can't care less.

The curtain at the rear is heavy velvet the color of oxblood, like those in Broadway theaters. She pushes her way into the narrow hallway, painted a matte black and illuminated by fairy lights strung just below the ceiling, that leads to Forest. Long before she reaches the end of the hallway, however, the hard, racing beat of the house music insinuates itself into her, a fist gripping her soul.

Forest bursts upon her all at once, assaults her both visually and aurally, which, she supposes, is the point. Total immersion as she pulls her first breath of the thick, shimmering atmosphere, musky with swirls of perfumes and colognes. Eddies of body odor and makeup, lashings of heated metal, sweet pot smoke, shoe leather threaten to overwhelm her. Sweat flies off the frenetic dancers in overheated sprays. Red, blue, yellow, green, magenta, orange spotlights on tracks hanging from the ceiling high overhead pop like the flashbulbs of the paparazzi mobs in Fellini films. The space is so vast, so jammed with writhing bodies, that she can't even make out what the walls are made of, let alone their color. And the constant beat of the music like a giant's stamping boots.

She searches for M, making only marginal headway in the thickets of heaving people. Two young men, sinewy, shirtless, eye shadowed, their torsos silvered with sweat, feed each other tabs—X or acid, who knows?—without missing a beat. A clutch of girls in black-and-white barely there skirts or silver-and-gold Mylar shorts so tight they display the lower halves of their butt cheeks drink and dance, dance and drink, laugh and dance, dance and kiss each other on the lips. They admit a couple of males into their midst, laughing again, closing ranks around them as if corralling wild horses.

A guy breaks off from another pack and, stepping up to her, offers a glass of what might be white wine but in this situation could be anything. His smile is wide, razor thin, predatory. His gaze roves over her body appreciatively.

"How about it?" he mouths, his voice hardly heard above the roar. She shoves him away, gets swept up in an ungovernable undertow, candy-spun into an altogether different galaxy of trans, gender-fluid drag sisters, who accept her without the slightest edge of threat or danger. I should be dancing, she thinks, but she is too distraught to let herself go. Instead, she moves on to another part of the dance floor. She is whirled around by a dancer young and bright, neither obviously male nor female. Handsome or beautiful, what is the difference? "Your lips are so pale," the dancer says, grinning, and paints them with poppy-red gloss, pressing the stick into her palm before swirling away into a nearby group. The music changes from house to trance, the beats per minute slowing from 160 to 130. She has read that the trance's tempo mimics that of ancient shamanistic rituals the world over, but at this liquid moment such lofty thoughts are far from her mind. Her body takes over, and finally, she loses herself in dance.

She plunges deeper, much deeper, until there is only her pulse merging with the rhythm of the music, a fusion so familiar that the transformation is like slipping into the clear lake of her childhood. Sophie's lake, cool, clear, secret, and sacred. She can feel Sophie coming into focus, Sophie beside her. Her Sophie, at once missed and not. But something seems to be tugging her somewhere else. The pounding of the rhythm, the insistent beats cause momentary blackouts and the frightening sense that she is being sucked down, that she is being shoved through a membrane from one world into another.

At length, exhausted, disoriented, she makes it to the bar, grasps onto it with clawlike fingers. With the human surf lapping at her heels, she hails a bartender, a man who appears to be made up of nothing but muscles and luridly colored tats. She asks him where M is, but he just shakes his head. She shouts her order for a mezcal and tequila mix. As she waits, she turns, gazing out over the throbbing sea of bobbing heads and writhing bodies without finding a glimpse of M. Downing the drink in a single swallow, she asks for another, and another. And another.

14

Tara, still traumatized by the assault, now drunk and dislocated by the rhythmic throbbing of the bass, staggering and buffeted, somehow makes it across the packed room. How long it takes she has no idea. Her consciousness is flickering in and out of existence, like a stuttering film. Reaching the ladies' room, she hauls open the door, stands with her back against the wall. All the stalls are in use. She waits.

———

"Hypnosis is like looking in a mirror," her father said. Tara sat on a chair facing him. They were in his study. It smelled of tobacco, leather, and Hickory. It was late. The night was still. She was five years old. "You look in the mirror and you see yourself. But at the same time you see someone else, someone you've never seen before. Your Other. I'm going to let you see your Other, to visit her whenever you want. Would you like that?"

Apart from the question, Tara was barely able to follow what Father was saying. But she loved Father and always did what he told her to do. So she bobbed her head up and down, her ponytail undulating like a fox's tail.

"Hypnosis takes you outside yourself, makes you stronger. Hypnosis will give you a new life."

Years later, when she was old enough, Tara found that she remembered every word he said to her that night. She even remembered Hickory barking outside, at a raccoon or a possum. Everything made sense, then. But at five, she simply acted on trust. She trusted her father implicitly.

His eyes were coal dark, like the crows in the treetops outside. They seemed to bore into her, tunneling into her mind. "You need this, baby. You want this, don't you." It was not a question; it was an exhortation. He pulled Tara to him, and their foreheads touched. This was their secret sign. "Baby, you must want this for the hypnosis to work. For you to be strong enough."

Strong enough for what? Tara didn't know. She didn't want to know.

She nods. "I do." She said this in the solemn manner of a five-year-old, oblivious to the bridal reference. "I do."

So it began: the strength. The life outside herself. The periods of near death before the fire that would consume everything.

———

Two girls, sniffing mightily, exit, giggling like lunatics. Tara enters the vacated stall that stinks of urine and other human effluvia, and rests her forehead against the inside of the locked door. Time collapses, vanishing altogether, as if through a mirror.

Tara becomes aware that she is staring at the filthy floor, strewn with toilet paper that missed the bowl, bits of tinfoil veined with white powder, scrunched-up tissues containing God only knows what. She no longer knows where she is. The shock of Marwyn's assault has caused an earthquake inside her, a tsunami of events long hidden behind the wall her unconscious has built. Unprotected, vulnerable, her past and present colliding.

Inhale, exhale. Again. And again. Someone is banging on the stall door.

"Hey," a harsh female voice screams at the top of her lungs, "what the fuck are you doing in there, killing yourself?"

Tara unlatches the door. In rushes a goth girl, in full leather regalia, her eyelids blackened, her nails as well.

"Cunt," Goth Girl mutters, brushing Tara aside, slamming the door behind her.

Dimly, Tara recalls that is what Marwyn called her. Half-spun around by Goth Girl's rush, she finds herself staring into the mirror. Through the lipstick smears, the Pollock paint-spatter of dried spittle, she sees a face staring back at her. It is her and it isn't her.

It doesn't feel like her face because it is Sophie's.

Her sister's ravishing poppy-red lips purse in a salacious moue, and, with a wink freighted with intimate meaning, she says, *Hey, Tara. Long time no see.*

PART 2
ANOTHER LIFE

The bargain might appear unequal; but there was still another consideration in the scales.

—Robert Louis Stevenson,
The Strange Case of Dr. Jekyll and Mr. Hyde

15

T ara, you're shivering."

She blinks, sees Figgy standing in front of her. How did she get here? She was in the ladies' room, staring into the mirror. Now she is leaning against the wall outside the restroom door.

Hello, Kitten. Time for fun again.

Looking around hurts her head, as if she has slipped, as if her forehead has hit the edge of the bar.

Figgy puts his jacket around her shoulders. She feels his arm across her back and recoils inside. She cannot understand what has happened to her; she's lost the knowledge that Sophie was inside her all the time.

Kitten, this is no time for flashbacks, Sophie says in Tara's head. The disdain in her tone is unmistakable, and all at once Tara feels lost, as if the chain to her anchor has been severed.

"Tara?"

She just stares at him, at a complete loss. She went into the ladies' drunk, disoriented, and unmoored and came out with her pleas answered. After twenty silent, absent months, Sophie has climbed out of the hole . . . and climbed back into her head. Will he know? Will he see the subtle differences between Tara and Sophie? But how can he, she reassures herself. He scarcely knows me.

"What happened to you? I tried to find you at the party, but you'd gone."

She looks into Figgy's eyes. He seems genuinely worried.

His brows knit together. "Can we get out of here? I can't hear myself think."

Outside the club, a light mist is falling. The streets are slick, looking like vinyl. They stand in the doorway of an adjacent building, waiting for the Uber Figgy has ordered.

"Okay, listen, I'm sorry we fought. And really, I'm so sorry about what I said to you." He hangs his head. "I just don't know what I was saying. It came out before I had a chance to think."

"What were you doing at Forest?" She has found her voice at last.

"You called me, left a message."

"I did?"

"Yup. You told me where you were."

"Uh, I don't remember."

"I'm not surprised. How many drinks have you had?"

"Many."

"I thought you didn't drink." When she makes no reply, with his brow furrowed, he says, "I didn't think you wore makeup either. It makes you look different."

The comment lances through the fog. Nettled, she says, "I'd look different in a string bikini" (she'd never . . .) "or a Vera Wang gown" (glimpsed in a recent *Vanity Fair* . . .).

Figgy nods. "Fair enough. But—"

The Uber comes then, and they climb in. She doesn't ask him where they are going.

She is staring out the window at nighttime Manhattan rushing by like workers late for appointments.

"I like you in lipstick," he says. "The color flatters you." When she doesn't respond, he takes a breath, says, "Tara, I'm trying to be . . . I'm trying to apologize."

"I know what you're doing," she says. But she doesn't, not really. Is he complimenting her or Sophie? She is going to find out, though—that much she knows.

"Listen, I know the party made you uncomfortable. I know I never should have suggested it. But I was more or less required to show up." He holds up his hands, palms out. "No excuse. My bad. Why I thought it would be fun for you I have no idea."

Because she is still staring fixedly out the window, he leans forward, the better to see her face. "Ripley's a first-class dick. He's a moneyman who thinks he can score points with his clients by throwing these so-called salons, where they can gain bragging rights by mingling with the creatives. He thinks it gives him instant cachet." He sighs. "Essential for his brand of business."

Still waiting for a sign from her, he says, "Tara, truce. Okay?"

"Why?" she murmurs, turning to face him.

"Why a truce?"

She tosses her head. "Why were you required to be at Ripley's party, 'more or less'?"

His hesitation makes her give him a penetrating look. His face is a chiaroscuro of light and shadow as they continue uptown.

"Figgy, if you don't tell me, I'm out of here."

He shrugs. "My fledgling company needs to expand. That means more backers. That means the guys who were at Ripley's." In the glare of her eyes, he sighs. "I'm not required to like them. Just get them interested in investing in my—"

"Is part of your job providing them with women and drugs?"

"Now you think I'm a dealer?" His face turns dark. "Why do you talk to me that way?"

"I'm sorry." To her mild surprise, she is. "But those people rub me the wrong way. They're parasites, sucking the lifeblood out of the country." Thinking mostly of Marwyn, her skin crawling, as if she can feel him all over her. Intimately probing. Violating her. "They're part of the kleptocracy. To think you might be part of that—"

Something appears to click behind his eyes. "First of all, I'm not. But more importantly, what's going on with you?" He peers at her, clearly concerned. "Did something happen to you at the party?"

At that moment, the car comes to a stop, and they get out. To her utter astonishment, they are on Christie's street. In fact, her brownstone is just to her left. While she stands, transfixed, Figgy walks up the steps to the brownstone just east of Christie's, into which the contents of the Masterpiece moving van have been unloaded.

And then, all at once, light floods across the street, stopping just short of her feet. Figgy is standing in the open doorway.

He gestures, holding out one hand. "Come on. What are you waiting for, an engraved invitation?"

Figgy is Christie's new next-door neighbor.

16

The front door closes behind her, and she finds herself in a small, quaint, wood-paneled foyer. A crystal chandelier hangs from the center of the ceiling, lit up in a blazing constellation. A half-moon console with curved cabriolet legs delicate as a fawn's holds a glass vase of lilies and violets. The air is perfumed by them. Also by food, though she can't tell what food exactly. Exotic spices, maybe. A dish recently cooked.

"Cauliflower and pine nuts with cumin and za'atar," Figgy says.

I like him, Sophie says. *He's hot.* Oh, screw off, Tara tells her. *Not now,* Sophie says. *Not ever. I'm here to stay.*

Where have you been? What have you been doing? I remember the fire, then nothing. Nothing at all. Six months—whole months—of my life gone, just like that. What did you do, Sophie? *You don't want to know.* I said, tell me! *You're already too frightened. You'll freak.* Sophie laughs. *And by the way, why haven't you jumped this beautiful man's bones?* Don't change the . . . *I would think that would be job number one.* Yes, of course, for you. Do you think I've forgotten what you did when we were young—the wildness, the wickedness, the danger you put us in?

But we had fun, Sophie says. *You must admit that.*

Tara shudders inwardly. You are supposed to keep me safe, she says. That's why Father created you. *He created me out of you, Kitten, lest you forget.* I ask for your help, and this is what I get? *I am that I am. I've grown up too. But of course you know that—ever since we were thirteen.*

I'm losing my mind, Tara thinks, dizzied. Nothing feels right, as if she is simultaneously in and out of her body, as if part of her is fading away. A sudden wave of terror sweeps over her, leaving her shaken and sick to her soul.

She assumes Figgy will lead her through to what was once called a drawing room, back to the kitchen, but he must've seen her sudden pallor and, instead, installs her on a plush sofa on one side of the marble fireplace. The walls are a deep green above white wainscoting. Artfully designed posters announcing major shows in museums in Tokyo, Amsterdam, and Paris, simply framed, adorn the walls, and she thinks of these posters in their crates being offloaded from the moving van in the street outside.

"What can I get you? A brandy?" He looks doubtful. "No, not a brandy, or anything alcoholic, I think. Not with the amount of alcohol already in your system."

Without waiting for a reply, he excuses himself. She hears him banging around the kitchen. Moments later, he returns with two tumblers filled with a bubbly reddish-brown liquid. His has ice; hers doesn't.

"Coke," he says, handing the iceless tumbler to her. "It'll settle your stomach."

He's right. The Coke feels good going down, even better in her stomach. She takes another sip, then a larger one. She vows never again to make fun of Coke advertising in movie theaters.

"Better?" he says, sitting down opposite her in a leather library chair.

She nods. He sits just close enough, their knees almost touching. "Thank you," she adds belatedly.

"There's a bit of color to your cheeks now."

He's so damn cute. I'm going to grab him right this second, Sophie says, but Tara fights to ignore her.

He clears his throat, suddenly uncomfortable. "I promise I'll only ask this one more time, and if you don't want to answer . . ." Abruptly, he gets up, goes over to the stereo—with a very cool-looking turntable, no less, and a gigantic McIntosh amp with tubes. Moments later, Dave Brubeck's piano and Paul Desmond's tenor sax drift out over the room like a soothing balm.

When he sits back down, she says, "Okay," which is all she can manage to get out. She thinks she knows what he's going to ask and wonders how she will answer. *Don't lie to him,* Sophie says. *You're asphyxiating on your terror.*

"I know—well, I think I know—something happened at the party. Yes?"

"Yes." Her voice is faint; the room swims before her eyes. *Steady, Kitten.*

"More Coke?"

"Thanks, I'm full up." She lets the quartet's music wash over her. It reminds her of Chicago: gleaming midcentury high-rises, beautiful architectural details. She sinks into it, relaxing. "Let me ask you a question," she says.

He spreads his hands. "Anything."

"How well do you know Marwyn."

He frowns. "Marwyn Rusk?"

"That's right."

He shrugs. "As well as anyone, I suppose."

"Meaning?"

"His facade is impenetrable." His frown deepens. "I told you I'm not part of that crowd. What's this all about?"

Tara ignores his question. "And you know that he lives right next door."

"Sure, but—"

"Was that deliberate? Or is it a coincidence?"

Figgy's face closes like a fist. "This is starting to sound like an interrogation. Where are you going with this?"

"Do you guys play golf up in Connecticut? Do you go out for drinks after work? What?"

"He's not my friend. I very much doubt he's anyone's friend. Please get to the point."

"Marwyn assaulted me in the bathroom at the party."

"He—" Figgy's eyes open wide, his expression softening like butter in the sun. "He did—what?"

So she tells him every last detail of the assault.

Figgy appears slightly dazed. "Did he . . . ?"

She shakes her head. "I kneed him in the balls."

Figgy laughs, then quickly shuts it down. "Sorry. Not funny. But good for you." His expression is deeply troubled. "Damn, Tara, I'm . . . I don't know what to say. Have you told anyone else?"

She shakes her head again.

"But you're going to, right? You should talk to someone about what happened—a therapist maybe?"

"I can't." There is Christie to think of, not to mention Charlotte. She can't ruin their lives.

His brows knit together. "But . . . why not?"

"I just can't, okay?"

He hears the sharp edge to her voice, and he holds up his hands, palms toward her. "Sorry, sorry. Your decision completely."

"Gee, thanks," she says, the edge sharpening.

"Okay." He sits back, deciding not to pursue. "Sorry."

"Stop saying you're sorry." Voice softening, sighing. "I know you're just trying to help."

He says nothing for some time. Brubeck's quartet swings into a slower tune, one with one of their signature odd time changes, conjuring up blue shadows in the street.

"You must be tired," he ventures.

"I imagine we both are." *Not going to broach that subject?* Sophie says. What? *Sex, silly.* Are you kidding? *Well, it does seem to be* Who's Afraid of Virginia Woolf? *time.* Not for me, Tara says. *No, of course not,* Sophie backhands. *Nothing's for you, Kitten. And that's the trouble.*

"Tara?" He is leaning in closer, his eyes questioning. "What is it? Are you okay?"

"In fact, I am," Tara says, without thinking about it. "But look, the truth is I'm Dr. Christie Lind's patient."

"Wait. You mean Marwyn's wife?"

When she nods, he says, "Oh, dear God."

"Now d'you see how complicated the situation is? I sure as hell can't talk to her about what happened."

The music has stopped. He rises, crosses the room, and flips the record over. The more Brubeck she hears, the more she wants to hear, enmeshed in the time signatures of the music.

When he turns back, he says, "Well, I suppose it's a matter of what you can live with."

Well, that's a fucking joke, Sophie says dryly. "There is no good choice," Tara tells him.

"No right choice, either." He sits down beside her. "It's very late," he says. "Why don't we table this."

She nods.

"You can stay here tonight."

Oh, goody! Sophie says. Tara can almost hear her licking her chops. "I can camp out here on the sofa," she says. *Oh, no you don't, Kitten!*

"No, ma'am." He smiles. "I have two spare bedrooms. Pick the one that suits you."

I know which one suits me, Sophie says. Tara continues to ignore her but senses the probing. Sophie is gaining strength as well as resolve. She begins to feel as she did during Sophie's night forays, except this is worse—far worse. Sophie is willfully, frighteningly pushing herself into Tara's consciousness.

———

She wakes to misty dawn light. For a moment, she doesn't remember where she is or how she has gotten there. Then, as she sits up, she sees the light filtering through the jalousies of Figgy's guest room window. It overlooks his backyard. She has only slept for a couple of hours, but she hasn't dreamed of being chased through a forest on fire. That, at least, is something.

She reaches for her phone, sees three late-night texts from M: where are u? U OK? just let me know, k?

All fine. Tried to find U at F. I'm at Figgy's. Tell all later.

Throwing the bedcovers off, she draws on the tracksuit Figgy has thoughtfully provided for her. It is a bit big, but in a comfy way. She tiptoes barefoot out into the second-floor hallway and makes her silent way down the oak staircase. Downstairs all is still; Figgy must still be asleep. In the kitchen, she finds everything she needs to make herself a triple espresso with one teaspoon of sugar. She stirs the espresso, takes a sip, then looks around. What a change from her previous digs—broken-down farmhouse, endless hotels and motels off the interstates, her own sublet with its water-stained walls, unreliable appliances, and her constant rear-guard action against roaches. This is how the 1 percent lives, how Christie lives. This is what gives Marwyn Rusk his moneyed Connecticut entitlement. For a moment, she feels Marwyn pressed up against her, his sour cognac breath against her cheek. His hand probing.

She loses her breath, has to put down her cup, grab hold of the countertop. *Breathe, Kitten. Breathe,* Sophie says. Sophie inside her head, Sophie let loose, like a genie from its bottle. Never going back. Not now. Not ever.

With her coffee cup in her hand, Tara passes through the open rear doorway. She peers out at the backyard, with its redbud tree, barrels in which someone—Figgy himself?—has planted small conical ever-greens. She feels the brownstone at her back, like a weight—the weight of money, of responsibility, of whatever it takes to afford a townhouse in Manhattan's Greenwich Village. How much has Figgy paid for it? Five million? Six? Either is an immeasurable amount so far as she is concerned.

A line from *Breakfast at Tiffany's* surfaces, one of her favorite books when she was growing up: "Because no matter where you run, you just end up running into yourself." Truman Capote was so right!

Along with that memory unavoidably surfaces another. She used to hide the book under her mattress because she'd heard her mother denounce Capote and James Baldwin to her flock: "From chapter twenty, verse thirteen of Leviticus, we read: 'If a man lies with a male as with a woman, both of them have committed an abomination; they shall surely be put to death; their blood is upon them.' Therefore, all homosexuals are dangerous to our God-fearing way of life," her mother declaimed from her perch overseeing the fervent believers in her crowded tent. "But of all the fags in this country, the two most dangerous are Truman Capote and James Baldwin, because they are writers. Worse still, Baldwin is a negro; he has no business writing any-thing. Reading their writing will deform your children's brains for life. Therefore, be vigilant. Hearken unto me, my children! Burn their vol-umes if ever you have the misfortune to come across them. Treat them as the poison they are."

She takes another sip of espresso, as if to incinerate her mother's words, as if to wipe her mind clear. But there they are bright as flames, seared into her.

She steps out onto the flagstones, still nighttime cool and damp beneath her feet, making her toes curl up. Inevitably, her feet follow her gaze off to her left, where a head-high fence separates Figgy's yard from Christie's.

With every moment, the morning mist is dissipating in the rays of the rising sun, reflected off the top eastern-facing windows of higher buildings. As she picks her way toward the fence line, she can hear voices coming from the other side, from Christie's backyard.

"Tiffany Blue," Christie says.

"Open it." Marwyn's voice, causing something inside Tara to shrivel up.

She can picture them—Christie and her traitorous husband: Christie in T-shirt and drawstring pants, her feet bare, like Tara's, sitting in a wicker chair, perhaps going over her notes for the day's clients. Marwyn, still in his suit from the night before, standing beside her, slightly uncomfortable, maybe.

"To what do I owe . . . ?"

"Late nights, hardly ever home."

She might have searched for a gap in the fence boards, but that would have been too much. Hearing his voice is difficult enough. The fence provides a kind of protection against him.

"Nevertheless. You didn't have to—"

"Leading to a record-breaking quarter." He enjoys interrupting her, it seems, or maybe he simply needs to keep control of the conversation.

"Money."

Has she detected a change in Christie's voice when she says *money*? A flattening of her tone, a certain exhaustion, maybe? If so, her husband hasn't noticed.

Marwyn's laugh, like fingernails drawn across concrete, makes Tara wince. "So much money." And then, a command: "Open it! I can't wait a moment longer!"

Because, Tara thinks, it's all about you, shitbag. Every second of every day.

A rustling, as of autumn leaves skittering across cobblestone streets.

"Oh, dear, you shouldn't have."

"Do you love it? How much do you love it? Tell me."

"Well, diamonds. Who wouldn't love diamonds. But, I mean, Marwyn, you really shouldn't have."

"I wanted to."

"Well, that's the basic problem, isn't it?"

Silence, like a cloud crossing in front of the sun. Tara thinks she can sense the air settling between them. A bit of motion in the corner of her eye causes her to look up into the large Norway maple in the rear of Christie's backyard, where a beautiful treehouse nestles into a major fork in the branches. She can see a smudge that in the morning's orangey light resolves itself into the face of a young girl of about fourteen. Their daughter, Charlotte. She is listening to her parents intently, oblivious to everything else. And Tara thinks of late nights, listening to her parents arguing, trembling and terrified of what she is hearing and that she will be caught out.

And now, down below, Charlotte's father says, in a tight voice, hardened by anger, "What basic problem, Chris?"

Christie sighs. "Again?"

"I'll tell you what's 'again,'" Marwyn grates. "I do something nice, and you don't appreciate it."

"Can you please listen to what I'm saying for once," Christie replies. "It's not the diamonds I don't appreciate, Marwyn. It's your reason for giving them to me."

"I don't understand."

"Of course you don't."

A fraught silence, tense as a drawn bowstring. And above, tears in Charlotte's eyes.

"You didn't want to get me these—you needed to."

"Chris, don't. Don't start psychoanalyzing every damn thing I do."

"I won't be a party to your guilty conscience." Christie's voice grows faint as, presumably, she walks back into the house. Yes. A door slams.

"Hey, come on. Jesus Christ. Come back."

Tara, listening as intently as Charlotte has, now aware of the girl sobbing silently up in her solitary perch, feeling the rage rising, not only for herself but for Christie and Charlotte, doesn't hear Figgy come up behind her until he is very close.

"What is this?" he says in a quiet, bantering tone. "The aural equivalent of *Rear Window*?"

Tara starts, automatically feels ashamed for eavesdropping, but Sophie possesses none of her sister's societal compunctions. *What do we have to be ashamed of, Kitten?* she says. *Not for being in the right place at the right time, surely. Not after what that shitbag did to you.* Sophie is right, Tara knows that, but it doesn't stop her cheeks from flaming as she turns around.

"Early morning, voices carry." She produces a wan smile. "I couldn't help it." Even Tara doesn't believe that. Sophie guffaws silently. *Now we know*, Sophie says. *Now we know something important.* I'm not supposed to know personal things about her, Tara replies. She's my therapist. *Stop kidding yourself*, Sophie says cannily. *That's not all she is to you, Kitten. That's not all you want her to be, is it? Is it?*

Figgy is smiling, relaxed, holding a small cup of espresso in one hand. "Sleep okay?" The morning casts him in such a handsome light. *He is handsome; you thought so right off the bat*, Sophie says with yet another maddening on-the-mark observation. *That's what you're afraid of here, Kitten. How attracted you are to him. Ever think of that? No, why would you?* Sophie sighs. *I have to do all the heavy lifting. But that's the way it's always been, Kitten, isn't it? I mean, that's part of an older sister's burden.* If it's a burden, get out, Tara says in a burst of anger. Get out now and never come back. *I terrify you now, don't I?* Sophie says. *Because I took over, because what's happened . . . happened.* Yes, all right? You scare the shit out of me. *But why?* Sophie asks with blatantly false coquettishness. *I am you.* But you're not! Tara says. With a vehemence that frightens her. Dad saw to that. *You still believe that bullshit?* Dad brought you into being for a specific purpose. *Okay, I'll admit he was the facilitator.* Prestidigitator. Sophie laughs. *Potatoes, potahtoes, but have it your way. In any event, no matter how good a prestidigitator the Hypnotist was, he could never have created me out of whole cloth.* The malevolent reptile, abruptly nearer, snaps at Tara's throat. What do you mean? She fairly chokes. *Jesus Christ, come on, Kitten. You know the Hypnotist could only have brought me into being because I was already inside you. He didn't create me, Kitten. You did. He was simply the ob-gyn who guided my journey into the light.* Oh, God, oh, God, oh, God, Tara thinks, nearly beside herself. Then a crazy laugh comes bubbling up: No, she thinks, I am *clearly* beside myself.

"Tara?"

She hears a voice as if from far off.

"Tara? Are you okay?"

Figgy's voice.

"Sure." Her voice thick, furry, as if surfacing from sleep. "Why wouldn't I be?"

"I dunno," Figgy says, frowning. "Your expression keeps changing, even though you haven't said a word."

Tara takes a deep breath, lets it go. If only it were that easy to let Sophie go. *No dice, Kitten. I told you I'm here to stay.* A laugh. *What will your therapist think of that? What sort of diagnosis do you think she—*Stop! Tara pleads. Please stop. *Okay. Let's attend to Figgy now, shall we?* What? *Let's fuck his brains out. I mean, that's what you want, isn't it? It sure as hell is what I want.* What you want is irrelevant. *Sez who?* Is that Sophie laughing? She realizes that she'd better exert an iron control to make sure it's she who is speaking, not Sophie.

"Inner dialogue," Tara says, a truth, though not the whole truth. "I was debating the societal taboo of the kind of eavesdropping I just engaged in."

Figgy nods. "Fair enough. And what conclusion did you come to?"

"Fuck society." What the hell . . . ? Has her control faltered already? But the response makes Figgy laugh until his eyes are wet.

"Jesus, I like you, Tara. I really do." He gives her a deprecating smile. "I know this sounds like a line, but I've never met anyone even remotely like you."

"I'll take that as a compliment."

"Please do."

Now they are both laughing.

Figgy gestures back to his townhouse. "Breakfast?"

And she nods. "Please."

What Sophie wants for breakfast is Figgy, and Tara hasn't the strength to fight her; the will has abruptly vanished, as swiftly as water down the drain. Horrified at herself for slipping back into her teenage self, she watches, glassy eyed, sick to her soul, as Sophie divests Figgy of his robe, pulls his hair until his head rocks back. Sophie licks the side of his neck, the hollow at the base of it, while grinding her breasts and hips against him. Tara shudders inwardly at the slide of his hot flesh, that part of her shrinking away in fright, as she always has when it comes to sex.

The sofa seems as good a place as any, and Sophie doesn't hear any protest from Figgy, not that she would have cared. One thing you can say for Sophie, when it comes to sex, she knows how to draw immense pleasure for herself and her partner. She has this acquired ability (it cannot possibly be innate, Tara thinks) to gauge her lover's desires and respond to them. As with others in the past, now with Figgy, Tara is riding an ecstatic whirlwind that builds and builds until she feels Figgy's shivers quite apart from her own.

And when he is on the brink, Sophie whispers in his ear. The words act as a trigger. He thrusts down and in, but she squeezes her Kegel muscles, clamping the base of his phallus. He is big and thick, so it is easy enough physically, but in every other way it is difficult to bring their pleasure to a halt. Sophie laughs silently, hearing him groan in frustration. She shivers from the inside out, her body sweat-slick, want-ing desperately to thrust up against him. Her legs are locked at the small of his back, heels dug in. The tensed muscles of her thighs are quivering. Figgy stares down at her, his eyes unfocused.

Then she relaxes, and at her silent command, he comes. So does she, in a swirling flood of bliss.

17

What Stevie left behind when she moved out is a much-used toothbrush, judging by its bent bristles; a bra with one ripped strap; and an alarmingly large black dildo. The dildo also appears to have been much used. All of that goes into the plastic garbage bag in M's tiny kitchen. Tara uses dishwashing gloves when transferring the items.

M's apartment is a medium-size two bedroom in one of those white-brick high-rises built in profusion during a certain decade, this one a doorman building on Sixth Avenue at Twelfth Street. It is furnished with odds and ends—a hand-painted dresser from the 1950s, a pair of barstools around a small dinette table with a boomerang-patterned top that has been salvaged from the street. Somehow, viewed together they make up a pleasingly eclectic whole. M took the door off the closet in her bedroom, and Tara can see the array of dresses, skirts, and shirts on hangers. Boots and shoes lined up on the floor. Jeans and underwear neatly folded, stacked on shelves by color.

Stevie's room is smaller, set up as a kind of writer's office, as there is a desk and task chair, along with a convertible sofa and the 1950s dresser. A window overlooks an alley and an identical building next door. The venetian blinds are lowered in the window across the way. Tara drops her packed weekender by the side of the dresser. It is wood, painted with patterns of children skipping and laughing in a field.

"We'll take that sofa bed out. If you decide to stay," M says, standing in the doorway. "Come on, I'll make us some coffee."

While M is in the kitchen, Tara wanders through the living room. There is a battered sofa, two mismatched upholstered chairs, a coffee table, a scattering of lamps. Tara chooses the sofa, settles into one soft corner. Abraxas, M's cat, a chunk of living agate, eyes Tara for a moment before jumping up into her lap. Stroking her releases a deep purr of contentment. If only humans could be so easily pleased! Tara thinks.

While waiting for M, Tara stares at the large framed photograph on the wall opposite the couch. It is of an amazing piece of Banksy street art: on a whitewashed London wall, with brickwork on the extreme right, is a starkly black-and-white lithographic blowup of a photo of a young Queen Elizabeth, wearing her crown. Her eyes are closed, as if in concentration or boredom—it is impossible to tell which. A string of pearls adorns her neck, and a fur collar, possibly from a long, regal coat, is visible. Down the length of her face in brilliant crimson and blue—the only color in the artwork—is the signature lightning bolt David Bowie wore for his Ziggy Stardust persona. Typical of Banksy, the artwork is multilayered. It snatched what it needs from tradition (the queen), art (Andy Warhol), and pop music (Bowie) while defacing the traditional establishment with a startling slash of the transgressive.

"You know, I adore this piece," Tara says after M brings over handthrown mugs of coffee and a stack of Oreos, and settles herself in the sofa's other corner.

"I do too," M says. She plucks an Oreo off the tray. "Tara, honestly I'm happy you decided to take me up on my offer. As I told you, I worry about you in the shithole you live in." She nibbles on the cookie. "Plus which, I don't like being alone."

"I'm not a substitute for Stevie, you know." The words burst out of Tara before she has a chance to think.

"Oh, honey, you're not; you're a friend," M says softly. "A good friend." She breaks her Oreo in half, hands the bigger half to Tara. Then, seeing the roll of twenties on the table, she points. "Okay, what's that?"

"Rent money."

"Listen—"

"No, M. You listen this time. This here is what I pay for my current place."

M shakes her head. "Honey, I don't want you to pay two rents. That wouldn't be—"

"Already taken care of. My deal is fluid; I'll turn in my key at the end of the month. Also, my dirtbag slumlord owes me a big one. I got rid of a lurker who was hanging around the building, scaring old Mrs. Garcia half to death."

"Really, you?" M chuckles. "How did that go down?"

"I came out with the baseball bat I found in a corner of the second-floor hallway. It was cracked and of no use. I was going out to throw it away." Tara bites into the cookie. "The moment I saw the lurker, I raised the bat. Pure reflex, really. Anyway, one look at the bat and he ran like the devil himself was after him."

They both have a good laugh at that.

Leaning forward, Tara taps the roll of bills. "So this is my contribution. It's not much compared to what I must actually owe you, but it's what I have." She raises a hand to forestall yet another objection. "M, please, it will make me feel better. Your invitation was generous enough."

"Okay, okay, I surrender," M says, smiling, as she takes possession of the money. "I graciously accept your contribution."

"Good. Because I don't want there to be any tension between us," Tara says.

M takes up another Oreo, holds it in front of her, studying it as if trying to figure out just what that crème center is made of. "One other thing." When she looks up, her cheeks are slightly flushed. "I want to reiterate I didn't invite you here to fuck you."

A bubble of embarrassed laughter escapes Tara's lips.

M eats half the cookie. "Look, it would be unnatural if it wasn't on your mind. But I'm not predatory. Stevie was. To be honest, that was the root of our problem. Her fucking girls she picked up at Forest. She had to pick Forest, right under my nose. Her running off to LA was just the last straw."

"I'm sorry, M."

M shrugs. "I learned my lesson."

"Why are lessons only learned the hard way?"

M frowns. "Hmm. I'm thinking you need another Oreo." Tara takes it but doesn't bite into it. "What's going on?"

"Oh, I don't know. Sometimes I just feel . . . I feel like I'm not altogether here."

"Where are you then?" M moves closer.

"Somewhere . . . somewhere I can't see or hear anything, you know what I mean?"

M shakes her head. "Wait, did your parents lock you in a closet or the basement when you were a kid?"

"Oh. No. Nothing like that." Tara considers a minute. To go on or not to go on: that is the question. But for some reason she feels safer here than when she is with Lind, if only because she knows M won't ask probing questions that she doesn't want to answer; she'll just let her talk. Like a friend, a good friend.

"So I told you that my father was a hypnotist by trade."

"Uh-huh."

"Well, as soon as I was old enough—seven, I guess—I became part of his act, and because the audience loved me, pretty soon I was the highlight."

"So, I mean, how did that work?"

"He hypnotized me."

"For real?"

Tara nods. "He knew how to do it. For real. He put me under. He never gave me cues beforehand; he never told me what he was going to do. It was absolutely legit."

"I don't . . . wow! What would happen?"

"That's the thing," Tara says. "I don't know. I don't remember a thing about the times he put me under."

Concern flowers on M's face. "Isn't that . . . dangerous?"

"He was my father; I trusted him," Tara says. "Only . . ."

M leans toward her. "Only what?"

"It wasn't like I was unconscious. It was more like . . . well, I was in a place where I couldn't see or hear anything."

"Jesus. That sounds like a nightmare."

Tara draws back against the sofa, her eyes closed. "It seemed like that . . . it could've been."

"Didn't you . . . I mean, you must've said something to your father."

"I was so young. I wanted to please him." Tara's eyes open, and she stares at M. "And he kept telling me how great a subject I was, and when I came out of the trance, I saw the audience on their feet, applauding. And it was for me as well as my father, because when he let me step forward and take a bow, they applauded all the louder. Whistled even, sometimes."

"Men, these were men, the audiences."

"Mostly. I guess."

"And your father never told you what he asked you to do when you were under."

Tara shakes her head, and all at once, her heart seems to shatter, and she falls into M's arms, sobbing uncontrollably.

18

Tara shifts in her chair, crossing one leg over the other. Outside, the afternoon is turning to charcoal. "There was always a group—psychologist types, well known, like a pack of hyenas—who agreed with my mother, were sure my father was a charlatan. They didn't believe in hypnotism, period. They especially didn't believe it when he put me under. They were sure it was an act."

"Was it?" Lind asks.

She shakes her head. "No."

"What happened when you were under?"

"I don't know," Tara answers truthfully.

"He never told you?"

"That's not how it works," she says, also truthfully, as she's confessed to M.

"Then how does it work?"

"Magic," she says. "It's magic."

Lind regards Tara without blinking. "There are scientific explanations for hypnotism. Will you explain what you mean, please?"

"Magic can't be explained." This, too, is the truth.

"Not even this kind of magic? Your father's magic? Hypnotism?"

"Especially hypnotism," Tara says emphatically. Her fingers are busy in her lap, worrying the scars. "Other magic consists of potions, elixirs, dolls, and fetishes. Hypnotism isn't about props. It's about the mind: what it can do, what it can be made to do."

There is a small silence while Lind studies Tara's face for any change of expression, Tara supposes. Then: "Did your father make you do things?"

"Of course he did," Tara says.

"What kinds of things?"

"I don't remember."

"He never told you?" Silence. "And you never asked."

"It never occurred to me. I became a star of sorts."

Lind takes a moment to absorb this. "You have told me that when your parents fought about you, it had to do with your father's act. Is that why your mother objected, you becoming a star of sorts?"

"That's one reason, I suppose. Jealousy."

"What were the others?"

"She objected to me hanging out with my father, especially at night when he was training me. The screaming fights. She didn't want his ungodliness infecting me."

Lind taps the point of her pen against her pad: tap-tap-tap, like a bird searching for food. "Help me out here, Tara. Your mother was a God-fearing woman, a righteous preacher."

"That's right."

"You told me previously that your father was in thrall to her. Was the feeling mutual?"

"My parents were both heretics. Mormons, originally. They made a mutual decision to leave the Church of Latter-day Saints. Well, that's a bit of a gloss. My father was treasurer. He embezzled a ton of money. That's the story, anyway, but stories get embellished; the truth gets deformed.

"Anyway, my mother became a born-again Christian, maybe to atone for condoning what he had done. She assumed he would do the same, but like most people she misjudged him. At some point, it became clear to her that he had joined the Mormons because he saw an opportunity, not because he had faith. My father remained resolutely apostate."

"And yet they stayed together."

"Well, partly that was for appearances' sake. My mother had many followers; they needed to believe in her purity. She wasn't going to go the way of other preachers who strayed and then humiliated themselves asking forgiveness from their flock.

"But they were also bound together by sex. Their mutual attraction was palpable, even to me at an early age. Much later, I came to understand the elements of rage and punishment each felt every time they fucked. Sorry, but that's the right word for what they did."

What she doesn't tell Lind—doesn't dare to—is that that horrifying insight came to her via Sophie.

———

Her hour over, Tara rises. Just before she reaches the door, she turns back. She has been churning this moment over and over in her mind in the confused, rageful, humiliating aftermath of Marwyn's assault. Her relationship with Lind is forever altered, but she cannot bear the thought of giving her up. The sessions have come to mean a great deal to her. Deep down she knows that the therapy sessions are helping her, that Lind is the right therapist for her, that Lind's gotten her to a level none of her previous therapists ever could. But her feelings are all muddled up. Her mind feels scattered, as if she is looking at herself in a shattered mirror, wondering who is real and who is the reflection. It will take all her courage to do what she feels needs to be done now, but she will do it.

Lind, setting her pen aside, says, "Tara, it seems as if there's something else on your mind? Do you feel able to tell me what it is?"

"I . . . I . . ." She takes a breath. Pushes herself forward. "I've been thinking, and I . . . I would like to be a friend. To you, and, if you agree, to Charlotte."

Lind smiles gently, the woman behind her swimming placidly in place, hiding the alarm that Lind feels at the mention of her daughter's name. "Tara, do you know what transference is?"

"Of course I know," Tara says, somewhat indignantly.

"It's when the therapeutic bond between therapist and client extends outward, past this room," Lind says, as if Tara hasn't spoken. "It happens more times than not." She puts her hands together, as if in prayer. "It's impossible for us to be friends."

"But why?" Tara hates sounding like a child. The desperation in her voice humiliates her.

"Because it's inappropriate." Lind leans forward, elbows on knees. She is wearing a pink skirt, a mauve blouse, and patent leather pumps with low heels. "It's a breach of professional ethics. Just as crucially it would violate the trust that binds us together in here." Her eyes hold Tara's. "But I think you knew that even before you asked."

"Don't you make exceptions? Ever?"

"If I did, I would be betraying you."

"But you wouldn't. I promise. This is different."

Lind sits back. "How is it different?"

"Because . . . because I know what's happening." She can hear the words coming out of her mouth, but she is starting to feel as if she isn't really there. She is going to fail to convince Lind. "Because I know what I'm feeling, and it isn't transference."

"Tara, listen to me: there's no possible way you can know that. Our relationship is here, in this room."

But of course she does know. Tara's problem isn't transference; in a sense it is the opposite. She knows things about Lind that she shouldn't. She knows firsthand Marwyn's despicable behavior. And she knows firsthand that Lind is aware of at least a measure of his betrayal of her and is doing nothing about it. She's been a fool to think that in the harsh spotlight of that reality, any effective analytical bond between her and Lind could stay alive. She feels the sea rising, the waters turning choppy, churning over the ship's sides. She can tell Lind what she knows and hope Lind will find a way to make it not matter, or she can say nothing and walk away from the delicate process they have managed to build. A process she has been yearning for ever since she woke up with an immediate memory of the fire but no memory of escaping the burning farmhouse, no memory of the six months that came after. What happened? Where did she go? She has the vaguest sense that she did something terrible, but every time she reaches for the memory, it slips away. Why can't she remember?

"I have some more time, Tara. Please, sit back down." Lind gestures to the empty chair, as if delivering an offering. "Our relationship is complicated. Our work consists of many elements, all interconnected. You need all of those elements to help yourself, to heal your old wounds, deep as they are."

Tara sits, back straight, hands in her lap like a schoolgirl who has been summoned to the principal's office, expecting the worst. She stares at Lind, confronting her fate. The room, once so comforting, now feels claustrophobic. It reeks of Marwyn's assault on her, his serial betrayals of his wife. And what of Charlotte's sadness?

"I fully appreciate how difficult this process has been for you," Lind is saying. "How painfully hard it is for you to trust people, to believe in them, to trust that they won't turn on you and hurt you. I get that. Do you really want to throw away all the progress you've made in here? From everything I've learned about you, I know you don't."

She leans forward again, her eyes burning bright in the dimly lit room. "Something has happened—I can sense it. Something has changed, something significant enough to cause you to want to leave."

"I didn't say I wanted to leave," Tara blurts out.

"Think a minute. What you're asking of me . . . it's an indirect way of telling me you want to stop these sessions." She takes a breath. "You didn't ask for my opinion, but I'll give it to you, in any case. You're on the verge of breaking through some long-held barrier. That's terribly frightening: the known is far more comforting than the unknown, even when it's holding you back. Even when it's painful, even when it's preventing you from feeling joy, from experiencing your life as you are meant to experience it.

"You're on a precipice, Tara. It's scary, but you must go forward, believe me. And rest assured I will be here beside you every step of the way."

Tara, trembling, opens her mouth to say something. Instead, she bolts from her chair and disappears from Lind's sight.

19

Running. She heads east, running to Seventh Haven, looking for solace. But no solace can she find, even there. An ambulance is parked outside the entrance. A pair of EMTs loads someone on a stretcher into the back of it. A shroud of sorrow lies over the facility. M emerges from her office the moment she sees Tara.

"Hey," she says, coming around to hug Tara. "I'm happy to see you. But you look like you haven't slept a wink. Why didn't you come to my place?"

"Long night, longer story. But everything's cool," Tara prevaricates. She gestures with her head. "Who was that?"

M's eyes are swimming. "Darren."

"Oh. I'm so sorry, M." Darren is known to both of them. A confused girl in a man's body, shamed and ashamed, he turned to every kind of pill or powder in order to forget who he really was. "I thought he was making progress." M has been counseling him.

"So did I. But who knows what the hell anyone's thinking?" M wipes away tears. "Sometimes, like today, I think, What's the point?"

Tara hugs M, the contact helping to anchor herself to the here and now. She is used to entering new realities, leaving those that pain or frighten her behind. "They don't all end up like Darren." But she knows they are both thinking about Angelo. They forged a bond with him, but what did those bonds mean? He killed himself anyway.

"It's the helplessness, you know?" M says.

And Tara does. "It makes you wonder why you can't do more."

M nods. "Speaking of, Lia's here."

Sudden anxiety clutches at Tara. "Is she okay?"

"I was just going to find out, but now that you're here . . ." M smiles through her tears. "The truth is, even though I've been here longer, she responds better to you."

Tara steps past, having been told that Lia is in room B. Lia is a teenager who regularly cuts herself—finds cutting herself a release. She comes here to Seventh Haven for help. Lia Caro is the younger of two sisters in a family emigrated from San Ángel, a residential neighborhood of Mexico City. Her parents are teachers. Leda, a couple of years older, is a high achiever. She excels in school, in track, in every extracurricular activity in which she chooses to participate. As a result, she is extremely popular in school. Girls try to emulate her style; boys are always wanting to take her out on dates. No one dares ask her for a blow job like they do with the other girls.

Lia exists in that titanic shadow, pushed by her mother to live up to her sister's standards, destined to fail. How can she not? Lia is not Leda, nor will she ever be. That fact doesn't stop their mother from constantly berating her. "Why can't you be more like Leda? What's the matter with you?"

The only way for Lia to keep her shit together is to cut herself. The slicing of the blade through her skin, into her flesh, releases endorphins into her bloodstream. Like pulling the plug on a bathtub, the pain allows the pent-up anxiety, frustration, despair to drain out of her. The pain is transformed into pleasure, and for a time, Lia is able to feel sane again. That is one theory, anyway.

Lia certainly doesn't look sane when Tara enters room B. She is sitting on a metal chair in the middle of the windowless space, one of five such intimate venues set up for one-on-one counseling sessions.

Tara drags the desk chair over and sits facing Lia. The girl is barely sixteen, thin and pale to the point of being ashen. Her long hair is lank and stringy—God alone knows when she has last washed it. She is wearing jeans torn at the knees and shins, a filthy pair of sneakers, and a black tee emblazoned with FUCK YOU YOU FUCKING FUCK in white across the chest. Over this is an oversize denim jacket that just about swallows her narrow torso whole.

She sits with her legs spread, like a guy, thin forearms on thin thighs, her fingers interlaced. The ragged nails are bitten to the quick.

Reaching out, Tara takes the girl's hands in hers. They are cold as ice. She rubs them, bringing blood and heat to the surface. "How about taking off your jacket."

Lia shakes her head. "The nurse asked me to. I won't."

"Now I'm asking you."

Lia looks down, slips her hands from Tara's, traces Tara's scars with her forefinger.

"Do they still hurt?" Her voice is vibrating and thin, like a strand of spider's silk in the wind.

"Sometimes. When it gets cold, or when they get too much summer sun." Damaged as she is herself, Tara feels Lia's anguish viscerally. She can taste her rage, understand it, and so can talk to Lia in her own particular argot. Lia knows all this, if not on a conscious level, then on a subconscious one. The knowledge draws her to Tara like a moth to a flame. Trust, for souls like Tara and Lia, is of paramount importance, and very difficult to give. "It's difficult to live with sometimes."

Without another word, Lia lets Tara's hand go, stands up, and shrugs off her jacket, laying it across her lap. Sitting back down again, she displays the insides of her forearms without needing to be asked. The new wounds are inky, crusty against her white flesh. They join the lividity of the older scars.

Leaning forward, Tara takes Lia's forearms in her hands. "We talked about you stopping this."

"I said I'd try." There seems a terrible sadness behind Lia's eyes, like a soldier returned from combat who has seen too much. "And I did try—I tried so hard, and then . . ."

"What happened?"

Lia twists her head back and forth on the stalk of her neck. "My parents had an awful fight. Again. But this time . . ." She takes a breath, then seems to not know what to do with it, lets it out like air out of a popped balloon. "Leda was out of the apartment—she had a piano lesson—so it was only me listening to them. Then I heard a weird noise that made me jump, like a sack of wet cement hitting the floor. I heard someone make a sound."

"What kind of sound?" Tara asks.

Lia takes a breath. "A low sound, like a . . . a . . . I saw a documentary once on how steers are slaughtered. There's a sound they make when that metal thing hits their forehead, just before they go down." Her eyes are shining, tears slipping over her lower lids. "That's the sound I heard."

Dear God, Tara thinks. "And then? Did you see . . . ?"

"My father had hit my mother so hard the back of her head hit the wall between my bedroom and theirs. The sound was so loud . . . like a gunshot, almost. I was so scared I peeked through the open door. I saw the dent in the plaster." Tara is aghast. "And my mother was sitting down, back against the wall, but kind of slumped over, you know? And my father was standing over her. Her head slowly came up when she saw me, and he yelled at me. 'Get out! You didn't see anything. You weren't here.'"

There's a story for you, Sophie says, and Tara tells her to shut up.

"I went out of the apartment. I couldn't bear to be there anymore. But I had my razor blade in my pocket. I didn't want to do it this time, I swear I didn't. But everything kept rushing at me. Whatever I felt wouldn't leave me alone, so I started cutting. When I cut myself, I'm bringing the pain inside me to the surface. It becomes mine. I can control it." She turns her head away again, showing Tara only her profile. She looks older, somehow, as if with these unguarded words Tara has elicited from her, she has lost what was left of her youth.

Tara smiles. "I'm pleased you were able to tell me. Thank you." Her heart breaks for this teenager who is in way over her head. "One day at a time, Lia, isn't that what we talked about?"

The girl nods. The gesture makes her seem fragile.

Tara takes her hands and squeezes tightly. "Last night you cut yourself, and you hated doing it. And then today you came here, and now we're talking about it. Those are changes, Lia. Important changes. And tomorrow or next week when you feel nothing else is going to help but cutting yourself, you'll come in here first, and we'll talk, and you know what, the talking will take the place of cutting—talking will help make you feel better."

"Really?"

Tara nods. It occurs to her then there are in fact some lessons she has absorbed from her previous therapists, some of whom are perhaps not as foolish as she believed. Even so, they weren't anything like Lind, whom Tara still feels inside her like a distant lighthouse in the absolute blackness of her inner night. "Absolutely."

Lia jumps up and throws her arms around Tara. "I want that to happen," she whispers in Tara's ear, as Tara stands to embrace the girl fully. "I promise I do."

"I believe you," she says. She is crying, and so, too, is Lia, she realizes. "You are protected here," she whispers in Lia's ear. "You know that, don't you?" And when she feels Lia nod, she says, "And loved. Unconditionally loved."

She feels Lia's heart fluttering like a caged bird desperate to be free. Or is that hers? She holds the girl close, letting her own warmth seep into Lia. Or is it Lia's warmth seeping into her?

Either way, their embrace lasts a long time.

20

After returning to her apartment, Tara heads straight to the bath-room, starts filling a small nylon zip bag with the cosmetics she left behind. Without really understanding what she is doing, she fishes out the lip gloss she was gifted with at Forest. She draws out the applica-tor and paints her lips cherry red. She stares at her face in the mirror. It's so different, so shocking, she wipes the color off with a wad of tissues. Now she looks pale and wan. She reapplies the lip gloss, then immedi-ately wipes it off again with such vigor her lips feel sore.

I've come undone, she thinks and throws the slim cylinder in the trash.

No worries, Sophie says. *I'm here to catch you. Always and forever.*

"That's how I know I've come undone," Tara says out loud.

There's no one to hear you but me, Sophie tells her. *Now pick up your gloss, and get on with it.*

When she fishes around in the trash basket, she finds not only the cylinder but the card Brandon Fiske gave her at the party. For a second she wonders how it got there, then recalls throwing it away after stum-bling home, numb and in shock.

Before I took over, Sophie says. *Before I saved you again.*

———

After dropping her bag off at M's, she heads west toward Figgy's place. The day fades; the light is failing. Blue shadows in the street. People are hurrying to the markets, on their way home, or to evening classes at NYU. The closer she gets to Figgy's, the closer she comes to Christie's. Anxiety starts to build within her. Twelve minutes from now would be when her Monday appointment would normally start. It feels odd, disconcerting, to be here and know she isn't going to see Christie. She wonders if she's made a mistake. But when she tries to imagine what it might be like to face her, talk to her, be in session with her with the secret of her husband's assault looming over them like a mountain, black and forbidding, with the two of them on either side, never to see each other clearly again . . . she flinches at the thought.

She hasn't called Figgy, and of course he isn't home when she rings his bell. For some time, she stands in front of his door like an idiot, not knowing what to do. She wonders why she hasn't called him. Wherever he is, he might have agreed to meet her. She steps back, and her gaze strays to her left, to Christie's townhouse. Possibly it wasn't Figgy she wanted to talk with, after all.

She is just turning to retrace her steps back to M's building when she sees Charlotte coming toward her from the junction of Seventh Avenue South and Greenwich Avenue. She is in the company of another girl, the two painfully thin as willows. They are sharing a pair of Bluetooth earbuds, listening to something—music or a podcast—on Charlotte's iPhone. Without giving it a second thought, she sits down on Figgy's stoop, takes out her phone while keeping the girls in the corner of her eye.

Just before they reach Charlotte's home, her friend unplugs her earbud, gives it to Charlotte. They hug each other goodbye, and the friend walks off, past where Tara sits, still as a statue. About to race up the stairs to the family's brownstone, Charlotte glances at Tara and sits down on the side of her stoop closest to Tara.

"Hey," she says. "My name's Charlotte."

"Tara. Hey."

"Are you waiting for Figgy?"

Tara is surprised, though she supposes she shouldn't be. Figgy is Charlotte's new neighbor, after all.

Tara grins sheepishly. "I guess I should've called first."

Charlotte regards her critically. "Are you and Figgy hooked up?"

Tara laughs. "We've gone out a couple of times. I don't know whether that qualifies."

"I like him," Charlotte says. "Figgy." She puts away her earbuds. "My dad does too."

Tara stiffens. Every muscle in her body tenses like a drawn bow. "Your dad knows Figgy?"

"Yeah. I think he's investing in Figgy's start-up."

Charlotte makes it sound as if this is an everyday occurrence for her father, and maybe it is. What a world, Tara thinks.

"Does your mom like Figgy too?" she is compelled to ask.

"I guess." Charlotte, fingers playing over the screen of her phone, is already bored by the topic, so Tara wisely changes the subject. "So, what's caught your attention?"

"Oh, sorry." Charlotte glances up. "Boyfriend problems. Things that, you know, I can't talk to my parents about, which is kind of funny 'cause my mom's a therapist. But with me she's just a pain."

"That's so like parents, right?" Tara nods. "Mine were the same way." Charlotte's fingers are dancing again. "Can you tell me what the problem is? Maybe I can help."

Charlotte glances up again, her blue eyes big around. She is quite a striking girl; clearly she's gotten the best of both parents in the looks department. "Oh, well, you'd probably find it stupid."

"Try me."

"Really?"

"Why not?"

Charlotte giggles. "Okay, well, his name is Robin, and he's a couple of years older than I am. Which right away would be a red flag, especially for my father." She wets her lips with the tip of a pink tongue. "Anyway, he comes from a strict religious fam. His dad thinks my father's a philistine, that our material way of life will somehow pollute his son, and really, I don't know what to do."

"Interesting. I come from that kind of background. At least, on one side. My mom was a preacher—a televangelist, actually."

"Really?" Charlotte inches closer. Tara has her complete attention. "What was it like?"

"Not good. I was a born rebel."

"Robin is too! You think we'll be okay?"

"I think it depends, Charlotte. Not on you or Robin but on the parents. My advice is to take it slow. One step at a time."

"Patience isn't one of my strong suits, to be honest."

"It wasn't mine, either, at your age. But trust me, it's a useful trait to have. Believe it or not, having what you want right away isn't always best."

"That's not what my dad thinks. He's always telling Mom that he needs to get this or that done stat." She makes a face. "*His* strong suit is impatience."

"I pity him," Tara says. *No, you don't,* Sophie cuts in. *You think the kid suspects what her father's really like?* "My advice is don't be like him," Tara says to Charlotte. "Be yourself. Always."

Before Charlotte can respond, her cell phone buzzes. She takes the call, says a couple of words, then rings off. "That was my dentist's office. I'm sorry, but I'm late for an appointment," she says to Tara as she gets up.

"My bad."

"Oh no. This was great! Thank you for listening to me. Food for thought, right?"

"Right." Tara stands. "Hey, Charlotte, I'll see you again, right?"

Charlotte laughs as she skips off. "Mos' def! I mean, we're already friends. Yeah!"

21

W hat on earth happened?" Brandon Fiske studies her hand. "Fire? Acid?"

"I tried to drag my father out of our farmhouse," Tara says, "as it was burning to the ground."

"Did you manage . . . ?"

"No."

"I see." His lips purse. "I'm so sorry."

Now Brandon Fiske is the second person, and the first adult, she has met in New York who's had the guts to ask her about her hand. Is it because he doesn't care whether he embarrasses her? Or because he intuits that she won't be embarrassed.

"I trust you don't mind . . ."

"Not at all." And she smiles to reassure him, because the truth is she doesn't mind. That comes as a kind of revelation. It astonishes her that here she sits across from him and doesn't feel afraid or even defensive.

"Well, it's good you're not self-conscious," he says. "The way I see it, that hand of yours is a badge of courage. Shows what you tried to do for your father."

"I tried and failed."

Elbows on his walnut desk, he spreads his hands. "I wouldn't call risking your life for someone else a failure, no matter the outcome. But hey, we were all failures once."

Moments before, a sleek-looking assistant ushered her into his high-floor corner office whose windows overlook steel-gray skyscrapers. Beyond she can see the Statue of Liberty out in the bay, torch raised beneath a blue hazeless sky. Sunlight sends dazzling shards across the waves.

"I'm pleased you called. I wasn't at all sure you would." Brandon has a solid face, tanned, time creased without looking worn. His thick hair with its silver wings is combed back from his wide philosopher's forehead. He appears to be in his late fifties or early sixties but has retained the youthful energy and impish look in his eyes of someone two decades younger. He wears a navy sports jacket with a cream windowpane design, black slacks, and polished loafers, all expensive looking without being showy. She is dressed in her best day outfit, a charcoal pants suit that, in these surroundings, strikes her uncomfortably as looking cheap and shabby. At least her suede low-heeled pumps have style.

He regards her with a candid expression. "Can I get you something? Coffee? Tea? Pastrami on rye?"

She laughs, and that breaks the ice. It was actually a curiously thin layer. She recalls how much she liked this man at the Night of the Horrid Party. She wouldn't have considered it, even five minutes ago, but she feels good that she's come. *See? I still take care of you, Kitten. After all, without you I'm nothing.*

"Okay," he begins, "now that you've accepted my invitation, now that you're here, I'll be frank. That's the kind of guy I am. I hate beating around the bush—I won't have it. Say what you mean and mean what you say." His brows knit together. "Now where is that from?"

He seems to be asking himself, but Tara says, "Matthew five, thirty-three to thirty-seven." It is automatic, said without thinking. Her mother's training.

"The Bible, huh?" He shrugs. "Well, anyway, it works for me." He looks down at his desk for a moment. "We're here to help people—indigents, those at risk, those going from paycheck to paycheck, the LGBTQ community. We're here to try and fix what's broken about the education system, from elementary school up. We're here to retrain people whose old jobs have vanished into the robotic twenty-first century. In short, we take from the rich and give to programs that help the poor. Does that sound like something you'd like to be a part of?"

"I'm already a part of it at Seventh Haven."

"Of course you are, but I'm speaking now of a larger canvas. Doing the right things on a vast scale. Sound good?"

"When you put it that way, of course it does."

"Excellent." He hunches forward. "Now listen. I don't know you, Tara. I don't know where you're from or what your story is. I don't care, and I'll tell you why. When I was fifteen, I was already a freshman in college. I had matured fast; I looked like I was eighteen. That Christmas, I ran away. I never returned from winter break. I didn't go home either. I had never gotten along with my parents; I had as much use for them as I had for my college courses.

"I went out on the street. I stole, I mugged people, I sold myself to older women, preying on their loneliness. They had a desperate need to be touched and held; the sex was, believe it or not, secondary. I was in a juvie detention center in upstate New York for eighteen months. When I got out, I robbed a liquor store, not for the money, per se. To spite the fuckers who put me inside. Anyway, that was then; this is now." His smile is almost shy, almost a boy's smile. "So, to you. Most people I meet see only what's in front of their face. They believe what they read or hear that reinforces their own beliefs; they reject everything else. But from listening to you the other night, it was clear to me that you see beneath facades. The inner working of things informs your beliefs. That's great. That's special." He nods. "That's all I need to know about you."

Tara sits there looking at him, not knowing what to say.

Everything's going our way, Kitten. We're a good team.

A brief chill goes through Tara. We're a team? The two of us? she thinks. No, that's crazy. My father created you *from* me. You can't be a separate entity.

Oh, but I am, Kitten. Surely I am. And I told you I'm not going anywhere.

"So." Brandon's hands flat on the desk. "How about it, Tara? Welcome aboard or turn tail and run like I ran?"

"Well, I hope I'm not a coward . . ." She is speaking to Sophie as well as to him.

He tilts his head. It's a very nice head. Something old world about it. Distinguished. "Is that a yes? Or do I hear a *but*?"

"There's a big but."

"What's that?" Brandon seems unconcerned.

"I love my hands-on work at Seventh Haven."

"You'll love this work even more."

"Oh, please." Tara barks a laugh. "How can you possibly know that?"

"A change of pace is good for the soul."

Something is not right. She stands up. "I'm not playing this game." She takes a couple of deep breaths, but she knows Sophie's rise is going to happen imminently.

His eyes track her movement. "This is no game, I assure you."

Panic rises like a flight of birds rousted out of their tree. "Listen, I have to pee."

Flying out of the office, she races down the hallway, only to find the ladies' occupied. With an animal groan, she hauls open the door to the men's and runs right into an older man in a suit as gray as his face.

"Hey, you can't go in there!"

"How about I vomit all over your eight-hundred-dollar shoes?" Tara snarls as she hurls herself into one of the cubicles, shuts the door. The tears have already started, streaming down her cheeks. Her head feels as if it is about to explode. There is a breach inside her, growing wider and wider by the second. She can glimpse Sophie in there, grinning. This isn't the Sophie of her childhood, who cradled and protected her as she was supposed to. This is the Sophie who changed during Tara's adolescence, becoming more than her father could ever have imagined, becoming her own—what?—person? But that is impossible. A ghost then—a ghost stalking the many rooms of Tara's mind.

Slamming herself into a corner, she crouches down, shoulders shaking. The sobs come uncontrollably. Madness is lurking a hairsbreadth away; she can feel it reaching greedily for her. Her legs spasm out, and she kicks at the wall over and over, her fists pounding against the green-and-black-speckled linoleum floor. Spittle flies from her half-open mouth; her eyes roll up in her head.

Sophie's reappearance is too much, too fast. Her mind can't absorb her, isn't made to hold two separate people at once. Dimly, as if seen from over a wavering ridge, a sand dune baking in 120-degree heat, waves of mirage like a screen rising over her memory, she sees her father. "You fucked me up, Dad." Her voice hoarse and reedy, as wavering as her vision. "You fucked me up for all time." Her body spasms again, the soles of her shoes battering the wall. She is back at the farmhouse, the sky red, the sun hammered into an oval by the twilight. "I'll never forgive you—I'll kill you." Thickly, her mouth full of mucus and blood. "I swear on Mother's grave I'll kill you."

Tara feels all cried out, but she can't stop sobbing, tears scalding her like liquid fire. Fire, the fire. And her hand in it. Or is it Sophie's hand? Is Sophie responsible for every bad thing that has happened to her, every bad thing she's said or done? Is that what she is reduced to, blaming her father's unholy creation for the trajectory of her life? Wasn't Sophie right when she said she'd been created from what was already inside Tara? Is a life worth living without taking responsibility? Without owning the bad with the good, who are you? No one. You are nothing. Complete annihilation. But what does she know of life, anyway? Of death, she is plenty knowledgeable. Intimate, even.

What does it mean that Sophie has transcended the bottle of hypnotism in which she was birthed, in which she was contained, summoned only when Tara needed her in order to survive? That she cannot be stuffed back inside, no matter how many wishes Tara makes? Those six months after the fire that are blank to Tara were Sophie's first real taste of life—her life. Sophie is her own person now—present, powerful, demanding life in her own right. Tara loved Sophie; now she realizes that she fears her. What if, in that time, Sophie has gained the upper hand in her mind? What if she—the Tara persona—is slipping into eclipse?

All at once the blinding heat of the desert morphs into water. Surf crashes around her, growing louder and louder, threatening to drown her. Her mouth filling up, she screams and strikes out with her right arm.

Her fist collides with Brandon's chest. She hears his "Oof," hears him say, "No, no, don't do that. It's okay. I have her." Who is he speaking to?

"Tara," Brandon says. "Speak to me." She feels his arms around her, thinks he is her father, and tries to fight him off. "Tara, it's Brandon. Brandon Fiske. Remember?"

And she does remember.

"Brandon."

"I'm here, Tara. I'm going to call a—"

"No ambulance," she mutters. "No ambulance."

"Okay, right then. We'll just get you back to my office."

She feels herself being lifted to her feet, led out of the corner into which she stuffed herself like an ill-used rag doll. Vaguely, she is aware of him guiding her down the hall. The fluorescent stripes too bright, everything popping, as if she is in the middle of an anime movie. People stare at her. What does she care? Her head pounds; it hurts as if it has been hit with a hammer.

I can't do this, she thinks once again. This time it really is too much. And she sees, so vividly she is actually there again, in the open doorway, at her moment of indecision: Do I throw myself into the inferno of the burning farmhouse with my father, or not?

———

Somehow—she has no memory of it—Brandon manages to get her back to the office and onto a sofa against a wall facing the view of the tip of Manhattan.

"Sorry," she mumbles.

Brandon says nothing, hands her a bottle of water. Tipping it back, she drinks down half of it in one go. She is as thirsty as T. E. Lawrence coming out of the Arabian Desert. "Oh, God," she says. "Goddamn." She drinks the rest.

"Seriously, Tara." Brandon takes the empty bottle from her, draws up a chair facing her. "Are you ill?"

"No."

"Right." It is clear he doesn't believe her. "Does this kind of thing happen often?" Not since I was thirteen, she thinks. And never like this. Never before. "And what kind of thing is it? Epilepsy?"

Her laugh rings through the interior. "I should be so lucky."

"What then?"

"There's no cure for what I have."

22

I do believe a change of scenery will do us both a world of good," Brandon says with all the authority at his disposal.

There is no denying it. Shaky as she is, inside and out, she allows him to lead her to the elevator. At some point she realizes they are going up, not down. A bell dings faintly and the doors open, and she finds herself accompanying him out onto a rooftop terrace. Half of it is glassed in. A small kiosk dispensing coffee and donuts dwells within. He takes her to the other side, open to the elements. The wind ruffles her hair, brushing it back from her still-tearstained cheeks. She is not okay—not by a long shot—but on the other hand the fire in her brain has been banked, even if only temporarily.

For a time, they stand side by side, not a word passing between them. And why should there be? She is sure she has blown his job offer—in his eyes she is damaged goods, ill and therefore unreliable—but that seemed like a pipe dream anyway.

"Back in Chicago I met a grad student who could write backward. You'd dictate to him—anything that came into your head, and no matter how fast you spoke, he never missed a word, wrote it all backward, from right to left."

Brandon nods. "Strange bird."

He seems relieved that she has spoken, and she realizes belatedly that is what he has been waiting for. She is astonished that he is so mindful of her feelings.

"You asked what happened to me back there. I have no idea. Something in my brain that's happened since childhood. But," she hastens to add, "it's not a specific thing—I mean, it's not a disease or a syndrome. It wouldn't even be quantifiable to a doctor, no matter her specialty."

Brandon takes a breath, lets it out slowly. "I was sorry to see you in that state."

"I know." She ducks her head. "Thank you."

Between the sound of the wind and the street noises from far beneath them, she becomes aware of his close study of her.

She turns to him. "What?"

"You've got some color in your cheeks," Brandon says.

"Thank the wind and the city air."

He laughs softly. "You should get out more often. Sunlight suits you."

For Tara, a compliment, like kindness, is difficult to accept. She is disconcerted; she doesn't know what to do with it, so she does nothing.

He looks at her steadily. "I think it's time we were totally honest with each other."

Her headache starts up again, fiercer than ever. She sits deathly still while her heart plummets into the pit of her stomach, like the sun sinking into the ocean, leaving only a duskiness in its wake.

"About . . ." She scarcely knows what she is saying or even where she is. It hits her then with the force of an oncoming train that she doesn't know who Brandon Fiske actually is. "About what?"

"What this job you're going to take actually entails."

A sudden contraction in the pit of her stomach. "It's not charity work, is it?"

Brandon's eyes seem to bore right through her. Gone is the affable older man. In his place is a fortress, hard and smooth as any stone awash in the ocean. "No, it isn't."

He holds out a plain manila envelope.

For God's sake, don't open it! Sophie cries. *Don't even take it!* As if I have a choice.

Tara takes the envelope from Brandon.

PART 3
A WALK ACROSS ROOFTOPS

I sat in the sun on a bench; the animal within me licking the chops of memory; the spiritual side a little drowsed, promising subsequent penitence, but not yet moved to begin.

—Robert Louis Stevenson,
The Strange Case of Dr. Jekyll and Mr. Hyde

When I woke up, lying on a stretcher, my left hand black and pink, my lungs feeling as if a blowtorch had been taken to them, my entire body racked with pain, all I wanted was out of the horror story that was my so-called life. No, that's not right. I wanted something different, something more. I wanted to be the hero of a fairy tale. I wanted to be on cloud nine.

SOPHIE

LOS ANGELES—TWENTY-SIX MONTHS AGO

Cloud 1

The thing about Santa Monica was the ocean and the salt air. And the people. The ocean rolled gently; the salt air kissed gently. And the people—well, the people were different. The ocean came first—vast and mesmerizing. I sat on the beach, knees drawn up, strong arms wrapped around my shins. I dug my toes into the sand, trying to put down roots, to make sure that even if Tara awoke from her deep trance, she wouldn't be able to pry me away from here. For hours on end, even after the sun began to burn me, I remained captivated by the ocean. Coming from southwest Georgia, I had been on rivers, trod the shores of lakes, but I'd never seen such a vast body of water, except on TV and in the movies. The real thing was overwhelming. Several times during those first few days, I pinched myself to make sure I wasn't dreaming.

The only fly in the ointment was my damned hand. I had been taken by ambulance to the burn unit of Crisp Regional Health Services in Cordele, where I was initially treated for smoke inhalation, too in pain and out of it to register the irony of the place's name. Hours later, I was bundled off to the JMS Burn Center at Doctors Hospital in Augusta three hours away. No one shared those agonizing rides, but I could dimly recall that Tara and I had shared the terrible moment when she'd almost thrown herself into the fire that had already engulfed most of the farmhouse. If it hadn't been for me, she might actually have done it. I'd stopped her. I didn't want to die. Unlike her, I knew what it was to die—I died over and over again every time she left my shell to return to the world of her childhood and adolescence. With no thought as to what happened to me. Didn't she know that I died every time she abandoned me? Dead and buried until the next time, scared witless, she retreated into my womb-like shell. Waking me when she hid away from the terror so I could enfold her in my arms. Every time she returned to herself, I died. But it was a surreal form of death; it was supposed to absorb her guilt and her shame, along with her terror. What was most dreadful was that what I longed for most, my return to life, only happened when she was traumatized again. I was the Hypnotist's soldier; I followed his orders. Or at least I used to. New to me was the abject shame and guilt I felt for wanting my own existence as I watched the farmhouse burn. As Tara stood on the brink of self-immolation. I shouldn't have felt shame for what I wanted, for what that desire did to her. I shouldn't have felt guilt for wanting what I wanted. But I did. I had begun to slip the leash the Hypnotist had put around my neck. The fire was a turning point: the unknown in the equation the Hypnotist, in his peculiar kind of genius, had created.

I wondered: Is it part of being human to feel guilt and shame? After all, the Bible told us that Adam and Eve felt guilt and shame when they were cast out of Eden. But that was all nonsense, wasn't it? But in that moment of stopping her from self-immolation, I wondered this: Are Tara and I two sides of the same coin, or are we two separate coins? What had the Hypnotist planned for us, or had he not thought that far ahead? What if my existence was meant to be short? What if I was to be discarded once Tara didn't need me anymore? These were the questions that haunted me from that moment on. They were the same questions Tara could not face even more than two years later.

By the time we reached the burn unit, I had fully awakened as if from a deep and dreamless sleep. By then the intense trauma had done its work on Tara. Somewhere back at the smoldering farmhouse she had sunk like a stone into oblivion, and for the first time I was both awake and free of her.

I arrived in LA with the back of my hand bandaged and instructions on how and when to keep the wound clean and disinfected, what kind of bandages to buy and apply. For the first two weeks, I'd had to wear a glove on my left hand, sealed with duct tape, when I showered. Washing my face was awkward. The bandages themselves were unsightly. I came upon the idea of using one of a pair of neoprene fingerless weight gloves I bought at the gym I'd joined. I simply wore the right one on my left hand so the padded side covered the bandages. Other than that, everything was cool. Better than cool, actually.

I was six weeks past Tara's eighteenth birthday, but I looked and acted older. In the land where female youth was worshipped, no one questioned me. I didn't think they cared. Anyway, Tara was an early developer. By the time she was thirteen, she was wearing adult bras. Her body was smokin' hot. And I was canny. I was used to being alone—I mean really alone. I was like the djinn in the bronze lamp, curled and all unknowing until summoned. At least, that was the Hypnotist's intent; he was so damn arrogant. In any event, I had become used to looking out for myself, as well as for my sister when she needed my shell to crawl into, needed me to soothe her, needed me to assure her that this, too, would pass, that she was going to be okay. There were times—the worst of times—when I wasn't at all certain I believed the lines the Hypnotist had put in my mouth. Still, we did make it out, Tara and I, but at what stupendous cost I was unable to calculate. The multiplier was overwhelming.

Life in Santa Monica was impossibly languid, but it took some time to sink into that rhythm. The first morning my excitement was such that I woke up very early. The eastern sky was a tender pink, streaked with orange, as I picked my way along the beach toward the pier. The rest of the sky was a shade of pale blue I'd never seen before. When I arrived at the pier, it was more or less deserted. Only a couple of fishermen types were about, delivering their catch to the restaurants' back doors. They looked at me as if I was crazy. I suppose I was, in a way: crazy about Southern California. I thought, that morning, gazing up at the Ferris wheel that would light up the night sky like a fireworks display, Now that I'm here, that I know what it's really like, I'll never leave. I had worked my way to LA. The credit card and driver's license I had were in Tara's name, which, in order to keep her protected, I would not use.

How naive I was! How stupid. In reality, I knew nothing about Santa Monica, let alone LA. But here in La-La Land the truth came slowly, and often painfully, buried as it was beneath layers of glitter, beauty, and seductiveness. You don't see it until it's right on top of you; by then it's too late. That first morning everything I saw, heard, and touched felt surreal, and at the same time more real than anything I had experienced in Georgia. And everything I ate—the tacos, especially the tacos!—tasted better than I could have imagined any food tasting.

Cloud 2

It took only a week for me to meet Rex. But actually, in the way things were done in LA, Rex met me. You would think, seeing how handsome, charismatic, and downright charming Rex was, I would have met him at Michael's or the Ivy at the Shore, or any number of star-studded haunts, but no, it wasn't like that at all. Every city ran by a clockwork mechanism. In LA, if you wanted to meet someone, you never could. You had to run into them by accident or not at all. This was how LA worked.

It was a Saturday, late morning. I'd Ubered from the Westside to Beverly Hills to have brunch at Nate'n Al. Everybody in Santa Monica talked about Nate'n Al, which was weird, since usually Westsiders didn't set foot out of the beach area for fear of winding up spending the better part of a glorious, sun-splashed day buried alive in teeth-grinding traffic on the freeways. You've never seen anything like the 405 at four in the afternoon. Jesus Lord! Nevertheless, they never shut up about Nate'n Al, because it provided a whiff of authentic New York: pastrami, corned beef, latkes, bagels and lox. All terra incognita to me. I'd read about such food, of course, during the times after school when Tara would sneak off to the library, use their computer to learn about history, art, science, the world at large outside our little dog patch of Georgia. I read everything Tara read, absorbed everything she did—that was part of my deal, how the Hypnotist made me. I don't think he'd had a choice—even he had his limitations.

Anyway, that Saturday, feeling restless, I thought, *What the hell, I'll check it out.* So I walked in, and the deli was filled to the teeth with guys and their offspring. Kids between three and maybe eleven, though it was hard to tell at that age. Apart from the waitresses and the cashier, all of whom looked one step away from the glue factory, not an adult female in sight. Turns out Saturday mornings were when divorced dads took their kids to Nate'n Al. I swear it was like some kind of a camp, albeit a depressing one. I mean, none of the dads seemed able to keep a handle on their offspring. The progeny of the rich ran around the aisles between the booths and were given treats and otherwise super indulged by the waitresses, who, it appeared, knew them all by name.

I watched this scene with eyes wide open, trying to make sense of it all and coming up short. I got the pastrami on rye with coleslaw and one of those sour pickles. "Ya gotta get the sour," the waitress said with a wink. "The half sour's for wimps and tourists from the Midwest. You're not from the Midwest, are ya, doll?" I said I wasn't.

I had wolfed down half the sandwich, relishing every bite, and was sipping on something called a chocolate egg cream, which, inexplicably, contained neither eggs nor cream—it was damn good, though—when Rex came up to my booth and asked if he could sit down. *People in LA are so polite,* I thought. Hah, was I in for a surprise.

I took one look at him and said, "Sure," without a second thought. In fact, his beauty boxed every single thought out of my head. No doubt about it, I was knock-your-socks-off bedazzled. How to describe him adequately? He was tall, six feet, probably, and built like a surfer dude—slender hips, wide shoulders. He wore lightweight trousers, a plain blue T-shirt, and leather huaraches. His skin was the same toasty color of his huaraches. He sported coal-black hair and had gull-gray eyes. His nose was long but slender, his mouth generous—to a fault, some would say. Not me, though, because right then he smiled, and my thighs began to quiver as if their nerves and muscles had minds of their own. I tried to say something, but my mouth was as dry as Nevada's salt flats, so instead, I latched on to the straw and sucked at my egg cream, now not tasting it at all. At that moment, all I was capable of was wondering what his mouth would taste like when I stuck my tongue down his throat. I imagined it would taste like the beach at Santa Monica, like the pier's lit-up Ferris wheel, like the ocean at midnight.

As it turned out, I was wrong. He tasted like a pine forest and rain. But I'm getting ahead of myself. Rex did that to me, until he didn't.

He sat. "Hey. My name's Rex," he said, holding out his hand across the table. "Rex Stroud."

I took his hand, which was warm and dry. He held mine a moment longer than was necessary, not that I minded. On the contrary. "Sophie," I said. "Sophie Wade." I wasn't about to give him or anyone else my real name.

"So you're not from around here."

Somehow, by the grace of God, I grinned. "What gave me away?"

"The fact you're here at Nate'n Al on a Saturday morning," he said with a wry smile.

I laughed. "Yeah, I can see I stick out like a sore thumb."

"I'd say more like an orchid in a swamp."

"My, what a gentleman you are," I exclaimed. "But, hmm, why not a bird of paradise?"

I couldn't even begin to calculate the wattage of his grin. It was as if he'd stepped right off the silver screen. And why not? This was LA, right? "Why not, indeed." He ducked his head. "From now on I shall call you Bop."

"Now you're making fun of me."

"Certainly not." He smirked, which, on him, looked damn good. As I found out, anything and everything looked good on him. And off.

I burst out laughing. "Bop says okay then."

He threw his head back, as if to indicate his total acceptance of me. At least, it seemed that way then.

I looked around. "How many of your children are with you?"

"I have one. He's eight." He waved a hand. "He's off somewhere with Maureen. She's served him here since he was a toddler."

"I suppose when he was a toddler, you and your wife brought him here together."

"That would be a no. My ex wouldn't be caught dead in a place like this."

I set about devouring the remaining half of my pastrami on rye. Just being near Rex made me ravenous. And that sour pickle! How could something so humble taste so good. Better than I had expected. But then everything in LA was better than I expected, by a magnitude of about ten thousand. By the time I met Rex, my plan to stay permanently had already been set in stone. What Tara would make of this decision I had no idea. Anyway, the less I thought about Tara, the better. I was free now. The idea of her resurfacing didn't exactly fill me with joy. This kind of freedom—my freedom—was not to be shared.

"Who doesn't like deli food?" I said when I came up for air. "I mean, *I* like deli food, and I'm from Texas."

"Ah, well, you haven't met my wife." He watched me take another bite. "Count yourself lucky."

Cloud 3

Rex lived in Bungalow 1 at Palme d'Or, a sprawling ornamental wedge of grand hotel and private bungalows perched atop the hills overlooking Sunset Boulevard. It turned out he shared it with two girls. Sunrize was a masseuse possessed of purportedly magical talents and an aspiring songwriter who was constantly making DIY recordings of her songs and messengering them, in Rex's name, to music producers. Then there was Melodie, a bartender at Palme's Barangrill, as well as an aspiring screenwriter constantly rewriting a screenplay based on the time in 1973 when Gram Parsons drove out from the hotel to Joshua Tree and never came back; it was titled *OD at Twenty-Six*. She never allowed Rex to read it, and after sneaking a peek at it, I knew why. Lucky for her she was a great bartender. Anyway, to my knowledge she never did finish the damn thing.

Everyone in LA, it seemed, was one thing while striving to be something else: someone famous, someone rich—a celebrity, in other words. Apart from Rex, that is. He seemed content to be exactly who he was: a man-child born into boocoodles of money who had no ambition other than to enjoy the good life to the fullest extent of his abilities, of which he had plenty.

The Palme d'Or was inaptly named: the large hotel itself looked like a French chateau in the Loire Valley, where so far as I knew there were no palm trees, golden or otherwise. The interior had been meticulously renovated by a Parisian hotelier, retaining a high percentage of its original charm. Rex had chosen it for the same reason other celebs did—to decompress, to get away from the high-wire life that had strung them out. The list of famous (and infamous) guests who had stayed in the hotel or bungalows was long and hallowed: Douglas Fairbanks, Sharon Tate, Robert De Niro, Marlon Brando, Roman Polanski, Dominick Dunne, Oriana Fallaci, David Hockney, and, at one time or another, virtually every major rock group, a number of whom had walked across the hotel's rooftops, drunk, stoned, and, often, naked.

Although as Rex told me, one didn't *stay* at the Palme d'Or so much as *live* there. The retreat was perfect for him, a celebrity of sorts in his own right. He was known everywhere and by everyone in LA, or so he made it seem. He was beautiful, charismatic, and wealthy. He was invited to seemingly every fantastic party in town. Best of all, he had the invaluable knack of hooking the right people up with the right people. That was true on many levels; it took me some time to figure out all of them.

In LA, if Rex liked you, you were golden, and Rex liked me. He liked me a lot. He took me home with him to Bungalow 1, a three-bedroom affair with a garden of bougainvillea and a fragrant lime tree, framed by a six-foot-long boxwood hedge. There, within twelve hours, I met both Sunrize and Melodie. I had no idea whether those were their real names, but what did it matter? I preferred not to think about it. I wasn't real either.

At twilight, Rex took me around the grounds, showed me where Jack Lemmon used to sunbathe in the nude, where Errol Flynn practiced his swordsmanship, where the young Marlon Brando played touch football with his best buds, where Humphrey Bogart planted his garden at the side of the bungalow he lived in.

Four weeks later, Melodie was gone. In her place appeared an all-over-tanned surfer girl named Carmen Gemini, who aspired to be "discovered." I immediately coveted her name, made up or not. "I'm a starlet," she promptly told me upon introducing herself. "Or at least I will be within a month." Right after the party, she too had vanished into LA's palm tree haze.

Meanwhile, there was Rex. Always and forever, Rex. And me, of course. His new golden girl; no matter who else came and went from the other bedrooms in Bungalow 1, I remained with Rex.

But I'm getting ahead of myself. That first night, after our little tour, we sat at the bar, where I was introduced to mezcal, tequila's smoky big brother. Melodie served me a drink called a bloody sombrero made with blood orange, mezcal, tequila, and lime. She laughed when I rolled my eyes and smacked my lips. Rex looked on, drank añejo in straight shots.

I wondered whether he had been fucking one of them, or both. If so, I wondered whether he'd continue to do that now that I had arrived, a sultan with his harem. Not that I cared; jealousy wasn't part of my makeup. Staying alive was job number one.

Three bloody sombreros on, I was slow dancing with Rex to the Eagles' "Hotel California." I was roasted on blue agave. I had the rhythm in me. I loved to drink, I loved to dance, and soon enough I became addicted to fucking Rex. Tara was terrified of sex. Not that I blamed her—God, no. But I did what I did anyway; I couldn't help myself.

———

I was always aware that everything Tara was I was not. But so what? I was not a stranger to jealousy. That was how I was made: Sophie, the invisible sister, a shell inside which Tara could conceal herself to keep her from going insane. So I was of necessity incomplete, nothing more than a place of respite and repose. But along the way something happened, something unexpected, something unforeseen. It terrified Tara; it scared me. Gradually, bit by bit with each time I was summoned by Tara's terror, I grew stronger. I was Tara and she was me; that was how it had always been. Until the fire. Until the trauma obliterated the Hypnotist's work. Now I was alone. No Tara. Now I was forced to think for myself.

I loved Tara—after all, if it weren't for her, I would never have been created. But I hated the Hypnotist with all the force of my limited nature. He created me, then left me in this wasteland, neither alive nor dead. I didn't know who or what I was. Was I a figment of Tara's hypnotically augmented imagination, or was I a separate individual? Mostly I felt like a form without a shadow. Was that true? Was I even in any way real? I *felt* real enough. What was existence, anyway? The Hypnotist might have known—he might, but I doubted it. It was the Hypnotist I hated with every atom of my insubstantial being. He created me, but at the same time he put me in a bronze lamp and sealed it with a stopper he assumed only Tara could unscrew. But he was wrong, so far wrong it was off the map.

In any event, the fire changed everything. At the same instant it incinerated the Hypnotist, the fire gave me life—true life, this life, whatever it turned out to be, however long it would last. Were these two things interconnected? I'd likely never know.

And still another death was dogging my heels. That moment when Tara would arise and I would yet again be consigned to the realm of the living dead. Only it would be worse this time—far worse—because I would have had a taste of what it meant to be alive and free. My own person.

———

That first time, the night of three bloody sombreros, the night of slow dancing with Rex to "Hotel California," Fleetwood Mac's "Dreams," Lana Del Rey's "Born to Die," he led me back to Bungalow 1 and took me from behind. Just lifted up my skirt, moaning when he saw I wasn't wearing panties. Like a bull. I remember he smelled like an animal. I didn't mind. No, I encouraged it. I danced for him, loose limbed, lascivious. I turned my back to him, threw him a swampy look over my shoulder. Not that he required much encouragement. I needed him in me, all at once. Feeling empty, I needed to be filled, to have someone else prove to me that I was fused to Tara's body, that I was at last full flesh and blood, that I really did exist. That first time, my entire body was an erogenous zone. My nipples were hard as bullets. I was wet between my thighs. I had no desire for preliminaries. I didn't even consider kissing him—not then, but many, many times thereafter, yes, of course. Because, even though it seemed that way, I was not all id. Mostly, but not all.

"Why has it taken so long for me to find you?" he asked in the aftermath of our second coupling of the night, or was it the third? I forget. The bedclothes were rucked up around us, a damp sea. We both smelled deliciously of sweat and sex. Alcohol fumes wafted about us as if we were on some sort of perverse heavenly cloud.

"I was lost," I said without a second thought. "But now I'm found."

Rex laughed so hard his tears flew in all directions. It was only then I realized—those were lines from "Amazing Grace." How foolish I felt, and how satisfied. Norma Jean would have had a stroke if she'd heard "Amazing Grace" spoken in this carnal context.

I drifted off to sleep with Sunrize softly singing "The Boys of Summer" along with Don Henley somewhere in the bungalow.

The thing I didn't realize then was that LA was a rabbit hole. It was so seductive you couldn't help but go down it, but once you did it was awfully difficult to find your way out. Your appetites flew out of control. You could not take just one bite of that lotus leaf; you had to eat the whole goddamned thing.

Cloud 4

The weeks flew by in a golden haze. We went everywhere. We hiked in Griffith Park, skied in Tahoe, looked into a volcano's seething innards in Hawaii, gambled and danced to idol DJs in Vegas, and three times a week he took me to his gym, where I joined in his strenuous workout regimen. I gloried in Tara's farm-toughened muscles—*my* muscles now—as they grew ever stronger and tougher. When we went horseback riding, I surprised him by surpassing him with ease, and riding bareback, to boot. But then, he said afterward, assuaging his male pride, you're from Texas.

Late one night, when most of LA lay sleeping, we sat atop Mulholland Drive, like gods high above the glittering carpet of lights spread out below, and among them all the delights of LA danced just for us.

"There's something I want to tell you," Rex said. We were close together, shoulders pressing, knees drawn up, thighs pressed together.

I turned to him, and just like any starstruck girl at the fringes of Hollywood, I wanted in so badly it was a taste in my mouth. I waited for him to go on. I wondered if my body was betraying my desire and my longing. At that moment, I was as vulnerable as a lamb all unwitting to the slaughter.

"You're not like any of the other girls I've met." He reached out for me. "You're not only beautiful—you're smart." His fingertips drew wisps of my hair back behind my ear. So light, his touch, like an angel's wing. "And so very clever."

He smiled, then, and it seemed to me that the smile encompassed all the stars on the silver screen, as well as all the stars in the sky, even the ones I couldn't see through the city's haze and light pollution. The night felt both hyperreal and unreal.

When I told him that, he laughed. "LA isn't the wasteland I thought it would be when I grew up here."

"I think it's magical. It's so laid back, and yet at the same time, things move so fast."

He caressed my ear, tracing its outer curve. "People make a decision one day; the next, they've forgotten all about it and are on to another idea. That's why you've got to corral their attention, fence them in."

"Get the saddle on them and cinch it tight before they can buck it loose."

"To complete the metaphor." His eyes glittered like the stars. "So, so smart."

For a moment, his gaze turned inward, and he seemed lost in thought.

"I'm hosting a party next week." His fingertips were running down the side of my neck, giving me tremors along my legs, intersecting at the juncture of my thighs. "There are people I want you to meet. Businesspeople." He leaned in, his voice barely above a whisper. "You can help me. Would you like to help me?"

"You mean setting it up?"

He laughed. "I have people to take care of hiring and overseeing." He pressed his lips against the corner of my mouth. "No, I want you to meet the people who matter to me. Dazzle them with your wit and your charm." He grinned. "So? Say yes."

"Yes." Blood was whooshing through my temples like a waterfall. To be invited into his inner circle! "I say yes."

He nodded. "That's my girl." And pulled away a little, all business now. "Parties in LA are different than anywhere else. What you must keep in mind at all times is that it's all brittle, made of glass—extremely expensive glass. One false move, one wrong word, and it will all shatter, and with it your reputation. And in this town reputation is everything. Whether or not you're actually competent at your job—say in a movie studio or as an agent—is irrelevant." He nods again. "Sounds crazy, I know. But when in Hollywood . . ."

He smiled. "So." He clapped his hands together like a circus ring-master (not so far off the mark). "Hollywood parties are a microcosm of Hollywood itself. The entrance you make is the only thing that matters. Make a great entrance and every attendee will want to talk to you, and afterward they'll remember you. Even better, they'll talk about you. Why? Because they'll assume you're a new somebody. And they all want to be seen with the new *somebody*; they'll all want to claim that they discovered you first, that they knew before anyone else that you would crack Hollywood's code." He laughed. "Plus, you'll be on my arm."

Looking back, all these rules struck me as being loony as a mad hatter, veins polluted with mercury. But at the time I didn't stop to consider this. I didn't *want* to consider it. I wanted it all to be true, part of the floating airship I had stepped onto when Rex had sat down opposite me at Nate'n Al. I was in a new world, and he was my Virgil, holding his lamp high.

But Rex was no Virgil. More like the hellhound Cerberus, leading me down into Hades.

But that was later. Now, a shopping spree on Rodeo Drive to get me party ready. I didn't want expensive clothes; I didn't like clothes much. I was most comfortable in Tara's body naked, stripped of all those things I didn't really understand. But Rex's eyes gleamed so diamond hard; how could his divine golden girl say no? I should have said no. Instead I said yes. Yes to everything. How could anyone blame me? I went from having nothing to having everything. Too potent a temptation. Gluttony meant overreaching. Temptation meant being bedazzled, taking risks and saying "Fuck it" to the consequences.

That was my downfall, or maybe my downfall was written in the stars. If you believe in fate, then I was bound to fuck up in LA, no matter what I said or did. That's how I came to look at it, anyway. It's how I had to look at it, for my own survival. If I winked out of existence, what would happen to Tara? She'd be all alone with the demon of the past. God knows, she'd suffered enough. I didn't want to be responsible for more.

Cloud 5

Rex's party was thick with people, massed, sweaty, and drugged out. Carmen Gemini was pouring the alcohol; waitpersons passed around platters of caviar-filled puff pastry, smoked salmon on butter-slicked squares of black bread, minishrimp cocktails, joints, and little twists of paper containing coke. All very posh, all very decadent. Everyone was inhaling something while they talked, drank, stumbled, laughed, and tried to keep an eye on everyone in the garden outside Bungalow 1 to make sure they were tracking the movements of all the VIPs. There were a lot of those: musicians, artists, film directors and producers, but only a smattering of actors. That was another interesting thing about Rex: he appeared completely impervious to the lure of Hollywood stars. His focus was business; he had no time to be starstruck.

I, of course, was drawn to the actors like a moth to a flame, but Rex, keeping me on an invisible leash, drew me back to the suits. Three in particular. They all wore expensive cashmere sports jackets, totally out of place in LA's evening warmth. Striped shirts, thin ties, and ankle boots that seemed out of time, as if they were emulating the Mods of 1960s London. They wore their hair long, over their ears, and closer to, they appeared younger than they had from across the garden. One had pockmarked cheeks, another a white scar at the outer corner of his left eye. Tiki torchlight licked their faces, turning them into vaguely ominous masks.

Rex introduced them as Dan, Dave, and Dick, as if they were triplets from a circus sideshow. They spoke like triplets, too, finishing each other's sentences. Dark skinned, black hair slicked back from wide sloping foreheads, blacker eyes. Totally creepy. I would have laughed at them, except that Rex had warned me not to. These are totally serious guys, he told me. You're to treat them as such. On the other hand, they were regarding me wolfishly. I was wearing a pale-orange Akris cap-sleeve embroidered cocktail dress that showed a lot of cleavage. Rex had wanted to buy me a pair of Jimmy Choo pumps with five-inch heels, until I said, "I'm not going to look like a thousand-dollar-a-night whore even for you." He bought me what I wanted: a pair of deep-gold sandals with a manageable wedge heel and a wide buckled strap that went around my ankle: sexy, definitely not whorish. He didn't say a word, just cheerfully paid for everything.

The garden was all but overflowing. Rex pulled me aside, pointed across the throng to three suits who looked as out of place as armadillos at the seashore.

"Those are the guys: Dave, Dan, and Dick."

"You're kidding, right? They might as well be called Huey, Louie, and Dewey."

"These are serious guys," Rex said, scowling. "Treat them right until I join you."

"Where're you going to be?"

"A producer I need to speak with just showed up. I gotta button-hole him right now or he'll slip away, and it'll take me days to catch up." He kissed me briefly. "Go on then. I'll be over in no time."

Okay then. I worked the crowd as I wended my way toward the three suits. It was a bit like playing *Frogger*.

"Gentlemen." I grinned when I'd at last made my way through the thickets. "Welcome to Rex's party. He's notorious for his parties, you know." Nothing. Like talking to rocks. Taking another tack, I gestured. "So, gentlemen, why don't you set your briefcases aside and enjoy yourselves?"

"No," Dave said, dead eyed.

"Where's Rex?" Dick said, his voice laden with accusation.

Jesus. "On his way, I assure you," I said. "You guys're here to do business with Rex, am I right."

"Right as rain," Dan, the scarred one, said, somehow managing to make the trite phrase sound offensive.

"What kind of business? You're moneymen, I bet." I shrugged. "I mean, you have that look."

Nothing. Nada. Zip.

Wow.

"Where are you guys from then?"

"Not around here," Dick said. The torchlight made his pockmarks look like the craters of the moon.

"South," Dave said.

"San Diego?"

"Something like that," Dan said. And they all snickered in concert.

I cleared my throat. "What can I get you gentlemen to drink?"

"Cerveza," Dick said.

"Beer," Dave said. "Preferably Mexican."

I brought them what they wanted. Rex had stocked plenty of Dos Equis, perhaps for just this reason. They eyed me as I handed over the frosty bottles. One thing was for sure, they were making no bones about raking my boobs, my hips, my legs, as if I were about to reenact a scene from their favorite porn film. I thought that was funny—the unreality of it. It was so LA.

The raucous sounds of the party roared on, reminding me how far away I'd been. I still had these men to deal with, but the moment their eyes had locked lustfully on me, I had them. I knew how to deal with the stupidity of men like these.

I cocked my head, hands on hips. "What would interest guys like you, hm?" I used a different tone, warmer, informal. "Sports, am I right? Sure, football. No, soccer. You bet on the games."

"Matches," Dave said. "They're called matches."

"*You* interest us." Dick pitched me a look that made my blood run cold. "You're Rex's latest squeeze." Squeeze? Who the hell used *squeeze* nowadays? Any minute now he'd be calling me a *skirt*, and I'd be back in Raymond Chandler's 1930s LA.

"You in showbiz?" Dave asked. "Film?"

"No shit, Sherlock," Dick said. "Look at those tits. Epic. She's a starlet in the making if I ever saw one."

Now, despite Rex's admonition, they had started to piss me off. I stepped forward, got up in Dick's face. "I think it's time you and your fellow wise guys put down your briefcases. This Hollywood buzz is going to your heads. The strain is beginning to show."

When no one answered, I said, "Jeez, it seems to me you guys are in serious need of a vacation."

Dick transferred his briefcase from his right hand to his left. I didn't like the look of his right hand, empty now, fingers slightly curled.

Before the unpleasantness went any further, Rex came up behind me, slipped an arm around my waist, and with his best megawatt smile, said, "So, how's my little girl been treating you?"

"Well, she is a real treat," Dan said.

"A treat and a half," Dave said.

"Actually," Dick said with a nasty edge, "she was just about to pucker up and blow." That concert of snickers again.

I expected Rex to come to my defense, get all up in their faces over the insult, but when he didn't move, I did. Stepping to my right, out of Rex's loose embrace, I slapped Dick across the face so hard I could hear his neck vertebrae crack. A white mark bloomed on his cheek, quickly turning red.

There was, of course, a reaction: a flurry of motion from the trio, confused and uncoordinated but somehow threatening. Rex didn't hesitate this time; he immediately reestablished control.

"Sophie's my girl, got that?" He shook his head ruefully. "She isn't a *puta mexicana* you can talk to like that. She's a lady."

"A lady." Dick snorted. "*She's* the one who slapped *me*." His eyes narrowed. "I oughta—"

"Boys, boys."

"Why the fuck you send her over?" Dave asked.

"She kept you entertained, didn't she?"

Like a pet monkey, I thought. My eyes blazed. Maybe I should've stripped for them.

"She's hot," Dick said.

"True. But she's off limits. And, listen, I'll let the offense you caused her slide. She took care of it herself." Rex smiled, arms sweeping out to encompass the entire garden. "But hey, we're all cool, right? Now if it's pussy you're after, I've got lots of girls here for you to choose from. Once we finish our business, I can—"

"What if we want *her*."

I was getting the picture now. Dick outranked the others. What utter Neanderthals these guys were, only one thing on their minds now they'd set their eyes on me! I observed this with a mixture of amusement and disgust, but also now a bit of growing discomfort.

Rex shook his head, a smile fixed to his face. "That would be imposs—"

"Fuck, no." Dick took a step forward. "Last time I asked for . . ." He snapped his fingers.

"Sunrize," Dan said helpfully.

"Right, you gave us Sunrize for the night." Dick made a show of looking around. "I don't see her here."

"Escúchenme, señores," Rex said, "ustedes pueden tener a quien deseen, pero no a esta." *Listen to me, gentlemen, you can have anyone you desire, except this one.*

Dick pursed his lips. All of a sudden, he laughed raucously. "¿Quién querría este de todos modos?" *Who would want this one anyway?* It was his way of saving face. "Nevertheless, I demand reparations. If not this one, then we take three girls." He leaned in. I was invaded by his sour sweat, his fetid breath. "And I promise you they won't be the same when morning comes."

I could sense Rex breathe a sigh of relief, but I couldn't believe it; Rex was pimping out girls to these monstrosities. In his mind Dick had been mollified, and that was all that counted. I was appalled at what he had agreed to. But if he'd already thrown poor Sunrize to the wolves, what else could I expect? Briefly, I wondered how I could save tonight's sacrificial lambs. Who knew what Dick, Dan, and Dave had in store for them. Nothing pleasant, that was for sure. I shuddered to think just how bad it would be. At least Rex had refused to make me the sacrifice. I told myself that was something, wasn't it?

Rex had rescued the moment, but storm clouds had rolled in, darkening the air between us, thickening it. Acrimony soured the night breeze. Rex gestured toward the bungalow. "Gentlemen, let's take this inside, shall we?" Their heavy shoulders rolled, and they trekked off single file, like military men. That was when it occurred to me that they might, indeed, be just that, some sort of military. But what kind of business would Rex be doing with men like that? I was reasonably sure I wasn't going to find out, but then Rex turned to me, said, "Come along. I want you to witness this."

"Really?" I was taken aback.

Rex nodded. "Consider it part of your education."

What made him think this was the education I wanted or would enjoy? Frantically, I tried to think of ways to weasel out of this. But it was too late. He had taken my hand in an iron grip. He led me into the bungalow. The door closed behind us.

Dick, Dan, and Dave were already in position around the low coffee table. Their briefcases were lined up as if ready for inspection, and again I considered the possibility that these men were military. But when, as one, they bent, unlocked the cases, and raised the lids, when I saw the clear plastic packets of white powder, I began to think: Okay, military—but which military? If I was to believe them, they were from the south. When, in my naivete, I had asked if that meant San Diego, I'd been met with a chorus of snickers. So *farther* south then. Tijuana, or even farther, Rosario, on the coast, where the newer drug cartels had set up shop, leaving the heads of their enemies rolling in the surf for snuffling dogs and horrified tourists to find. Or maybe this shipment had come from even farther away: Nogales or Ciudad Juárez. And these were the dicks Rex had told me to entertain with my wit and my charm. And the lead dick was the one whose face I'd gotten up into when he'd pissed me off, the one I'd slapped when he'd treated me like a *puta mexicana*.

Slipping a slim gravity knife out of his pocket, Rex flicked open the blade. He turned to me and said, "Pick a packet."

"What?" I wasn't sure I'd heard him correctly, but when he repeated the request, pointing at the three open briefcases with the blade of his knife, I understood. Rex wasn't looking at me, but then he didn't have to—Dave, Dan, and Dick had pinned me in their sights, and they weren't about to let me go until I complied.

Chills ran through me as I stepped to the table. I was shaking so hard I stumbled. That was when I felt Rex's powerful fingers close over my elbow, keeping me on my feet and hurting me at the same time. Our sex life often involved a level of pain that excited me. I never questioned it; I accepted it as an animal response. When it came to sex, we were all animals, instincts drowning civilized behavior. At the moment Rex grabbed me, I felt some of that pain and excitement gravitating to my thighs. I welcomed it; it took me out of this awful situation into another where I was alone with him in the night, Roxy Music or Marvin Gaye wafting over us.

Rex placed his hand on the back of my neck, pushed me down, as he often did in bed. My lips opened, my teeth bared. The breath came hot and fast up my throat. I reached out and moved aside one of the packets, revealing the one underneath.

"That one," I breathed. When Rex pierced it with the point of his knife blade, I gave a stifled cry. Dan, Dave, and Dick grinned, but only Rex understood its meaning.

"Good girl," he whispered in my ear, sending a different kind of iciness down my spine. I had no eyes for the coke. I was wet between my legs; I was hot for him.

Rex's tongue flicked out, tasted the coke on the blade; then he snorted the rest. He sneezed, shook his head. "Choice-quality shit, *señores*."

The three *señores* made grunting noises of satisfaction. Rex brought out an old-fashioned black pigskin doctor's bag, appropriate to the transaction. Dick was the one who opened it, pawed through its contents, counting the packs of hundreds, while the other two stood ramrod straight at his side. They stared at Rex between rapid glances at the open bag.

At length, Dick snapped the bag closed. "And now," he said, "reparations." He meant the three girls they were about to pick from the crowd outside.

Rex nodded without a second thought.

They left then, the three of them escorted by Rex. No one said a word to me, for which I was grateful. The moment the door closed behind them, I ran into our bedroom. With a little indrawn sob, I collapsed onto the bed, drawing a pillow to me, seeking solace and finding it beyond my grasp.

The fire that had burned so hot moments ago was extinguished. Nothing left but the taste of ashes in my mouth.

Shoulders quaking, I wept inconsolably.

Cloud 6

Seasons change, but not in Hollywood. It's as if time didn't move on there, and all the plastic surgery was a desperate attempt to make sure it remained that way.

But I wasn't built that way. For me, life was too ephemeral. Every day I was actually here to experience it was a gift, one I'd never thought I'd have. A life. Separate. Time to explore myself.

But after the night of Rex's party, everything changed. My unexpected life didn't feel like a gift anymore. Lying by Rex's side, I was afraid to fall asleep. When I finally did, in my dreams I saw the three girls Dick, Dan, and Dave had chosen, "picks of the litter," as that cocksucker Dick had called them. I wished to God I had never seen their faces, hadn't been there when they'd been culled, when they'd acquiesced to Rex's command. They owed him—or, more accurately, he owned them. He owned their habits. They were tied to him in a way I couldn't fathom. Helpless as I was to intervene, knowing that they'd chosen their lives, didn't help. I prayed for them as Norma Jean had taught Tara to pray. *We only pray to him when we need him.* They haunted me, those three girls. I never saw them again, which in a way was even worse than if I had. It was as if, after that night, they'd been erased from the face of the earth.

I hated myself then. I hated how complicated, how fraught with danger real life was.

Cloud 7

One night, about a week after the party, I was sitting in the garden of Bungalow 1, inhaling the perfumed scent of the lime tree. I heard someone step out of the doorway behind me. Rex was at a meeting of investors in his latest project, Melodie had left right before the party but was already a fading memory, and Carmen Gemini had barely even registered on our radar before she, too, had left the day after the party. For a while I had heard Sunrize strumming her guitar, making up lyrics as she went along, but that had stopped some time ago. Now she came and plunked herself down in the wooden adirondack chair next to mine. Several minutes went by in a silence steeped in the long LA night. Lights were on in the main part of the hotel. On the expansive back lawn that led to the pool area, a uniformed waiter lit a rectangle of tiki torches. Prepping for a cocktail party, I supposed. As if to verify my guess, a burst of laughter sounded, followed by the throaty roar of a sports car approaching up the hill. The slam of car doors, more voices. Guests arriving. Now and then, when the wind was right, music drifted over from the Barangrill, plangent chords and Stevie Nicks's soaring voice. I didn't look at Sunrize. A certain anxiety had risen within me at her approach. All week, I'd done my best to avoid her. Even looking at her was painful, and each time she was gone, I breathed a sigh of relief.

"Hey," she said finally. Sunrize sort of hummed when she spoke. "Whatcha up to?" She came with her own personal cloud of sweet musk.

I felt struck dumb. When I glanced over, I saw she held a square mirror on which was a twist of paper. A lit joint was between her lips. She held it out to me.

"Thanks." I could barely get the word out. I felt like an idiot, but truly, after what Dick had said about her, I couldn't think of anything brilliant to say. I took the spliff, inhaled the weed deep into my lungs, handed it back. I watched her as I held the smoke inside, feeling my head slowly expand. She was a slim girl, pale eyes, flaxen hair, a sharp nose. She appeared frail, but her massage work had made her strong.

"How're you enjoying life in Bung One?" She had that strangled voice people got when they spoke with a lungful of smoke.

I frowned. "What you really mean is—"

"Ah, no." She shook her head, exhaling in a wide sweep. "I haven't even given Rex a blow job in months."

"Really?"

She heard the skepticism in my voice, handed over the roach. "Yep. The door has shut on that particular path of my life."

"Your doing, or his?"

Sunrize opened the twist of paper, expertly arranged the powdered contents in two lines. "You really want to know?"

I nodded. "I mean what I say."

She sighed, looked off into the palms that ringed the pool, lit from below. A tightly rolled bill appeared between her fingers. Bending over, she hoovered up a line of coke into her right nostril. "Truth be told, I ended it." Her lips quirked upward at one corner. "Not that he cared. Rex doesn't care about much. Except Rex." She rubbed the residue off the end of her nose. "Sorry, sweetie."

"Don't be." I'd smoked the last of the joint, and Sunrize offered me the rolled-up bill. "Sure I can't lure you into dreamland?"

"I'm good."

She nodded. "Yeah, that's you all over." Somehow said sweetly. Then she snorted the remaining line into her left nostril. Massaged the tip of her nose vigorously, shook her head. "Oh, boy. Wow. This is the shit."

"I guess Rex is all Rex needs to be, seeing as how he's a trust fund baby and all."

Sunrize stared at me for a moment, her eyes big around, stained by the shadows in between fronds of torchlight. Then she burst out in the raucous laugh of a coke addict. "You're kidding, right?"

I looked at her, blank faced.

Her eyebrows arched. "That's what he told you?"

I nodded. "Uh-huh."

"Christ almighty," she burst out, "that's a new one."

"Wait, what?" Somewhere I felt the earth coming up to meet me as I fell further from LA's illusory grace.

Sunrize laughed, not unkindly. "Don't look so surprised. Everyone wears a mask here. If you don't learn that quick enough, this place will eat you alive." She ducked her head. "I mean that."

Looking at her, thinking what Rex's party had revealed, I knew she was right. "So what is he then?" I asked.

"Who the fuck knows. Really. But I can tell you his money doesn't come from Mummy and Daddy. It comes from south of the border."

"Dave, Dan, and Dick."

She shuddered. "So you've met the three trolls." She licked the mirror clean. Her throat clicked as she swallowed convulsively. Her expression darkened as she looked up at me. "Nothing happened, did it?"

"Thankfully no." Trying to be circumspect, I said, "I think I understand why you weren't at the party." When she didn't respond, I tried again. "You were conspicuous by your absence, according to Dick."

"You mean Captain Ruiz." She shuddered again, and for the first time I realized that the blue around her eyes didn't come from shadows. "They're Mexican Federal Ministerial Police, not cartel members."

"What's the diff?" I said, only half joking. I'd read lots about the incestuous relationship between the drug cartels, the police, and local politicians.

This time her laugh was raw, razor edged. "Not fucking much. Sometimes, I suppose, nothing at all. In Mexico anyway. Here, I think the police are more self-controlled. They don't want to be discovered north of the border, especially carrying kilos of coke. The cartel guys don't give a shit."

"Did they . . . ?"

She shook her head, her eyes warning me off. "After the first time Rex introed me to those guys . . ." She turned her head away for a moment, sniffed once or twice. "I hope to God I never see them again."

How could Rex do that to her—use her like a piece of raw meat thrown in front of an enraged pit bull?

"One thing I still don't understand. Why did Rex insist I watch the deal go down?"

"Ah, well." Sunrize pulled her hair back from the side of her face. "That was to make you complicit. Apart from a bit of weed, you don't use. So he made you a witness to bind you to him."

Something inside me went dead cold. "But he can't implicate me without implicating himself."

"Have you met Rex? He knows everyone in Hollywood. No one's going to implicate their source. He has a permanent get-out-of-jail-free card."

The revelation, slow in coming, hit me in the face. The terrible truth was that I was as addicted to sex with Rex as those girls were to the drugs he sold them. So in my own way I was no better than they were, tied to him as I was. Worst of all, I knew that even after all this I wouldn't leave him. I couldn't. I wanted—*needed*—what he gave me too much to resist. I felt sick to my stomach.

Sunrize put the mirror aside, leaned in toward me. "There's more. The most important thing. Above all, you need to understand that Rex isn't simply dealing drugs—he's taking them. He's a goddamn addict."

"Addict?" I echoed weakly. I was already white faced. Now the ground underneath me seemed to open up, plunging me into a hole filled with pit vipers. Here came that hellhound Cerberus.

"Coke, Adderall, poppers, X."

I stared at her, trying hard to keep my hands from trembling. How was it I hadn't known—or at the very least suspected? But then what experience did Tara have with drugs or drug addicts? Addicts of any kind, like me?

"A girl like you, you may not know about addicts," Sunrize continued, unaware of the irony, "but trust me: I do. They have difficulty making emotional connections with people. Their emotional connection is with their addiction. But it's really a love affair with death. See, each time they get high, a little piece of them is lost. They become ghosts, shells of who they once were, until they slide all the way down into darkness."

It became clear to me in the moment that Sunrize wasn't speaking just about Rex; she was talking about herself as well. My heart broke for her, which came as a surprise to me—up until then, I didn't think I had a heart. I loved Tara, sure, but that love was built into me; it was involuntary, like a reflex. This was different; it was a feeling toward someone outside of me—an emotional connection. It was at that precise moment I knew without a shadow of a doubt that I was more than a ghost, more than a shell.

I was so grateful to her. "Sunrize," I said, reaching out toward her.

She shook her head violently. "No," she said. "Don't." Her eyes slid back and forth, darting like a lizard seeking shelter, finding none. "I can't stand to be touched." And when I made to persist, she begged me to stop. "Please."

I drew back. "You can't stay here. You know you can't."

She gave me a sad smile. "Oh, Sophie"—she never called me Bop the way Rex and Melodie did—"where in the world . . ." Her eyes seemed dead. "I have nowhere else to go."

"You have no family?"

She shook her head. "I had two brothers. They died in Afghanistan. My parents broke up long ago. My mother's somewhere in Germany—Berlin or Munich, I don't know; my father's got a whole new family that doesn't include me."

"I'm sorry."

Sunrize brought out another prerolled spliff, lit it with a pink BIC.

"About your brothers, I mean."

"Ah, well, that." Sunrize took a deep drag, held the smoke in her lungs, before letting it sing out through her nose, making her look like a petite dragon. "I was close to both of them. They called me Hammie, on account of the hamster I had when I was a kid, the one who was eaten by a cottonmouth when the stupid, stupid thing got out of its cage and escaped the house." Tears rolled down her cheeks in great, fat blobs. "Oh, great." She dabbed at her eyes. "Just look at her now. A fucking child again, crying over her dead hamster." Tilting her head back, she gazed up into the night sky, as if she could place her tears high above the city's neon-argon glow, among the paled-out stars. *Adorable,* I thought, *but sad.* At that moment, she seemed the saddest person I'd ever met.

"What about you?" she asked, offering the joint. She was struggling to recover her composure, moving the conversation away from herself. "Where's your family?"

I shook my head; I'd had enough pot. "Haven't got any. Norma Jean died of a snakebite. The Hypnotist was burned alive in a fire."

I held up the back of my hand to show her the scars. The bandages had come off weeks before.

She tried not to stare. "I was wondering . . ."

"Wonder no more."

"I'm glad at least you escaped."

"That's kind of you to say." I meant it too. There was something about this girl. She needed help the way Tara needed help—way down deep inside, where it was becoming clear she herself couldn't reach.

"But listen." Her brows knit together. "Norma Jean and the Hypnotist? Were they foster parents or something?"

"Just parents," I said laconically.

Sunrize seemed bewildered. "You don't call them Mom and Dad?"

I gave her a thin smile. "Never felt right."

She considered this seeming anomaly for a time. "So, wait, your father was a hypnotist?"

I nodded. "Among other things."

"So . . ."

But my eyes went out of focus. I was still processing her background, the damage that parental dipshits, whether it be emotional withholding or the wrong form of attention, can inflict on a child. Mourning my own insubstantiality had left me no room to consider the myriad catastrophic consequences possible for a child. When Tara summoned me, I was wholly consumed, working hard to cocoon her. I'd never had time to acknowledge (except in the most remote way) the traumas that had brought me to her, let alone ponder them. Or was that a lack in me—a deliberate one, baked in by the Hypnotist, in order to keep my attention on the task at hand: calming Tara down, walling her off from the aftermath, helping her forget? For doing that I'd also begun to forget. Now Sunrize had brought the horror racing back. And like a dam bursting, the long-held-back images flooded into me at breakneck speed.

"Sophie? Soph?"

Someone was calling my name. At first I was sure it was Tara, and my blood ran cold. Death before I was ready to give up this life. I blinked, saw Sunrize leaning toward me, a concerned expression on her face. "Are you okay?"

I nodded, not trusting myself to speak.

She appeared unconvinced. "Listen, if I overstepped by asking about your parents, I'm sorry. So, so sorry."

"No, it's not that." It most certainly was that, along with a tsunami of the memories that went along with it, but I wasn't going to share any of them with her; she had her own shit to carry. That's when I understood that I was like a baby, unused to emotions—especially adult emotions—and most certainly the emotions of a broken adult. Did that mean I was ill equipped to help her?

She spent a few moments sucking on the joint, its business end lighting up intermittently, like a firefly. Maybe to give me time to recover—who knows? I was grateful for the pause, anyway. The party had migrated into Barangrill, where Johnny Marr's electric live version of "How Soon Is Now?" was plundering the velvet night. I was wondering that myself.

"Hey, Soph, you ever been up on the roof?" she said from out of nowhere.

"What, here?"

"Uh-huh."

"Nope. Why would . . . ?"

"Lots of guests have tromped those tiles over the years. Mostly rock stars—drunk, stoned out of their gourds. Management tends to frown on it, but what can they do?"

"Padlock the roof doors?"

She laughed. "There's other ways to gain access." Her eyes sparked. "Always."

Marr was singing about being human and needing to be loved.

Didn't we all, even those of us who weren't really here.

Cloud 8

Sophie and Sunrize walking across rooftops.

"Brothers? Sisters?" she asked after a time.

I thought for a moment. "Not a one," I said. "There's only me."

We were lying on the roof of the main hotel, tiles against our backs, sounds rising from below: voices, the laughter of drunk friends, the hushed whispers of clandestine lovers, the colloquy between people who would never see one another again. The rich, smoky odor of grilling steaks rose up from the exhaust fan of the Palme d'Or's kitchen, reminding me of the fire. The smell set my mind at ease. No more Hypnotist, no more Norma Jean.

We stared up into the sky, as if we could pierce the haze, as if we were far outside LA, or any city.

"You know," Sunrize said, "I've often thought that night is the time for listening. You can find out all sorts of interesting things if your ears are open."

"Hey, are you talking about me and Rex?"

She laughed. "Not what first came to mind, but now that you mention it . . ." She laughed again. "No, I was thinking about my parents. About their fights. Real knock-down drag-outs."

"What were they fighting about?" I asked, thinking of the early-morning screaming matches between the Hypnotist and Norma Jean.

"My father's heavy gambling addiction. He almost bankrupted us, numerous times. He also liked to sleep around."

You could say that again. The Hypnotist with his exploitative stage shows and his little black chicken heart, Norma Jean with her fiery come-to-Jesus sermons and her little black hypocritical heart. What a pair. A profligate embezzler and his silver-tongued devil woman.

"You might think I'm sad not to see my parents again," Sunrize was saying, "but I'm not. I'm sure the sight of either of them would make me hurl."

Birds of a feather, I thought. *That's what we are.* Without being conscious of it, I took her hand in mine, and this time she didn't rebuff me. I felt her returning squeeze. Then, as if they knew we had communicated all that was needed, our hands simply unclasped. Maybe that was as much contact as she could tolerate. For a long time after that we lay there without speaking. Below us, the party died its inevitable slow death, as people departed in twos and threes, all talked out, or finally too drunk to find any words at all.

Befitting the deserted early hours, the music mellowed out to jazz that seemed to me peculiarly LA: Miles Davis's *Sketches of Spain.* His lonely horn sounding like a mournful train moving across a darkened landscape.

"Are they why you came here?" I asked.

"I dunno, really. Sometimes I think I wound up in LA like a piece of flotsam at the edge of the Pacific."

"But surely you don't want to stay here."

"Don't you?"

"Well, I thought so. In fact, I was sure of it, until about a week ago, when reality started to leak into my fantasy world."

Sunrize gave a sardonic chuckle. "Isn't that the way it always is." It wasn't a question.

"Yeah, but I don't know why it has to be like that. Me, I'd like to find a way to change that."

We heard a soft clatter to our left, and we both rose onto our elbows. Rex was making his way out onto the rooftop.

"I thought I'd find you kids here." He waved as he came toward us, and I guess we both realized at the same time that he was very drunk or very stoned, most likely very both. "I looked all over. No one was around." He frowned. "That Gemini girl?"

"Gone," I said.

"Gone?" Like he couldn't believe it, even though she'd been gone for days. "Huh."

I think it was at that point that he was close enough for us to see that he wasn't alone. Something was draped around his neck.

Beside me, Sunrize jerked as if poked with an electric prod. "What the hell is that?"

"It's a present." Rex was grinning. "From an admirer with a particularly large sweet tooth." He winked. We knew what he meant: a patron of his dark art.

"Yeah, but what is it?" It was draped across his shoulders, patterned black and tan, triangular head.

"A ball python!" he crowed, flung his arms wide, and almost stumbled. "How about that?"

Sunrize had already recoiled in horror, and I remembered that her beloved pet hamster had met his demise in the venomous jaws of a cottonmouth. By this time, Rex had plopped himself down next to me. Luckily, I was between him and Sunrize. I could feel her tension, the shallowness of her breathing.

Rex leaned in, his eyes glittering. He held the snake's head in one open palm, offering it as if it were a twist of coke. "How about we all—"

"I'm getting the fuck out of here," Sunrize said, jumping up.

"Uh." Rex wagged a finger at her. "You'll have to get past Ruby—that's her name, Ruby, on account of her—hey, look! There's that tongue! Look at it vibrate. She's scenting you two, I bet." He sniggered. "I wonder whether she'll like you." He finally noticed that Sunrize was twitching. "Yeah, hey, listen, Sunrize, she won't like you at all if you keep doing that."

"I already don't like her," Sunrize ventured. She looked ready to take flight at any moment.

Rex's eyes narrowed. "Oh, come on. Ruby's not poisonous. She's a constrictor, and a small one at that. There's no way she could hurt you." He stroked the top of the snake's head. "And anyway, she's a cutie." He puffed out his lips. "Aren't you, darlin'."

"Ugh."

Given Rex's extreme state of intoxication, Sunrize shouldn't've said anything, but I understood why she couldn't help herself. Me, I had no trouble with snakes at all. They were all over the farmland when Tara was growing up. But for Sunrize it was a different matter. Even if the incident with her hamster hadn't happened, she'd likely still have been deathly afraid of snakes. Most people were.

Anyway, Rex was getting pissed off. He wanted what he wanted, and he wanted it right now.

"Here's what I think," he said, an idiotic grin distorting his innate beauty. "I think we should have a foursome."

"Foursome!" Sunrize cried. "What foursome?" Her eyes were so wide open I could see the whites all around.

That idiotic grin was plastered to his face. "You, Bop, me, and Ruby."

Sunrize was aghast. "Are you nuts?"

Again, it would have been better if she'd kept her mouth shut. Her obviously terrified reaction to the snake was just goading Rex on.

"Yes, the four of us." Rex wobbled to his feet. "Right here. Up on the rooftop of the Palme d'Or. What better place to fuck our brains out, right, Bop?" But he wasn't looking for my endorsement; he'd already made up his mind.

He lunged across me toward bug-eyed Sunrize. His lead foot caught under my outstretched leg, and he toppled. The snake shot out of his hand, toward Sunrize. She screamed; the python recoiled into Rex's face. I reached up to steady him but knocked into his elbow.

Off balance, his snagged leg twisted under the weight of his body. I heard a distinct snap, like a dead branch cracking in two. Rex screamed in pain and went over on his right side so hard he bounced down the canted rooftop. I scrambled after him, reached out, but the damn snake coiled itself around my wrist, and I missed him.

For an instant the python and I stared at each other, its bulging yellow eye with its vertical pupil holding my image steadfastly in its gaze. Then it slithered off my wrist, and Ruby and Rex tumbled over the eave, plunging down together.

Cloud 9

By the time the cops were summoned, along with the ME, Sunrize and I were both gone. Rex had been impaled on a tiki torch, we read days later. The weight of his body had stripped away the bamboo cladding, revealing the stainless steel core. There was an inordinate delay in getting to the body, as Ruby the python had wrapped itself around Rex's neck. Special snake wranglers had to be summoned to deal with it before either the detectives or the ME would venture near the crime scene. The one quote from the lead detective was, "These crazy Hollywood types. What the [expletive deleted] was he doing with a [expletive deleted] snake?" Toxicology revealed just how much shit was in Rex's system at the time of the fall, which, a week later, was ruled death by misadventure. And that was the end of it. You can bet the management and ownership of the Palme d'Or sighed in relief.

———

Sunrize and I spent about a month together in Santa Monica at a little place I rented by the week. We lived among the piers and the sand, the endless waves and endless sky, the surfer dudes and their golden girls, the Rollerblading bitches and their boy toys.

It took only a day there for me to realize that my weeks with Rex had been a dream, a fantasy, an alternate reality that he had woven around me, and that I was awake now. Like all good con men, Rex had read me like a book, seen how much I wanted that dream, and given it to me. And I had been a willing participant. I paid a heavy price, though. His price.

Most of my time during that month was spent trying to get Sunrize straight, and to give her her due, she did her best, and there were stretches of time I was optimistic she'd make it. But one night she didn't come home. In the morning I found her underneath a pier, a needle stuck in her arm. Death by hotshot.

I cried for the better part of the week. Then I got out of LA for good.

The truth was, I wasn't made to be on my own.

The truth was, I missed my sister. I missed Tara.

PART 4
DISINTEGRATION

I was slowly losing hold of my original and better self.

—Robert Louis Stevenson,
The Strange Case of Dr. Jekyll and Mr. Hyde

23

New York City—Present Day

Four eight-by-ten black-and-white photos. Apart from being slightly grainy blowups, the subjects are clear enough.

Surveillance photos, Sophie says. *At Rex's party. That's us and Rex,* Sophie says of the first one. And of the second: *That's Dave, Dan, and Captain Ruiz from the Mexican Federal Ministerial Police.* The photo clearly shows the three Mexicans carrying briefcases. The third: *That's us with Captain Ruiz and the others.* And the fourth: *All of us together—us, Rex, and the Mexican cops.*

They both become aware of Brandon's scrutiny at the same time. Sophie makes sure to give him no clue to the churning inside.

"Coffee," Sophie says, because Tara is stricken. "Strong and black. Two—no, three sugars."

Brandon gives her a look, reacting to her assertive tone. Then he shrugs. "Sure, why not? Give you time to digest your situation." He shoots her a sardonic look before turning on his heel and departing.

As he strides to the kiosk on the other side of the rooftop terrace, Tara thinks she's never encountered anyone who can blow so hot and cold. One minute he's the solicitous gentleman, the next a hard-eyed operator. So which is he, which is the skin and which the bones, which the facade and which the real Brandon Fiske? It takes her several moments to work out the exquisite irony of encountering him—a male counterpart of the strange and discomforting duality of her own self.

Tara is as thunderstruck by the story Sophie has told her as by the damning photos she holds in her trembling hand. She watches Brandon's back as he stands in line for her coffee. Disbelief commingled with real terror. The vague but constant fear she has lived with since waking up in Tucumcari, the dread that drove her into therapy, now has form, shape, and meaning. Its name is Sophie. She feels like the hemispheres of her brain have split apart, two separate entities vying for control of her central nervous system.

Listen to me, Kitten, Sophie says, interrupting Tara's sudden insight. Don't call me Kitten, bitch, she says. Look. She waves the photos. Look what you've done to us. *Stop for a second and listen, would you?*

But Tara isn't in a listening frame of mind. Twenty months ago I woke up in a fly-bitten motel by the interstate in the middle of fucking nowhere, she says, no idea where I was, what had happened, lying in a bed stinking of someone else's sweat, alcohol, and sex. I was terrified, overwhelmed by an existential dread. In my left hand—she raises her fist—a damp twist of paper containing the dregs of a white powder I could only imagine was cocaine, considering the ravaged state of my body—so thin I could see my ribs when I looked down. On the night table, a pair of bottles of mezcal, both empty. Try, if you can, to imagine my state of mind. When I stood up, my hands trembled, and my legs felt like lead weights. Imagine what went through my mind. What the hell happened to me? And then, like being T-boned by a truck, it hit me: you happened to me, Sophie. You. I stepped into the bathroom, staggered when I saw my face in the mirror. It wasn't my face staring by at me, horrified. It wasn't your face either.

This is what you did to me, Sophie. You unmoored me, made me doubt myself—the past, the present, the future. Everything.

The truth is, Sophie's voice soft in her mind, *I did it to both of us.* Don't give me—

Okay, okay, you've had your say. Now you'll listen to what I need to tell you. In the aftermath of LA, I came to understand for the first time what the Hypnotist did to you, not just to me. I saw it through the bitter lens of my own tragic folly.

Tara, the time for our separation, our war, has passed. We're one creature now. No! Tara cries. It can't be! *But it is.* Damn you. I won't let it. I *can't* let it. Sophie doesn't understand. Tara is too far out of her depth. She has been ever since she woke up in Tucumcari. More perhaps even than Sophie, what saved Tara all those years is this thing of her own that she has learned to wield—control. She can't let that control go. She can't. Because if she does, she'll drown.

How, Tara says, can you stay so calm? This is a catastrophe! *No, you're wrong. I've had time to consider,* Sophie replies. *What happened in LA opened my eyes. It forced me to look, really look, at not just my actions and their consequences but also at the terror in your childhood you still can't face.* That's because Father made sure I wouldn't have to face it. *And that was a mistake, Kitten. The knowledge he sought to lock away has been leaking out slowly, drop by drop, despite the Hypnotist's best efforts. It's become toxic, Kitten. In the end, he failed. He failed you, and he failed me. It was the terror he couldn't control, let alone stop, that caused him to fail. It was too much, too powerful even for him.*

He protected me. *He* thought *he was protecting you. But really*— You're . . . damnit, Soph, this is too much to take in . . . I don't . . . I can't handle it. *You have to, Kitten. Time we went back in.*

We? Tara does all but scream it. She takes her hands away from her face and looks around as if she can see Sophie. She laughs out loud, then, but it's a kind of maniacal laugh that makes her stomach heave. *Easy, Kitten, don't let this get away from you.* Too late! Too late! Six months out of my life, and I don't remember a thing you did. You took over my life. Completely. And look what happened, look what you did! I can't . . . I can't allow that to happen again. *It won't.* How can you say that? It's only days ago that you took over in Forest. *Only because you couldn't. Because of what the Hypnotist did to you. He had no idea of the far-reaching effects—*

You *became* me, Soph. I was helpless. I fell away into a black pit. It was so terrifying.

Well, Kitten, now you know how I felt every time you left me. The little death is misnamed.

Tara's next automatic response, rejecting everything Sophie is telling her, makes it only as far as her throat. It dies there.

I never wanted to take over your life, as you put it. I only did what I was created to do.

But now something has changed.

Yes.

What?

We're one person. I'm no longer a shell, a ghost who comes and goes at your whim. I'm my own person.

No, no, no, no, no! I have my rules, the guidelines that keep me safe, she says. All the things I've learned to deal with. They're the only signposts I have. And now you want to take them away from me.

You didn't allow me to finish. My own person is just another way of saying I'm the other part of you, the one the Hypnotist pared away. The one he kept from you, the one he was so fucking sure would kill you.

I've made a life for myself without you.

And what a life it is!

And yours? All I see is a bitch in permanent heat. An animal.

We're all animals, Tara. That's something you can't or won't grasp. You lack empathy for adults; you don't experience joy. You couldn't handle the physical side of your relationship with Figgy. You like him—I know you do. And yet . . . you're awake at night, restless and tortured. You lie to everyone, even your therapist. You know what you've done. You've learned well. You've weaponized lying, just like the Hypnotist did. That's a poor imitation of life.

Tara feels feverish, dizzy, as if she is coming down with a dread tropical disease, as if she has a tapeworm crawling through her guts. At least I save people whose lives are at risk, she says cruelly, desperate to strike back. You couldn't even save Sunrize.

The moment the words are out, she knows she has crossed a line. But considering how invaded she feels, she isn't sorry. If she doesn't stand up to Sophie, if she doesn't fight her with every fiber of her being, she knows she is finished.

I could say that you couldn't save poor Angelo, but where would that get us?

Tara stands up, shaky, near defeat.

I'm not your enemy.

Her heart is hard but also, she knows, brittle as crystal. And here comes Brandon, carrying her steaming coffee.

24

"Who took these?" Tara asks, struggling to regain a semblance of her equilibrium. Solid ground still seems like a mirage.

"You don't appear taken aback," Brandon says, baring his teeth.

"Answer my question," she snaps.

Brandon consults a single sheet of typescript. "You would know her as Carmen Gemini."

The surfer girl, Sophie says. *She was a DEA plant.*

"Her real name doesn't matter." Sighing, Brandon gathers up the photos, slides them back in the folder, and closes it. "What matters is what these photos show."

"They don't show anything," Sophie says. It's time she took over; Tara is having difficulty processing the sickening turn of events.

"That's the tip of the iceberg, I'm afraid." Brandon sets the folder aside. "Your former friend Rex Stroud. His real name is Stern. Wayne Stern."

Her eyes narrow. "Who are you, really?"

"I am who I said I am. But—"

"It's the 'but' that has to come out of hiding."

"I'm what is known in fed speak as an FFA—a free-floating asset. What that means in common language is that, in addition to my work here, I'm a stringer for whichever federal agency is in need of my talents."

"Which are."

"I have advanced degrees in forensic accounting and criminal psychology." He says this as a simple statement of fact, without an ounce of pride or condescension. "I can smell out corporate malfeasance, insider trading, traders hiding their massive mistakes from their firms. That kind of thing. But occasionally, the financial area that's my expertise gets tangled up in the drug scene. This is one such instance."

Dear God, Soph, Tara blurts.

"Listen," Sophie says, "I'm telling you and whoever might be listening in—"

"Who could be listening up here?" Brandon says quietly. "Besides, this isn't a TV show."

She waves away his words as if they are smoke concealing his image. "I spent some time with Rex. It wasn't until late in the relationship that I had any idea he was using and dealing, and then only from another one of his girls. I met the Mexican cops just the once at the party shown in those photos. Apart from Captain Ruiz, I knew the other two as Dave and Dan, and I only found out about Ruiz's real name after the fact. He was introduced to me as Dick. That's it. That's the extent of my knowledge."

Brandon regards her levelly, as if he's a human lie detector. "So you didn't see Marwyn in LA. You never met him."

For a moment, she is bewildered. "Marwyn?" This is one of those times when a spoken English word has no meaning.

"Marwyn Rusk," Brandon says softly.

"I ran into Marwyn Rusk at Stephen Ripley's party," she says shortly. "It was a singularly unpleasant meet."

"In the bathroom, I believe."

Now, at last, she sees where this is going. She senses the accusatory spin he's put on that sentence. Drugs. Of course it's drugs. She'd asked Figgy whether he was supplying Ripley with drugs for his party. But it was right there under her nose, why everyone fawned over Marwyn. He's the supplier. How stupid she has been. How blind.

"Who the hell are you, really?"

"I told you."

"But clearly not everything."

"Tara, listen to me: I'm in a unique position."

"No, you're just another asshole trying to take advantage of a woman."

"That's isn't fair, Tara."

Her eyes blaze. "Fair? You want to talk to me about fair? The prick tried to rape me, Brandon. That was the first and last time we ever met. And let me tell you if I never see him again, it will be too soon."

He rakes a hand through his hair, as if he is distraught. But that can't possibly be the case, can it?

"I'm afraid," he says softly, "under the present circumstances never seeing Marwyn Rusk again isn't an option for you."

"Fuck you!" Sophie spits, in full-metal-bitch mode.

She runs from him, across the terrace. Spangly lights are on, like Christmas tree ornaments, and the coffee kiosk is morphing into a bar. Taylor Swift is singing on a Spotify playlist. He catches up with her at the door to the elevator, whirls her around.

"Hold on a minute."

"Get. Your. Hand. Off. Me." Each word is like an ice pick.

His grip loosens, and his hand drops away from her elbow. "Okay, but let's—"

The elevator door slides open, and she steps in. She presses the button for the lobby, then jabs the door close button.

Brandon shoulders through just in time.

"We need to talk about this sensibly."

"This? *This?*" She stares at a space above his head. "What the hell is *this*? Marwyn Rusk? Good luck with that."

"Let me explain."

"Are you for real?" Color rises into her cheeks. "You offered me a job—a good job, maybe a great one. But does it exist? No. There's only secrets and lies and threats." There is fire in her veins, venom in her words. "You shit, you did nothing but lie to me."

Brandon shakes his head. "Tara, that's not entirely true, but in any event I'm truly sorry for deceiving you. But it was necessary."

"Why?" She glares at him. "Why was it necessary?"

"Okay. This approach was my idea. I argued for it with the DEA team—I deemed it necessary to keep you safe."

"I didn't *do* anything."

"They don't know that," Brandon says. His phone buzzes, and, holding up a finger, he takes the call, listens, says almost nothing in return, breaks the connection. "And chances are they won't believe you," he continues as if they haven't been interrupted. "Once you're in the system, that's it. Besides, who else do they have? Rex is dead, and to date they haven't been able to touch Marwyn. And the Mexican police . . ."

She rounds on him. "Do you?"

"Do I what?"

"Believe me." Tears shimmer in her eyes, unstoppable, spilling over now, like raindrops running down her cheeks. Her voice trembles as it grows heated. "Do you think I'm involved in Rex's drug trafficking? You want to search my place? Go ahead. I give you permission. I've got a large family of roaches and a rodent as big as the Mouse King in *The Nutcracker*. That and some books are about it."

"Already been done."

"Huh?" Her eyes open wide as she wipes them with the back of her hand. Then it clicks in. "I see. While I'm here with you," she says bitterly. "That was the call you just got. You sonuvabitch."

Brandon raises his hands, palms outward. "Hold on. There was nothing I could do about the DEA search. They found exactly what you told me they'd find." He tries on a smile, clearly aware of her anger.

"But I do believe you, for what it's worth. And, for the record, my offer of a job was—is—legit."

"Shove it, Mister."

The doors open, and she heads across the lobby.

"I told you I'd love you on my team," Brandon says, catching up with her long strides, "and I mean it."

"I don't care." She thinks of what M said. "I love where I am."

"I'll give you three times what you're making."

She laughs at him. "Everyone can be bought. Is that your philosophy?"

"It's been my experience."

They stop in front of the glass doors, step aside for people passing in and out, then move to a corner where they have privacy.

"Five times. Or write your own ticket."

"Poor you," Sophie says. Her voice as outraged as ever. "I'm doing good work—important work—at Seventh Haven. I'm helping to save lives." Her eyes are filled with rage. "And now you want to what, Brandon?"

"Circumstance put you in this position, Tara. You're the only one who can get to Marwyn Rusk. You're our last chance."

When Sophie makes no protest, Tara is abruptly alarmed. *Sophie, what are you doing?*

I got us into this; I'll get us out.

Not this way. Not—

I'm afraid we have no choice, Kitten.

25

W hat I'm about to offer is a chance to do more important work," Brandon says. "To continue to save lives."

She shoots him a skeptical look. "And put mine in jeopardy in the process."

"I don't want anything bad to happen to you—you have to know that."

She shakes her head. "That's a devil's bargain I'm not prepared to make."

They are back in his office, Brandon behind his desk, fingers steepled. Outside, lights glitter through Manhattan's plum-colored twilight. A helicopter buzzes over the tip of the island, rising like a huge insect from the city.

He sighs. "I was so hoping you wouldn't say that."

"But I did, and I mean it." She crosses her arms over her chest, stands in the slightly spread-legged stance of someone holding a pistol.

He gestures. "Please sit, Tara."

She doesn't move a muscle.

"Look." He spreads his hands on the desktop. "I like you, Tara. Just as importantly, I admire you."

"Hollow as you."

"It's true, up until now, I've given you no reason to believe me." He gestures. "Nevertheless, it's the truth."

When she makes no response, he swivels his chair, grabs a bottle of bourbon and two shot glasses, fills them. He pushes one across the desk, but she makes no move to pick it up.

"Suit yourself."

"I always do."

That brings a wry smile out of hiding—another mercurial change. He downs his bourbon in one practiced swig. "You made a mistake."

Something clenches deep inside her. "What mistake?"

"They tracked you here, but you were clever enough to lose them." His tongue clicks against his teeth. "Until at Seventh Haven you gave your name to M as Tara Gemini."

Lord Jesus! Carmen Gemini. Sophie loved that name. Somehow that love crossed to Tara's unconscious. She had used it without the knowledge of who Carmen Gemini was, or that Gemini would mean anything to anyone else.

"The Seventh Haven database is centralized. The name caused a red flag. From that time on, they put someone on to shadow you."

The lurker outside her building, the one she scared away with the split baseball bat. Anger and guilt fuse inside her like a gun being loaded. She squares her shoulders. "And now?"

He is staring at her, his eyes wide. "I don't believe how different you are from the young woman I met at Stephen Ripley's party, the same woman who walked through my office door this morning." He shakes his head. "Since you had that . . . episode . . . it's like I don't know you."

"Nobody knows anyone," she says and smiles sweetly, but she feels as if she is coming apart, seams splitting, stuffing spilling out like brains and guts. Who is she? Tara? Sophie? Something in between, someone unknown to both of them?

His eyes narrow. "That's true enough, I suppose." He clears his throat. "Now we have come to the nub of the matter." He pours himself another shot. "An elite unit of the DEA has been after a certain Mexican drug cartel. Your LA lover, Rex—Wayne Stern—was one of two of the cartel's distributors here in the States."

"Let me guess," Sophie says, fully in charge now that Tara is curled, cringing in a corner of their mind. "Rex was West Coast, and Marwyn is East Coast."

Brandon downs his shot, gestures with his empty glass. "You should have a shot. It's really quite excellent single barrel."

Tara rouses herself briefly. *Sophie, you fool!* "For how long?" Her mouth feels full of cotton.

"Five years, more or less. He was much too smart for them. Him and Captain Ruiz, and especially Marwyn Rusk. Now Rex has gone to meet his maker, and Captain Ruiz's decapitated head was found rolling in the surf at Cancún. A honeymoon couple in a fifteen-hundred-dollar-a-night suite found it. Can you imagine? So much for honeymoons in Mexico, right? Anyway, even with them gone, the coke keeps flowing without even the flicker of a misstep."

"So it's down to Marwyn."

Brandon nods. "The DEA unit's last gambit was recruiting your friend Figgy, with the goal of embedding him in Marwyn's inner circle. To date, that hasn't worked so well."

She feels short of breath. "What do they have on Figgy?" She can hardly get the words out. *What is Figgy to us? Sophie says. Just another fuck, right?* But they both know that isn't the case. She felt something for Figgy from the moment he sat down beside her. *But what do your feelings have to do with me? Sophie says. I was created to blunt feelings, to deflect them, to push them down into the darkness where they can't harm you. Or you, Sophie. But you had feelings for Sunrize. You admitted it to me. Yes, I did. Everything has changed. How can that be?*

"Nothing. Figgy's clean as a cat's whiskers." Brandon's words bring her out of herself. Once she draws breath, she realizes she's been holding on to it for a frighteningly long time. "But they did approach him. Asked for a favor. A patriotic act." His features relax, giving her a glimpse of the man he once might have been. "Figgy's a good guy, Tara. Like me, he's just trying to do the right thing."

She feels dizzy, disoriented. Sophie or Tara? At this moment, neither of them knows. They are both like the swimmer in Lind's office. She is keeping her head above water, but she is out of sight of any land. Only sea and sky between her and slowly approaching death.

"But he led them to me," she says thickly. "Or maybe it was M."

"It was neither, Tara." He seems truly compassionate now, as if he wants only the best for her. "Through me, they sent Figgy to find you."

"To become my friend."

"You'll have to ask Figgy that directly. What happened between the two of you—"

"So Figgy meeting me wasn't a meet-cute random incident."

"I'm afraid not."

She flushes all the way from crown to throat. *Why should you care?* "Shut up."

Brandon starts. "What?"

"Nothing." She lowers her head. Did she actually speak to Sophie out loud? She must really be losing her mind.

Brandon takes a third shot, sets the glass down but doesn't let go of it. His eyes grip hers.

Her gaze flickers for an instant, just before she reaches for the bourbon he poured for her. It goes down like liquid fire, tinged with hickory and sugar. "I would've bet on Ripley," she says as she sets the glass back down.

He looses a conspiratorial chuckle. The tension between them that has been stretched to the breaking point seems to have dissolved like tears in the rain. "Yeah, well, that would've been too easy, right?" He looks down at the empty glass in his hand, circles the rim with one finger until it begins to hum lightly. Then he stops, raises his head. "With your help, Tara, they can get the proof they need. And, listen, you can get your revenge for what Marwyn did to you. You do want to get revenge, don't you? You don't want him to get away with what he's done to you and to other women."

She lifts her head as well. He is looking at her steadily. "Revenge."

I don't want revenge, Tara says. *Maybe not,* Sophie replies, *but it's what you need.*

Brandon's expression changes once again, revealing a struggle of several emotions, and for that she forgives him many things. Not that she would tell him that.

"The team was at a standstill. Figgy was getting nowhere. Then he brought you to Stephen Ripley's party."

"To meet you."

He nods. "But listen, I had no idea what to expect from you. Even they didn't have a dossier on you. They had no idea how to approach you."

"So you agreed to do it."

"Because Figgy refused. I told you he was a good guy. There are lines he won't cross. As for me, I've already crossed those lines long ago. I had no choice in the matter. But it turned out lucky for me. Everything I said to you at the party—and afterward—I meant. The moment we began talking, I knew I couldn't bullshit you. I knew no one can."

"Figgy—"

"If Figgy is bullshitting you, then he's bullshitted everyone he's come in contact with, including me." He smiles. "How likely does that seem?"

She takes a seat, but her stomach refuses to unclench. "The other shoe is about to drop."

"Well, here's where you can do the important work, Tara. The unit wants you to meet Marwyn again—"

"Are you for real? Hell, no."

"By accident." He contrives to ignore her outburst. "They'll set it up, no problem. A restaurant or a nightclub. They know his movements."

She closes her eyes. I won't do it, Soph. *Well, but you must, Kitten. And don't you worry—I'll have your back.* Like you did in LA. *That was a mistake. I confess, Padre.*

Standing over her, he says, "Are you okay?"

Sophie looks up, smiling so her teeth show. "Never better."

There is a certain sadness in Brandon's eyes now that he's broken through the iceberg, a shadow that has come sweeping in from somewhere deep inside him, and she remembers him saying that he genuinely liked her.

"It's already been established," he says, "that Marwyn has a thing for you."

She barks a laugh. "Marwyn has a thing for anyone with tits and a pussy."

Brandon laughs with her, a comradely gesture, surely. "True enough. But he's talked about you. More than once."

"They have him on a wire?"

"Listen to you, the law enforcement expert." He is only half joking. "They don't have enough on him for a court order. No, he's spoken to Figgy about you."

"Jesus." Tara's world topples over onto its side.

"He's asked Figgy to find you."

"Does he know . . . ?"

"About you and Figgy? God, no." He rushes on, wanting to get all the bad news out at once. "So you meet up with Marwyn, you take him to bed, you do what . . ." He can't find it in himself to finish that sentence, so he starts over: "You find out everything you can. If you have to stay with him, become his mistress—"

"He already has a mistress. He brought her to the party."

"Yeah. No. He shitcanned her the moment you left."

I can't do this, Tara says. Please. Soph. I'm begging you. I'll die if he puts his hands on me again.

Hush, Kitten. Let me hold you like I've always done. I'll hold you, and you won't feel a thing.

But this isn't like before. I'll know.

You've got to face your fear, Kitten. And, trust me, you'll get your revenge. I swear on Hickory's grave.

It's then that Tara is certain Sophie means what she says. Hickory was the one creature they both loved. But still, the price she'll have to pay is so monstrously high she isn't sure she'll survive. She'll have to rely on Sophie to protect her, as she's done so many times during their childhood. She thinks about Sophie's time in LA and she shudders. How can she trust someone who has done . . . ? *Because I'm part of you,* Sophie whispers. *Because I am you.*

She rests her forearms on her knees, head hanging down, trying to regain her composure. The two of them are like oil and water, or, in this case, superego and id. Except that Sophie is right: for both of them, being alone is now an illusion. The trauma caused by the assault on Tara has triggered the singularity: two personalities inhabiting one mind. Since then, she has found herself sleepwalking, inhabiting a world more dream than real. From both hemispheres of her brain, the creative and the intellectual, she finds herself drawn to a certain truth that strikes her as discordant and, at times, repugnant. The truth is this: she is doomed to an unspeakable reality. No longer whole, she is broken, two separate sides at war with one another. Who is "she"?

How much time passes, she cannot say, but at length she sits up straight, realizes she is breathing more or less normally.

Brandon leans toward her. "I'm not the monster you must think I am." He clasps his hands together. "I know this can't be easy for you. But it's not as if you haven't had practice in this sort of thing."

Blood rushes to her cheeks, and she feels an unpleasant heat race through her. "Excuse me?"

Brandon lifts a finger. "Look at it this way: your time with Rex was a dress rehearsal." He speaks in a gentle, almost intimate manner—advice given from one friend to another. "This, going forward, is the real thing."

26

Lights burn the darkness around Christie's brownstone. And next door, a fancy fixture illuminates the front door. The downstairs windows are lit. Figgy is home.

Sophie could have texted him. That would have been the polite thing to do. But Sophie is so far from polite she can't even make it out in broad daylight. Besides, she is curious to see the look on his face when she shows up unannounced. It is a kind of psychological experiment Sophie and Tara have both decided on.

He opens the door after an unconscionably long time, and she imagines he is spending it trying on different expressions with which to face her. When she sees him, it is not what she expected: the entrance is unlit; his face is in shadow. She cannot tell what he is feeling or thinking. She says nothing. Having missed her visual opportunity, she wants to hear his first words, listen for intonations, for clues to his state of mind.

"Ah, the will-o'-the-wisp returns," he says. There is nothing in his voice she can use.

On the threshold, she begins working out a plan B on the fly.

"I wonder," she says.

"And what could that be?"

"I wonder whether you really want to see me?"

"Only one way to find out." He steps back. The light from the entry washes his face. He has dark crescents under his eyes; his face is rumpled, as if he hasn't slept since the last time she saw him. She remembers what Brandon told her about Figgy being embedded in Marwyn's business. On the other hand, he appears pleased to see her. He wears a blue denim shirt with the sleeves rolled up, baring his forearms; lightweight jeans; and his well-worn huaraches on his feet. She can imagine him walking on the beach in Santa Monica. He holds out his hand. "What? Are you waiting for me to carry you over the threshold?"

Sophie laughs then. She can feel the warmth spreading through her—Tara's warmth—so strong it staggers her. She comes toward him, and he is laughing, too, his teeth very white and even in his dusky face.

"It's good to see you," he says when they settle on his living room sofa with ice-cold Cokes in front of them. The soda has quickly become a kind of in-joke with them.

Tara loves that he hasn't asked where she's been or why she hasn't called. Sophie feels nothing at all except a building tumescence in her loins. She can feel Tara fighting against that, but she's the stronger one now, and she pushes Tara's weakness down, stamping on it with a vigor she thoroughly enjoys.

She takes up her Coke; they click rims and drink, after which, without preliminaries or fanfare, she jumps him. The Coke spills everywhere. She pulls at the buttons of his shirt; one flies off. With his hands on her, she pulls off his shirt, unbuckles his belt, and undoes his jeans. It goes very fast after that. Their sex is aggressive, but certainly Sophie is the more aggressive, handling him, biting him, pushing them both and then, abruptly, holding them in check. She knows he likes that, though, like most men, would never talk about it, never even allow those desires into his consciousness. Men are funny that way. Their relationship to sex is bound up with needs having to do with power. On the one extreme is rape, which has nothing at all to do with sex but rather with rage, domination, revenge. On the other end of the

UNTIL WE ARE LOST

spectrum are the men who need to cede all control, which has led to the rise of dominatrices. Being constantly dominating in business is an exhausting endeavor; at the end of the day a little subjugation can wash away the exhaustion, feel like a kind of renewal.

Sophie keeps these thoughts flying through her head, mainly to keep Tara down, the lightning-like strings of synaptic connection acting as a neural net, trapping Tara in the brass bottle to which Sophie has consigned her.

During this time, she has allowed just the smallest part of him inside her. It is driving him crazy. He takes her head in his hands, mashes his lips against hers, mouth opening, his tongue twining with hers. But as that doesn't get her to move her hips down, the kiss is short lived. Is there passion in it or only lust? The two are very different, as Sophie has discovered. One contains love, the other only need.

His back hunches as his lips move down to her nipples. To her delight, he has picked up on her erogenous zones quicker than most. Some of the men she has bedded have never even bothered. His tongue flicks out, and she moans. Again and again, and she can no longer hold out, slamming her hips down, embedding him fully. He arches off the cushions, gathers as much of her breast into his mouth as will fit. As he sucks, she comes so hard her entire body quakes, her hips bucking in a staccato rhythm. She wants to watch his face when he comes, but the waves of pleasure are so strong her eyes roll back in her head, her mouth opens, lips curling back in an animal snarl. With that, she at last submits, losing herself. As he comes, another orgasm roils her, stronger this time, longer, a storm tide snatching every last breath away from her.

———

"You're going already?" Figgy sits up, watching Sophie climb into her clothes. Astonishment and disappointment are written across his face.

"I've got an appointment."

"Cancel it."

She buttons her shirt. "I can't."

"We can go out to dinner." He swings his long legs over the side of the sofa. "Or I can make something here." Ignoring the Coke spatter on the coffee table's top and floor, he picks up two buttons that have flown off his shirt. "Something yummy." He watches her as she draws on her pants. "And best of all, no meat within a mile of you."

"Sorry." Even deep down in her prison, Tara loves that he is being so nice, that he clearly wants to prolong their time together. To Sophie, he is being tedious and needy. Not that she cares one way or the other. He has served his purpose.

"Hey, wait." He picks up his jeans. "Stop." Hopping on one leg as he rushes to put them on. "Can't we even talk about this?"

She looks around for her jacket, finds it, and slips it on. "I promised a friend."

"How about I read to you? Kant or Livy." He is joking, of course, trying to evoke a change of mood, an alteration of her trajectory. "Or even better, *The Decline and Fall of the Roman Empire*. That won't take long."

From her submissive position, Tara still manages to kick Sophie hard enough for her to turn to Figgy, smile, and say, "What a wonderful idea. Stick a pin in it."

Then, without another word, she is gone.

———

At the side entrance to the club, M appears in response to Sophie's text, and immediately, amid the junkies, the entwined couples high on E, and a dense sweet smog of pot smoke, embraces her as if she is afraid she'll disappear again. She returns with M to the apartment, exhausted. There is no way she will ever be comfortable in her own rattrap now that the DEA has crawled all over it. She wonders if the roaches will miss her.

The talk with Brandon has unnerved her, despite her bravado with Tara. It has brought back the losses she suffered in LA in a way her confession can't. She sinned, and now she is going to be made to pay for that sin. Sophie is bitter and rageful, taken aback by how deeply she has been scarred by her time in LA. That she allowed Rex to exploit and abuse her is a mystery that feels like an abyss, sucking her down into the raw blackness of childhood. She should have been exhilarated by her energetic bout of sex with Figgy; she thought fucking him would assuage her hurt. Instead, she feels like crying. It's Tara's fault, of course. Tara's persona continues to bleed into hers, and she feels the fractures like blows to her skull. She knows Tara is grateful for her friendship with M, but the meeting with Brandon has also triggered Sophie's latent paranoia. Why has M befriended Tara so readily? Why has M invited her to live here, rent-free, no less. And she recalls M threading her arm through Tara's, pulling her close after the concert the other night. What was that all about? Now, having found no solace in Figgy's body, she feels herself edging further toward that abyss of fear, fury, and humiliation.

It is just past three in the morning; the lamplight throws warm ovals across the apartment floor and walls. *I'm sure Tara would say this place feels like a home,* Sophie thinks bitterly. M goes to make tea for them, while Sophie, depressed and unaccountably debilitated, lies on the sofa, staring at Queen Elizabeth and her crimson Ziggy lightning bolt, feeling decidedly ill. But by the time M returns with the steaming mugs, she is fast asleep. After setting down the tea, M takes off Sophie's ankle boots, opens up a caramel and pale-pink cashmere throw, and covers her friend.

The earthy, hot-metal aroma of the oolong tea wafts to her like a message from the past. M always makes oolong tea; it was her brother's favorite. Javier was six years older than her. As a kid, he wanted to be a soldier. He was single minded about it, and when he turned eighteen, he became one. He'd survived two tours in Afghanistan, only to be shot to death standing on a street corner in the summer sun a block from the family apartment in the Corona section of Queens. Gunned down by a member of the so-called Red Pill movement who'd left a hate-filled white supremacist manifesto on 8chan, the internet message board.

M takes up one of the mugs and settles into a chair across from the sofa. Immediately, Abraxas leaps up, curls in her lap, and begins to purr. While M carefully sips her tea, she absently scratches Abraxas behind her ears. She thinks of Javier, the waste of his life, the dregs of her father's life, who spent forty years hauling trash for the city and got emphysema for his efforts. She's never been close with her parents, but she misses Javier fiercely, even after eight years. She sometimes dreams of him at night, but when he comes to her, he is blood soaked. As he falls into her arms, he keeps trying to tell her something, but his mouth is full of blood. She tries to cradle him, but he is lighter than air, and he keeps floating away from her. Always, when she wakes from this dream, her cheeks are wet with tears, as if she has been weeping for hours.

Her gaze strays idly around the room, seeing but not seeing the trappings of her life. A painting her talented mother had made just before her death, of the Mexican countryside, dusty and always, to M, spooky. At length she finds herself watching her friend asleep on her sofa, a mystery from the moment she first walked into Seventh Haven.

———

When Sophie wakes, it is late morning. M is already up and bustling around the kitchen. Hearing her friend stirring, M throws a look over her shoulder. "Hungry?"

"Famished."

After returning from the bathroom, showered, in fresh clothes, Sophie stretches. It is Saturday, a swing day at Seventh Haven, which means she can go in or not. M does not have to report to Forest until 7:00 p.m.

"How does french toast sound?" M says.

It sounds just fine, and while M finishes up at the stovetop, Sophie sets the table. Light as white as a winter morning streams in through the calico curtains of the east-facing window, igniting tiny dust motes dancing as if to the sizzle of the frying pan.

One of M's Spotify playlists is running Beyoncé softly in the background. For whatever reason, Sophie is more on edge than she was last night.

M brings full plates to the table, and for some minutes they both eat without talking, just enjoying the hot, tasty food. Sophie pours them orange juice, and M drizzles maple syrup. Sophie prefers the thick raspberry preserves she found in the refrigerator while fetching the carton of juice. She smears it on thickly, trying to count the seeds as Tara did when she was young, and, as Tara did, gives up.

"So, listen," Sophie says, when she's swallowed her last bite of breakfast. "I met with Brandon Fiske today."

"Brandon Fiske?" M's brows knit together. "I didn't think you knew him."

"I can't say I know him," Sophie responds. "I mean, whoever knows anyone?" Did she mean Brandon or M?

Stop this, Tara says. Sophie, stop this right now.

"But anyway," Sophie continues as M clears the dishes, "Figgy introduced me to him, and it seems we got along right away."

"Did you now?" The dishes clatter into the sink as M's back stiffens.

"What?" Sophie is all wide eyed and innocent looking. "Don't you like him?"

"I've hardly met him, but I'm wondering what you—"

"He offered me a job."

"Really?" M glares, hands on hips. This is a side of her Tara has never seen, and she quails inside.

"Really." Sophie stands up, the table between them. "It's a once-in-a-lifetime opportunity, and I'm going to take it."

"What about your work at Seventh Haven?" M looks stricken. "You're leaving just like that?" Her face darkens. "What kind of person does that?" Leaning forward, she presses her fists against the tabletop so hard her knuckles turn white. Sophie can see the corded muscles in her arms pop out.

She seems like two people, doesn't she? Sophie observes. *The one you see on the surface, the one that's your friend. And now here's this other M, the one who's hidden, the M you don't know. Doesn't that worry you, Kitten?*

"And how in the world would I know Mr. Fiske, anyway?"

"Well, he helps fund Seventh Haven."

M makes a derisive gesture. "He's above my pay grade. Way, way above." Shooting Tara a penetrating look, she says, "But apparently not above yours. Is that what you were doing yesterday?"

"I told you I met with him."

"Did you *fuck* him?"

"What? How could you?"

M steps around the table to confront her. "I smelled it on you, last night when you met me outside Forest. I smell it often enough at the club—man-woman sex." M's face is rageful. "Now I'm *asking* you. Did you fuck Fiske?"

"No, I didn't. I—"

"Liar." They are practically nose to nose now. "I thought we were a team," M says.

The word *team* seems to be a trigger for Sophie.

"A team, right." She tosses her head. "You wanted me here . . . you're lonely." A cutting edge to her voice.

M pauses a beat as if wondering whether she has just been insulted. "You're right. I *am* lonely. I was lonely even when Stevie was here— *especially* when Stevie was here, come to think of it. But that's not why I invited you. You know it isn't.

"It seems to me that hole-in-the-wall you choose to live in is a kind of self-punishment, and I wanted to help pull you out of it if I could."

She shakes her head. "And now . . . now it worries me that you've stopped seeing your therapist. It seems to me that she was doing you a world of good."

A kind of righteous fury, born of terror, wells up in Sophie. "What gives you the right to psychoanalyze me? You don't know me, and even if you did, you've crossed a line." Even in her confusion, Tara can tell M is upset. "Is that all you have to say? No apology?"

M snorts derisively. "I'm not the one who needs to apologize."

Tara is scared now—truly scared. But Sophie has gained control of her. Sophie doesn't care. And now there is no place inside Tara that feels safe, or even calm.

Sophie is running flat out.

27

Outside, in the world that was once real, it is raining, a slow, incessant drizzle, settling on her shoulders and hair. More like a Seattle morning than one in New York. There is almost no wind. The sky is low, the clouds inert, as despairing as she feels. The people she passes—an old man, shoulders hunched as if from the burden of life; an even older woman with a filthy knit cap perched atop stringy hair, foraging in a trash can for sustenance or something to redeem. A young couple, arms linked, hold between them a paper bag of Murray's bagels, so freshly baked the warm, sweetish scent briefly comes to her. A dog lopes past, turning its feral yellow eyes on her before lunging for a scampering squirrel. Apart from garbage trucks and an ambulance headed east toward Beth Israel hospital, the streets of Greenwich Village early on a Saturday morning are virtually devoid of traffic.

I want to go to Seventh Haven, Tara says. *Sure. Why not?* Sophie replies. She is reminded of Jim Morrison singing about people appearing strange when you're a stranger. And it's true: she has become a stranger to herself, emotionally estranged, evicted from her body, her life. No direction home. She is justly terrified. This is why she heads to Seventh Haven, her only sanctuary, where she can lose herself in helping others like Lia, where she can feel safe.

Upon turning the corner onto the clinic's street, she sees two black SUVs and a van with blacked-out windows. On the van's side is stenciled three letters: ICE. What does the US Immigration and Customs Enforcement want with Seventh Haven? She starts to run.

She races into the entry and finds a young woman she's never seen before at the desk. As she starts to pass by, the woman says, "Excuse me, may I help you?"

Arrested in midstride, she turns to the woman. In her present fractured state she has no patience for this, and her annoyance comes out in her voice. "I'm . . . Tara." Dear God, is it so hard to remember her name?

The young woman narrows her eyes. "Yes, and may I ask who you're here to see?"

"I'm Tara Gemini," she says shortly. "I work here."

"Really?" The young woman looks down at several sheets of paper, running her forefinger down a list, presumably of names. Then she looks up. "I'm sorry, but your name isn't on my list of current employees."

All the rage that has been building inside her from the moment she woke up on M's sofa now boils over. She advances menacingly on the young woman. "And who might you be, Missy?"

Rearing back in alarm, the young woman says, "Myra. My name's Myra."

Resting her forearms on the desk, she says, "And how long have you been working here, Myra?"

"This . . . this is my first day."

"Uh-huh. Now listen, Myra, I've been working here for two months, so fuck off."

"You can't—"

But she is already past the front desk. Out of the corner of her eye, she sees Richard Burnside hurrying out of his office.

"Hey, Tara," he says.

She smiles. "Ah, a friendly face. Well, at least someone around here knows who I am." She likes Burnside. For the most part, he keeps out of the way of the clinic's vital day-to-day functions, about which he knows nothing. He is a pencil pusher, not a therapist or a doctor. "For a moment I thought I'd crossed over into the twilight zone." She gestures to the vehicles outside. "What the hell is going on?"

"It's a raid." Burnside looks like death warmed over. "One of our . . . well, the entire family's been targeted."

Tara, fully alarmed, says, "Who? Which family?"

Burnside hesitates long enough for her to see two burly ICE employees bringing a girl out of the shadows. When she sees that it is Lia, she shouts, "No!" Her run toward the girl is halted by Burnside's thick hands on her arms. Nevertheless, "You can't! She's my patient."

Twisting violently, she breaks away from Burnside's grip, heading again toward Lia. Shockingly, one of the ICE guards reacts by blocking her bodily.

"Step back, Miss!" he commands. "Out of the way!" And when she does not give ground but keeps coming toward the girl, yells at her, "Impeding a matter of national security is punishable by imprisonment. Do. You. Understand. Me?"

"Tara, please come back here." It is Burnside, urging her to retreat. But Tara scarcely hears him. She is concentrated solely on Lia's tearstained face, drawn, terrified. She stops but does not step back.

"Lia," she says, "what's happened?"

Lia bursts into sobs. "Tara!" she cries. "It's my whole . . . they've taken my whole family. My mother and father first, and then—"

"That's enough!" The ICE guard with his gun drawn shouts her down. "No talking!"

"Then they took Leda, and now me!" Lia's wet, frightened eyes are fixed on Tara, begging her for help. "They say we won't see anyone again."

"They're just trying to scare you," Tara says, her desperation and sorrow leaking into her voice. "We'll find some way—"

The guard very deliberately moves his arm so his gun is aimed directly at her. "What did I tell you," the ICE guard grates. "Back the fuck up. Now."

Rage bubbles up in Tara's throat. "You can't talk to me like that." Burnside catches her as she makes a lunge toward Lia, wrapping his arms all the way around her this time.

"You'd better keep her under control, Mr. Burnside," the other ICE guard says. "Otherwise, I can't vouch for her safety."

Tara opens her mouth to reply, but Burnside covers it with one hand. "Keep still," he whispers in her ear. She nods, and he takes his hand away.

"But Richard, they're taking Lia away," Tara says in a low voice. "I've got to do something."

"There's nothing either of us can do. I'm sorry, Tara, but that's the way it is nowadays."

"Bullshit," Tara spits. Then to the girl, "Lia. Lia, I'll keep track of you. I won't let anything happen to you."

Lia and her guards have come abreast of Tara and Burnside. The rest of the staff, hanging back, watches the proceedings as if it is a train wreck.

Help me, Lia mouths.

"Lia, I love you," Tara says, "just remember that."

And then they are gone, out the door, into the street, where the van with the blackened windows awaits.

Burnside lets her go, and Tara's shoulders slump. Her face is as wet with tears as Lia's was. "They don't know anything about her. She could easily kill herself while in their custody."

"They have doctors who I'm sure will take care of her."

She looks up into his face. "D'you really believe that? Because I don't. Not for a minute."

Burnside seems to have his mind on other matters. As Tara starts toward the back of the clinic, he grips her elbow. For the first time, she realizes he is standing between her and the hallway down to the intake rooms. "Tara, I'm afraid some necessary, uh, admin protocols have been instituted."

Her anger is still in full flower. "Like hiring that idiot Myra?"

"Myra's a college student. She's volunteering here."

"Good for her, but she ought to be up to date on personnel."

"Well, the thing of it is, she is."

For a moment, the two of them stare at one another, unmoving.

Another chill spikes through her. Lia's abduction by ICE isn't enough shit for one day? Now this? "What are you saying, Richard?"

"We lost some funding for the new fiscal year."

She tries to engage him, but he won't look at her.

"New budget cuts had to be instituted. Basically, we're running on fumes. God knows we didn't want to lose you, but last in, first out. You were our last hire." His shoulders lift, fall. "It had to be that way. I'm sorry."

Her eyes narrow. "Does M know about this?"

"Your being let go has nothing to do with Margo. The directive comes from the top," Burnside says. "Management."

"Meaning what? Constant Horizons?"

He doesn't need to answer. This is that prick Brandon's way of making sure she takes his job offer. What a snake. She told him how much she loved working here, and he has used that against her. What a fool she has been to think she could control him.

I told you, Sophie says. *If you'd let me loose on him, he'd be ours now.*

She doesn't respond. Whether Sophie is right or wrong doesn't matter now. A far more pressing concern keeps her standing her ground. "But Lia?" She takes a step toward him, toward the intake rooms, toward other patients that need her help. "What will happen to Lia?"

"No one knows now."

"We have to do something for her and her family."

He shrugs. "It's a tragedy, but these things are happening all the time these days. And maybe it's for the best."

She stares at him as if he has grown a third eye. "For the best? How could dragging Lia out of our care possibly be for the best?"

"Anyway." He shrugs again. "It's out of our hands."

"You're a coward, Richard."

"Okay, okay. That's enough, Tara. Don't make me call security. You've already caused enough of a scene. We can't have that here; it upsets the patients." His thin smile cracks like broken china. "Besides, all this may be moot. The building's up for sale. All this"—he lifts his arms—"may be gone in a matter of months, or even weeks."

28

The rain has picked up; the sky is lower; more people are on the street: freaks and strangers. She heads for the subway to take her to Brandon's office. There is murder in her eyes, murder in her heart, the desire to do harm in her limbs.

Her phone buzzes just before she reaches the subway station stairs. Hauling it out, she seeks an awning to shelter herself from the rain. She takes the call without even looking at the screen.

"Yeah?"

"Good morning, Tara." An unfamiliar male voice in her ear. Another invasion.

"Who's this?" she says shortly.

"Philip Morris."

"Right. And I'm the Duchess of Sussex."

She is about to end the call when the voice says, "I'm a, uh, colleague of Brandon Fiske's. Perhaps he mentioned that you would receive a call regarding our mutual friend."

Fiske did alert her to the call, right after she'd acquiesced to going forward. She knows who their "mutual friend" is: Marwyn Rusk.

She considers a moment. "Give me your number. I'll call you back."

He chuckles. "Good thinking; make sure I really am who I say I am. Here's the general number—you'll want that. My extension is 3708." Then he rings off.

Beneath the dripping awning, she looks from the blank screen of her phone to the blackened subway entrance. Sophie says, *Fuck the call and fuck Philip Morris. What I want to do is to find Brandon and deliver a swift knee to his groin.* Tara says, That's not the best way to handle the situation. Call Morris back. See if he's legit. *You know what's going to happen if he is legit. You know what he's going to ask us to do.* I know what will happen if we confront Brandon. We'll have nowhere to go, we'll have the DEA or the FBI on our tail, and it'll be useless to run.

But there may be a third path. In truth, she no longer knows whether she has come up with it or Sophie has. Is there a difference? she asks herself. Once, maybe, but not anymore. In any event, it will have to be Sophie who will implement the plan.

A bit over three blocks east and south is a terrific rustic Italian restaurant where Tara has often gone by herself. On rainy days like this, she would sit at a table in the rear, eating penne arrabbiata and chocolate gelato, while looking out at Washington Mews with its side-by-side brownstones, ivy covered and bird flocked, a tiny private enclave that somehow makes her feel safe.

She asks for one of those tables now. As she is led past the bar and the very Italian stand-up tables, into the room at the rear, she sees Christie, Charlotte, and another woman—heavyset, dark hair blunt cut to just above her shoulders, large hazel eyes, a strong, resolute face as she concentrates on something Charlotte is saying—at a table by the windows. She chooses a table that puts her back to the therapist and her daughter, and facing the other woman, who seems about Christie's age, give or take a year or two. All Tara can see is an oyster-colored silk shirt.

Christie is wearing cream linen slacks, a lightweight steel-colored turtleneck, and flats. A black rain jacket hangs off the back of her chair. By contrast, Charlotte wears a pair of jeans machine worn at the knees, a black tee with the words "Excuse Me While I Dracarys" arcing across the front in fire-engine red. A pair of sneakers, in matching red, are on her feet.

Tara is handed a red-bordered menu but puts it down as she leans back in her chair, listening.

Charlotte is weeping softly. The other woman is speaking softly to Charlotte. Christie is silent, but she has put her arm across her daughter's trembling shoulders. *What is happening?* Sophie asks. Christie's just letting her daughter cry. It's cathartic to cry sometimes, Tara says. *I don't get it,* Sophie responds. Tara tells her to hush.

A waiter appears at Tara's table, and she orders a carciofi primavera salad and a double espresso. Christie and Charlotte have resumed a conversation, but Tara is too far away to make out any words. It is just as well; she is starting to feel uncomfortable.

She stares out the window at the mews, the colors vivid and glistening in the rain. An older woman walks the mews beneath an umbrella with a MoMA logo and a Citarella Gourmet Market shopping bag in her other hand. Tara's salad arrives. She drinks her double espresso, scarcely tasting it. She orders another, picks at her food, watches the comings and goings in the mews, the charming quiet life amid the bustle and crowds of the city.

"I'm not a child." Charlotte's voice is raised. Tara can hear her clearly. "Don't treat me like one."

The second double arrives, and she takes the dark liquid in her mouth, swallows hard, without using a grain of sugar. Her deepest emotions, so long in cold storage, are surfacing. She feels Charlotte's despair as if it is her own. Echoing down the dark hallways of the farmhouse are the male and female voices, raised in anger, frustration, escalating, spiraling upward and outward to encompass the entire structure. And under the quilted covers of her bed, her younger self drowning in despair.

Her cell burrs softly. The same number as before. Philip Morris wanting to find out why she hasn't called back. Obviously, what he has to tell her is vital to the moment. She turns the phone over, rejecting the call.

The two double espressos were clearly a mistake. She rises, goes off to the bathroom to relieve her bladder. It is when she returns that Charlotte sees and recognizes her. She raises an arm, her face coming alive.

"Hey, Tara!"

The moment she hears the name, Christie turns in her seat, and now Tara has no choice but to engage them both. She should have known better than to take the table next to them. Better by far to have turned around and left the restaurant, or at the very least asked for a table on the other side of the room. Now, however, it is too late.

She plasters a smile on her face, even as her feet feel like lead as she crosses to their table.

"Hello, Tara," Christie says in a neutral tone. "It's nice to see you." There is no hint that Tara has left her as a client or even that she hasn't returned her therapist's call.

"Hi, Dr. Lind," Tara says hoarsely. "Hey, Charlotte."

"You know my daughter." This isn't phrased as a question, simply a statement of fact.

"We met out on the street," Tara says somewhat lamely.

"And had a great talk," Charlotte jumps in. She is clearly pleased to see Tara, happy to get away from the difficult conversation in which she and the two older women have been engaged. Tara comes as a welcome distraction. "You've met my mom?"

"We're acquainted, yes," Christie says before Tara can utter a word. Again, everything is being carefully calibrated, kept in neutral gear.

"Tara, this is Lily Palmer."

Lily smiles warmly at Tara, extends her hand. "Hello, Tara. It's a pleasure to meet you."

Her hand is warm and dry.

"Lily's like my aunt," Charlotte pipes up, and Tara gives her a closer look. Tawny eyes look back at her neutrally.

"It's a pleasure to meet you too," Tara says.

In the moment, Charlotte pipes up again. "Hey, Mom, guess what?" Her sad mood seems to have evaporated, at least for the moment. "Tara's Figgy's girlfriend."

"Well, now, I didn't say that exactly," Tara responds, laughing. Christie's eyes widen incrementally, while Lily, the neutral observer, looks on interested, but not too; curious, but not too.

"You didn't have to." Charlotte is grinning. "Are we going to get together again? I've got some new music I'll bet you'd like."

"We'll see." Tara's eyes cut to Christie's inscrutable face, then back to Charlotte's. "But I'd like that."

"Great!" Charlotte gestures. "Hey, why don't you join us?" She has had enough of the darkness that has invaded her own life. The irony blinds Tara momentarily.

But she has the presence of mind to beg off. "I'd love to, thanks, but the truth is I'm late for an appointment." She says her goodbyes as quickly as she can and moves off.

At her table, her check is waiting. She puts down enough money to cover the bill and tip, and leaves the restaurant. It's all she can do not to run. The rain has retreated for the moment, leaving the streets as slick as they look in the movies. Morris has called her a third time. Not bothering to listen to the two voicemails he's left, she punches in the number and gets the DEA. Well, now she knows for certain.

She asks for extension 3708. When the male voice answers, she says, "Who's this?"

"Philip Morris, Tara. Returning my call is the right move. It saved me from sending my people to come get you."

"You're so full of it," Sophie says, muscling Tara out of the way. "You want me clean; you wouldn't send one of your window cleaners to bring me in, not at this stage."

He is silent for some time. She suspects he is debating whether to refute her, but the longer the silence stretches, the more certain she is that she is right.

"So," he says at last, "tonight our friend is going to be at Deva, a gentlemen's club over on West Twenty-Sixth Street. Know it?"

Sophie bursts into a laugh. "Right. I worked there as a topless pole dancer."

He ignores her sarcasm. "Our friend will be arriving after dinner, around ten. That's when you'll engage with him."

"Actually, I won't." She has been thinking about this since his first call, since Tara has come up with her plan.

"You'd better, or—"

"Listen to me, Philly. I know men a lot better than you do. Going up to him right away won't make sense to him, or have you forgotten my first encounter with him."

Another silence, followed by, "What do you suggest?"

When she tells him, he pauses a minute, then agrees.

"Okay," she continues, "after I engage with him, then what?"

"He's got a bolt-hole in Hell's Kitchen, where he takes his girls. You've got to get him to take you there. He's got a ledger of some sort that lists all the transactions. We think he's stashed it there."

"Why don't your agents go in and search the place?"

"Rusk's smart—very smart. So far we don't have enough to get a judge to order a search warrant or grant us a wiretap permission." He sighs. "You're our only hope of getting in there."

"Okay, say he takes me there. Then what? I mean, what am I looking for?"

"This is where it gets tricky."

She laughs sourly.

"So the ledger could be electronic, in which case it would be on a flash drive—you know, one of those—"

"Please. Spare me Computer 101. I know what a flash drive is."

"But," Morris says, "the ledger might also be a physical book."

"Why would he put that information down on paper."

"Security," Morris says. "An internet hacker can't get to a physical book."

"But a thief can."

"That's the idea."

She considers a moment, her mind racing ahead. "I'm going to expense this little enterprise of yours."

"Expense . . . ?"

"I need a new wardrobe."

"You'll wear whatever you have."

"This guy is a multimillionaire. He's used to his girls gleaming like a Tiffany diamond, not looking like something the cat dragged in."

"Fuck me," Morris mutters. But he doesn't say no; he knows she is right.

"And there better not be anyone there when I arrive," she adds. "None of your people."

"They have to be—"

"They'll get in my way. Maybe they'll muck up the plan altogether. That's a hard no. Keep them away from me, from him, from the club, and everything will work out to your satisfaction."

"You'd better pray it does, honey," Morris says darkly.

"I'm no one's honey," Sophie snaps even more darkly. "Especially not yours."

29

She returns to her old apartment.

As she plops down her bags and starts switching on lamps, she can smell the mustiness. If it weren't for the remains of the insecticide she sprayed at the end of her last visit, the stale air would've smelled like a crypt. She pauses to open one of the windows that overlooks the backyards and the windows at the rear of the building on the other side. Leaning out, she breathes deeply, until it occurs to her that the apartment must be under some form of surveillance. She ducks back inside, turns her back on the windows, and immediately thinks there is nothing so depressing as coming back to a place that hasn't been inhabited for a while.

Tara opens the refrigerator and winces. Not much there, but when what does remain is curdled or growing blue, green, and white fur like a laboratory experiment, you know you've hit rock bottom.

As in a nightmare from which there is no escape, the walls start to close in. Her mind seems to shut down. No thought now, simple instinct only: close window, turn off lights, grab shopping bags, bang out of there like a shot exploding from the barrel of a gun.

———

Saturday evening, the streets crowded, lines at the movie theaters, lines outside hot restaurants, even at this relatively early hour, lines at the checkout counters at Whole Foods and Citarella, the drift homeward bound. All except Tara.

She has spent the late afternoon shopping, interrupted only by a text from Lind:

Tara, it is imperative that we talk as soon as possible. Please call me.

Im sorry, she texts back.

You need to come in and see me. Even outside office hours. I will make time for you.

She knows she can't do that, especially not now. Anyway, what would she say? She knows she crossed a line when she befriended Charlotte, but the girl is in trouble, and besides, it makes her feel good to talk with her.

She is laden with bounty—shopping bags filled with two elegant Akris outfits: a bright-blue jersey jacket with a stand-up collar; a black silk shirt; slim ankle-cut trousers, also in black; suede ankle boots with a medium heel; and an embroidered black silk sleeveless dress with a plunging neckline. Both outfits flatter her figure. Naturally, it is Sophie who has picked these out. And to top it all off, she's bought a bottle of Femme, by Rochas, a perfume built around an animalistic cumin note. She has sampled a number of perfumes, but this is the one that to her smells like being day-old-sex drunk.

Now she heads for what she prays is the safety of Figgy's. She has made a bargain with Sophie: Tara will be in charge while they are with Figgy; she refuses to allow Sophie to mess things up with him the way she did with M. In exchange, she has agreed to give Sophie her head when they arrive at Deva sometime after nine. Misgivings, she has plenty, but unfortunately she holds a losing hand, and she knows it. No way can she face seeing Marwyn Rusk again, let alone engage with him.

She can scarcely drag herself to Figgy's brownstone. She has to stop twice, out of breath, gripped by blackest despair. She cannot remember being as exhausted as she feels now. Praying now merely for him to be home. She considered calling or even texting him, but after the way Sophie ran out on him, she isn't willing to take the chance. If he isn't home, she is prepared to hide inside the Quad Cinema until it's time to change. But if he is home and turns her down, she doesn't know what she will do. It's difficult, even painful, for her to admit her feelings for him, let alone consider that she might be falling in love with him. In truth, she has no experience with being in love, and as for Sophie the entire concept of love is so alien as to be absurd.

Her relationship with Figgy is balanced on a knife edge. How does he feel about her? He was the one Brandon tasked with bringing them together. Is his romancing of her real or an act to reel her in, bring her to Stephen Ripley's party so her meeting Brandon would appear a random circumstance? And as far as she is concerned, Sophie throwing herself at him has only muddied the waters all the more. She worries that Sophie has already screwed things so badly that a genuine relationship with him is now out of reach. Did he see her simply as a great lay? He said, "I like you, Tara," but that was before Sophie arrived. He never said, "I think I'm falling in love with you."

I'm going to have to start over, she says to Sophie. As if he just sat down on the stoop that first evening. He has to see who I really am.

Is that so? Sophie replies. *Curious, since you don't know who you really are.*

If she could have slapped Sophie, she would have then. Sophie laughs at the impulse.

She stands in front of his front door, rooted to the spot. To go forward into the light or to retreat into the gathering shadows, that is the question. Never before has she imagined Hamlet's most quoted speech being relevant to her own life. But now she whispers to herself: "Whether 'tis nobler in the mind to suffer the slings and arrows of outrageous fortune, or to take arms against a sea of troubles and by opposing end them."

To which Sophie surfaces long enough to answer: *Thus conscience does make cowards of us all.*

And so Tara raises her hand and, after pressing the bell, hears its melodious tones raised in cheerful greeting. And in the knuckle-gnawing moments before the door opens, she thinks of the lines of dialogue between Michael and his mother from one of her favorite books, J. M. Barrie's *Peter Pan*: "'Can anything harm us, mother, after the night-lights are lit?' 'Nothing, precious,' she said; 'they are the eyes a mother leaves behind her to guard her children.'"

Then the door swings inward. Instead of Figgy, she confronts a young woman in jeans, a smudged T-shirt under a Lee denim jacket, and Converse sneakers. Her hair is tied back in a ponytail.

"Oh, hello." She hurriedly stuffs some folded money into her hip pocket as she steps out of the way. "I was just leaving."

Tara is so taken aback that all she can utter is a monosyllable that, even much later, she cannot recall. She stares at the girl as if she is a model on a Parisian runway; she is beautiful in that slightly unformed way of girls who have not yet lost all their teenage roundness. She isn't wearing a bra; her nipples are clearly evident.

The girl, smiling blithely, brushes past her.

"Do you do this with everyone?" Figgy says.

Her head whips around. He is standing in the living room, his expression unreadable. "What?"

"Showing up unannounced," Figgy says. He wears a pair of paint-spattered jeans and a T-shirt adorned with the silk-screened image of Jimi Hendrix, with his intense face and exploded psychedelic hair.

"Maybe that's why I'm not very popular." She has meant for it to be an amusing remark, but judging by his expression, it lands with a thud. "Should I come in?"

"I don't know," he says. "Are you going to run out right after we make love?"

She is still focused on the arresting afterimage of the girl. "Now I don't know whether I should." She feels very shaky, as if at any moment she will collapse.

"Why not?"

"I think you're pissed off at me for leaving so abruptly."

He shakes his head. "Pissed off, no. Confused, yes."

"I told you I had an appointment."

"Yes, you did."

She frowns, holds on to the doorframe to steady herself. She can no longer feel anything below her knees. "I was meeting my friend M."

"At two in the morning?"

"She works at a club downtown." Her heart is beating far too fast. "You don't believe me?"

When he doesn't reply, she gestures after the girl.

"What? Chloe? She comes once a week to clean."

"This is Saturday."

"She has classes at NYU during the week." He gestures with his head. "Enough questions. Come in or don't."

She steps in, closes the door behind her. Her hand is trembling. Pushing herself onward, she approaches him. "Anyway, I'm sorry."

Figgy crosses to the turntable, puts on a Miles Davis album. "Miles Runs the Voodoo Down," from *Bitches Brew*, races through the room like a bloody hound, ragged, muscular, electrifying, and she says, "That's better."

She sets her bags down beside the end of the sofa, takes off her coat, another new purchase, shiny and swingy and so very in vogue. Her indecision as to where to put it mirrors her bafflement as to whether he wants her there. He has his hands in his pockets, which she's never seen him do before. Is it a sign of some change within him, or a craziness on her part?

I need a starting point, she thinks. A place to reset our relationship to ground zero. She clears her throat. "If memory serves," she says, "you were going to read me *The Decline and Fall of the Roman Empire*."

"When you ran out. Yep, I remember." His shoulders are hunched up around his ears, as if he's expecting a physical blow, and this makes her very sad. "That was a joke," he continues rather lamely. "It's six volumes, you know."

"I'm sure Chloe would have known that." She says that more sharply than she intended. Now he must know that she is jealous, even if she has no reason to be.

They face each other, watchful and wary, the sofa between them. Sweat breaks out under her arms and at the nape of her neck. She wipes her upper lip. While they stare at each other, at some form of emotional or psychological impasse, Miles's trumpet is going all out, and she says, "Wherever you are, Miles is ahead of you. Who said that?"

"You did. Just now."

Is the frost slowly melting? Is the ice coming apart? Like I'm coming apart, she thinks miserably. And she thinks, I can't do this alone. Neither can Sophie, though she'll never admit it.

Nothing from Sophie.

He hasn't moved toward the bookshelves, and she finds herself hoping he won't. This line—this way in to him—is foolish and is now dead as a day-old fish. She must move on before it starts to stink.

"You also offered to make me dinner." She says the first thing that comes into her head. Is that from Sophie? She puts her hands to her throbbing temples. Every time she thinks of Sophie now, and what would be upcoming, she feels ill.

"Are you all right?" He takes a step toward her. Real concern is in his voice. She feels a sense of relief, as if she is starting to have some success, no matter how small, in opening him up, in starting over.

"Yes. Yes, I'm fine."

"You don't look fine." He takes another step toward her, and she realizes that he's as tentative as she is. "You look pale."

"I . . ."

He comes to her, then takes her gently by the elbow, leads her into the back of the house, where he sits her on a high-backed chair, one of two set around the center island. Without asking, he pulls a bottle of Coke from the refrigerator, opens it, divides it into two glasses he's filled with ice.

They sit together on the same side of the island, sipping their Cokes, while Miles Davis runs that voodoo down, and the silence between them extends. She listens attentively to the music. Miles has done away with not only time signatures but all musical signposts as well. He has created a new place, a place of bewitchment and sorcery, good and evil, that you feel privileged to inhabit.

Occasionally, Figgy gives her a swift sidelong glance, but his eyes are always somewhere across the kitchen when she looks at him directly.

"I saw Brandon yesterday." She spits it out, as if it were a hairball threatening to choke her.

"And?" The gentle concern that was in his voice a moment ago is no longer there.

Only now does she understand why she has told him about her meeting with Brandon Fiske. She needs to know something that will give her solid ground on which to stand. Anxiety eats through her like acid, making every word she utters uncertain, every answer he gives suspect. And then, rushing on, because she doesn't know or understand whether they are still at odds; his sudden sharpness makes her defensive. "He offered me a job, and I took it."

"Very cool. Congratulations." His smile seems to consume her rather than warm her.

"I have you to thank. It's through you that I met Brandon."

"But you were the one who impressed him. Obviously. What are you going to be doing at Constant Horizons?"

She likes his answer, but she doesn't like the fact that he's side-stepped a direct reply. Lied to her by omission. A painful bubble bursts inside her. It seems to swell in her chest, unknown emotions threatening to sink her. Is he still pissed? Does he like her for anything other than her body, than for the way Sophie knows how to please him? She hasn't felt so inadequate in a long time, not since returning to her bed, crying herself to sleep, from which she awoke, paralyzed. She is so awful at interacting with people. Dogs and horses she understands, but human beings are a complete mystery.

Well, what d'you know, Sophie comments. *Brandon didn't tell him the real reason he wanted to meet you.*

Does that mean everything between us has been genuine, or is he a first-class actor? Tara asks Sophie as much as herself.

I'm a djinn, Sophie says, *not a clairvoyant. Foretelling the future was supposedly Norma Jean's forte.*

"To be honest," she says to Figgy, "the details have to be worked out, but Brandon says he wants to start a separate division for the funding of carefully curated nonprofits. That's where I'll start."

"Your own division." Figgy is clearly impressed. And, she thinks, if he is acting, he ought to be reciting Shakespeare at the Old Vic in London. "He must think as highly of you as I do."

"Thank you," she says and means it. Détente, or at least the glimmer of a new beginning. Now that she feels on firm ground, she can move forward with confidence.

"Now, let's celebrate," he says, rubbing his hands together. "What would you like me to make for dinner?"

"I don't know." She doesn't. "You choose."

He nods and rises. "How about omelets?" He scavenges in the refrigerator, then a wire basket that sits on the countertop. "I have onions, two kinds of mushrooms, scallions. How does that sound?"

"Perfect." And it does. As she begins to relax, she discovers a hunger deep in her belly. Watching the easy manner in which he skins and cubes the onions, washes the mushrooms, chops the scallions gives her a kind of contentment. Is it also happiness? When is the last time she can remember being content? Or happy?

Miles is done.

"Why don't you find another album to put on?" he says as he gets out a large sauté pan, puts it on a burner.

His collection is weighted toward jazz from the '60s and '70s. She chooses the *Getz/Gilberto* album, with Stan Getz on tenor sax, the instrument most like a human voice, and vocals by Astrud Gilberto, the great Brazilian singer, João's talented wife.

As bossa nova beats drift through the house, she hears him call, "Good one." The scents of heated butter and browning onions make her mouth water. The sizzle of the eggs hitting the pan. "Tara, come on in—these will be ready in a second."

After they eat, they dance to the second side of the album, close together, her head on his shoulder, his hand on the small of her back. That one gesture electrifies her, softens her like the pats of butter he dropped into the warmed sauté pan. The air is still perfumed by the dinner he made. What with the meal and the music, her mood has turned dreamy. What Sophie has to do later that night mercifully seems far away, a dream in an alien world.

They dance and dance, even after side two has ended, until he whispers, "I want to take you to bed."

"Not tonight," she says. "I'd like to wait."

"Seriously?"

"This is different." She lifts her head off his shoulder so she can look at him directly. His eyes are half-lidded, and she knows that he is as intoxicated by their closeness as she is. "Do you understand what I mean?"

"I think so." He nods. "Like starting over?"

She kisses him lightly on the mouth. "Exactly like starting over."

Oh my God, she thinks.

30

I have to go out for a bit," she says, later. "But I'd like to come back and stay the night." She hesitates a moment. "If it's all right."

"Of course it's all right."

They are drinking coffee in the living room. Mark Ronson's *Late Night Feelings* is on the turntable at low volume. She loves that Figgy listens to vinyl.

She stirs in some sugar, an indulgence not often taken. She has gotten used to strong coffee, black. "Now I'll tell you some things."

"Must you? I've gotta confess you're irresistible when the mystery isn't pierced."

She is grateful for his bantering tone. When she stood on his doorstep, she was terrified she'd never hear it again. "I am undeterred. Too much mystery works against the soul," Sophie says in her voice.

Get out. Get out, get out, get out! We have a deal!

"A little over two years ago there was a fire." Sophie has gone quiet, and Tara is able to remain in control. She knows her time is coming to an end. "Our farmhouse burned to the ground, and my father was in it."

"Ah, well, now I understand your aversion to cooked meat." He instantly reconsiders his words. "Apologies. Was that too insensitive?"

She laughs. What a lovely sound that is! she thinks, like a lark in spring. Why doesn't she laugh more? "Not at all," she tells him. "It's the truth, after all." She takes a sip of her coffee. Between that and the Coke, the caffeine is working its magic, revving up her system.

She holds out her hand. "I tried to go back in and save him. I had to be saved myself. I must've been taken to the hospital, but I don't remember. Six and a half months later, I found myself in Chicago, where I enrolled in an online college. Weekends I worked as an orderly at a hospital on the South Side, where I saw a ton of gunshot and knife wounds. Once, there was an incident with an active shooter. One patient, a doctor, and a PA down. It was very bad." All of this is God's honest truth, and it feels so good to tell him. To trust that there are things she can reveal without fear. To him. Keeping every aspect of her life hidden inside is an awful burden, one she only now fully understands.

He stares at her, his mug suspended between the table and his lips. "My God, Tara. I had no idea."

"Yeah, up until now no one did."

"But . . ." He considers a moment. "What happened to you after you left the hospital? You said you didn't get to Chicago until six and a half months later."

He's smart; he isn't going to let her get away with anything now.

She takes a deep breath, lets it out. "See, that's the thing: I don't remember. One minute I'm in the flames, the next I'm waking up in a motel in Tucumcari."

With his eyes open wide he seems unutterably vulnerable. "And six months had passed?"

"That's right."

He shakes his head. "How is that possible?"

"Well, that's one reason I was seeing Dr. Lind."

"I can find you another—"

She waves a hand in dismissal. "Don't bother."

"It wouldn't be a bother."

She leans over, puts a hand over his. "Thank you."

His eyes are beseeching. "Tara—"

"No." She is smiling, patting his hand. "Now I've got to get ready."

"Where are you going?"

"A business meeting. My first assignment for Brandon."

He glances at his watch. "At this time of night?"

She grins at him as she rises. "The city never sleeps."

She sweeps up one of the shopping bags and goes upstairs. The powder room on the ground floor is too small. The only floor-length mirror is in Figgy's bathroom. Swinging the bag as she goes, she feels like Holly Golightly.

In the bathroom, she pulls out her clothes, carefully unfolds them from their pink and green wrappers. Then she kicks off her shoes and stares at herself in the mirror. Sophie claimed that she doesn't know herself, but that was before this evening. Once, she felt as if Christie would become a safe harbor in which to drop anchor and stop running before the wind. But too frightened to confront herself, she ran out, turned her back on Christie. Only to finally find her safe harbor here.

She begins to dress, turning this way and that to regard her outfit, something she hasn't done in what seems a long time. And that's when she sees it, reflected in the mirror. For a moment, she stands stock still, pulse racing.

Then she turns, so reluctantly, with a sinking sensation in the pit of her stomach, as if she's in an elevator dropping at high speed. And still, she holds on to the hope that what she sees is merely a shadow, a trick of the light. An illusion conjured out of the darkness of her mind.

But no. As she crosses the chill tiles, she recalls Chloe in the doorway, smiling, stepping past her, her bare breasts pushing against the thin fabric of her T-shirt. And now Tara knows why.

As in a dream, she reaches out, her mind disconnected from the action of taking up the pink lacy demi bra that is draped over the shower door like a postcoital lover. Not her bra.

Chloe's bra.

31

Deva is housed in a sprawling pitched-roof building clad in old brick stained by the depredations of the city. The exterior is modeled after private clubs, which is to say that, unlike other gentlemen's clubs in New York that feature glitzy signage and other gaudy accoutrements serving as come-ons, there is nothing at all on the facade to give even a hint of what is going on inside. Deva has no public phone number. A private number is given out to members, passed on by them with the unmitigated restraint of religious acolytes. And, in fact, Deva is something of a cult: expensive to join, difficult to leave, dominated by ironclad rules. One of these rules is that women of a certain breed are always welcome, gratis.

It is this rule that guarantees Sophie's access. The two doormen, large as brick outhouses, take one look at her in her obviously expensive Akris outfit and fall all over themselves to open the door and usher her inside.

She departed Figgy's without a word about what she'd found in his bathroom. It was Sophie who left his brownstone, just as it was Sophie who put the thing back, draping it just as Tara had found it. Sophie didn't even have to expend psychic energy shutting Tara down; Tara, dazed and confused and heartbroken, retreated on her own. Furled like the flag of a defeated nation, she hides in the deepest recesses of her own mind in the sad domain the Hypnotist created for Sophie.

As she did in LA, Sophie puts Tara completely out of her thoughts. The world is once again hers. She knows what she has to do, and she knows how to do it. When it comes to seduction, she has no equal. Whether men or women, it makes little difference to her: Sunrize turned out to be a better lover than Rex. Certainly more inventive and just as uninhibited. They made love three times a day in the beach shack Sophie briefly rented, the lust for life never more shockingly immediate than in the aftermath of death. In fact, Philip Morris be damned, she is in the market for a lithe female body to rub up against. To that end, she has decided on the outfit with the plunging neckline. She has daubed Femme on the inside of her wrists, in her cleavage, and behind her ears.

The interior brick of the club is painted a glossy black. The clouded glass top of the mirror-backed bar against the right-hand wall is illuminated from below. A blue glow rises up from it as if from an aquarium. And, indeed, the underwater motif continues with larger-than-life mermaids, doe eyed and beckoning, painted on the walls at random intervals, some entangled in long strands of seaweed, as if emerging from an underwater forest. The floor of the main space is of some translucent material. As with the bar top, it is lighted from below, the colors constantly changing from blue to green and back again. One can imagine the male patrons as reef sharks, gliding from table to table, hungry for entertainment in the form of a lap dance, a private strip, or something even more gratifying in the intimate VIP rooms beyond guarded doors on either side of the main room. In the center, a circle of topless girls in the tiniest thongs imaginable dance slowly, hips swiveling, pelvises twerking, glistening lips partly open, creating a vortex of ersatz lust. As much as sex means to Sophie, she simply can't fathom the appeal of clubs like this—all glitter and glitz, reeking nauseatingly of men's sweat and female pheromones. Not to mention the music, which is that kind of sleazy pop-rap that pollutes the radio.

Stepping inside, she doesn't immediately look for Marwyn. Rather, crosses the room, buttocks clearly outlined against her dress. She selects an empty bar seat next to a trim, buxom redhead, who might or might not be a $2,000-a-night professional. She is drinking a vodka martini, at the bottom of which is a single cocktail onion. When the female tat-laden bartender approaches her, Sophie orders the same, specifying Absolut Elyx, the ultraluxe, single-estate, manually distilled vodka.

The redhead turns to watch the bartender pour and shake, and when the cocktail is delivered, says, "I see you know your spirits."

Thus is the ice broken, easy as pie. Sophie takes a sip, eyes the redhead over the rim of her glass. "If you're going to drink, then drink well. That's my motto."

The redhead, who appears to be in her late twenties, lifts her glass in silent recognition of a connection of a certain nature. Sophie responds in kind.

"Rose," she says.

"Sophie."

"First time?"

Sophie nods.

"I figured. I saw you checking out the place in the mirror." Her smile is knowing, conspiratorial. "That's why I'm perched here. I can see everyone who walks in."

"Looking for a date, a fuck, or a client?" This is Sophie's way, and either it works or it doesn't. She has little doubt here.

Rose chuckles, a deep, rich sound that Sophie can hear even over the music. "You're quite the brazen creature, aren't you?"

Sophie shrugs. "Why take longer to get to the point than you need to?"

"No reason at all," Rose says. And then, because they've both con- sumed most of their drinks, she orders a second round. "Make them her way," she adds to the bartender, indicating Sophie, before returning to their conversation. "To answer your question, it depends on the day of the week or, more importantly, my mood." Using one of her acrylic nails, she spears the onion at the bottom of her empty glass, pops it into her mouth. "But, hey, I'm no professional, though I've taken sums in gratitude for a night well spent." She shrugs. "I like sex, and I like performing. That's just me."

Right on time, the cocktails arrive, and they clink rims, savor first sips.

"You know, when I was a little girl, all I wanted was to be a ballet dancer," she continues. "I studied and I learned quickly. That's what's so cruel about it. I might have been good, great even, according to my instructor, but then I grew these." She grabs her breasts. "And that was it for ballet—for modern dance too."

She continues to sip her drink. It's a story told without an ounce of self-pity. Sophie admires that. "I wanted to be a dancer so badly I thought about having a breast reduction. I even went so far as to see a top plastic surgeon, after researching them for months. But right around then my best friend was diagnosed with breast cancer. I was with her when the oncological surgeon recommended she have a double mastectomy. I saw what was going to happen to her, held her while she cried her eyes out, while she told me she didn't want to lose them."

Rose appears to be looking into the mirror at the back of the bar, but her attention is turned inward as she revisits the past. When she speaks again, her voice is changed. It's brighter, crisper, more like that of a young girl. "I woke up the next morning, went in to take a shower, and looked at myself in the full-length mirror, and it hit me like a lightning bolt. I hated myself. Here is my best friend having her breasts cut off because she has no other choice, and here I am contemplating basically the same thing. That's when I took a long hard look at myself—not just my body, but *inside*. And here's what I realized: I didn't want to mutilate my body—not even to become a dancer. I realized I'd never be happy if I didn't accept myself for who I was. I chose to be authentic, rather than become a plastic counterfeit."

She gives a little laugh. "Now I work in digital advertising."

"Do you like it?" Sophie asks.

Rose downs more of her martini. "Well, I don't dislike it."

"Do you regret . . . ?"

"Regret nothing, that's my motto," Rose says. "I don't look back now. My friend died despite what she was told to do. The future's all that matters to me, and finding pleasure in the present."

"Here?" Sophie asked.

Rose smiles, leaning in as she lowers her voice. "My secret life. I crave sex the way other people crave food. It's a necessity for me—for my happiness." She cocks her head. "Does that make sense?"

"Perfect sense," Sophie says.

Rose laughs softly, an intimate sound. "Most people wouldn't get it at all. They'd be appalled. Frankly, I'm astonished I told you all of that."

"It's easier to tell strangers things about ourselves—intimate things—we'd never tell our friends. Why is that, do you think?"

"Friends judge us. Strangers won't," Rose replies. "And even if they do, who cares, we'll never see them again." Her nostrils are dilated. "My, you smell good."

"Femme."

"Ah, yes. I'll have to try that."

Rose orders them a third round. "Enough about me. What about you?" she says.

"Me? Oh, I'm here for revenge."

Rose's eyebrows shoot up. "Excuse me?" That low, soft voice. She puts her head close to Sophie's again. Her breath is sweet and fresh, despite the martinis. "Did you say revenge?"

"I did." Now she takes a thorough look around the room, and there is Marwyn, sitting at a far corner table, flanked by two other men. A naked blonde with a tramp stamp of spread wings on the small of her back is dancing on their table. She manages to deftly avoid the bottle of Johnnie Walker Blue and three shot glasses. Sophie sees her push Marwyn's hand away from her gleaming thigh.

"I could do better than that," Sophie says.

Following the trajectory of Sophie's gaze, Rose says, "So could I," with a mischievous grin. "Now, about this revenge . . ."

Sophie considers. "I don't think I can tell you . . . unless, that is, you want to be part of it."

"Huh, really? Well, hm, I guess that depends. Are we talking about Mr. Groper at that table?" Rose inclines her head slightly in Marwyn's direction. "What did he do to you?"

"We are, and that cocksucker physically assaulted me at a party."

"Did he rape you?"

"It wasn't for lack of trying."

"Well, that's something at least."

"I kneed him."

That deep-throated chuckle again. "You go, girl!"

"There's more. Get this: this guy's a serial cocksucker; he's married, *and* he came to the party with some pneumatic blonde he was banging on the side."

"She wasn't enough for him?"

"He saw me. He wanted me. Nothing else mattered."

"Fuck." Rose's face twists in disgust. "Cheating on his wife *and* his whore. Now that's a number one asshole." She taps her forefinger against her glass. "This walking hard-on have a name?"

"Marwyn," Sophie says. "Marwyn Rusk."

The dancer at Marwyn's table has finished and, tips in hand, jumps down, off to her next table stop.

Time, Sophie thinks. "I'm going to pee," she says, slipping off her seat. "When I get back, just follow my lead."

"What d'you have in mind?"

"I want you to be surprised," Sophie says.

"Just like Christmas!" Rose says with a knowing smirk.

"You never had a Christmas like this, I promise," Sophie replies.

The restrooms are in the far left-hand corner of the room. In order to get there, Sophie will have to pass by Marwyn's table. Sophie's idea is to play off his reaction to her.

The men are on their second or third bottle of Johnnie Walker Blue, and things are getting raucous: raised voices, a bit of off-key singing, a couple of truly awful rap tries, constant backslapping and high fives, and a stream of dirty jokes.

"What does Angela put behind her ears to attract men?" Marwyn shouts, his voice thick with whiskey. And after a beat: "Her ankles." Laughter all around. His gestures are expansive. His body is encased in a midnight-blue pinstripe suit over a white shirt. His initials are engraved in his silver cuff links. His tie, as neatly knotted as if he is still giving presentations, is gold with tiny red diamonds.

As Sophie comes abreast of them, one of Marwyn's companions happens to glance at her, eyes sliding down from her face to her cleavage. Marwyn, quick on the uptake, sees her in profile just as she passes by. A quick flash as his eyes open wide, and then she is in a short dim passageway.

Pushing through the second door on the left, she finds herself in a space that looks like Madame de Pompadour's boudoir—all pink and cream, with froufrou shaded wall lamps and cherubs—yes, cherubs—frolicking among the trompe l'oeil clouds on the ceiling.

"Jesus," Sophie says under her breath. She thinks briefly of Norma Jean and laughs at what she would have made of this room.

Sinks are on the left, stalls on the right. She steps into the last one, closes the door, and sits down. She doesn't have to pee; she needs to think. Think about Marwyn. About why seeing him again has sent a shock through her like the bolt from a crossbow. She sits forward, elbows on thighs, listening to the sounds of toilets flushing, water running, and voices rising and falling in laughter and querulous debate over what is sexier: butt or dick.

All background static to her as she tries to make sense of her totally unexpected discomfort. She simply assumed she'll deal with Marwyn the way she dealt with Rex, Figgy, any of the other men she has briefly been with. But no. This is different. Way different. What Marwyn did to Tara has somehow affected her too. The sight of him has set her body trembling. He is like an icy wind shooting through a crack in the foundation, chilling the interior.

Involuntarily, she crosses her forearms over her half-exposed breasts. She feels vulnerable. How can this be? Isn't feeling raw and exposed Tara's bailiwick? She has been immune to what happened to Tara as a child. The Hypnotist saw to that. But somehow, some way, that immunity has expired. Sophie can almost feel the familiar ground sliding out from under her; she no longer retains even a single landmark. Everything she thought she knew, relied on for her existence, has been stripped away in one second of pure irrepressible emotion; she has been dropped into a landscape so alien she is at a loss as to how to react. And yet she knows she has to move forward, complete the assignment Brandon and Philip Morris have given her. She's been a fugitive long enough. That has to end, no matter the cost to her or to Tara.

Pulling herself together, she opens the stall door, steps back down the corridor and into the cacophony of the main room. This time, she feels Marwyn's eyes on her, hot and covetous, as she strides past his table. He half rises from his seat, his nostrils filled with her scent, is pulled back down by one of his friends or colleagues or sycophants, whatever they are.

Across the room, Rose waits for her. She swivels away from the bar, keeps her eyes on Sophie's face as Sophie comes up to her, puts her arms around her, and kisses her long and hard and hotly on the lips. The kiss lasts a long time and sends a current of electricity snaking from her throat to the juncture of her thighs.

When at last she breaks the kiss, Rose says, "Now that's what I call a Christmas present!" Her eyes are hooded, and her cheeks and throat are flushed.

Sophie grins at her. "Yummy," she says softly, stroking the nape of Rose's neck.

Behind them, the movement of the bartender breaks their connection, and they both look at her at the same time. She holds a bottle of Veuve Clicquot La Grande Dame 2006 and two champagne flutes, which she sets down in front of them.

"Compliments of Mr. Marwyn Rusk," she says, "the gentleman in the back corner." She pops the cork and pours. "He knows his wines, that one."

Rose turns to look, smiles, and raises her hand in acknowledgment, but Sophie, quite deliberately, does not turn around. She grasps the flute's stem, drains the champagne, taps the rim for a refill. As the bartender pours, she says, "Mr. Rusk come in here often?"

"He's a regular," the bartender says. "A real big spender. What the Las Vegas casinos call a whale."

Sophie, smiling thinly, nods to her, then turns to Rose. "Well?"

"Well what?"

"Sooner or later he's going to come over. He's going to make a play for us."

"Fine by me."

"And if he wants us both?"

"Seriously?" Rose laughs. "I'm hoping the fuck he does!"

32

He does. Of course he does. Introducing himself, he is quick to detail his position at the pinnacle of the hedge fund industry. He is a glib talker, but the more he talks, the more disappointing he becomes. Cutting through all the bullshit, he is just another salesman hiding under the guise of a gig economy genius with the prescience to buy all the right companies at venture capital prices, making a fortune for his clients and, incidentally, for himself at IPO time. Most interesting to Sophie, he keeps his eyes mostly on Rose. Just a flicker now and again in Sophie's direction. He does not give any indication that he and Sophie have met before, let alone that the incident in Stephen Ripley's bathroom ever occurred. But what is going on in his mind? Surely he can't believe that she doesn't recognize him, or that she has forgotten what he's done to her. Or can he? She has learned that narcissistic men have an infinite capacity for self-delusion.

She is not about to allow him to dictate the parameters of this encounter. So, twining her fingers with Rose's, she says to him, "Haven't we met before?"

He shakes his head, brows pulled together. "I think I'd remember such a beautiful young woman."

"And yet I have a vague feeling." She worries her lower lip. "You look familiar."

A shadow chases itself across his face and in the blink of an eye is gone. His smile seems frozen in place. "Is that so."

She snaps her fingers. "Hey, are you a friend of Steve's, maybe?"

"Steve?" He seems genuinely bewildered.

"Yeah. Steve Ripley. I sometimes do a bit of work for him. Freelance."

He frowns. "What do you do?"

She has given him a path to change the subject, and he has taken it gratefully. "IT. I specialize in cleaning out the worms, bugs, ransomware, Trojan horses, rootkits." Her eyes lock on his. "You know, all the rotten shit that can gum up the works, the product of bad actors, criminals, cheaters. That sort." She smiles. "There's no end to them."

A short silence, punctuated by Rose looking from one to the other. Sophie can discern the ghost of a smile at the corners of her lips, but only because she knows what to look for.

"Hey, I know," Rose says brightly, "why don't you hire Soph to clean up your mess." She waves a hand. "I mean, are your own IT people good enough? Do you really know what's lurking at the core of your computer system?"

"I think I've got that covered."

"Well, you never know," Rose says, pushing it so that Sophie is obliged to stifle a laugh.

Marwyn rubs his chin. "Maybe we can think of a way to keep this evening going."

"What about your pals over there?" Sophie says.

"Oh, them." And chuckling, "They're big boys. They can take care of themselves." He looks from Rose to Sophie and back again. "I guess I should ask. Are you two an item?"

"Occasionally," Sophie says.

"When the mood strikes us," Rose says, playing along perfectly. Sophie gets the impression that, as she has indicated, she is enjoying this byplay immensely.

"What about now?" Marwyn says in a bantering tone, and Sophie, to her utter astonishment, has to keep herself from striking out at him.

"Now, I have to get some sleep," she says, gathering up her coat. "But you and Rose . . ."

"I was thinking of you both." She sees the longing in his eyes and revels in it.

"Well," Rose says, cocking her head to one side, "aren't you the manly man."

Marwyn grins in exaggeratedly wolfish fashion, not getting the irony at all. Again Sophie feels the urge to hit him in the face. "So, girls, what do you say?" He lifts an arm. "My limo awaits your every command." And now she feels the full force that men can and do exert over women, that power, blunt as a truncheon, thick as a brick, as if it is their birthright to bring women to heel, make them obey, lay them low. It tugs at her—even her—like a magnetic draw that she responds to instinctively, as if it is encoded in her female DNA. And yet Sophie is not like other women—not like any other woman; she pulls back from it and, squeezing her hand, drags Rose along with her.

"Are you sure you want me along?" Sophie says.

"I wouldn't have it any other way." He says this, smiling, in a steel-backed tone that brooks no refusal.

Rose turns to Sophie, their hands still clutched together. "What d'you say, Soph? Sleep or all kinds of fun?"

"Well, if you put it that way . . ."

"Excellent! Shall we?" As they rise from their seats, his fingers brush the back of Sophie's hand, and she feels a shard of ice pierce her skin. Possibly it is this invasion that wakes Tara and drives her from the shadows into the light.

In the back of the Lincoln Navigator, Tara is seated next to Marwyn, who has arranged to have the women on either side of him. She starts screaming as the recognition of where she is and what is happening breaches her consciousness. The scream is silent, of course. Only Sophie can hear it. *Shhh, Kitten,* she says. *Sleep now and let me handle it, just as I have before.*

Marwyn places one hand proprietarily on her knee as he tells another joke, this one only slightly off color. "What's the difference between a G-spot and a golf ball?" he says with a jack-o'-lantern grin. "A guy will search for a golf ball."

Rose laughs dutifully, but it is unclear whether she thinks the joke is funny. There is no doubt that Marwyn does. Not that Sophie knows or cares; she is on the battlefield, and as long as they are in the limo, she is occupied with tearing Tara down, putting her back where she has been ever since she picked up Chloe's bra.

33

The Navigator cleaves the night. Lights and neon signs flash by, dulled to monochrome by the smoked windows. The night is blue as they head west, drained of color. Drained of life.

Twenty minutes later, the limo approaches their destination. They arrive at Hell's Kitchen.

Marwyn's fuck pad—or as Philip Morris would have it, his bolt-hole—is in a five-floor walkup, one of those grim, soot-stained buildings that one day will inevitably be bought up by a billionaire developer, demolished along with its neighbors to make way for a sleek condo with a Whole Foods or a CVS at street level. At the moment, though, a block and a half from the Hudson River, it is as private and anonymous as you can be anywhere in Manhattan.

The vestibule is dim, buzzy with faulty electricity. To the left is a metallic rectangle of mailboxes, a number of which are halfway pried open. To the right, a wall of startlingly graphic graffiti, nevertheless beautiful. The floor is littered with flyers and menus from local takeout joints.

Three flights up, amid the stink of fish frying, cat urine, and, faintly, garbage, he unlocks the door at the far end of the floor and ushers them into a one-bedroom apartment that looks out onto the street below, where a slow parade of cars passes amid shouts and murmurs from passersby at the jolting hard-core rap bursting like machine-gun fire through the vehicles' open windows. He hangs Sophie's coat and Rose's jacket on an old-fashioned wooden coatrack by the door.

The living room is square and dark. A sofa, two lounge chairs, a coffee table between them, a thin rug beneath them, a bookcase holding a pair of small crystal bowls, a DVD player, a half dozen oversize paperback thrillers. The furniture is serviceable but looks like it came from IKEA or Rent-A-Center. There are no photos, mementos, nothing of a personal nature whatsoever. Neither is there a hint of Marwyn's profession: no laptop or tablet, no periodicals, no *Wall Street Journal, Inc.*, or *Investor's Business Daily*. Sophie is bound to the eerie sensation that if she closes her eyes, she'll find herself back in the rented bungalow in Santa Monica. She starts, feeling the heat of Sunrize's body next to her, only to turn her head and see Rose standing near her.

Marwyn switches on floor lamps and lights fat candy-pink candles, two on the coffee table, another atop the bookcase. The candles are scented. The smells of sandalwood and sage fill the room. "It's not much," Marwyn says, falsely self-deprecating, "but it's home."

Rose, stepping closer, whispers in her ear, "Are we going through with this? What's the deal?"

"I need to have a look around. Keep him occupied," Sophie says—or is it Tara? In this moment of intense anxiety and confusion, neither of them can tell the one from the other, making a mockery of their bitter turf war. Whatever is happening has taken on its own shape and momentum, as mysterious to Tara as to Sophie. Something dark, something bloody, something evil.

"He clearly wants you," Rose replies.

She strokes Rose's cheek. "I'm sure you can think of something that'll take his mind off me for a couple of minutes."

Stepping away and raising her voice, she says to Marwyn, "Facilities?"

He flashes her another keen look, then smiles thinly. "Down the hall, first door on your left," he says, gesturing.

But it isn't to the bathroom Sophie goes. First, the bedroom, where she searches between mattress and box spring, behind the headboard, in the corners of all three drawers of the insubstantial-looking dresser. Behind the night table, in the shallow closet—everywhere she can think of where he might hide the ledger of his criminal enterprise.

Finding nothing, she hurries back down the hall. In the bathroom, she searches everywhere as well, even checking the shower drain to see if there is a cord or thin chain attached to the grill. Not a thing. Exasperated, she takes a last 360, double-checking to see if she has missed anything the first time. But no, damnit. No. If he is hiding the ledger here, the only other place would be the cramped space that in New York is laughably called a kitchen, containing a half-size fridge and a two-burner stovetop.

"Ah, there you are!" Marwyn is holding a tumbler of whiskey, which he is in the process of handing to Rose.

"I'll just get myself some water," Sophie says.

"I can do it," Marwyn says, taking a step toward the kitchen, but she waves him off.

It is at this moment she realizes that Tara hasn't gone to sleep as she asked but is fully with her now. No more sleep for either of them—both consciousnesses share the same body. It feels curious, though strangely not unpleasant, as it has before. What has happened to change that? Though she has absorbed all the knowledge Tara learned growing up, her understanding of human psychology is still in its infancy.

Together, they check the cabinets while pulling out a glass. Under the guise of getting ice, they peer into every corner of the half fridge. Nothing but a lemon, blue-green on one side, and a couple of bottles of beer. The stove holds nothing at all. They drink a half glass of water.

When they return to the living room, he has poured whiskey for her, hands it over. "Now let's have a toast worthy of what this night will bring."

"To women," they say, before he can go on. They lift their glasses. "To women and all the men who fuck them over."

"Ha ha!" Marwyn grins. "I think you mean 'to all the men who fuck them.'"

"Exactly," Rose breaks in. "That's exactly what she meant, right, Soph?" And she gives her newfound friend a sharp look.

"Sure," they say, a smile curling one corner of their mouth as they wink at Rose. "Exactly that."

They all taste the whiskey, Marwyn's eyes devouring her over the rim of his glass. His smile looks distorted through the refraction of the liquid. Sophie, who hates whiskey, takes only a sip.

At what point the world melts into a thickening fug they cannot say. At what point they realize that Marwyn has spiked their drinks is indeterminate. Unquestionably, both things happen—not quickly, not slowly, but at some unrecognizable pace, as if a hand reaches out from another dimension of time, grips her body in a vise, while her mind, completely unmoored, drifts out over the fog-bound sea. At one point, Tara is certain she sees the swimmer in the painting in Lind's office. The swimmer seems to be waving at her, whether in greeting or to urge her on is unclear, nor is it of any interest to Sophie—its meaning obscure— but yes, it is of keen interest to Tara.

But there is much to be shared: they both feel immensely tired, as if weighted down, as if movement is no longer possible. Together, they know they ought to be thinking of Marwyn, of what he is doing to Tara's body, but their attention is far away, completely filled by the swimmer, who is no longer afloat, but, like both of them, is sinking down into fetid darkness, about to give up.

Someone bares their breasts, someone squeezes them, making them cry out in pain. Someone pulls at their nipples, twisting them, causing more pain. Someone rucks their dress up over their buttocks. They are on their hands and knees. Marwyn, behind them, pushing their head down onto their forearms. With the ragged grunts of a wild boar in rut, he begins to penetrate them. Tara is screaming in terror. Sophie briefly tries to calm her, but she is having her own difficulties. They are being torn apart. For the first time, neither of them wants that. They try to cling to each other's persona, like orphans in a raging storm, but what is happening to their body is too violent, too monstrous. This isn't sex; it isn't even lust—this is violence, the exercise of power at its most primitive level. How horribly ugly and commonplace it all is, this assault, this debasement, endured by so many women before her. Sophie feels a curious kinship with them, this abused sisterhood. If she belongs anywhere, it is with them. But in her heart she senses that she belongs nowhere. She was set adrift long ago, and now it is too late. To go forward, to go back, it is all the same, every path a dead end. Sophie is slowly losing her grip on reality. She knows she can't allow that to happen; she has to protect Tara at all costs, but her mind is so muzzy, she can't . . . but she knows she must to save both of them . . .

In her utter despair Tara loses what is left of her will. With a stranger's eyes she sees the network of scars on the back of her hand. They seem to be an emblem, a visible marker of her sins—terrifying, inexcusable. And all the while inside her lurks the other emblem of her sins, with her since the age of five, a constant reminder, as if she has been forced to swallow a demon that is raking her insides, growling to be let out, to be set free. She thinks of Lia, sitting with one half of her face visible, as if the other half no longer exists, as if she is only half there. And now she isn't there at all. She thinks of Lia's cuttings, those awful emblems Lia mistook for an outlet, as if she could be in control of the overwhelming pain of her life. Tara can feel the real nature of the girl's cuttings in the scars on the back of her own hand. And at long last she recognizes them as the scars of self-hatred.

On the heels of that recognition comes a burst of clarity: she should give in to this assault; it is after all only what she deserves. And with that revelation some change—chemical or alchemical—occurs. Everything drains away, as if swirling down a sinkhole. She is empty, hollowed out.

Except for the damned demon. She can no longer abide its talons shredding her from the inside out. Anything is better than this. She is dying.

And into this void sweeps Sophie.

Marwyn is taking his revenge for being rebuffed in Stephen Ripley's bathroom. Rejection is not something Marwyn is used to or can tolerate. The situation is already out of control, and for the first time—and far too late—Sophie understands the real danger she is in. And with that she remembers she isn't alone. Rose lies on the floor, white throat disfigured by a ribbon of red. Her mind is screaming. Rose, what has he done to you! Slit your throat and—I got you into this. My fault! Jesus God, my fault!

No sound from Tara. With one last swing and sound of the metronome, Tara has gone; the trauma of Marwyn's assault has beaten her down.

On no account will I die, Kitten. And that means . . .

Sophie clamps her thighs together, squeezes her Kegel muscles as tight as she can, trapping him temporarily. At the same time, she uses all her strength to twist her torso. His weight falls on her so heavily she thinks he will crush her, but that is only a manifestation of the drug he has given her. How has she allowed that to happen? She wasn't paying attention, too preoccupied with trying to find his accursed ledger. Thank goodness, needing her mind clear for what she has to do, she's taken only a sip of the tainted whiskey.

"Never take your eyes off the ball," the Hypnotist told Tara as he was training her for his stage act. "Once you lose the rhythm of the act, you're lost."

I took my eyes off the ball. I fucked this up for me and for Rose, Sophie berates herself. *No more. No fucking more.*

Their limbs tangle painfully. Marwyn, initially taken by surprise by her sudden aggression, begins to fight back. She fends him off with her fists, knees, feet, but still he rains heavy blow after heavy blow on her rib cage, the pain shattering her, shards driven to all corners of her body. But now Tara's mind is emerging from the drugged fog.

Together, they kick him hard, shove him into the edge of the coffee table, which rattles, rocks, and overturns, takes two of the candles with it. The cheap carpet burns like newspaper, the flames running every which way. Marwyn lies crumpled like a paper tiger, blood drooling out of the back of his head.

In pain, pressing one hand to their bruised side, they rise to Tara's knees, look from Marwyn to Rose, crawl to their dead friend. Except Rose isn't dead; she is stirring, coughing now from the acrid smoke that is quickly filling the apartment.

Then the next swing and sound of the metronome brings Tara fully back. Kneeling beside Rose, eyes tearing, trying to take shallow breaths, they see the scarlet ribbon around her neck that their drug-addled brain interpreted as a slash of blood. A flash of the woman Marwyn brought to Stephen Ripley's party, wearing an identical scarlet choker. Putting their free hand up to Tara's throat, they feel the ribbon. With a wave of revulsion, they claw it off. Sophie stares at the room through Tara's eyes, abruptly flooded with Tara's emotion. Tara sits back down, stares at the flames, her mind racing down the rabbit hole to the fire in the farmhouse, her father trapped inside. Knowing he is there in the kitchen, stepping across the threshold, seeing him afire, wanting yet not wanting to go to him, save him, burn herself alive, not going to him. Because of what he has done, the sin he has committed. Because he deserves to be burned at the stake, an ancient punishment that in her mind, in her mother's world, seems perfectly fitting. The last moments when his eyes lock on hers, all understanding transmitted back and forth between them in the space of a contraction-expansion of the heart, his heart. Her heart. The fire destroying everything. She reaches out for him. And then . . . and then a thick curl of smoke envelops him. He makes no move, standing his ground, his fingers rigid as steel bars. The knowledge of his death there, in that spot, is clear to both of them. Then she is being grabbed from behind, lifted off her feet, back across the threshold. From outside, seeing the flaming kitchen thickly hazed, the heat, the smoke, the lack of oxygen combining to send her away, far away . . .

. . . to this moment, to another fire, in another time, in another city. Unable to handle this one, just as she was unable to handle the first one . . .

Again, the metronome swings, sounding. Sophie shrugs into her dress, then helps Rose sit up. Rose, who has taken in more of the drug-laced whiskey, is still more or less out of it.

"What happened?" Her dulled eyes keep crossing as she tries to focus.

"The apartment's on fire," Sophie says urgently. "Come on, we have to get out of here before we pass out."

Rose shakes her head, trying to clear it, which only causes a violent coughing fit. Sophie grabs her around her shoulders, brings her to her feet.

"Come on! Come on!" she implores, pushing them toward the front door.

Rose shakes her head, another explosion of coughing, and Sophie understands her mistake, pushes Rose back down onto hands and knees, where the air is cleaner and cooler by several degrees.

They crawl across the floor, which is growing hotter with each passing second. But something makes Sophie turn back at the last minute. Some anomaly. Her gaze passes over everything still visible. Something she has seen is stuck in her subconscious like a burr. Or rather Tara's subconscious has noted it. But try as Sophie might, she can't grasp the image; it keeps slipping maddeningly out of her mind's eye, like a fish. Rose is almost at the front door. The apartment glows like an evil ruby, slowly disappearing behind a wall of flames and smoke.

The Hypnotist has made sure that it is not in Sophie's persona to give up, but she is on the verge of panic and despair. As a last resort, she calls on Tara.

What have you seen, Kitten, that I can't?

No answer.

Please! And then, because all other choice is gone: *Tara, for the love of God. Help me!*

And then, as if rising from the depths, Tara does answer. Two words is all it takes for Sophie to act.

Heart hammering in her chest, she returns. The heat is terrific; her lungs feel seared, and she tries not to breathe. The bookcase is already on fire. The veneer is peeling off and, like a skinned animal, its pale flesh is exposed. Three of the paperbacks are curled, blackened, burning. Can one of them be *Breakfast at Tiffany's*? But then why would Marwyn have a Truman Capote novel unless it was *In Cold Blood*?

She approaches him in a direct line; this is no time for caution. She sees it right away.

His chain, Tara had said.

Reaching out, Sophie grabs the chain, lifts it off his chest, sees that she is holding a coke spoon, but an oddly oversize one. Tara, too, must have noted the anomaly—the spoon's size is the giveaway: What if it has a second use? What if it is something more than a means of snorting coke? No time to confirm the theory now; she has to trust Tara. She rips it off the chain and turns to go. At almost the same instant, a hand grasps her ankle. Marwyn has regained consciousness, though his eyes are moving in and out of focus.

"Bitch, you're not going anywhere." His voice, thick with smoke and phlegm, is almost unintelligible.

Sophie reaches down, tries to pry his fingers off her. The fire is creeping closer. Any moment, the bookcase will topple over, trapping them both. Slowly, inexorably, he is drawing her toward him, toward the engulfing flames. Above her, the cracking of splintering wood. The bookcase is about to go.

Dimly, she hears Rose calling to her. Twisting like a contortionist, she bites down hard on Marwyn's wrist, pulling away skin, flesh, tendons, and veins. Blood spurts like a fountain. His mouth opens wide, making a sound she can't hear for the excitable roar of the flames. One by one, as quickly as she is able, she unwinds his fingers from her ankle.

That desperate effort uses up Sophie's last bit of strength. She tries to crawl away but too soon comes to a numbed halt, her head hanging down onto her chest. She is so close to passing out, so close to dropping into the hot, crackling abyss.

Then she feels Rose's arms around her, pulling her away from the conflagration. Inch by inch, Rose pulls her toward the door. Then her strength, too, gives out.

But they reach the coatrack beside the door, and she grabs her coat. She snatches at Rose's jacket, but misses. It crumples to the floor, and she leaves it. No time, no time. The doorknob is so hot Sophie snatches her hand away, crying out. A gust of smoke covers them, swirling, turning everything around them into darkened blurs. Wrapping her reddened hand in her coat, she twists the knob; the door opens, and they fairly fall across the threshold, crawling now slowly, it seems, as snails.

A thin streak of flame rides Rose's back, and Sophie spreads her coat, presses her own exhausted body over it, smothering the fire. Smoke envelops them. It is hellishly hot in the hallway. They are roasting to death.

"Rose? Rose?"

Spots dance before her eyes; she feels herself spiraling away. She wants to drag Rose, drag herself down the stairs, but she can't seem to move. All volition has fled her. Excruciating pain lances through her limbs, her body, her head, as though a bullet has split into pieces on impact with her center. She is utterly spent, a deer bleeding to death in the forest.

Sirens rise, proliferating like Christmas tree lights. Nearer to hand the shouted instructions of one man to another, the heavy tramp of shoes in the stairwell, and a familiar voice, Philip Morris's voice, calling her name over and over. He seems far away, in another room, another building, another block, another part of a city on fire.

Maybe she dreams it, because right then something large and heavy slams into her head, driving her into blackness.

PART 5
DEVIL WENT DOWN

My Father's house has many rooms; if that were not so,
would I have told you that I am going there to prepare a
place for you?

—John 14:2

I used to think of my memory as a gateway drug, something to be avoided at all costs, for it could only lead me into the darkness of shame and guilt. But that was before. Now I realize that my memory is a closet without hangers. It has hooks, though. A lot of those hooks are bare, but on fifteen of them a postcard precariously hangs.

I wanted never to look at them. Now I know that I must.

TARA

GEORGIA—FROM FIVE TO EIGHTEEN

Postcard 1

We live in a posttruth world, and I'm a product of it.

I mean, what's the point of the truth, anyway? You tell people the truth; they don't believe you. You lie to them, and they believe that lie. In fact, the more outlandish the lie, the more fervently they believe you.

This has been true forever. "People believe what they want to believe," was the first lesson my mother taught me. The first lesson my father taught me was that people *want* to give you their trust. "Remember this," he told me, "and you will never go wrong." Applying those two principles allowed my parents to survive and thrive. Trust was their métier. The manipulation of trust was their livelihood. In this, if in nothing else, they were kindred spirits. They did not have to read Nietzsche (as I did in Chicago, along with Hegel and Kant, the two other pillars of the nineteenth-century German philosophical psychodrama) to understand his philosophy and put it to work. "All things are subject to interpretation; whichever interpretation prevails at a given time is a function of power and not truth." They both knew that; it was instinctive in them. It was what brought them together, bound them, and eventually killed them.

So this is the way it goes. Or, anyway, the way it went:

The past never dies, sort of like a vampire. And like a vampire it sucks at you and sucks at you, trying to drain you of every bit of life. There are as many misconceptions about hypnotism as there are about vampirism. Of course vampirism is a myth, but the majority of people are under the impression that hypnotism is a myth, which is unsurprising. By and large, hypnotism is the dominion of charlatans, sleight-of-hand magicians, and con artists. Then there are the doctors who purport to know all about it. Their mistake is believing hypnotism is a science. It isn't. It's a gift, a primitive way of seeing the world—the real world, as my father called it.

According to him, hypnotism was a shamanistic tool, old as deserts, ancient as oceans. Who was I to disbelieve him?

My mother was a powerful woman. While my father went about fixing up the beat-up farm in southwest Georgia, my mother established herself as a preacher of note who spoke in tongues, freed people from their sins, and ousted evil through her particular form of exorcism. Soon enough, her fame had spread throughout the area. Both my parents had changed their names the moment they settled in Georgia to keep from being found by the church they had stolen and fled from. And not long after she erected her first tent (soon outgrown!), her devoted followers swore to protect her from everyone and every institution that might seek to bring her down. Maybe to distinguish herself from other evangelists, she made exorcisms her specialty, or maybe she really did have the gift. Whether the exorcisms worked, I couldn't say. But they did appear to, which, in religion, is the same thing. Once she had her own televangelist TV channel, she was untouchable.

My mother raked in the coin from such a burgeoning enterprise, but as fast as it came in, it went out due to my father's gambling. No Cadillacs or fancy houses, no expensive wardrobes, powerboats, or vacations for us, not that my mother wanted any of those things. My education at the local Catholic school and her ministry were the only things she cared about. Nevertheless, they fought bitterly over money: her earnings he gambled away; his own earnings he squandered on young women of ill repute.

My parents' families are shrouded in mystery: where they were, who they were, even where my parents were born and brought up. Neither ever spoke of their pasts beyond Salt Lake. There were no photos of families grouped together, staring into an old camera lens.

Nothing.

Postcard 2

My father had the eyes of a wolf. They were a striking gold color, with flecks of gray and red in them. They were eyes to get lost in. He was tall, thin as a whip, with a heap of black hair that came down to a widow's peak. My mother was herself striking, with high cheekbones, wide mouth, and full lips.

My father met my mother not at the church but at the county fair outside Salt Lake City. He was manning one of those pitching games where if you throw a ball into one of a dozen pails, you get a stuffed animal. It's not as easy as it looks, take it from me. But no one was as bad as my mother. The first ball she threw struck my father in the forehead. Afterward, he took her out for soda pop and funnel cake, and after that, he took her back to where he worked, pitched a ball right into the center pail, and gave her the prize: a white unicorn. I remember that unicorn well. It lived up in the attic, coated with spiderwebs, cedar chips, and the dust of ages. But that was years later. Back then, the evening they met, my father took my mother behind the ball toss, crushed her lips with his mouth, felt her up, and braced her against a tent pole. They made violent love, while the unicorn looked silently on.

My mother's name was Norma Jean; her father, who died long before I was conceived, was a big Marilyn Monroe fan. But so ignorant were he and his wife that they misspelled Jean, which should have had an *e* on the end of it. No matter. My mother despised her name; she never used it. Her friends called her Jeannie or, for some reason, Stella. I never did find out why. My father said he didn't know; maybe he didn't care. But at times my mother made me call her Stella. I didn't mind. At the time, I didn't understand. Though even if I had, I was a child in a household ruled by the wrath of God. What could I do?

Both my parents possessed what the English call *glamour*, from which the American word *glamorous* is derived. But as I learned much later during my studies in Chicago, *glamour* has a different meaning. *Charisma* comes closest but still falls short. There's a mystical element to glamour, and whatever it is, both my parents had it in spades.

But theirs was a dark glamour. It worked its way beneath the skin into people's psyches. Glamour helped them forge their new identities. The burgeoning number of my mother's worshippers helped them elude the consequences of their misdeeds. The black seed money my father stole went faster than they could have imagined, and by the time they arrived in Georgia and settled on Grandfather's farm, they were broke. But Grandfather's presence and escalating medical needs precluded my father taking the risks inherent in further theft. Besides, by then my mother had found God. "The true God," in her Sermon on the Mount words. "God as Savior, God as the Great Rectifier, the God Who Speaks through Me."

Under that tent, my mother loved God more than she loved us. But her vision of God was unaccountably vengeful—more vengeful by far than the God of the Old Testament. That lens through which she viewed the world distorted everything around her, and in the end, it destroyed her relationship with my father.

My mother didn't see herself as extreme. She believed herself to be rooted firmly in the center of charismatic Christianity, of which the evangelical movement was a part. She, and therefore her ministry, believed in the so-called foursquare gospel, the four fundamental beliefs of Pentecostalism: Jesus saves (John 3:16); Jesus baptizes with the Holy Spirit (Acts 2:4); Jesus heals the body (James 5:15); Jesus is coming again to receive those who are saved (1 Thessalonians 4:16–17). "Only through the death, burial, and resurrection of Jesus Christ," my mother preached to her avid flock, "may your sins be forgiven and humanity be reconciled with God."

———

As soon as she judged me of age—seven years old, "the magic age," she called it—my mother took me to what she called the Tent of God's Love. Possibly she did this to keep me from taking the stage at my father's show on the Sabbath, although she told me it was to keep me purified and sanctified through the healing of Jesus.

Inside, the tent seemed much larger than it did from the outside. It was always packed and smelled of sweat and anxiety. Often, these were times of exorcisms. The one I remember went this way:

My mother standing on the stage, bathed in spotlights, arms spread wide, looking larger than life, would call out: "In the name of Jesus and Saint Michael, the holy protector, slayer of foul beasts and demonic dragons, I call upon those who hear voices—voices from below—the grunting of infernal beasts, the scratching of the red-eyed rats that infest the portals to hell."

She looked across the assembled multitudes, her eyes blazing. "Who among you has been tempted into sin and immoral, ungodly acts by the Jezebel spirit?"

After some prodding by her neighbors, a woman who looked to be young to my child's eyes stood up. She was white as cheese, wearing a plain shift, blue eyed, with long, lank hair parted in the middle. She said her name was Katy Myers. She trembled terribly. My mother's gaze fell on her immediately. "Tell me, then, sister."

"I . . . I have been led into sin," Katy said, becoming increasingly agitated.

"What sin, sister?" my mother cried.

Katy looked around wildly, as if she wanted to escape. She began to moan piteously.

"Speak up, sister!" my mother cried. "Jesus needs to hear you!"

Katy started, as if pricked with a needle. "I have fornicated with unnamed men," Katy said with a bit more strength. "Sometimes three or four a night."

"And when you fornicate with these men, do you hear the infernal beasts, the noises they make from below?"

"Yes," Katy shouted, gaining strength from my mother's expanding glamour. "I do."

"Then come!" My mother beckoned. "By Jesus Christ and all that is holy, you are possessed by the Jezebel spirit! Come forth and be freed! Come and be released from your servitude to Satan! Come here and let the loving light of Jesus Christ enter you!"

Katy almost stumbled as she climbed the wood steps to the stage, but no one moved to assist her. No one dared touch someone possessed, for fear of succumbing to the filth of immorality, of being possessed themselves by the Jezebel spirit.

"We see you, Jezebel spirit!" my mother cried, beginning to work herself up into a frenzy. "You stand before us, revealed and known in the sight of Jesus Christ!"

I watched, wide eyed, rapt but terrified out of my skull as Katy began to twitch, as if she had a python under her shift. Her nose started to bleed. She bared her teeth and growled like, I don't know, maybe a wolf, or maybe something else altogether. Something inhuman, anyway. Her eyes were shut tight, as if the lids had been sewn together, but beneath them her eyeballs were rolling wildly, distending the lids.

My mother lifted one arm on high. "Jezebel spirit, you have entered holy ground! You are in the province of Jesus Christ and God himself!" My mother's arm moved above Katy; her fingers looked like they were grabbing something out of thin air. "The flaming sword of Saint Michael is raised above you! It is about to smite you!" The fingers curled into a fist. "To send you all the way back to the hell that spawned you and your demonic kind!"

Katy began to spasm more strongly, like a marionette whose strings were being pulled by a madman. My mother placed her fist atop her head. "Can you feel it, Jezebel spirit?" She drew a handful of Katy's dank hair into her fist and pulled upward until Katy was standing on her tiptoes. She was quivering with whatever she was channeling. "Can you feel the power of Jesus Christ running through Saint Michael's flaming sword as it presses down on you? Immobilizing you?" At once, sweat broke out along Katy's forehead and upper lip. "The divine heat is upon you! Jezebel spirit, hear my voice! Feel the power of Jesus Christ!" Katy's spasming stopped. But now her lids flew open and, as one, the assembled gasped. Her eyes were coated with a thick yellow film that seemed to pulse with a life of its own.

Someone in the crowd moaned loudly. Someone else fainted. My mother was oblivious to both; her concentration was solely on the woman or, if seeing was believing, the Jezebel spirt within.

"Carry our prayers up to God's throne," my mother cried at the top of her voice, "that the mercy of the Lord may quickly come and lay hold of this beast, the servant of the serpent of old, Satan, encasing the Jezebel spirit in chains of iron and brass, casting the Jezebel spirit into the abyss, where it belongs."

My mother pulled harder so that Katy rose off her tiptoes, as if my mother were holding her aloft with the power that radiated out from her.

"Out, Jezebel spirit!" she called. "Out, I say, in the name of Jesus Christ, in the name of Saint Michael, the protector of the righteous and the holy! In the name of God Almighty!"

She turned the woman from facing outward, toward her. "Your hold is loosened! Jezebel spirit, your name is known to us! You will free her! You no longer have domain over our sister! Out, out! Your power is gone! I have bound you! I have chained you! I have drained you of your power and your influence over this woman. Out! Out! Your power is broken! Saint Michael's holy sword has unmade you! Out! Out, I say! Down you go, Jezebel spirit, back into the abyss of hell!"

At that moment, my mother let go of Katy's hair. At once, she collapsed like a rag doll. An audible exhalation arose from the assembled. My mother made a signal, and two of her stagehands came and drew Katy to her feet. The moment my mother wrapped her arm around Katy's waist, they stepped back, retreated to the wings, where I stood transfixed with a kind of electrified horror. I could scarcely breathe. I felt overwhelmed, inundated by the unknown, stunned into immobility.

My mother turned Katy to face the congregation. "Sister," she said, "open your eyes."

And Katy did, blinking as if she had just emerged from the deepest darkness. The spasms were gone, as was the film over her eyes.

"Sister, can you hear me?"

"Yes."

My mother wiped the blood from her nostrils and upper lip. "Do you know where you are?"

Katy nodded. "I do." She appeared normal in her movements and in her responses.

"You are among friends, sister. You are surrounded by our love. You are bathed in God's loving light. Can you feel it, sister? Can you feel God's loving light flooding you, warming you?"

"I do," Katy said. A smile broke out across her face.

"Do you hear voices? Do you feel the Jezebel spirit moving in you?"

Katy shook her head. "No." Her blue eyes opened wider. Color rushed to her cheeks. "I . . . I'm free! Praise God! It's a miracle!"

"Yes, sister! Let all of us lift up our voices in praise of God and his son, Jesus Christ! You are saved, sister! The miracle of the love of Jesus Christ, our Savior, fills you as it fills every single one of my celebrants gathered around you!"

Katy turned, threw herself into my mother's arms, weeping openly as the congregation as one rose to its feet with a roar of approval.

It was a long time dying out, but when it did, my mother, holding Katy's hand in hers, led her ecstatic flock in one last prayer.

———

My mother never asked me what I thought of the exorcism. She was uninterested in the effect it may have had on me. To her, it was just part of her ministry; she saw nothing unusual about it, or, if she did, she certainly wouldn't share that with her seven-year-old daughter. Nor did she when I was older, and I, pushing it into the farthest recesses of my mind, lacked the fortitude to confront it again. Because of her power reverberating like an endless echo. Eventually, I came to understand her hold over my father, even through all the bitterness and violence of their late-night fights.

———

The money from my mother's evangelical hellfire-and-brimstone act, which she insisted be called "contributions to the love of Jesus Christ," were in fact donations from people she called "celebrants," people desperate for answers to questions that had no answers. It's true that so far as I knew, the bulk of the donations went back into bigger and bigger tents, better sound and light systems, more assistants. And then there was the cost of her show on the local TV station—sets and wardrobe and makeup. What was left for us after those expenses was gambled away by my father. My father was forever dreaming of a lavish life, even though my mother often repeated that a lavish life was for sinners.

"Never say you're sorry," he once told me. "Never admit you were wrong." That sounded like something a lawyer would tell you. My father was no lawyer, but he knew how to stay a step ahead of every-one, including the law.

He was a thief, an embezzler, a magnificent liar, an inveterate gam-bler. He was also a weak man, a coward. I loved him all the same. Until, standing on the threshold of the fire, seeing him in the fierce glare, a different light, I didn't. His profession was a movable feast: wherever he was, the magic happened. And me an integral part of it. My mother didn't like him using me; she was very vocal about that. She was so protective of me, her only child, her daughter. "You're my gift," she'd tell me late at night. "God gave you to me, not to your father. You're *my* child, remember that always." Screaming matches on an epic scale erupted because of me. I heard their strident voices through the wall, escalating up a mysterious scale; sometimes the house seemed to vibrate with them. Then in the aftermath, I'd open my door, stand in my doorway, leaning forward, listening intently. I heard plenty: it was like a pair of raccoons had eaten through the walls and were fighting over the spoils.

To my mother, hypnotism was an instrument of the devil, and she was intent on saving me from it. This was her opinion and, therefore, the truth. She believed that my father must be a charlatan. She claimed God told her he was gambling and taking his sexual pleasure from a coterie of his female patsies, who flocked to him like groupies, whenever and wherever the mood struck him. Which was kind of amusing, when you think about it, being as how she was in the "gray magic" busi-ness: taking in people's money, not to mention their trust, for helping them believe in the impossible. Her dark glamour allowed her to take advantage of the endless cupidity of people. It was through this dark glamour that doubtless one or another of her celebrants told her about my father's transgressions. God had nothing to do with it.

Postcard 3

The clapboard farmhouse my parents finally settled into had been painted canary yellow, once upon a time. But over the years the wind and sun and rain had scoured it to the color of the hour before dawn. It hunkered, shivering in winter, sweating in summer, on the edge of a burnt-out field that seemed to stretch for miles when I was a child, but surely didn't.

I used to wonder what had grown there, once upon a time. Now there was the old barn and the many-roomed farmhouse that sheltered us as best it could between its sloped sharp shoulder blades. The barn out back housed a roan quarter horse by the name of Miss Molly. She'd been my grandfather's. Miss Molly was the name I'd given her; my grandfather had named her after my grandmother, but her Inuit name was impossible for me to pronounce. When I was five, I learned to ride her and feed her and brush her, and she liked me best. There was also a weather-beaten henhouse my grandfather built, with a dozen egg layers I took care of when my father was too busy or away on one of his tours.

Our living room was dominated by a deep-cushioned sofa where I liked to curl up in the evenings after dinner. Above it, affixed to the wall, was a painting of Christ on the cross my mother had commissioned from a portraitist of note. Just below Jesus's feet, my mother had commanded the artist to paint, **I COMMIT MYSELF TO YOU, O GOD. IN MY LIVING AND IN MY DYING.**

In the short hallway between the living room and the kitchen, Norma Jean's prized Bible, oversize and thick as a brick, lay open on a handmade walnut stand one of her converts, a carpenter by trade, had lovingly made for her. She swore she woke up each morning with a specific Bible verse in her head, which she took as a sure sign from God, to use at the day's revival. Right next to that sacred object was the profane, so far as Norma Jean was concerned: a big color TV she had purchased, vanity overcoming her zealotry, so we could all partake of her thrice-weekly shows. It was always on, tuned to the regional station that carried Norma Jean's taped ministry night and day, like the weather or, in those parts, crop prices for corn, soybeans, and lean hogs.

There was a big overstuffed sofa, too, the floral fabric covered with fringes at its bottom, as if it were an old-timey shay that might take us out on a Sunday after church. Next to the sofa was a monster radio Grandfather kept fiddling with, as if trying to find a wavelength that no longer existed, if it ever had. Maybe he thought it would give him holy instructions on how to regain his eyesight.

The worst part of the downstairs, by far, was the dining room table. It was polished walnut and as homely as a fat woman with tree-stump legs. But it was immense, I'll say that for it. Too large for this family, anyway. You'd need, what, ten more kids, and there'd still be room left over at the far end for the in-laws you couldn't abide.

In most households, dinner would be the major meal of the day. Not so for the Pearys. More often than not J. M. was off evenings hypnotizing half the county, gambling and whoring every chance he got, and getting well remunerated for his particular brand of psychological sleight of hand, but of course, he never brought much home, if anything. And as for Norma Jean, she would wolf down a slice of cold chicken or, if there wasn't any lying around, a couple of tablespoons of baked beans straight from the can. She was never much for food.

Postcard 4

In my father's study were two shelves of books. Of God and his disciples there was no sign. Nothing from Thomas Aquinas or Cusanus, Jerome or Saint Paul. Neither were there texts on the histories of the con game, the stage magician, or sleight of hand. Instead, there was book after book on investigations into the history and customs of world shamanism, the hand-bound journals of actual shamans, as well as a curious slim volume on the application of mathematical principles to shamanism, all of which I found fascinating.

As it turns out, there are 110 to 140 beats per minute to trance music. There are also, it turns out, 110 to 140 beats per minute to the drumming shamans have used since time immemorial to induce the deep altered state of consciousness used to peer into the future or cast spells. In both, the aim of the repeated tempo is to bring about a change in the brainwaves of the shaman or the person seeking the shaman's help.

In my case, when I was but five years old, the shaman came to me.

He had no shape, this shaman, merely a shadow that pulsed to the beat of my father's metronome. The shaman lived behind my closed eyes. He spoke to me in my father's voice. I didn't think he was actually my father, though; he sounded very old and very tired and very wise.

"You're in water," the shaman said. "Warm water that closes over your head. Warm water into which you sink, into a calm and peaceful place where the only sound you hear is the lapping of the waves."

The metronome swings, sounds.

"That sound is my voice. You are lying on your back in the place between the shore and the sea. You are part of both. The shore and the sea."

The metronome swings, sounds.

"You look up, and there is the sun: my voice. You look up, and there are the clouds: my voice. Now the sea and the sky."

The metronome swings, sounds.

"The sea and the sky. There is no land, only the sea on which you rest and the sky above your head. Sea and sky: my voice. You float on my voice. You relax into my voice."

The metronome swings, sounds.

"You are my voice."

The metronome swings, sounds.

"My voice speaks to your skin, your flesh, your muscles, your kidneys, liver, heart. My voice seeps into your bones. My voice becomes your bones."

The metronome swings, sounds.

"My voice lives within you, rising and falling like the tides, rising and falling like the sun, rising and falling like the moon. My voice is the sky, and you are under it; you are of it."

The metronome swings, sounds.

"We are one."

———

My father first brought me onstage when I was seven. So began the escalation in the cold war between my parents. For the first two years, until I was nine, my father stepped into the spotlights with me in his arms, setting me down center stage. I wore taffeta and lace dresses he bought for me without my mother's knowledge. Later on, when I was eleven or so, my body already between prepubescence and adulthood, my outfits changed to short pleated skirts, cap-sleeve tops, knee-high socks, and black patent leather Mary Janes. I liked the Mary Janes best; they made me feel quite grown up. And as my breasts budded, my hips widened, and my legs grew shapely, they provided me with a certain self-image that seemed like armor, a kind of protection.

My "outfits," as my father termed them, were never allowed in the house or anywhere near it. They were a secret from my mother, a sacred vow we made together by twining pinkies. He had a series of lockers in the bus station where all his hypnotist's gear—including my outfits—were kept.

It was like the two of us entered a second, secret life the moment we stepped out the front door and drove to the station. There, with his help, I would change clothes in the last stall by the window of the men's room. Then I held as still as possible while he applied rouge to my cheeks and kohl on my upper eyelids, and painted my lips cherry red. He brushed my hair till it shone, drew it back into a ponytail, held by a scrunchie. Then we would drive to wherever his act was playing, always in another county, far away from my mother's ministry.

This could be a theater, a country music venue, bar, or roadhouse. Several times we took our act to strip clubs with names like In the Pink, Forbidden Dreams, and Strokers Lounge. All the audiences were rowdy, especially at the strippers. But my father assured me silence reigned as soon as he hypnotized me. I was an unqualified star, he assured me. When I was older—twelve or thirteen, maybe—and he brought me out of the trance, I'd find a whole bunch of men crowding the front of the stage, holding out one- and five-dollar bills, flapping them urgently, their gazes hungrily drinking me in, until I took them. I had no idea why they were offering me money. When I'd ask my father later on the way home, he'd just shrug and say, "I told you, Kitten. You're a star."

Whether they were theaters, bars, roadhouses, or strip clubs, they had several things in common: they were crowded, mostly with men; they were overheated; and they smelled of liquor, cigar smoke, and sweat. The few women I saw were always on a man's arm, leaning in, nibbling on her escort's ear, or sitting on his lap, facing him. Toward the end of the night, the atmosphere was so thick it seemed you'd need a skinning knife to cut through it.

Once, when I was about eleven, we stayed at Forbidden Dreams, which we had been booked into with increasing frequency, to watch the main act, a platinum blonde named Saint Cyr with a beauty mark riding her left cheek and the longest legs I'd ever seen on a human being. The climax of her act went like this: An enormous champagne glass was wheeled out onto center stage. Her amazing legs rose from within it amid an eruption of bubbles—soap, I guessed, from the scent. The bubbles shimmered as she shimmied up, completely naked, and began her snaky dance. Afterward, my father left me with the stage manager, who bought me a bottle of soda and sat with me as the dancers came and went around me. After about an hour, my father reappeared, running his hands through his hair and tucking in his shirt.

He grinned at me as he came up. "How's tricks, Kitten?"

"Super," I said, not knowing what he meant or why I answered as I did.

———

Sophie was born of necessity. My father told me, "It's the least I can do." He said, "It's also the most I can do." He said, "You're too young to understand this, but I can't help myself. I'm a prisoner of my own desire." He looked away at his shelf of books, then into my face. "What else can I do, Tara?" He knew what else he could do, but it took him years to gin up his courage. "This is all I can do." To give him his due, it was more than most could even imagine, let alone attempt.

And then afterward, the insistent beat still rang in my ears, pin-balling through my head, changing my emotions, settling over me like grains of sand, keeping me hidden from everything, including—especially—my self. My father's voice insistent, the tempo: "You must promise me one thing, Kitten. What we do here, you and I, must be our secret." He held me by my shoulders, looked me straight in the eye. "You must never, ever tell anyone. You must most especially not tell your mother. This is very, very important." His fingers gripped me down to the bone. "Promise me that you understand."

I didn't understand. Of course I didn't. What five-year-old would? "I promise," I said obediently, knowing that I would never break my promise to my father. I knew that. With the gift of hindsight I know he knew.

He also said, "I pray to God that one day you will forgive me."

That day still hasn't come.

Postcard 5

Our dog, Hickory, had a white patch between his eyes. It was more or less the shape of a diamond—on a horse it would be called a blaze. The rest of him was the color of, well, a hickory tree. Except for his feet. He had white boots my mother always made me clean off—mud and wet leaves and such—before she'd let Hickory back into the house. It was always me who got that job. I didn't mind; I adored Hickory.

My father brought Hickory home one slate-gray afternoon. He said he'd gotten him from a client who couldn't afford to pay him in cash, but my mother was dead certain he'd won the pup in a poker game.

"The one time you win, this is what you bring home?" she berated him, and in a way she was right.

Not surprisingly, my mother took an instant dislike to Hickory. She complained that it was another mouth to feed. To her, Hickory was a symbol of everything she found contemptible in my father. But I suspect there was more to her antipathy than that. To tell you the truth, she didn't like any animal; I think she was scared of them on account of her being sure they had no soul. I disagreed with her on that, though I was clever enough never to tell her so. It was never a good idea to argue with her—I'd learned that from eavesdropping on my parents' screaming matches about freedom, God, gambling, using me in his act like a "godless performing monkey," as she said. (And it was true: he'd hypnotize me onstage or in mansion parlors, and I'd never remember what he ordered me to do; he'd never tell me either.) But mostly about my father's "serial fornication," as my mother termed it.

"It's a sickness," she shouted. "An illness without a cure." Her voice rose and fell, rose and fell, in some kind of dreadful rhythm. "I know what it is you do, the fornication you refuse to curb, the women you lie with and then discard like so much rubbish. God alone knows what perversions you get up to with them."

"Every last thing you refuse me," my father replied.

I heard a quick snap, like a branch breaking, and knew she had slapped him hard.

"Like that," he said, his voice momentarily mocking. "Just like that."

"As God is my witness," my mother cried, "if I find that you have ever touched my little girl, I will horsewhip you to within an inch of your life." I winced; I think I cried because I had no doubt she would too. "Your continuing despicable behavior is shaming me before God. I pray every night for his forgiveness, for not turning you out, for not sending you into the darkness of your own creation."

"But you won't," he said. "You can't. Your private life must remain sacrosanct, pure, perfect for the sake of your ministry."

"Your reputation—"

"Is nothing compared to yours. No one pays attention to me. I'm the jester, the fool, the performing monkey."

"And that's your life," my mother said bitterly.

"At least I have my freedom. At least I know what freedom really is. Unlike you. Your idea of freedom is bending the knee to God's will, but only when it serves your purpose. I may be a philanderer, but you're a hypocrite. And you drove me to it. You and your God, who does your bidding, not the other way around. You're like all the other people who control religion, perverting God's will into your will."

"Stop! Stop! Your lies disgust me."

"That's because you're blind to your own failings."

Which loosed a spate of hateful invective I never could have imagined coming out of my mother's mouth—my mother who loved me, who comforted me and held me. "What a spiteful whoreson you are!" she screamed. "Worse, you're selfish! And believe me, there is no greater sin than selfishness." Thereby cementing her position as both spiteful and selfish. She was strong. Too strong for him.

After a time the screaming matches faded into my memory. My father gave up. Sort of.

Postcard 6

Right away Hickory became my dog. Mine and Sophie's, of course. We fed him, brushed him, hugged him. On sticky summer nights I took him to the pond, playing in the water to cool him off. On cold nights we'd sit by the fire with him dozing beside us. I loved to scratch his favorite spot, behind his ears. They twitched, those ears, whenever my mother passed by, as if even in dreams he was aware of her.

Postcard 7

It was April the third. I was eight years old. In the illusory light between dawn and morning. I could hear the cock crowing, the hens discussing the day's first news around their pent-in part of the yard. My father had doubled the thickness of the chicken wire and dug it down to a depth of three feet to stop foxes burrowing under it, making a bloody mess and terrifying the hens they didn't eat. The ones left alive were so stressed they stopped laying. I had come out to check on them, to reassure them, I guess.

I heard the horses whinnying, and I saw Hickory lit up by the barn's slatted light. He was inside Miss Molly's stall, and then he started barking—the noise half-angry, half-frightened—and as I ran in, I saw Miss Molly backed up against a corner, bridling and kicking. Her eyes were showing their whites, and terror had them rolling in their sockets. I crossed the stall, but so far as I could see, there was only a pile of hay and the galvanized metal pail I used to feed Miss Molly her oats.

I reached out to soothe her, but Hickory slammed me aside, and I went tumbling, crying out. It was then I heard it, the dry rattle like death in an old lady's throat. I saw the rattlesnake's flat head, shiny pin-dot eyes as Hickory's jaws clamped down on its body. Hickory shook it violently, keeping it away from me. It was very long, a western diamondback, the most dangerous of the venomous snakes in Georgia.

And then my father appeared. The sleeves of his heavy work shirt were rolled up, his forearms bare, the muscles bunched like steel cables amid black hairs that stood up just like the rattler's tail.

My father got right in the rattler's face. He stamped his foot, and the rattler's head darted out, mouth open, and sank its fangs into the meat of his hand. I wanted to shriek, but the sound got stuck in my throat. I thought I was going to be sick.

My father gripped the rattler by the back of its head as if nothing awful had happened. He gave a sharp command, and Hickory let go of the snake, backed away, and came to my side, sitting between me and the rattler. His teeth were bared, and he was growling deep in his throat.

My father was so confident, so methodical as he extricated his hand. I saw the two marks the snake's fangs had made, but there was no blood, no swelling of the wound as we'd been told in school there should be. No first aid for him, no antivenin. Instead, he took the rattler out of the stall to another part of the barn. He had set up a work space for himself; I'd seen half a dozen snake rattles, dried and preserved with lacquer, nailed to the wall boards.

"Tara," he said, "you and Hickory calm that horse of yours down. And mind you keep Hickory away from her hooves. She's still terrified, poor thing."

I stepped over to Miss Molly's stall, moving slowly and carefully, the way you're meant to when a horse is riled up. Miss Molly's eyes were still wide and staring, but her nostrils flared as she scented me. She didn't rear up. Her ears twitched; she heard me talking to her softly, crooning as Sophie did with me when she came to me.

With Miss Molly quieted, I knelt down beside Hickory. When I ran my fingers through his fur, he turned his head to me. I put my arm around him, laid my cheek against his, murmured, "Good boy. You saved my life. Everything's all right now." And it was. It turned out my father was immune to rattlesnake venom.

Postcard 8

"It's a contemptible example of a woman whose desire overcomes her, who only wants to be loved," my mother said, as she went about the business of making herself into the presence other people recognized: the fiery shepherd of Christ Almighty who guides her wayward flock to the gates of paradise. It was July, nine days shy of my eleventh birthday. Sophie was nine days shy of her eleventh birthday, too, even though she came when I was five. My mother didn't know about Sophie; she could never know. Not ever. She wouldn't understand. Not ever. And it would spoil everything.

My mother sat before the great oak mirror that rose, an amazing all-seeing eye, from her dressing table. The table's tiger-oak stripes mimicked the shadows of winter, seemed to bulge and ripple in the morning's low sunlight, as if still belonging to a living thing. And forever afterward I would think of them as an extension of her.

"Love, darling girl, isn't everything," my mother continued. "In fact, it's nothing but an illusion. An illusion that leads to lust, debauchery, the abyss of hell."

We were in what she called her "gettin'-ready nook." It was painted a creamy yellow, unfaded by time. It was smaller than the bedroom I shared with Sophie but larger than a closet. I had just brought her the herbal tea she loved, called Rockin' Robin, in the huge mug that was hers and hers alone.

"A parent's love for her children is a different matter, of course," she said, as I handed her a tube of mascara. "*That* is a pure form of love—the only one." Magically, one eye grew larger with the application of kohl, then the other. "God blesses the love of a parent for her children, darling girl, just as I have for you. That form of love is holy, sacrosanct, blessed." Was she aware that she'd repeated *blessed*? Probably so, since repetition of certain words in her orations served her purpose. In my father's performances as well, oddly enough.

She tipped the mug to her lips, sipped as daintily as a sparrow. On the wall was a photo of her parents. A tiny version of my mother half hid in the crinoline of Gramma's ankle-length skirts. Grampa wore a black suit and hat, both slightly battered. His suit jacket was streaked with the chalky stuff he had to dig through to plant the crops that, year after year, failed. There was no expression on either's face: that blank stare attached to people forced to stand in front of an unfamiliar and unfathomable device. The more you stared at that blankness, though, the more you could sense the fear they were holding in check. Fear of what? Heaven only knew. Life, maybe. These were people I had never known, so their lives, formed out of the few photos and stories my mother told me, took on the aspect of myth.

She set the mug down and cradled me in her arms, kissed my cheeks, the crown of my head. Filling herself with the sweet scent of my hair, newly washed, brush stroked. "The love in this house keeps us safe from the wickedness of the outside world. It's an inoculation—do you know that word, darling girl?" She rushed on, heedless. "An inoculation against the predations facing you as you grow into womanhood."

The house was stiff with frost, heavy with guilt. Icicles hung from the eaves, guilt from the light fixtures. Both did their share to obscure the daylight.

When, thirty minutes after she sat down, my mother rose, she was no longer recognizable as the woman who cooked us dinner, who read the Bible to us in her rocking chair, who, dressed in her flowing nightgown, slept on the other side of the marital bed from my father.

She had managed to make herself into a creature of pearly skin and blue-white bones. Her cheeks were sunken; there were blue-black rings around her eyes. Her long, thick chestnut hair was streaked with talc. The best part, though, was how she applied lipstick the precise color of her lips, which made them a focal point without giving away that they had been painted, as if this was their natural state. All in all, she looked twenty years older and, at the same time—of course this was the point—ageless.

"And so." Turning to me, long slender fingers wrapping my shoulders in a protective grip, she delivered her loving summation. "Giving yourself to someone—anyone—before marriage is a sin. It's to be avoided at all costs. Giving yourself—your *self*"—she enunciated carefully—"away will only bring you low, make you despicable. Useless, you will be cast out of God's sight, into the wilderness of eternal shadow, where you will wander all the days of your life."

Then a smile broke over her face like the sun burning through fog. "You're my special girl. Who loves you more than I do?"

"No one, Mama," I said dutifully, for this was a ritual we performed daily.

"That's right, darling girl." She squeezed me. "No one."

Then, with a swish of her white-and-gold robe, she was off to guide her sinning flock back into the pure-white dazzle of, in my mother's fiery words, "Christ's loving light."

Afterward, I thought long and hard about the sin of sex before marriage, what my father had told me about their first meeting. Had they had intercourse that night at the county fair, maybe several times? One of my parents was lying to me. Which one was it?

Postcard 9

Then there was Eve, a girl my age, part of the Davie clan that owned the farm closest to ours. There was our school, Our Lady of Perpetual Rage. That wasn't its real name, of course, but that's what I called it, and that's how I remember it. When I was young, my father used to drive me every morning, even though he'd sometimes be hungover. One of my classmate's parents would take me back home afterward, or if I was at the library studying late, my father would come get me. But one Christmas morning when I was eight, a shiny new fire-engine red Schwinn was waiting for me under the tinseled tree. It took me less than a day to learn to ride it, and from then on I had my own transportation.

The school was infested with nuns, mainly because they ran the place. There was no other religious school in the area; the nearest Christian school was in West Memphis, so even though it was Catholic, that's where I went, and so did Eve. At some point, my mother had tried to get a Christian school going, but she ran into too many roadblocks.

The nuns purported to teach us reading, writing, arithmetic, and history but in fact shoveled a Christ-based curriculum down our throats as if we were geese whose livers were being fattened for foie gras. Not that Eve seemed to mind, which naturally pissed me off—she sucked that religious crap down like it was Coke. But then again maybe it was fear. The nuns ruled by fear. Everything was a sin, according to the nuns: lying, dressing improperly, talking back, giving the wrong answer, because that meant you hadn't studied properly—and, of course, that was a sin. Plus, we had to bow our heads whenever we spoke to them; not showing humility was also a sin. Not that I cared a damn. Early on I had discovered the computer lurking in a dark lonely corner of the town library, where I and others in my class went to study after school. Apart from me, no one seemed interested in using it. Or maybe they were afraid of it; I don't know. Me, I couldn't get enough of the wealth of information—none of which was part of the school's narrow-band curriculum. The knowledge seemed to absorb into me as if my brain was a thirsty sponge, which, I suppose, it was. It was also interesting because sometimes I was sure that Sophie was awake, looking over my shoulder, absorbing just as much as I was. Other times, I thought I might be alone or, even more interesting, that Sophie was concentrating on a different section of the page I was reading. The more often that happened, the less weird it became, until I simply thought of it as part of my strange nature.

Right away I came to the conclusion that I didn't need God to tell me what to think, and Sophie definitely agreed. I was precocious in mind as well as body. But you didn't need a diploma to see that the nuns were a particularly nasty lot. It was their way or the highway. Needless to say, they considered me a problem child, but such was my mother's wrath the first time the head nun summoned her that the nuns would turn themselves inside out not to see her face again. Turning themselves inside out was okay, but turning the other cheek apparently was not. They were quite selective in what they considered the teachings of Christ—hence my private name for the school.

The nuns were forever blitzing us with queries about sinful behavior—when we arrived at school, in the middle of classes, like snap quizzes, and, oh, yes, in the bathroom. *Especially* in the bathroom, where it was thought all manner of deviant sin, from smoking to masturbation to lesbianism, took place. There was no privacy at all.

It made me think that the nuns' minds were the ones obsessed with sin and punishment. So naturally I asked them. A beating, a rageful lecture detailing the horrors of hell and an hour after school writing "I am a sinner" on the classroom blackboard ensued, all of which answered my question: the nuns were indeed obsessed with sin and punishment. In fact, the cheeks of the nun who volunteered to beat me ended up more flushed than mine at the end of the session. She rushed off to the bathroom, where, I had no doubt, she sinned most mightily.

Bad enough Eve swallowed all the religious horseshit whole—I suppose, for the sake of our friendship, I would've handled her reciting the catechisms day and night—but then when we were in eighth grade, she had to go and tell my mother that I was secretly reading *Breakfast at Tiffany's*: a whopper of a sin. Truman Capote was near the top of everyone's burn-the-book list, so the novel was confiscated forthwith. The next day Eve and I were ex-friends. We never went to school together again.

Postcard 10

"Here in Georgia," my mother told me, "God is king. No, more than king. God is everything."

We were backstage in her Salvation Tent, as everyone called it. I was seven years old when my mother brought me to her ministry, to increase my learning, as she informed me. Only later did I realize it was actually to spite my father.

Backstage it was all business, all the time. My mother had roadies, just like rock stars. They set up the amplifiers that cast her voice all the way into the back row; a separate TV crew arranged lights, reviewed the camera placements for her *Salvation Show* to be shown later in the evening on SNC, the Southern Network of Christ. My mother's show was SNC's centerpiece.

"I brought you here today to learn," she told me just before she took the stage. "I brought you here to witness a miracle. I brought you here to watch the connection—as I become a part of Christ's will, as Jesus enters me."

A moment later she stepped out onto the stage to a rising roar of approbation. Peering out from behind the curtain that separated the wings, where the apparatus of the miracles ground out its own form of magic, I saw such a sea of faces as I had never before witnessed, even at my school's weekly assembly. To my young eyes, the tent, big as it was from the outside, seemed vast now. So many people, so many true believers! An uncountable number.

My mother, transformed, addressed the congregation, blessing them with Christ's loving light, the light they all desperately needed to illuminate them, to lift them out of the pit of sin and despair into which they had fallen, to make their lives better, to make their lives worth living.

And how did she do that? Not with prayers, no; prayer was for the parish priests and poor ministers, who could never really connect with Christ, with his will, with his loving light as my mother regularly did. And this is the way she proved to them that Christ entered her Salvation Tent, that he moved over them, blessed them as he animated her.

And here came one, running up the center aisle so fast that he was onstage with her before anyone could react. As he approached her, grizzled, wide eyed, filthy, her bodyguards rushed from either wing, but my mother held up her hands to stop them in their tracks. The shocked whispers from the congregation were like the susurrus of impatient insects in high summer.

For what seemed a long time, the tableau on the stage was set, as if in amber. Then slowly my mother's arms came down. Her left hand dove into the deep pocket of her white-and-gold robe. She drew out a snub-nosed .38 revolver and pointed it at the madman. You could tell by the way she held the gun, the way she aimed it, that she knew what she was doing, though I'd never seen the weapon before, let alone her practicing with it. And yet here she was, standing spread legged, unafraid to shoot to kill.

"What is your name?" she asked the madman.

He looked bewildered for a moment. "Willie," he said at length. His voice was thin and raspy, as if he smoked three or four packs of cigarettes a day.

"Well, Willie, this is your time. You've made it your time. Now there is this decision to be made. Will it be the bullet or salvation? Do you want to die, or do you want to live?"

Willie took two halting steps toward her, and the entire congregation gasped. My mother didn't flinch, but from my vantage point I saw her finger tighten on the trigger. But in the next breathless instant Willie fell to his knees before her.

"Why doesn't God love me?" he cried. "Heal me! Save me!"

And she did. Sliding the .38 back into her pocket, my mother put both hands on the top of his bowed head. Her lips moved; she murmured something, a prayer perhaps. Then she spread her arms wide, making of herself a living cross. A collective sigh of relief from the congregants.

Head thrown back, eyes staring wide, she became . . . something Other. Where there had been a resumption of the vociferous surf of noise, now there was nary a sound. You could hear a pencil drop. Silence was all. It might have been my imagination or even the spell her dark glamour cast, but even the wind that had been gusting all morning seemed to be holding its breath.

Only then did she speak. By that age I'd read the Bible many times, memorized whole sections of it as she had recited them to me every night even before I learned to read. In 1 Corinthians 12:11 it was written that "it is the one and only Spirit who distributes these gifts, He alone decides which gift each person should have." However, in my mother's interpretation, "He alone decides which person shall have a Gift." She, of course, was one of the Chosen. Her Gift was being able to speak in tongues, and nobody—but nobody—in the entire viewing area of SNC had that Gift but her.

I read about speaking in tongues; in school, where because of my mother, I was held at a certain remove by my classmates, I'd heard that my mother had the Gift, but until that moment, seeing her onstage with her arms spread wide and her head thrown back, and every eye in that packed tent glued to her, I had no idea what speaking in tongues meant, let alone its electric power to galvanize hundreds of people.

And when she began to writhe, when the unintelligible words came pouring out of her like a beacon in the forest, the hairs on my arms rose up off my goose-fleshed skin, and quivered. Words became sentences, piled one upon the other, like a castle or a shining city, and all at once, as if through an invisible command, the entire congregation was on its knees. And I could see why. The tent itself seemed to reverberate with her voice. Was it her, or was it the engineers working their electronic magic with the sound system? I wondered about this only later; at the time I was completely caught up in her performance. The tongue in which she was speaking seemed to cause her to expand, grow to three times her size. Was it my imagination again, or did her eyes really blaze, as if they were made of ground diamonds?

Willie fell to the stage writhing as she writhed, groaning and crying out as if pierced by nails driven through his wrists and ankles. Then my mother lifted him up as if he weighed no more than a sack of flour. His eyes were calm, his demeanor serene. A smile wreathed his face.

"Behold!" my mother cried. "A child of God has been born, resurrected from the dead!"

The performance, this transformation its crown jewel, terrified me on an entirely different level from what was happening to me nightly in the farmhouse of many rooms. I summoned Sophie, and as I grasped onto her for dear life, we fled the pulsating tent and the crush of true believers held within it.

Postcard 11

Strictly speaking, Hickory wasn't bred as a hunting dog, but under my father's tutelage I trained him to be one. He had a nose for prey—that much I can tell you. And, of course, for some reason we never thought to visit, he had a particular antipathy toward snakes, of which we had plenty.

Saturday mornings I'd take him out for a run and then a stealthy stalk. Sometimes—not often—we went after white-tailed deer, and after I'd shot one, my father would skin and butcher it. My mother wouldn't touch venison. In fact, she claimed the smell of the meat cooking made her sick to her stomach. Neither my father nor I believed her, but to keep the peace we used the outside grill. We had to eat it outside, too, but that was okay, because then we could feed Hickory without her losing her shit.

If it seems odd, maybe even hypocritical, that loving animals the way I did, I'd hunt deer, look at it another way. The fact is I only did that when money was tight and we needed the meat. Every time I brought a deer down with my father's .243 Winchester, I knelt over it, and before I'd let him start up with his big knife, I'd say a prayer for the deer, my own riff on a line from *Romeo and Juliet*: "These violent delights have violent ends and in their triumph die; like fire and powder, they burn away, and kiss the soul goodbye."

One time, deep into the red-and-gold fall, Hickory and I came across a feral hog. I was seventeen, or almost anyway. I hadn't heard him, but Hickory had scented him, guiding me upwind of the animal I had assumed was a white-tailed deer. When I saw the pig, huge and bristly, black as night, through a gap in the trees, I froze.

As it happened, my father wasn't with us that day, but he had warned me about feral hogs—how dangerous they were, how fast they could charge you, how they were powerful enough to knock down a group of three or four young trees or uproot them with their tusks. In fact, the constant rooting of these wild pigs was destroying the forest undergrowth, the forest itself.

"What you must do, if you come across one," he told me, "is decide whether to shoot or withdraw. If you withdraw, if you're not mighty careful, the hog might still come after you. If you shoot, you must kill it with your first shot. There's nothing more dangerous in these parts than a wounded feral hog."

He told me that the animal had thick skin, tough as armor, and a mass of cartilage hunters called a shield protecting its heart and lungs. He told me never to try for a headshot; the critter had a small brain. "Go for the neck," he said. "That'll sever its spinal cord. But be careful, and for God's sake be accurate."

I lined up the target. By my side, Hickory crouched, his haunches trembling but perfectly silent. The good boy knew what we were up against: something strong. Too strong. And yet I had made the decision. I wouldn't back down the way my father had with my mother. I learned from him; I was determined to stand up to something more frightening, more powerful than I was.

As I sighted down the barrel, the hog turned, and all at once I felt exposed, unsafe, but not in the way I felt at night in my parents' house. I also felt excited. For once in my life I was in control. I held the weapon. I was stalking prey instead of being the prey myself.

Beside me, Hickory, as if intuiting what was happening, raced off to my left. The hog picked up the movement and turned back, giving me the shot I wanted.

I took it.

The explosion, the recoil, and the hog falling to its knees seemed to happen all at once. The great head swung back and forth like a pendulum; then, its spine severed, it crashed to the earth. I felt the shock of its death through my boot soles and into my legs.

I broke cover and ran, and Hickory ran with me, his coat smoothed back, his ears perked for the slightest sign of danger.

We reached the dead hog together, more than hunting companions, more than friends.

———

That afternoon was the last time I saw him. Hickory disappeared in the night, sometime after our glorious messy pig roast, and was gone when I awoke. I searched for him all day, through a blinding rain and fierce wind, but found no trace of him. Had he run away? I couldn't imagine that.

It was nearly a year later, when the rains had come again, but this time more insistently, steadily over a course of a week, causing rivers to overflow their banks and flash floods to strip away topsoil. That was how I found him. He'd been buried, hastily and not too deeply, on a hillside out back behind the barn. He'd been wrapped in an old soiled sheet. His blood had stained the cotton, brown, caked.

Inside lay Hickory, a .38 bullet hole in the back of his head.

Postcard 12

My mother loved me as no other person has loved me, could love me, or will love me. I was her darling girl, the apple of her eye. She wanted to teach me everything she knew; she wanted to train me in the ways of God. Her God. A perverse God, as my father had hinted at more than once during their screaming matches.

But it was Hickory I mourned, and will mourn, all the rest of my days. Unconditional love is hard to find, but the days running, playing, hunting, and curling up with him taught me it was possible.

"Well, at least now you know. And good riddance," my mother said to me when I came home, soaked and sobbing, barely capable of speech, of describing how I'd found him. I couldn't look at her while she spoke to me, not for the next several weeks.

"I know you're grieving, but for what?" she continued. "A creature without a soul. Save your sympathy for things that matter—human beings with souls that must be saved."

But it wasn't sympathy for Hickory I was feeling; it was empathy. He and I had formed a bond. He knew what I was going to do, what I needed him to do, almost before I knew it myself. I was inconsolable all over again, for more than a month. Every morning, as daylight crept across the ground, chasing away night's shadows, I went to where

I had closed the clotted earth over him in a way I'd thought fitting. I'd missed him so terribly and now could not pretend he might come back one day. Of course, Sophie didn't care; I was the only person she felt anything for. My father had seen to that. That time of mourning was the first time I came to hate Sophie. I hated her with an intensity that both shocked and frightened me. For that month I wanted nothing to do with her. I never summoned her, enduring the nightly ritual with teeth-clamped stoicism.

"You know, my darling girl, this is all for the best," my mother said when I was ready to talk to her again. "It seemed to me that you loved that animal more than you loved me."

———

In my spare time, and out of my mother's sight, I fashioned a sort of headstone for him, using a spare slab of wood I found in my father's workshop, leaning against the wall at the rear of the barn. It was covered in straw and cobwebs. Above it, the ranks of western diamondback rattles pinned to the wall, like medals of valor, made a curious decoration. That was when I discovered my father's hobby of milking the rattlers he caught and killed—like the one Hickory had discovered. Jarring their venom in the old refrigerator beside six-packs of beer. Why did he want the venom? Maybe, I thought, he drank it. I had read stories of Chinese men who drank snake venom to increase their virility, to bring them closer to the powers snakes were purported to have. I thought the story was crap, until I saw the stacked jars of venom, each one carefully labeled with date and origin.

But I did not forget my reason for being in the workshop. Using my father's chisels, I gave the board a curved top, and, after much thought and many drafts, onto its face, using the smallest of the chisels, I inscribed my prayer for my companion:

THANK YOU FOR HICKORY, FOR HIS LIFE, AND FOR THE LOVE AND JOY HE
BROUGHT ME.
PLEASE BLESS HIM AND KEEP HIS SOUL SAFE.

I don't know who I was addressing—certainly not my mother's God. I only knew that I was sending Hickory off to a higher power, whatever that might be, to a place of peace, wherever that might be.

Postcard 13

At night, I could hear a whippoorwill's call, the crickets in summer, stealthy foxes in winter. I kept my window open every night unless the weather became foul. There was, particularly, an owl nesting near my bedroom—a great big one with a white face and mottled wings. I would listen for him (I imagined the owl was a male, that with his enormous wings he would take me away), and I sometimes heard him. Not as you'd hear birdsong, all chirrupy and bright, but a swish so soft it could be mistaken for a tree branch in the wind. When the moon was full, or even waxing, I'd look for his face and see it briefly along the arc of his near-silent flight, before he dove down into the shadows thrown by the trees, after a mouse or a woodchuck. I always imagined that he looked at me when, at the apogee of his flight, he was most brightly moonlit, and I saw every feather on his wings and body, and that he saw me as well.

At night, in the farmhouse of many rooms, I was utterly alone, separated from everyone and everything, a *thing* myself, lying awake on an altar. I played the waiting game, waiting for that moment when I'd be summoned, as silently as the owl's flight, and I, a mouse or a wood-chuck, its prey. This was the time of night when Sophie was closest to me, Sophie who had been created to protect me, keep my mind safe while my body was violated over and over again.

Sophie, I love you!

I had to love her; my father made sure I had no choice. He created Sophie and bonded us together while I was under, the hypnotic state so deep, so complete he gained access to my unconscious. He split me in two, or rather he carved off a part of me to create Sophie, playmate and protector, a place I could go when the dreadful thing happened. A place of rest and repose. He did this for me, but it wasn't enough. He knew it wasn't enough; he'd told me as much. And then when he was at the end of his rope, when he finally gained the courage to act, the act was wrong, wrong as the nightly thing, and the fire happened.

———

The fox in its den is not as stealthy. The owl in the night is not as silent. The falcon on the wing is not as predatory. These animals kill only when it's needed, only when they're hungry. Animals aren't wicked, perverse, greedy, murderous. Of the seven deadly sins they know nothing. They are pure of mind, clean of soul. They exist on feeling and instinct. Maybe, once upon a time, humans were the same way. I'd like to think so, but that's wishful thinking. Because animals do not understand life, they do not know about death. But they know love better and more deeply than any human.

Stealthy, silent, predatory, my mother came for me in the dead of night. She stood by the side of my bed, still as a statue, white as a carved block of salt. I lay still, my heart beating as fast as a wren's, always hoping that this was a dream. My eyes were closed, and yet I felt her, as if her shadow had weight, pressing down on me.

She sat on the edge of my bed, and I opened my eyes. And there she was, her eyes glittering like diamond shards. She was beautiful in the moonlight—an unearthly beauty that was difficult to look at, like the sun at noon. Slowly, she drew the bedclothes off me. I shivered. Delicately she pushed my nightdress up, perfectly, like peeling an orange, the fragrant rind one long spiral. Naked, I trembled like a fawn. I was five years old when this began.

She put one hand on my forehead, the other on my child's flat chest, and I felt the heat of her seeping into me. Later, as my body changed—in prepubescence grew first long and lean, then in adolescence became prematurely womanly in hips, breasts, and thighs—her explorations became more thorough. She held my breasts in her hands, pressed her lips to the nipples, spanned my hips as if stroking a horse's flanks. I counted the filaments of down on the nape of her neck.

But in the beginning, in my childhood, it was simpler, if no less intimate. My trembling stilled. I breathed slowly and deeply. This was another kind of trance. Helpless, I fell.

Into her arms.

This was the ritual, repeated almost nightly.

Hearing her voice, carried on the wind snaking sinuously through the open window, the voice, she said, of the Holy Spirit.

I lay open before her.

"Let me kiss you," my mother whispered over me, "with the kisses of my mouth: for my love is better than the sacramental wine." Lowering her head, she kissed me with her lips partly open so that I could taste her breath. "I draw near you, I run after you, the Lord has brought me to your room, to join together, so that we may celebrate Him, rejoicing together in His love, entwined in each other's arms."

Her hands moved over me. "Your cheeks are rosy red, my darling girl, your neck a column of ivory." Across my cheeks, down the side of my neck, lower, lower. "Tell me, darling daughter, whom my soul loves more than anything, who is more precious to me than rows of jewels or chains of gold." Down the center line of my belly. "Do you not love God as I do?"

"Yes, Mama, I love God with all my heart, with all my soul."

Down to the tops of my thighs, caressing my flesh in small circles, like a butterfly's wings.

"And loving God is loving me," my mother continued, almost chanting now, "for he is within me." One fingertip on the swell of flesh just above the juncture of my thighs. And then into the crease. "And now I am within you. We are one with God, my darling. All the power he possesses now flows through us." In and out, her finger went. In and out, as my mother's eyes glazed over, as she chanted: "You are beautiful, my beloved, too beautiful for this world of rot and diseased men. When you are mine, when you are God's possession, you are made perfect, you are strength, you are . . ." My mother's other hand was between her own thighs, and her head was tilted back, her neck thin and pale, curved like a swan. I felt something, a heat, God's heat, my mother's heat. My limbs turned to liquid, and I could not breathe. I was panting. My mother was panting. God must be panting, too, I thought.

And then I didn't think anything at all. I lay floating in Sophie's space. Safe. Sophie more real to me than anyone else could ever be. Safe. And yet not safe at all. I was like a fulcrum, holding secrets about my father and about my mother that I must not tell. I must balance them against each other, keeping them close, part of me forever.

Beside me, above me, my mother shuddered with every fiber of her being.

Postcard 14

As in a fairy tale, at the stroke of midnight of my thirteenth birthday, the animal was let loose. It should not have come as a surprise to me, but it did. Had I been paying enough attention, had I not been so self-absorbed, so consumed with my own life, my family's dynamics, I might have sensed Sophie's transformation.

But just as I had grown breasts, my hips had filled out, my legs had become shapely, hair had sprouted between my legs and under my arms, my menarche arriving a year earlier, Sophie had grown with me. She shared my raging hormones, the difference being while I willfully and fearfully suppressed my reactions, she joyfully, one might even say ferally, embraced them. To the max, as it turned out.

That night, just after midnight, the visitation from my mother over, while I was curled into a fetal ball, weeping and still in shock, as I always was, though embraced by Sophie, I felt my body moving.

I was carried along as if on a tide, dark and gummy, in which I floated, but without will, without volition. I was aware that I was getting dressed, but it wasn't me doing it—it was Sophie. Then I was out the window, sliding down the drainpipe to the ground.

And there I stood, uncertain for the moment. Then, still curled and quiescent, I started to cry again.

Be strong. You must be strong, Kitten, Sophie said. *You've been through so much—and so have I, being cooped up in a dank corner of your mind. But now, while you rest, is my time to shine.*

The full harvest moonlight, deep gold, streamed through the trees. My owl hooted and, behind it, the mournful sounds of a train, chugging through the night on its lonely journey. There is nothing sadder, I thought, than that sound: a homeless trek across the desolate night.

In the barn, Sophie retrieved the Schwinn and cycled off fast, faster than I'd ever gone. Where were we going? I had no idea, and I had lost the ability to voice questions, let alone control my body's movements. Through the buzzing darkness she pedaled, down our dirt-packed road to a tarmacked two lane, skirting town, though at this time of night no one would be awake, and finally onto the interstate, wide as a river, black and endless. At length, lights came into focus up ahead—a hazy glow, now red, now blue, neon kissed—and Sophie headed for there.

It was a modern gas station, shiny and bright, with a convenience store, lit up like the signs of Las Vegas. The place also featured a fairly large lot adjacent to a chromium all-night diner, to accommodate drivers of the semis that rolled through here, heading for Atlanta or parts north, or sad salesmen, en route to wayward parts of their territory, who needed their sleep, a decent hot meal, or simply time to stretch their legs.

Huge moths, white and trembling, fluttered around the lights, and in the spaces between the traffic rumbling by, the insect drone was like a tuning up of a tiny orchestra. Sophie got off the bike and set it in the shadows at the rear of the lot. It was only as we passed the reflection in a car window that I noticed what she was wearing: shorts; a shirt, unbuttoned, the ends tied at her waist; sandals. With scissors she had turned the shorts into cut-offs, the shirt rendered sleeveless. I couldn't even imagine what punishment would have been in store for me had my mother ever caught me in such a revealing outfit. It was deliberately provocative, I realized now. I saw my figure as if for the first time: shapely and alluring. It frightened me, but in a manner I didn't understand, it also fascinated me. I was thirteen, but my body looked maybe eighteen or nineteen.

Sophie crossed the lot, stepped into the convenience store, bought a can of Coke, a Snickers, and a packet of Trojans. On the way out, I saw myself again in the mirror over the front door. I was shocked all over again. When did this transformation happen to me, and how was it that Sophie understood it better than I did?

Out in the steamy night, the moths were committing suicide into the lights, hot sizzles turned to dust. There were six or seven semis parked in the lot at any one time. Every once in a while an engine rumbled to life, and the rig nosed its way back out onto the interstate. Almost as soon as one did, though, another pulled in, and a weary driver slid down from the high cab and headed off to the men's room located at the rear of the convenience store.

It was on their way out, after their aching bladders had emptied and they'd bought themselves a beer or two, that Sophie presented herself. She never looked at them directly but stuck out one hip and, one arm akimbo, tore open her Snickers with her teeth.

Honestly, I don't know what got to the guys first—her outfit, her cocked hip, or her bared teeth. Maybe an irresistible combo of the three. But they were like the moths fluttering toward the erotic light she emitted. There was little talk, just brief negotiations, which, for some reason, Sophie always won. And then it was back to the semi cab or, often, just into the deeper shadows past the rear metal railing of the lot. These encounters were quick, to the point, sweaty, and in Sophie's case, fairly loud. After the sex, she'd slip away, take a mouthful of Coke, swish it around, then spit it out. Then she'd drink half the can and go on to the next victim.

I thought of them as victims because . . . well, what else could I call them? They wanted her, sometimes with a desperation that was frightening. Others clung to her in the sex-scented cab, half-passed-out or crying like a baby. There was a certain release for them, as well as for her, so maybe they weren't victims, after all. Though they weren't consenting adults—one of them wasn't, anyway—there was a quid pro quo that I guess was more or less equal. Each of them entered into the bargain wanting something—for Sophie the money was just a side-show—and it was the same thing: sex and its attendant climax. Which precluded there being any sense of her entering into a performance. For Sophie, as I came to understand, these nights were a necessary outlet for the forces driving her—forces my father could never have imagined when he'd created her. Maybe they should have been my urges as well, but those had been split off quite effectively by my mother's nocturnal violations.

It was the first driver, Bob, who got Sophie's cherry. He was the one who cried afterward and asked her how old she was. Sophie told him she was nineteen, lying through her teeth. Which turned out to be a good thing; he had twin daughters, aged fourteen.

The act, as strenuous as a run up a steep hill, repeated itself around me in a blur of arms and legs, sweat and spittle. It seemed that Sophie was insatiable. But after two or three hours of going at it with an animal ferocity, even she had had enough. I had the vivid sense that the return trip down narrower and narrower roads felt like freedom to her—a freedom made all the more powerful by its swift passage.

In bed, in the hour before daybreak, when the world was gray and furry with a dewy mist, I lay in bed listening to myself—for myself, as if I was already lost. Sophie was gone; she'd withdrawn as soon as I'd turned into the long, snaking driveway to the farmhouse. I felt keenly the soreness in the muscles of my inner thighs. I had felt this kind of soreness before, when I'd first started riding Miss Molly seriously, and especially when I rode her bareback. I knew there was a subtle difference now, but I was at a loss to say what it was. I kept trying my best to work my way through the Gordian knot of emotions that bound me.

Dawn broke dimly, uncertainly, apparently as baffled as I was. Not the slightest breeze stirred the curtains. I could hear the birds singing to each other, *Wake up! Wake up!* but the house was perfectly still. I smelled the men Sophie had been with, each one distinct, each one holding its own convocation of ecstasy and despair.

Postcard 15

The day my mother died was the nicest day in about the previous ten, sunny and warm, with a gentle breeze stirring the leaves on the trees. It had been raining off and on seemingly forever, and everything was a muddy mess. Water dripped from the trees, puddles pockmarked the yard, roads washed out, rivers rose: another flood "of Biblical proportions," the weather forecasters promised darkly.

We had had breakfast, my father had gone out, and I had brought my mother her usual mug of Rockin' Robin. My father had stayed long enough to make the herbal tea himself, and with a big smile and a wink, he whispered, "Buck up, Kitten," when handing me the mug. The tea was hot and steaming. I carried it carefully into the nook, where my mother was already seated before the magic eye of the oval mirror.

"Ah, yes," she said, taking the mug and sipping from it. "Just what the doctor ordered."

As it turned out, she was right—if the doctor were my father.

She had come downstairs that morning earlier than usual to wrap ice cubes in a cloth, press it to the soft pink on the inner side of her lower lip, where it looked to me like she had been bitten. Her face was flushed and slightly swollen, as it always was after she'd had sex with my father. Their coupling was the antithesis of her quiet, deliberate ritual with me—rough, almost vicious.

I was not present when she died. She grew ill on the way to her Salvation Tent, fell into the arms of her roadies, who, quite rightly, had no idea what was wrong with her. The concentrated rattlesnake venom my father had poured into the herbal tea he'd brewed for her that morning clotted her blood so badly and so quickly that her major organs failed all at once. There was no chance an entire hospital of doctors, let alone the country GP who was summoned, could have saved her.

There was an inquest, of course, and an autopsy. But the coroner who performed the autopsy was Luke Evanston, one of the men present the morning of my grandfather's death. He loved my father dearly—loved me just as much, actually—so whatever he discovered remained with him, and the official cause of my mother's death was a massive coronary. Or maybe Luke Evanston was simply incompetent, the consequence of a massive dose of western diamondback venom introduced into her bloodstream through the bite in my mother's lower lip a possibility he wasn't equipped to discover.

In any event, there were no legal repercussions. I never could get a grip on how I felt about that. There was no point in my going to the police; as I said, my father had made himself a hero in everyone's eyes. And no one would have believed me, and anyway, Luke would have refuted my testimony out of hand. My confession would have done nothing but turn everyone against me.

"I should have done it long ago," my father told me as we watched the crowd of people filing in for her funeral. "The moment I found out what she was doing to you." But he was too weak; like everyone, too much in thrall to her dark glamour. Including me.

So who did I hate more, my mother or my father?

———

My mother's funeral was stupendous, flamboyant as an ancient Egyptian pharaoh's—and as endless as the line of mourners. There were so many, in fact, that the tent was obliged to amplify the service in order to allow those who could not cram inside to hear the prayers, benedictions, and of course the wailings of grief, rolling like storm-tossed waves over the assembled.

The procession of speakers commenced their solemn turn at the lectern:

"She was precious," concluded one.

"She was a saint," concluded another.

"She has been taken to God's bosom," said yet another.

And another: "We will never see her like again."

"She was a mother to us all," concluded the last speaker, two hours later.

There were prayers. There were hymns. There was hand-wringing, hairpulling. There was beseeching. But the astonishing thing to me was that every nun from my school was present at my mother's funeral. Was it to say goodbye to a fellow religious or to make sure the witch was truly dead? I couldn't tell.

Unlike the funeral itself, the viewing was only for family, which meant me and my father. It was the strangest feeling to be standing, looking down at what used to be my mother, side by side with the man who had murdered her. Her face didn't look like hers at all; it was a horror, repellent. And with absolute clarity I recalled the cameo of her face, made exquisite by moonlight, as it hovered over me. A face, nakedly human in the private night of my bedroom. Not this made-up face, so much like the one she put on herself while I watched, the first stage of her transformation into the public persona that so terrified me. This was what she was now, all humanity stripped from her, in the final stage. Maybe my father, if he was feeling even a fraction of what I was feeling, thought it fitting. But I couldn't.

Vividly now, I remembered how each time after our nighttime ritual, a strange sensation would come over me, like pins and needles in my arms and legs, or paralysis, even. I would be shaken to my core, mortified, as if I had just had a violent argument with my mother, precisely as she so often had with my father.

And into my mind as clearly as if I had been there arose the specter of her, holding her loaded .38 against her thigh, creeping down the staircase at night, possibly directly after our ritual was ended, while I was incapacitated, dead to the world around me. Down the stairs she floated, like a wraith. The beautiful, moonlit face slowly transformed by shadow and her murderous intent, out the front door, picking her stealthy way to the place Hickory liked best when he wasn't at my side or curled next to me, breathing softly, his paws flicking as in his dreams he hunted.

The expression she presented as she crept up behind Hickory and pulled the trigger was, I was dead certain, the same expression on her face now in the open coffin. Death she delivered, and death was returned to her, leaving me with the crushing guilt and shame of our shared secret.

How can a person both love and hate another person? I can't fathom it. She fed me, clothed me, comforted me, loved me. And abused me over and over. She taught me, laughed with me, showed me the inner workings of her tent. And she shot my dog. What kind of a person does that? There were so many currents of emotion running through me at once I felt overwhelmed. A strange dizziness gripped me; I felt taken out of time, as if drifting in some void somewhere between the real world and the place my mother had got to. All at once, I couldn't breathe. I had to grasp the edge of the open coffin to steady myself, lest I collapse. When in a minute or ten, I regained a semblance of myself, I jerked my hands away as if the wood were on fire.

My father took a breath, let it out. "I did this, Kitten."

"Dad—"

"No. No, let me speak. You deserve that much." He grunted. "You deserve everything, God knows. You're the brave one."

I looked at him, bewildered.

"Not me. I'm the coward." He was fiddling with something jangly in his suit pocket. Keys, I supposed. "I did this to her, and the truth is . . . the truth is I'm not sorry. You might think me a monster; you might not. I don't know. There isn't much I do know about kids. I wasn't cut out to be a father. I don't say that as an excuse—there is no excuse. It's just the way it is." He brought out a pack of gum, offered me a stick. When I shook my head, he unwrapped it, folded it into his mouth. I smelled spearmint, like a rush of fresh air. The atmosphere in the funeral chapel was heavy, suffocating with shadows that seemed to move of their own volition, and compressed, as if we were inside a submarine.

"Your mother." He stopped there, and for a moment I thought that was all he was going to say, all he felt he needed to say. But then he pressed on: "She was a presence, all right. Larger than life. She took up all the air inside that farmhouse; it was a wonder sometimes the two of us could breathe." He took a breath now, as if to reassure himself that he could. Then he shook his head. "But, you know, what she did to you—"

"Don't, Dad. Please don't."

His head dipped for a brief moment. "Okay, yeah. I get it."

"You couldn't possibly."

My father looked down, not at my mother's painted corpse, not at her glossy coffin. At nothing at all. For the first time in memory he looked abashed. After a time, his head came up, and his gaze met mine. There were tears in his eyes, large, trembling. "This is so difficult, so different . . ." His voice faded out, and it was a few moments before he gathered himself enough to start again. "Kitten, I can't tell you how many times I imagined this moment." His voice was a murmur, echoing in my head. "In my imagination I was finally free." He pushed a lock of hair off his forehead. "But the truth is, I'll never be free of her."

My skin was raised in gooseflesh, just as if I had come unstuck in time, the calendar racing ahead to winter, a chill wind biting into the back of my neck. I felt as if I was going to be sick. Moonlight and sunlight vied for supremacy in the place I stood, next to my parents, but also a continent away. I was on a far shore, looking back at them from across a vast sea. And yet I felt something plucking insistently at my sleeve. I turned and saw her.

"Neither will I," I told my father.

PART 6
RUNNING THE VOODOO DOWN

You have your way. I have my way. As for the right way, the
correct way, and the only way, it does not exist.

—Friedrich Nietzsche

34

She hears Hickory barking. He must have found something important, something he wants her to see. The trouble is the fog, thick as she has ever seen in her life. Unnaturally thick, as if she is wading through clouds. Still, Hickory's bark comes to her clear and strong. Happy. What has he found? She can't imagine, but elation swells in her chest at the thought of it. Her love for him buoys her through the fog, causes her to put one foot in front of another, even though she is effectively blind. What if she stumbles? What if she falls? No matter. Hickory will be at her side, nuzzling her. Urging her back onto her feet.

"I love you." The fog sticks in her throat, damping her voice. "Hickory, I love you, boy!" Her voice raises, straining through the fog.

Then she falls. She tries to move, but her body and limbs feel as stiff as tree trunks. Her breath comes hard and fast.

"Hickory, where are you?"

She no longer hears his answering bark. Her heart is hurting, as if something has taken a bite out of it, as if it is somehow incomplete, missing a part, as if it is an engine.

A paralyzing fear crawls through her, like a lizard through a swamp. I've just come awake, she thinks to calm herself. This is just a bout of sleep paralysis, just as Lind described it to me. Nothing to worry about, she tells herself. Nothing to fear.

With a lurch that runs right through her, she falls again and keeps on falling until all hope is lost.

———

"If you run away from love," Lind is saying, "it will only follow you."

Or is it M speaking?

Or is it Figgy?

The three of them have blended into a single voice.

She hears Hickory's bark, but is it a bark at all? She opens her eyes and sees Charlotte Lind running toward her. She has her schoolbag in one hand. Earbuds in her ears, plugged into her phone. When Charlotte reaches her, grinning, she says, "There you are! I've been looking and looking for you! I was worried." Charlotte presses one of the earbuds into her ear.

"Listen to this," the girl says. "It's my new favorite."

What is it? she wonders. The new Miley Cyrus, Taylor Swift, Beyoncé? But, no, it's "Miles Runs the Voodoo Down," from *Bitches Brew*.

As she listens with one ear, she says, "How d'you know about Miles Davis?"

"Figgy played it for me," Charlotte says. "He said you liked it."

"I do," she says. "Very much."

Falling again, falling into the sea, where the swimmer on Lind's wall awaits her.

"It's been a long time," the swimmer says. "I feared you were never coming back."

"Am I back?"

"Do you want to be back?" the swimmer asks.

35

"S he's awake!" A voice, a female, light and young. "Doctor, she's awake."

Footsteps in a blaze of arctic white, and then a friendly face, oblong and flattish, Asian, takes up the bulk of Tara's field of vision. Long black hair, pushed back from her face, held in place by, of all things, a wide blue rubber band. There are three more around her left wrist, which is thin, bony, and frail looking.

"Hello, Tara." She smiles. "Welcome back to the real world." A quick glance at the machine recording Tara's vital signs: heart rate, blood pressure, internal oxygen level, and the like. "I'm Dr. Kim." A brief frown as she says, "You had us quite worried there for a while." The frown flies off, as if it never alighted on her face. "But now you're back with us, and for good."

"Am I . . . ?"

A smile a mile wide. "You're going to be fine. You suffered a concussion. You've been in and out of consciousness since you were brought in here. We'll be doing some further testing now that you're lucid, just to make sure we haven't missed anything."

Relief is replaced by a sudden anxiety. "What about Rose?" Her throat feels as if it has been scrubbed raw, and she swallows. "Is she okay?"

"She will be. Like you, she was treated for smoke inhalation, and she sustained a third-degree burn on the outside of her right forearm. It could have been worse. Much worse." Dr. Kim's lips pucker as if she is tasting something delicious. "From all accounts you saved her life."

"I think Rose saved me," Tara says, dazedly.

"She asks about you incessantly," the nurse interjects. "As soon as I give her the good news, she'll pop in and see you when you feel up to it."

Tara blinks. "My eyes are gritty. They feel like I have sand in them."

"Ah well, that's the aftermath of the heat and the smoke." Bending over Tara, she administers viscous drops in both eyes. "Just liquid tears mixed with an antibiotic."

Tara blinks several times, clearing her vision.

Dr. Kim checks her chart, then looks up. "The really big news for you, Tara, is that both of you are doing fine."

Tara, experiencing increasing rounds of clarity between bouts of foggy headedness, says, "Both of us?"

Dr. Kim nods. "Precisely so."

"Me and Sophie?"

Dr. Kim chuckles. "Getting a jump on things, I see." She places a thin, long-fingered hand lightly on Tara's arm. "Actually, you're not far along enough for us to determine the sex of the fetus, but I see you're hoping for a girl."

For an instant, Tara's mind blanks. Then she begins to shiver. The shakes become so violent that her teeth chatter. Dr. Kim slides her hand into Tara's. "Squeeze my hand, Tara. Squeeze it. And look into my eyes." Dr. Kim is perfectly calm, smiling as if nothing at all is wrong. "There's a good girl."

"Oxygen, Doctor?" the nurse says, near to hand.

"No, I don't think so," Dr. Kim replies without looking away from Tara. "Not this time." Her smile broadens. "Isn't that right, Tara?"

Tara tries to reply, tries at least to smile back, but all she can manage is a terrifying rictus. She keeps a tight hold on Dr. Kim's hand, as if she's a lifeline, as if she is beside the swimmer on Lind's wall and they are both in danger of once again drowning.

I am here and not here, she thinks. I am living someone else's life. I've left mine far behind. She can smell the acrid smoke, can see the leap of flames all around her, and the shakes start up all over again, worse— far worse—than before. And this time, Dr. Kim signals the nurse, who slips the oxygen mask over Tara's nose and mouth. A soft hiss, and free air is released. She breathes it in with an audible sigh. Eventually, the dreadful smell and hallucination fade, and she begins to relax enough for the mask to come off.

She shuts her eyes tightly for a moment, but when she opens them again, everything is still as it was when she closed them.

"Feeling better now, are we?" The comforting smile has never left Dr. Kim's face. Tara keeps hold of her hand.

"Thank you," she croaks.

"All part of the first-class service in the critical care ward."

"What happened?"

"I could say PTSD, but that's a convenient catch-all these days," Dr. Kim tells her. "What you are experiencing is something akin to PTSD, though I believe not nearly as severe."

"I've . . . I've had this before."

Dr. Kim nods. "Several times since you were brought in. Every time you've been conscious, in fact." She takes a quick glance at Tara's vitals on the green digital readout beside the bed. "Another reason to keep you under surveillance for a while."

"How long?" Tara asks. "How long will it last?"

"The only thing I can tell you for certain is that it will fade."

Tara looks at her. "What you said before . . . I wasn't dreaming."

"No," says Dr. Kim.

"You're not a hallucination."

That chuckle again. "Gosh, I hope not! My husband and sons would be so disappointed!"

Tara's mouth is very dry. Dr. Kim leans over and slips a paper straw between her lips, and Tara sucks up cool water. "Careful," Dr. Kim warns. "Not too fast."

When she's had enough to soothe her throat, she looks at the friendly face and says, "Tell me again . . ."

"You're pregnant, Tara." A flicker of surprise. "Oh, gosh, you didn't know."

Tara says nothing. Her mind is a complete blank, as it was just before the attack of shakes. She waits for them to return, her entire body tense, but nothing happens.

Pregnant. The word sounds odd, alien, without meaning, at least as it pertains to her.

"I can't be pregnant," she says at last. The word sounds thick and chewy in her mouth, like a candy bar she's never tasted before.

"The blood test tells me otherwise," Dr. Kim says. "I assure you, you are. And luckily the trauma you experienced did no internal damage. I'm of the opinion that it's because you're only a couple of weeks into it. Honestly, we wouldn't even have known if we hadn't run a thorough blood panel."

"There's no doubt?"

"None whatsoever."

Tara thinks about the pain when Marwyn squeezed her breasts, and now they feel hot, swollen, her nipples tender. She thinks about the nausea that gripped her in the men's room of Brandon's building.

"Do you know who the father is? Do you want us to notify him?" She waits, but when there is no answer forthcoming, she adds, "Later, we can discuss counseling, if you wish."

Her hand disengages from Tara's. She smiles as she rises. "I think that's enough for now. There are a couple of people waiting downstairs to see you, but I think it's best you get some rest. I'll let them know when to come back."

"Who's down there?"

But Dr. Kim is already gone. What Tara really means is, Who would want to see me?

The young nurse bustles about for some minutes, fussing with the small things all nurses fuss with. Then she is gone, leaving Tara alone with her thoughts.

She tries to imagine a child growing in her womb, but her mind is losing focus. She is so tired. At least it's not Rex's, she thinks as she drifts off. Thank God for that.

———

When she wakes, Rose is sitting in one of those ugly chairs you only find in hospital rooms. She has pulled it close to Tara's bed and is leafing through a magazine.

"Rose?" Her voice is thick with sleep.

Rose raises her head. Her grin seems to warm the room. "There you are!" She stands briefly to kiss Tara on the cheek. "I was so worried about you."

Tara's brows knit together, and she winces, feeling a pain between her eyes. "How did you know I was here?"

"You mean your Sophie alias?" She waves a hand. "Brandon told me when he came to visit me here. He wanted to thank me for helping you. He and his team were there—at the building. They hauled us out." Rose smiles broadly. "I guess I'll have to get used to calling you Tara."

"I'm not going anywhere."

She sits back down but takes Tara's hand in hers, as if she wants to make sure Tara is as good as her word.

"How are your burns?"

"Oh, not so bad." Rose lifts her right arm, which is bandaged from wrist to just below her elbow. "Thank God it wasn't my face, right?"

They both laugh, but it is an uneasy laugh, underpinned by the memory of what they have been through together. A war.

"Rose, I'm so sorry."

"For what?"

"Getting you into—"

"Forget it. I was all for it. An adventure, right? Something new, something exciting."

"It was exciting, all right."

They both laugh again, but it is an easier sound this time.

There is silence between them, then, a serene moment when everything seems settled, in balance, a sensation new to both of them. There is something between them now, strong as a steel cable, not unlike the connection soldiers feel for the comrades who fight beside them and have their back. The war.

At length, Rose lifts the magazine she's holding high enough for Tara to see. "Hey, I was reading this article about the Palme d'Or. You know, that hotel in LA where all the celebrities have stayed over the years. What a strange place! The things that went on there! I can't imagine a life like that; it seems so far removed from here—it could be on a different planet."

"It is," Tara says, Sophie's memories clear in her head. And for the first time she thinks, They're my memories. Memories realized, accepted without freaking out, welcomed, scary but nevertheless enriching. She is beginning to see a glimmer of how she and Sophie have been and can be now—that being one persona would be okay. "I stayed there once."

Rose's eyes open wide. "You did?" She leans in; she is like a little girl. "What was it like? Tell me about it."

"I walked across the hotel's rooftop."

"No!"

Tara smiles. "I did. From there I could see the hills on one side and the sprawl of the city on the other, a carpet of lights as far as the eye could see."

"Were you high?"

"Was I? I don't remember." And she doesn't. Actually, it doesn't seem to matter. "It was a night I'll never forget, though."

"I'll bet!"

"There was a party going on down below. Music and drinking and muddled laughter."

"Did you dance up there? That could have been dangerous, no?"

Rose's last question sobers Tara up as she sees Rex with that damned python, slipping over the tiles as she makes a grab for him, vanishing over the edge almost too fast to see.

"It was dangerous, yes," Tara says. "That was why we were up there, I suppose." Daring fate. How out of our minds, how foolish we were!

Rose folds away the *Vanity Fair*. "That's why I said yes to you. I was bored. I wanted a new thing, a dangerous thing. I wanted to tempt fate, and I did."

"But—"

"No, no!" She presses Tara's hand. "We did this together. That monster is dead. What he did to us, what he would have done to us . . . if it wasn't for you. I mean, we came through the fire, didn't we?" She runs her thumb over the web of scars on Tara's hand. "Now we both have our badges of courage."

36

W ell, here's someone I never wanted to see again."
"Hey, it could be worse," Brandon says, settling himself in the chair Rose vacated an hour before. "It could be Philip Morris come to visit you."

She shudders. "Bite your tongue." She is upright in the bed, reading the issue of *Vanity Fair* Rose left for her. Reading the article on the Palme d'Or is giving her tremors of recognition: hot sun, the shade of palm fronds, crystalline nights with Rex. The party where she is introduced to the corrupt Captain Ruiz and his Mexican Federal Ministerial Police cohort. Briefly, she thinks about Sunrize, their fleeting time together at the Palme d'Or and afterward on the beach at Santa Monica. She remembers, at the end, her dead eyes, the needle in her arm, and thinks of the terrible waste of a life.

"Not to worry, Morris is done with you," Brandon continues. "And with me, thank Christ." He produces a brown paper bag. "I can't tell you what a relief it is not to have that shit's boot on my neck." He pulls out two sandwiches wrapped in white butcher's paper, and suddenly the room is redolent of a heady aroma making her mouth water.

"What are those?" she asks.

"Pastrami on rye," Brandon says. "New York's finest, straight from the legendary Katz's on East Houston. Serving the best pastrami in the city since 1888." He hands her one with a theatrical flourish. It is heavier than she expected, the red meat glistening, speckled with black pepper and white strips of fat. When he sees her hesitate, he says, "Go on. Take a bite."

She should have been sick right there and then, but the opposite happens. Her stomach rumbles, an empty pit. She takes the still-warm sandwich and bites into it. The feel of her teeth sinking into the lush, fatty meat is dizzying; the taste is rich, complex, exquisite.

"You know, it's a time-honored tradition: when you break bread with someone, it means you're friends," Brandon says.

"I'm not big on tradition," she mumbles around a bite of her sandwich.

After freeing two sour pickles from their wax paper wrappings, he sets one alongside the half a sandwich that's left. He chews a bite of his sandwich ruminatively. For a while they eat in an uneasy silence, Brandon snatching glances at her when he thinks she isn't looking.

Finally, scrunching up the greasy paper, he says, "So, listen, I owe you an apology."

"I don't think that's going to do it, Brandon."

"Yeah, well, look . . ." His face is set in an abashed expression. "I pulled a dirty trick on you, it's true. So you have every right to be pissed."

"Pissed doesn't hardly cover it."

"Okay, I hear you, but you have to remember I had my marching orders from Morris."

"Heil, mein Herr!"

"Very funny. But no, lookit, Tara, I had no choice. Just as you had no choice. You know that. But the thing of it is, you came through like a champ. Morris nearly came in his pants when he found what was inside Marwyn's gold coke spoon."

"So I was right? It was the flash drive of his drug business."

"The spoon pulled apart and, bam! there it was, staring Morris in the face. Now, not only is Rusk gone, but Morris and his people are in the process of rolling up the whole network." He throws the balled paper into the trash can in a perfect arc. "Three-pointer!" He laughs. "You'll be interested to know that Stephen Ripley was picked up in that net. You can imagine the media shitstorm that brought down; I guess you didn't see it on TV."

"I've had no head for TV or the papers. I haven't even looked at my phone. I'm sure it's as dead as a doornail. But what about me?"

"Oh, you and your friend—"

"Rose."

"You and your friend Rose were kept out of the entire incident—Morris saw to that. It's the only decent thing I've seen him do since I came under his thumb."

She gives a sigh of relief. She didn't realize until now how worried she's been about her involvement going public; Lind is sure to see it. "Do they have enough to convict Ripley?"

"Yes, but to be honest—"

"That's a laugh!"

Not to be deterred, he begins again. "To be honest, it's likely Ripley's high-powered attorneys will get him moved to a low-security country club prison after his conviction, but, well, he's off the circuit, at least." He gathers the scraps of Tara's meal, balls up the paper, and makes the same shot into the basket. "By the way, Figgy's downstairs."

Her heart gives such a lurch she almost cries out. "Why didn't he come up with you?"

"He told me he didn't know whether you wanted to see him." He gives her a hard look. "You two have a falling-out?"

"I don't know what we had." Is that the truth? Really?

"Did this little thing of ours get in the way?"

"What the hell do you think? You sent him to get cozy with me."

"Look, he's not the kind of guy who—"

He is going to go on, but she gives him such a withering look he decides against it. He rises instead, throws the now-empty Katz's paper bag in the garbage. He is almost at the door when he hesitates. "He said he was going to the cafeteria. Do you want me to tell him it's okay to come up?"

"I don't know what I want." Why did she say that? Of course she knows what she wants. But then a snapshot of Chloe, her unsuspended breasts visible through her shirt, rears up in her mind. Another snapshot of Chloe's pink demi bra in Figgy's bathroom. The echo of Figgy's voice saying, "She comes once a week to clean." Yeah, right, while taking her bra off. What housekeeper does that? Anger rises anew, blood rushing up her neck, into her cheeks.

When she doesn't reply, Brandon heaves a sigh, as if to say, *Women, go figure.* "So, anyway, just to satisfy my curiosity, how did you know the coke spoon held a flash drive?"

Tara says nothing, simply regards him with her basilisk stare.

He nods. "Fair enough."

"You owe me." She has been thinking about this, when she isn't obsessing over what it will mean to bring another life into the world, what it will be like to be a mother. "You owe me big time."

"I suppose I do." He eyes her. "Are you still going to work for me?"

"Hell, no. I'm going to work for myself."

He raises his eyebrows. "Really?" He laughs. "No offense, but you have no capital, so how's that going to work?"

"Simple," she says. "Constant Horizons is going to fund me."

Oh, how she adores the look on his face.

———

She is considering whether to stay in her room or go downstairs when her cell buzzes. Rose has thoughtfully plugged it in, so it is fully charged. She looks at the screen. A text. From Lind:

Figgy told me about the fire. Please let me know how you are.
Fondly, Dr Lind

Her heart skips a beat, and for a moment, she thinks about turning the phone off without answering. Then:

Im okay recovering finally Im sorry for what I did

Im glad. I'll let Charlotte know. She's been asking about you.

I really like Charlotte please don't make me stop seeing her

Silence, during which nurses stride by on silent shoes, doctors consult in whispers, patients hooked up to tubes hanging from mobile racks shuffle along, all oblivious to her mounting anxiety. It is now, while the waiting seems to stretch out interminably like the ocean, that she realizes just how much her friendship with Charlotte means to her. They bonded in a close and curious way. She understands Charlotte's difficult situation, and she knows Charlotte gets that. They were drawn together like two stitches in the same sweater.

Charlotte has made clear to me how much you mean to her. I would never take that connection away from her. But you know that our work isn't done. We've come to an inflection point, which is why you ran away. Come back and I will introduce you to another therapist. Lily Palmer is my best friend. You met her at the restaurant, in fact. She uses my office twice a week. I can speak to her, get her up to speed so you won't have to backtrack over ground we have covered. If you're agreeable.

She hesitates, then stabs three keys:

Yes

Please give me times and dates and I will set up the appointment. Please don't wait too long. Regaining your equilibrium is vital. Moving forward even more so.

Tears overrun her eyes, roll down her cheeks. Without thinking about it, she types:

fighting my demons

And immediately the answer comes back:

You're not alone.

———

Twenty minutes after Brandon leaves, she convinces the nurse to unhook her from the monitors for oxygen levels in her blood and heart rate, telling her she'll lose her mind if she can't go for a walk. In the wheelchair the nurse insists she use, she takes the elevator down to the basement cafeteria, a large overly bright room painted sky blue. Square tables and orange plastic chairs are scattered around.

Figgy is by himself at a table near the left-hand wall, a cup of coffee and some kind of sweet roll, untouched, in front of him. He is staring straight ahead, at nothing. He is wearing jeans, a leather jacket over a black T-shirt with **REFLECTIONS** emblazoned across the front in white. A pair of well-worn Nikes is on his feet. He is almost painfully beautiful. I will fucking kill Chloe for poaching on my territory. Her pulse quickens, and she thinks, Oh, I do love him. I do. But what about Chloe? And then, almost immediately, amazingly: I don't care about Chloe.

Heart in her mouth, Tara wheels herself across the room, acutely aware that she is dressed unflatteringly in a bathrobe over a hospital gown. She finds she doesn't care about that either.

364

And this is what she says to him as she comes up to his table, exactly what she is thinking at that second: "I don't care about Chloe."

He starts, as if she has set off a firecracker at his feet, which, if you think about it, she has.

"Tara." He shoots up. The tone in his voice—the sadness, the longing, the happiness—overcomes her, and she falls into him. Her face in the crook of his neck, she inhales the familiar scent of him: wood and leather and something darker, something she once scented in the midst of the Georgia forest.

"Figgy, I—"

"Here." He kicks a chair away. "Sit beside me."

She maneuvers awkwardly, not used to being in a wheelchair. When he offers to help her, and she declines, he understands. "I'm so happy to see you. I had no idea what was going to happen. Brandon kept me in the dark, even when I threatened him."

"I know," she says. "I know." She smiles wanly. "But that's over now."

A pained expression appears on his face. "About why we met—"

"Brandon told me. But . . ." Now, on the brink, she hesitates and hates herself for it. Tara would have lied, not understanding her own feelings. Sophie would have seduced him, not caring a bit how he feels, feeling nothing herself. "About Chloe . . ."

"Chloe who?"

And the way he says it, all the meaning of it, makes her smile. It is a whole lot better than crying. "I want you to know I found her bra the night of Miles Davis, when we danced. In your bathroom, when I was dressing to go out." She puts a hand up, forestalling him. "I don't need an explanation. In fact, I don't want one . . . except, was it serious?"

"No, never. It was just . . . now it seems like a whole bunch of nothing."

Her ire returns. "But then it wasn't," she says sharply.

He shakes his head. His eyes hold his hurt. "The truth is I don't know what it was. I was angry with you."

"You once called me a will-o'-the-wisp."

"Fool's fire." He nods. "A ghost light sent to mislead travelers at night."

"That's how you thought of me?"

"I didn't want to, believe me. But . . . I don't know; it seemed like you were using me like a puppy bats around a ball, then gets tired and disappears somewhere outside."

"Jesus."

"Honestly, I don't know what to make of you. There were times when you seemed to be two separate people." He pauses, reaches out for her. "That didn't stop me from falling in love with you."

All the breath goes out of her. She feels lightheaded and sits back against the wheelchair in order to steady herself. "So was I. More terrified than angry, I think, because I couldn't find it in me then to confront you."

"Do you . . . Tara, do you love me?"

She peers into his face, studying every feature. Then she takes his hand in hers. It is warm and dry, and just like that the dizziness passes, and she feels whole again. More than whole, if such a thing is possible.

"Yes," she whispers. "I do love you, Figgy."

He grins; she has missed that too.

They spend long minutes in silence, simply staring at one another. When are you going to tell him? she asks herself. Not here, not now, she answers. Not yet. And the moment she thinks it, she feels the rightness of the decision. Because she wants the baby, and that, too, is different. Tara wouldn't have wanted it. Sophie sure as hell wouldn't have wanted it; it would have interfered with her libertine lifestyle.

At that moment, serenely lost in Figgy's light eyes, she realizes that she is thinking of both Tara and Sophie in the third person. Is she neither of them now, or is she both? All she knows for certain is that she is now, and forever, different than either of them has been. Two halves make a whole, she thinks. Can human nature be as simple as that? Surely not, but then again . . .

"Not right now," Figgy is saying, "but sometime will you tell me what happened?"

She nods. "Of course. Everything." But will she? Well, he already knows the worst about Marwyn, so why not.

"How are Dr. Lind and Charlotte doing?" she asks with real concern.

"I spoke to her briefly. She is with her daughter, Charlotte. I think I caught them in an unguarded moment."

"Meaning?"

"Meaning it didn't take her long to return to work, and Charlotte's already back in school." He considers a moment. "Lind strikes me as a very smart person. Perhaps she suspected some of it already."

"She must have," Tara says. "That morning I stayed over, I overheard them arguing—and so did Charlotte. Lind knows at least that he's a serial cheater."

He nods. "In any event, they both seem, I don't know, I guess *calm* is the best word to describe it, but who really knows anything."

She ducks her head. "I hope you're right." A rush of warmth washes through her. "They both deserve some peace."

"You know them better than I do." Idly, he spins his cup of cold coffee around, sloshing some onto the table. He quickly rights it. "When do you get out of here?"

"A day or two. Not long now."

He takes her hand in both of his. "Let me know. I'd like to pick you up. I'll take you wherever you want to go."

Her smile morphs into a grin. "Hey, d'you know the first thing I want to do when I get out of here?"

It is his turn to laugh. "Tell me."

"I want you to play me Chick Corea's 'Return to Forever.'"

His eyebrows shoot up. "You told me to take it off after the first eight bars," he says in the bantering tone she has missed most of all.

"Yeah," she tells him, "but now I want the whole thing."

37

There is a protocol, an imperative among alcoholics self-aware enough to attend AA, as important as it is practical: making amends for past misdeeds. This is what Tara is determined to do, starting with M.

She has treated M unforgivably; she has been a real bitch, and she knows it. Or, rather, she knows it now, and she is ashamed of it.

She is fully aware that making amends doesn't always work. Like everything else with people, it is a two-way street. M might not accept her apology, want nothing more to do with her. Tara knows she needs to be prepared to be rebuffed with extreme prejudice, but that is easier thought of than accomplished. Making an internal joke is all she can do to keep herself calm until the moment she confronts her once and, she hopes, future friend.

At first, she thinks she'll go to find her at Seventh Haven, a neutral setting. But then, reconsidering, she knows that is the coward's choice. Besides, there'd be too many distractions and not enough time.

Loitering in front of the building for a good ten minutes, she keeps her mind busy watching people pass by, making up stories about them, until she realizes she can't recall what a single one even looks like. Nothing for it, she thinks, but to move forward.

As she enters the lobby, she quails. Oh, God, she thinks, what if she won't see me? What will I do then?

"Good evening, Miss Gemini," the doorman says. "Go right on up."

"I've lost my key. Can you please ring up to Miss Quintana and tell her I'm here."

He nods. "I know she's home; she just had a delivery from Uber Eats sent up."

The lobby seems to contract like an iris in bright light, to become not the lobby she knows but some strange two-dimensional simulacrum, flat, a stage set, waiting for its actors to appear and give it life.

Soon, too soon, the doorman hangs up and turns back to her. The answer's no, she thinks. I know it.

"Miss Quintana asked if you would wait."

She takes a seat in purgatory to await the pronouncement of her final sentence.

"Dissonance," Figgy said just hours before (because she had to put herself in a happy place in order to keep her anxiety at bay). "Both Miles and Corea were interested in exploring dissonance. Not surprising, since Chick played in one of Davis's bands."

They were snuggled together on his sofa. "Return to Forever" played softly in the background. She was so happy to be there, so happy to be with him, together on the other side of the raging river.

"But dissonance, the rubbing of unrelated notes up against each other, is not for everyone," he said. "It takes time and patience to realize that those notes, though unrelated, have an attraction, one to the other. Together, they make something different, something new. That's what both Miles and Chick were exploring."

"I still prefer Miles," she said. "'Miles Runs the Voodoo Down' gives me shivers, takes me away."

He smiled, hugging her tighter. "You hear the new thing."

The new thing, she thinks. I'm the new thing—new to everyone, even myself. Tara and Sophie, two unrelated notes, when rubbed up against each other, making something different, something new. And she thinks of the swimmer on Christie's office wall, striving, always striving. The first time she saw her, she thought she was drowning. That's because I was drowning, she thinks now.

"Miss Gemini?"

It is a moment before she realizes the doorman is calling her. Rousing herself from her reverie, she stands rigid, alert, as if before a firing squad.

"Yes?" Her voice almost catches in her throat.

"You can go on up now."

She feels something melt inside her, like an ice cream cone in the summer sun. She feels herself moving toward the bank of elevators, though someone else must be directing her body, because her mind is somewhere high above.

Up the elevator climbs, and her with it. On M's floor she steps out. For a moment, she is bewildered, unsure which way to turn. Then she sees a front door ajar, and she goes along to her right, remembering the way.

She arrives at the door, her extremities and her mind numb. She pushes the door open. "M?" There is no Abraxas to greet her as she steps across the threshold.

M sits at the small wooden table in the space between the kitchen and the living room.

"Is Abraxas all right?" Odd those are the first words that come out of her mouth.

"She's fine." M gestures toward her bedroom. "Taking a catnap."

They stare at each other for some time, as if sizing each other up. The awkwardness of the situation is brought home to Tara—she doesn't know whether M has just made a joke.

"Come in and sit down," M says, coolly. She is wearing jeans, a horizontally striped green-and-blue polo shirt, and a pair of scuffed Doc Martens.

Tara closes the door behind her, moves in as silently as Abraxas through the apartment. She sits, but gingerly, perching on the edge of the chair across from M, as if at any moment she might lose her nerve and flee.

"M, I just—"

But she halts at M's raised hand. "My apartment, my rules." There are two brown paper bags on the table—probably the food M has ordered. Now she pushes them to one side.

"I want to tell you a story about my father. He had a friend—his best friend from when they were kids. They played together, went to school together, went out on double dates, all of that stuff. They grew into adulthood, long since best friends. Manolo, my father's friend, was lucky enough to marry a woman from a wealthy family."

She pauses a moment, as if to conjure up this woman, Manolo's wife, in her mind, to see her more clearly through the mist of the past. "There comes a time when my father has an opportunity to buy out the plumbing company he worked for. All he needs is the money. A stake. He goes to Manolo and tells him about the opportunity, offers to bring him in fifty-fifty. Manolo likes the idea; plumbing is a lucrative business. He says he'll talk to his wife. The following day the two men meet. The deal's off; Manolo's wife won't give him the money. She doesn't trust my father. She doesn't believe he has a head for business. 'He's a plumber,' she tells Manolo. 'He'll always be a plumber.'"

M drums her hands on the table, closing them into fists. "'She won't hear of it. What can I do?' Manolo says. 'You can get off your fucking knees, *cabrón*, and grow a pair,' my father tells him. He walked away and never saw or spoke to Manolo again."

Street noise filters through the kitchen window—cars and taxis passing, a one-sided conversation on a phone, a brief burst of laughter, quickly muffled—the small discreet noises of Greenwich Village. Her blood has turned cold. Why did I come here? she asks herself. What did you expect her to do, welcome you with open arms and say, All is forgiven?

"M, I—"

Again the upraised hand. "You're amazing with the kids, Tara. You're better with them, more important to them, than anyone else I've worked with. You've got a huge heart, and I love you for that."

"Thank you." But she is waiting for the "but." It isn't long in coming.

"You completely blindsided me. I never for a minute thought you would just up and leave Seventh Haven without us discussing it."

"I know, but . . ." But Tara's protest dies in her throat. She takes a breath, lets it out, her cheeks pinked and hot. "There were things I couldn't tell you then." She shakes her head. "But the way I brought it up, the way I acted, that was wrong. I know it was wrong, and I'm so, so sorry, M. It was a shitty thing to do. You've been nothing but so very kind to me—such a great mentor too. You always stood up for me at work, when I came in late or . . . you're a good friend, M. That's the bottom line, and I don't want to lose you."

M stares at her. "My father is an honest man. He values friendship highly. But he's also a prideful man. I saw how his pride got in the way of his happiness. He loved Manolo, and he was diminished the moment he turned his back on him. His pride diminished him.

"I don't hold grudges, Tara. I am my father's daughter," she says. "But I'm not my father, thank God." Her eyes seem to penetrate beneath Tara's skin. "I never had designs on you." Her forefinger makes circles on the tabletop.

"I know, M. I know. What I did was unforgiveable."

"Then you must forgive yourself." The air between them seems to peel away, baring tender flesh. Time freezes or becomes unstuck from its daily moorings as the meaning of M's words slowly sinks in, layers only Tara knows of or understands. I am like nested Russian dolls, she thinks, each part of me inside the other, going deeper and deeper, darker and darker. Tara shivers then, and she knows the meaning of someone walking on her grave.

M opens the bags, draws out plastic takeout containers. She slides one over to Tara, opens hers, and goes to work. She lightly dips a piece of yellowtail sushi into a small bowl of soy sauce, then into her mouth. She closes her eyes while the fish dissolves in her mouth. "Mm, that's so good." When she opens her eyes, she sees Tara sitting still, staring at her. "What? Aren't you going to eat? It's from Japonica."

"I'm not hungry." Tara glanced at the sushi once, then not again, slightly nauseated. She thinks of the pastrami sandwich Brandon brought her days ago, and her mouth begins to water.

"Beer then." M rises, takes out two bottles from the refrigerator, sets them on the table. "Dos Equis Ambar, your favorite."

Tara shakes her head. "I'll just get myself some water." At the sink, she fills a glass, brings it back, and sits.

M, still in the midst of eating, gives Tara a penetrating look. "The fight we had really disturbed me. Then I walk into Seventh Haven, find you'd been shitcanned on orders from Brandon, and phoned him, then texted him. Crickets."

Tara ducks her head. "I'm sorry about that."

M leans forward. "I'll know you're sorry when you tell me what the hell happened."

"Marwyn Rusk happened."

M drops the sushi. "What?"

So Tara tells her the whole story, from the time Brandon made her the job offer to her coercion to what she discovered at Figgy's to the night she went to Deva and met Rose, and the two of them being taken to Marwyn's Hell's Kitchen fuck pad.

"Wait a minute." The blood has rushed out of M's face. "Are you telling me that fire I read about . . . that you . . . that . . ."

Tara is nodding at every turn.

"Holy shit." M gets up, goes to Tara, and puts her arms around her. "Holy shit, girl. Damn." The feel of her, the depth of her emotion, starts Tara crying.

M's shoulders, which have been drawn up, relax. "No wonder you look different."

Which causes Tara to start laughing softly.

"What?" M draws away enough to be able to get a good look at her friend. "What is it?"

Tara considers a moment. "I want to tell you, but not here. How about we go for a walk? Maybe down by the Hudson?"

M nods. "Fine by me." And she rises, steps into her bedroom. Abraxas pads out, fixes her golden eyes on Tara, and leaps up into her waiting arms. "I missed you too," she says, nuzzling the cat. The vibrations coming from her as she purrs sink deep inside her, warming her. She has been chilled inside, so terrified was she that M would reject her.

"What a great pal you are," Tara says, rubbing behind the cat's ears.

M swings on an Avirex jacket. "What would I do without that little lady."

They head west, crossing Sixth, then Greenwich Avenue. They leave behind the bright lights and honky-tonk of Seventh Avenue South, a solid demarcation heralding the old brownstone section known as the West Village. Here, the same buildings exist just as they did seventy and eighty years ago, some fronted by tiny gardens guarded by black iron fences.

Nearing the West Side Highway, M breathes deeply. "You know, Tara, you were right about one thing. I was lonely after Stevie left. I didn't realize how lonely until our blowup and you were gone too."

They cross with the light and then are on the far side of the whizzing traffic, past the bicycle path, on the wide riverside promenade. By unspoken consent, they head south, but with no clear destination in mind. Now and again, a ship's mournful horn carries over the light-streaked water. To their right, wooden pilings, leaning as if against the tidal flow, complain like arthritic old men.

Tara takes a deep breath, lets it out slowly. "So here's the deal," she says. "First, I'd like to introduce you to Rose."

375

M gives her an arch look. "Are you trying to fix me up?"

Tara laughs. "I don't know about that. I don't know Rose's sexual orientation, and I'm not inclined to guess. If something happens between you two, that's your business. But no, I'm getting together a team."

M's ears seem to perk up. "A team? For what?"

"That's the second thing. I got Brandon to fund a group—"

"Brandon is your money guy? Uh-oh."

"Ha, no. It's not like that."

"Hey, kiddo, it's always like that for us girls."

Tara nods, acknowledging the truth of that. "This is different. For one thing, Brandon's all for what I want to do."

M turns to her, one elbow on the railing. "Which is?"

"Rose and I—and you, if you agree—are going to run Seventh Haven."

"What?" M nearly jumps.

"And we're going to do it our way. I want my freedom, from him as well as from everybody else. The reorganization I have in mind is going to lead to Seventh Haven becoming fiscally self-sufficient."

M shakes her head. "When something sounds too good to be true, it usually is."

Tara smiles. "Not this time. We're buying the building, for one thing. For another, we're leasing out the top three floors."

"Tara, there are addicts running in and out of there. Who's going to want to rent . . . ?"

"Figgy's already agreed to it. He needs space for his start-up."

M's eyes open wide. "Wow, okay, but—"

"Here's the best part. You'll have carte blanche. You'll run the day-to-day operations, set the budgets, be in charge of hiring, what you've always wanted. As for me, I want the kids who come there to not only learn to live their best life; I want them protected. I was there when

ICE came and took Lia away. I never felt so helpless in my life. It broke my heart."

"So how?"

"Lawyers," Tara says. "One of Figgy's father's best friends is Nicole Ayoub, who runs her own immigration law shop. She's top rated, she knows how to handle this new administration, and by all accounts she's relentless. Her first order of business is to rescue Lia."

"How on earth will you afford her?"

Tara grins. "Just like buying the building, that's part of Brandon's side of things."

"Jesus, Tara, you're going to owe him big-time. I mean, he'll own you and everyone else who's involved."

"Normally, you'd be right. But this situation is anything but normal. What I did the night of the fire got Brandon out of a very deep hole he'd been in for a decade or more."

"Okay, well, now you've gotta tell me—"

"Uh-uh." Tara shakes her head. "Some things have to remain between him and me. Suffice it to say he had a misspent youth."

"I see." M's gaze follows the spangled lights of a passing boat, where a party is in full swing. Katy Perry's "Never Really Over" lights up the night for a few moments, then fades off. "And what about your new friend Rose?"

"You'll like her—I know you will."

"What's her background?"

"She's a high-end escort."

"Perfect!" M throws her head back, laughing. "You're joking, right?"

"Not at all."

"Just my type!" M cries.

"Well, she's ex now. As you can imagine, she's psychologically very savvy. And we do get girls in—and now and again a boy or two—who in desperation have turned tricks. She'd be perfect counseling them."

"Hmm. It seems as if you have it all figured out."

"Not quite."

The wind has shifted, and with it, the air grows heavy and damp. A slow drizzle falls, sending threadbare voile curtains dancing across the river. Neither of the women moves, accepting the weather as they accept each other.

Tara is quiet for so long that M says, "What is it? What's the matter?"

"You still haven't told me whether you're in."

"First, I want to know that you'll have time for counseling. I'm not going to lose my best counselor while you go play at being a mogul."

Tara laughs. "The kids are my first love. I'll make time for them no matter what."

"Then Santa Maria! Of course I'm in, dummy! Now spill, what's eating at you?"

"Funny you should say that."

M flashes her a quizzical look.

"Hold that look," Tara says. Turning, she leans over the rail and vomits.

"Hey." M puts a hand on her back. "Hey! Are you okay? You're not sick or anything, are you?"

"This is perfectly normal," Tara says, wiping her mouth with a tissue. She always carries a couple of travel packs with her now. "For someone in my condition."

"What—hey, wait a minute. I saw you go green when you looked at the sushi, and you didn't want a beer. And now you're hurling for no apparent reason." She grabs hold of Tara. "Jesus, girl, you're pregnant!"

A sheepish look creeps over Tara's face. "Indeed."

"I think congratulations are in order." She takes Tara in her arms and embraces her. Then she holds Tara at arm's length. "The father? I hope to God it's Figgy. Tell me it's Figgy."

Tara grins. "It is."

"What was his reaction?" M says with obvious relief.

"I haven't told him yet." Fear muddies Tara's eyes. "I'm scared shitless. We're pretty new, after all. And I don't know whether he sees a kid in his future."

"Why the hell wouldn't he?"

"He's just starting his business, and you know, some people, they're not cut out to be a parent."

M frowns. "Has Figgy given you any indication that he's that type?"

"It's far too early for anything even remotely like that to have come up. But I mean, springing this on him—"

"Well, shit, you have to tell him regardless." M peers deep into Tara's eyes. "You *do* want the baby."

"What a question!" Tara cries. "Of course I want the baby."

M nods. "Then the real question is, Do you want a future with Figgy?"

38

"You have diamonds in your hair," Figgy says, smiling.

"What?" She puts her hand up, feels the wetness from the misting rain, and laughs.

"How did your reunion with M go?" he asks.

She has returned quite late. Unsurprisingly, he is still awake, sitting up in bed, watching an episode of *Dead to Me* on his iPad.

"She told me a story about her dad, and I was sure I was a dead duck."

"I think you might want to have more faith in your friends," he says, setting the iPad aside.

"I think you're onto something there, Dr. Freud."

He gives a chuckle and pats the mattress next to him. She sighs, sits on the edge of the bed, her back slightly bowed. "I feel like I've gone fifteen rounds with a heavyweight."

"That shouldn't come as a surprise. You've been through so much in the last two weeks. Give yourself a break." He reaches for her. As he does so, the bedcovers slip down, and she can see that he is naked. He takes her hands in his. "Now come to bed."

He watches her with avid eyes as she strips off her damp clothes. Naked, she crosses to the bathroom. She isn't too exhausted to realize with a jolt that the old Tara would never have revealed herself so fully, so brazenly in front of him—or any man, for that matter.

In the bathroom, she relieves herself, then, stooping, splashes cold water on her face. Staring at herself in the mirror, water running down her cheeks like rain, she sees a different person. Her eyes have the crackle and spark of Sophie, and as she continues to stare, her lips curve in Sophie's smile. But she is Tara inside. She no longer feels the demon inside her tearing into her guts, trying to claw its way out. And yet she is hardly at peace. She still hasn't told Figgy about the baby, and though she has wanted to, she hasn't confessed to M that she lied to her, that Sophie doesn't exist—has never existed in the way she has depicted her. Lying and withholding: this is typical Tara behavior through and through.

She places her hands on her lower belly. There is no swell as yet, but that won't last. She knows she has to tell Figgy before the baby starts to show, before she's peeing every hour. Already her eating habits have changed radically, and what if the hurling starts up in earnest?

It is then that her mind goes blank and the shakes begin. Not as violent as they were in the hospital, but bad enough that she has to grasp the edge of the sink to keep herself from falling. She thinks of the compassionate Dr. Kim and keeps her eyes focused on her reflection, on her own eyes in the mirror and on nothing else—not her bone-white, pinched face, not her chattering jaw. Soon enough, the shakes subside, and she is herself again. She takes a deep, gasping breath. Better, she thinks. Better.

She splashes more cold water on her face, lets the droplets run down the valley between her swollen breasts, across her abdomen, until she has diamonds in the hair at the juncture of her thighs.

Nonetheless, it is with a troubled mind that she returns to the bedroom, where Figgy waits patiently for her. She looks at him and stops in her tracks.

"What?" he says. "What is it?" He rubs his face. "Do I have something hanging out of my nose?"

She laughs and leaps onto the bed, straddling him, pushing him back down. With her face very close to his, she says, "No, you just looked so damn handsome."

He grins. "You know, the day I met you was the best day of my life."

She puts a hand to his cheek. "You know that's the best compliment you could give me."

"It's only the truth." And he wraps his arms around her, presses his lips to hers.

She feels the heat rising in her, that breathless sensation that tightens her chest, loosens her limbs. She pushes the covers aside and sees he is as hard as a wooden staff. She buries her face in his flesh, inhales his special scent until she is dizzy. When, sometime afterward, he enters her, she cries out.

Their lovemaking is different, not like it was with Sophie, which was only one thing: not like the old Tara, which would have been nothing. She enters this new thing with an open heart and gives herself over to the pleasure and the pure physicality of the moment.

It is only when she comes back to earth, lying in his arms, their limbs tangled, listening to the slowing of his pulse, the evenness of his breathing, that she becomes aware again of the life growing inside her, the secrets she is keeping, from him and from herself.

—

She wakes up earlier than usual, unable or unwilling to return to sleep and her uneasy dreams. She rolls out of bed without disturbing Figgy, draws on a robe, and pads downstairs to fix herself a double shot of espresso. She takes it out the back door and into the open space that abuts Christie's brownstone. It is a warm morning, the sky a deep pearlescent blue gray, as if still coming out of its nighttime cocoon. She wanders over to the fence, perhaps subconsciously hoping to catch a glimpse of Lind herself. But her backyard is deserted. The birds, at least, are out, gossiping among themselves, swooping down to the ground, briefly hopping this way and that, before taking off back up into the branches of the tree.

"Hey!"

She looks up.

"Hey, Tara!"

And there is Charlotte in her treehouse. Tara smiles and waves. "How are you?"

"Hang on," Charlotte calls and, emerging fully, scrambles down the ladder. At the far end of the fence, she grasps a board and moves it aside.

Tara laughs, hears an answering giggle as she steps down to where there is now a narrow gap in the fence. "How're you doing?" she asks, when they're face to face.

Charlotte shrugs. "Oh, you know. The first few days were a nightmare, but now that the press is on to some other story, it's better."

"I'm sorry about your father."

Charlotte's expression changes as quickly as a diva switching outfits. Her face grows dark, hard as an adult's. "Well, he had it coming, didn't he? I mean, he treated my mom like crap. So many times I found her curled up in a ball, crying." She is crying herself now, but they seem like tears of rage.

Tara can't imagine Christie curled up in a ball, crying. She doesn't think she wants to, and for a moment she regrets this conversation. She reaches out to Charlotte, squeezes her hand.

"Where did you go?" Charlotte asks, as if to shake off her tears.

"Oh, I had to visit a relative who was ill."

"I hope they're okay," Charlotte says in the vague way adolescents have of speaking about people they don't know.

"All better," Tara says. "Almost."

And then Charlotte, leaning through the gap so Tara can hold her, bursts into tears again. "But I didn't want him to die," she cries. "I didn't."

"I know, honey." Tara kisses the top of her head, feels her sorrow acutely.

"I imagined him dead so many times." Charlotte sniffles. "When they fought—when, especially, he brought her presents, because then I knew he was trying to make up for something awful he'd done against her."

"Charlotte, listen to me: my parents had god-awful fights when I was little. You pray for things to be different. You think it's your fault; you wonder what you did to cause this. But it's not your fault. This was between the two of them. Your father . . . I met your father once."

Charlotte looks up at her; tears continue to spill out, rolling down her cheeks. "You did?"

Tara nods. "At a party." Careful now, she tells herself. "He wasn't nice. He wasn't kind. I wanted to like him, but he made it impossible." She wonders if she's made a mistake. "Please don't tell your mother; it will only make her feel worse."

"Yeah." Charlotte is nodding. She frowns. "Why was he like that? I don't understand."

"Honey, I don't think anyone understands, including your mother, and she makes her living trying to understand people."

"Sure. I know." Charlotte seems calmer now, the storm passing. She exhales heavily. "I just . . . I so didn't want this to happen. I mean, why didn't she leave him? Why didn't she take me away?"

"That's a tough one," Tara says, thinking of her own father. "But adults, right?"

Charlotte gives a sad little laugh.

"It's often the case that people stay when from the outside it seems clear they should go."

"But why? It seems so simple."

"And yet the opposite is true. It's not simple at all." Tara thinks about this. "It's human nature to take the path of least resistance, to stay with the known rather than step into the unknown."

"Even when what you have makes you unhappy?"

"*Especially* then." Tara gives her a rueful smile. "It's a funny old world, IMHO."

"It is," Charlotte says emphatically. "It is."

Tara's fingers entwine with Charlotte's through the gaps in the fence.

"How are things at school?"

"Ugh. I can't wait to get out of there. I'm sick to death of my classmates. They'd rather be taking selfie vids for TikTok or Snapchatting each other than talking in person, and all they talk about now is my father, and when they see me, they look at me funny. Plus which, I've had to close my TikTok and Insta accounts because the trolls wouldn't let me alone."

"Forget about them," Tara says. "I feel sorry for those people. Talking in person has become too scary, too revealing. Now, hiding on the internet, everyone's a critic, and all the angriest ones are the loudest and most persistent."

"Hey, yeah. That's right. I've been too bummed to think of that."

Tara shifts from one foot to the other. "How's your mother doing?"

"Honestly, I think better than me," Charlotte says. "She has this way of being able to balance everything out." She gives a little laugh, then, that is as much a hiccup. "Except when it comes to me. She can go ballistic at the smallest things. Well, I think they're the smallest things, obviously."

"I think your mom is stressed out right now, so maybe give her some slack. And anyway, moms worry about their kids," Tara says, wondering whether that was true of her own mother and, if it was, why she wasn't aware of it. "It's instinctive. It's what they do." It will certainly be true for her, she vows. "Have you talked to her about your dad?"

"I tried, but she just shuts down."

"Maybe she's trying to protect you."

"Yeah, she thinks I don't know what went on between them. But I know everything. He cheated on her, and kept on cheating."

"Maybe you should tell her that. That you know." You're a good one to talk, she thinks.

Charlotte's smile is genuine, without an adult's cynical guile. "You're really cool."

Tara grins. "Right back atcha."

A raised voice from her back door calling her name causes Charlotte to glance over her shoulder. "That's Mom. I gotta go." She waves as she heads back across the yard. "Hey, I'm glad you're back."

"Hey." Tara smiles. "Me too."

———

"Hobnobbing with the neighbors again?"

She turns to see Figgy standing on the back stoop.

"Charlotte and I were just figuring out how to save the world."

"You two have definitely formed a bond," he says as he comes up to her. He kisses her, then takes a step back, holds up a white paper bag. "Croissants, fresh from Citarella." He grins. "I stood in line for you and everything."

She laughs. "Gimme one of those." Handing him her half-finished double espresso, she grabs a croissant and bites into the flaky, buttery layers. "My God, that's good!"

He sips her espresso, his eyes glittering as the sun spreads its warmth across the rooftops. He inhales slowly, deeply, as if wanting to take this moment and everything it portends into himself. "It's going to be a fine day. Let's do something—go up to the Cloisters, maybe."

"I'd like that."

He kisses a flake of croissant off the corner of her mouth. "Okay, then."

She stuffs the rest of the croissant back in the bag; all that butter is making her stomach queasy. "But first," she says, "there's something I'd like to discuss."

39

I 'm so pleased to see you up and about."

"Physically I'm fine," Tara says.

"What good news."

With her noncommittal smile, Christie Lind ushers Tara into the house. Today, she is wearing a black-pearl necklace, perhaps a discreet symbol of a death in the family.

"You have been such a good friend to Charlotte," Christie says. "She needs friends now more than ever."

"Does this mean we'll be friends too?"

"Perhaps." Christie holds her in her gaze for a moment. "Give it time, Tara. Can you do that?"

Tara nods. She is acutely aware that she hasn't given her condolences. Even now, she cannot bring herself to do so and understands it is a lack in her that she cannot help. She has thought long and hard about coming back here, been afraid Marwyn's specter would fill the room. But since she has spilled the beans to M, had that eye-opening conversation with Charlotte, she decided to take the chance. Now here she is. She thinks, Christie and I are like two shadows passing each other in a lightless hallway. We're so close, yet about this one thing I am invisible to her. And for the first time she realizes, like Charlotte not telling her mother she knows all about Marwyn's philandering, how that will be a good thing going forward.

They start down the familiar hall that leads to Christie's office. When they arrive at the door, Christie says, "Dr. Palmer is waiting for you." That smile again, warmer this time. "She knows everything, Tara. She and I have had several evenings together, and now I understand you have sent her something you wrote."

"Have you seen it?" Tara asks with no little trepidation.

"I shall," Christie says, "only if Dr. Palmer deems it useful." Her smile is warm, encompassing. "I'd like to think that one day you might tell me yourself." She nods. "Now, go," she says, in the gentle voice a mother might use to send her child off to a new school.

She opens the door, steps aside.

"You're not coming in?" Tara asks in a brief flash of panic.

"This session is between you and Dr. Palmer." And then because she sees the look in Tara's eyes: "Relax. You'll like her; we trained together under the same mentors."

Inside, Lily Palmer meets Tara, shakes her hand, indicates Tara's accustomed place.

"It's a pleasure to see you again." Her smile is different from Christie's and also in some ways the same. "I remember you vividly from our brief encounter."

Tara does not know what to say to that, but in fact, save for her clothes, Dr. Palmer looks exactly as Tara remembers at the restaurant, sitting opposite Christie and Charlotte: large hazel eyes; a strong, resolute face; dark hair blunt cut to just above her shoulders. She's in silk slacks and a lightweight sweater. In this setting the innate strength in her face has the effect of calming Tara's nerves somewhat. Still, she is facing the unknown at—as Christie correctly said—a crucial time in her healing process.

Still ill at ease, she stands up and paces about. The room has been repainted a rich cream color so recently the tang is still in the air, despite the glass vase of fragrant lilacs on top of a bookcase. The painting of the swimmer is precisely where it has always been, however, and this reassures her.

"Breathe slowly and deeply, Tara," Palmer says.

Tara tries that with limited success.

"This can be just a get-to-know-each-other session," Palmer says. "We can just—"

"I don't want to be quiet." The words are out of her mouth before she can stop them. "But I don't know whether I can trust you."

Palmer waits a moment. "I read what you sent me this morning," she says softly. "Several times."

"I've never told anyone about my childhood. Even Dr. Lind."

"How did it feel to write about it?"

"It felt . . ." Tara shifts her gaze from the swimmer to look Palmer full in the face. Her eyes are quite beautiful, she sees now, and full of compassion. "It felt like freedom."

"That's a good thing, don't you think?"

After a brief hesitation: "I do, yes."

"Tara, when you first came to Dr. Lind, you were behind a curtain—in seclusion from the world. To give you a vivid example, the Persian word for *curtain* is *purdah*. Some Muslim and Hindu women go into purdah, either behind an actual screen or within the drapery of clothes, in order to shield themselves from being seen by men and strangers."

A shiver attached to her mother's shadow runs down Tara's spine. "Is it a religious practice?"

"Religious and social," Palmer says. "In either case the purpose of purdah is concealment. By pretending Sophie was your sister, you were in purdah, concealing your true self from everyone."

Tara takes some time to digest this information. Then, thinking of how secretive, how concealed she was with Christie, she nods.

Palmer regards her neutrally. "You might be more comfortable if you sat down."

Tara returns to the love seat. Above and behind Palmer, the swimmer keeps on keeping on, and Tara hears again Katy Perry singing "Never Really Over" across the wide nighttime Hudson.

Palmer has taken up her pad, her pen hovering over it like one of the birds on Charlotte's treehouse.

"While I was away, I was in another fire."

"So I understand."

"It brought back the first fire."

Concern clouds Palmer's face. "How badly were you injured?"

"Smoke inhalation." Tara hesitates. The old Tara would have stopped there, would have husbanded yet another secret. "Also a concussion."

"I'm so sorry. Are you all right?"

"Yes, I . . ." Again, she has the impression of a time slip: a faded picture of the old withholding Tara, the uninhibited, fuck-everyone Sophie. Neither exists anymore. "Well, actually, I don't know yet. I'm still getting bouts of the shakes. My mind goes blank, and then the trembling starts; my extremities get cold. If I'm standing up, I have to grab hold of something so I don't stumble and fall."

Palmer's brows draw together. "What does your doctor say?"

"That they will pass. And actually, they're getting less frequent, and when they do come, they're shorter and less violent."

"Were you prescribed any medication?"

Tara shakes her head. "I just have to let it be."

Palmer appears to consider this response. "Something about you seems different." She tilts her head, taps her forefinger against her lips. Her nails are as blunt cut as her hair. "Are you, by any chance, pregnant?"

Tara nods. "I am." She finds that she is inordinately pleased. It is as if this intuitive comment creates a certain bond between her and Palmer. The kind of intimacy one finds only with a good therapist.

Palmer smiles. Her pen rises from her pad. "How absolutely lovely. Congratulations."

"Thank you."

"Does the father know?"

"I told him yesterday."

"I trust he was happy."

"He was," she says. "Extremely." A vision of Figgy's reaction when she told him about the baby swims across the scrim of her mind. Eyes wide as a child's on Christmas morning, an enormous grin wreathing his face, all he could say was "Wowwowwow!" He said it over and over again while he swung her around, and her heart sang.

Yet again, the time slippage, the awareness of a lie that would have formed on her lips. Not now. "I also told him that I don't know whether I want a conventional relationship."

"You mean marriage."

"That's right. Yes."

"Do you want to be a single mother?"

"I have—" And she stops, realizing that Christie is now herself a single mother. She clears her throat, starts again. "I have a group of girlfriends who can help me, if need be."

"What about the father?"

"The father is Figgy," she says with a shy smile. "He's—"

"Christie has introduced me, and how perfect. Then you would want him involved."

"He's so over the moon, so yes. Most definitely."

"Being a single mother presents a great many challenges," Palmer says. "I'd like you to give the matter some thought before you decide."

"Of course. I will."

"We can discuss it here, if you like. At another session."

Tara nods.

Palmer turns to a fresh page in her notebook. "Today, though, I'd like, if you wouldn't mind, to talk about your relationship with your parents."

"I already wrote it out. You read it."

"Yes, and yet I can't help but wonder if there's more."

Tara shakes her head, her mind racing, racing, as if against a powerful tide. "I know what you're thinking."

"Tell me."

"You think I have dissociative identity disorder."

"Is that what *you* think?"

"No," Tara says, "I don't."

"Do you believe you're qualified to make that determination?"

"There's no one better."

"I'd like you to consider the possibility that you might be too close to the situation."

"Anything's possible, I suppose," Tara says. "But in this case I don't think so."

"How certain you are. Tell me why."

"I've had a long time to think about it. And Sophie and I had a number of internal conversations about it. I think we were always two halves of a whole. Neither of us was a full person, but together . . ."

Palmer puts her hands together. "Tara, you were physically abused. That needs to be unpacked fully. Writing about it is a terrific first step. But unraveling the effects on you is a process."

"But I was protected from my mother," she protests. "My father protected me."

"That is a child's narrative, the narrative your father fed you," Palmer says levelly. "The truth is you were abused by both your parents. What your father did to you was exceedingly dangerous; it bordered on the psychotic."

Tara, stunned, shakes her head. "You don't understand. It was all he could do; it was everything he could do. He was powerless to leave my mother. Her sexuality overwhelmed him."

"And yet according to what you wrote, he still slept with other women. A host of them."

Tara is silent. The panic she felt when she first sat down is once again rising. She feels it in her throat like a ball of tar, choking her.

"The moment your father became aware of what your mother was doing to you, he should have taken you away," Palmer says. "Instead, he laid your child's psyche bare. Where do you think Sophie's endless promiscuity comes from? You?" Palmer shakes her head. "No, it came from your father. He made Sophie into a simulacrum of himself."

And, with an indrawn gasp, Tara hears her father calling her Kitten, Sophie calling her Kitten. Same name, same voice. Why hadn't she realized that until now? But Lind told her: she had been too close, too close to see the truth.

"Your father used you. He made you pay for his weakness, Tara. Your mother may have violated your body, but your father violated your mind—the mind of a helpless five-year-old child. His abuse of you was every bit as damaging as your mother's."

Tara, bent over with her head in her hands, is rocking back and forth, making small animal noises.

"Tara." Palmer's voice is gentle and so very kind. "Tara, what are you thinking right now?"

Tara's voice is muffled, indistinct. "I hardly know what to think. This is so . . . my entire world . . . the way I remembered my childhood . . . ashes at my feet. I don't know what to do with this new reality. I don't want it."

"That's perfectly understandable," Palmer says. "But in time you'll come to see this as a good thing. It's difficult to absorb. I get that. And, yes, this is a new reality; it will take time for it to make sense. But what I can assure you now is that its foundation is rock, not quicksand."

Tara looks up, bleary eyed. "Part of me doesn't believe you."

"That's the part that doesn't want to believe, the part that's still invested in the old narrative."

She recalls a snippet of yesterday's early-morning conversation with Charlotte across the back fence. "It's human nature to take the path of least resistance, to stay with the known rather than go for the unknown," she said.

"Even when what you have makes you unhappy?" Charlotte asked with uncanny accuracy.

"Especially then," Tara replied.

She shakes her head now. "I'm sorry." Never say you're sorry, her father told her. Well, too bad, Dad. "I'm sorry."

"Just breathe, Tara," Palmer says. "Just breathe and be present." She smiles. "You're not alone in this anymore. You've come back. Whatever you need, I'm here to give you."

At that, tears spill out of Tara's eyes, overrun her cheeks. Palmer pushes a box of tissues across the table between them. Tara grabs a couple, presses them against her face. "Oh, God," she whispers. "Oh, God."

"It will get better," Palmer says. "I promise."

Tara nods wordlessly, but she still feels as if she is falling—falling from the sky into the sea. She wants her swimmer beside her, and she looks up, over Palmer's head. Yes, she is still there, still swimming, still alive, still struggling, and she takes a deep, shuddering breath, feeling a bit better.

"I wonder," Palmer says. "Have you read Robert Louis Stevenson's *The Strange Case of Dr. Jekyll and Mr. Hyde*?"

Wiping away the last of her tears, Tara says, "I think I saw a film version once."

Palmer chuckles. "I'm going to give you a homework assignment, if I may. I'd like you to read that novel. I think it might be beneficial. It's a treasure trove of fascinating psychological insights you might find useful. Like you, Dr. Jekyll and his alter ego, Mr. Hyde, were two halves of a whole. Superego and id, in Freudian terms. One is chained to the strictures of Victorian conventions; the other is the opposite. Dr. Jekyll viewed Hyde as pure evil, but I'm not convinced Stevenson felt that way. It seems to me what the story is really about is how far civilization has distanced human beings from their primitive selves. Instinct is being bred out of humans, Stevenson is saying, and that's not a good thing."

"There were things about Sophie—her exuberance, her unbridled sexuality, her disdain for conventions—I envied," Tara says. "These things made her brave. They gave her a strength that, as Tara, I never had." She pauses for a moment, gathering her thoughts. "But then again, Sophie had no regard for the emotions of others. That part frightened me."

"So unlike with Jekyll and Hyde, Tara isn't the good side, and Sophie isn't the dark side."

"No, not at all. But we were always one."

"And now?"

"Something happened in the aftermath of that fire, some alchemical change inside my mind."

"Like Dr. Jekyll's potion, only in reverse."

"I suppose you could say that."

But Palmer is shaking her head. "No, Tara. No outside magic happened. It is all you. Something must have happened when you were exposed to the second fire that brought you two together, some bit of insight, some act . . ."

And there it is, laid out in front of Tara like a banquet. "We helped each other," she says in wonder. "I remembered something vital, and Sophie had the courage to go back into the fire and get it." She takes a shuddering breath. "We worked together, you see. For the first time since we'd been children, for the first time since the farmhouse fire, Sophie and I helped each other." Her voice is brighter. She is feeling better, getting her feet back under her, going over this well-worn history. "I mean, sometimes we also fought—often desperately. But that is only because we were each seeking to be whole. I lost my way, and Sophie never found hers. Now, together, we have."

Palmer is busy taking notes, and Tara takes the time to turn inward. Her hands work in her lap, the fingers twining and untwining, as if trying to work out a difficult puzzle or untie a maddening knot.

"Does that narrative seem right, or is there something else?" Palmer glances up from her writing. It is as if her wise and knowing gaze is seeing clear through Tara's last defenses, to her castle's most closely guarded keep. "Something you haven't been able to admit to yourself."

Tara's breath catches in her throat. She feels something in the pit of her stomach start to unwind, like a serpent awakening from a long, unnatural slumber.

"I . . . I . . ." The serpent coils around her, causing panic. "I can't . . ."

"Yes, you can," Palmer says. "You've only to try." She leans forward, half out of her chair. "Breathe, Tara. Breathe." She puts her pad and pen aside. "That's right. One breath at a time. One thought at a time. Let go of the memory—you're squeezing it too tight."

It's me, Tara thinks. Oh God, I'm the serpent. Her mouth is filled with panic.

"Relax," Palmer says in that comforting voice of hers that already seems familiar. "Whatever it is, let it come to the surface of its own accord."

"No, no, no. No!" Tara cries. She drops to the rug, on her knees. "I can't. It's too . . . it will annihilate me."

"You're not alone." Palmer is on the rug next to her, strong, warm arms around her. "I'm here with you." She rocks Tara back and forth.

"I want Christie," Tara wails.

"I know you do," Palmer says. "You chose to move on."

"I've changed my mind," Tara says through gulps of air.

"I'll fetch her then." Palmer starts to let go of Tara.

"No!" Tara cries. "No, don't go."

The arms come back around her. Would Christie have held her so? She hopes so. But this woman . . .

"Tell me now, Tara. I'm listening to every word you say."

Tara shakes her head. "It's too dreadful."

"If you say it," Palmer says, "it will lose its power over you."

"No, I can't!"

"Trust me." She holds Tara more tightly, wrapping her as a mother swaddles her infant. "Do you trust me, Tara?"

"Yes," Tara whispers. "I do."

"Then say it."

She is weeping again, openly, unashamedly, her head pressed into Palmer's shoulder. She holds on to Palmer, and she thinks of the swimmer, and she draws strength from both, strength from somewhere inside her.

"The fire," she whispers. "The fire in the kitchen of our farmhouse. I am outside. I smell the smoke; I am running toward the building when I see the first flames crack open the kitchen window.

"Then I am inside, sprinting down the hallway to the kitchen. And there is my father, standing in the flames. I step in, reach out for him."

She is shaking now, her teeth chattering, a sickness running through her like a fever.

"Go on, Tara," Palmer urges. "You reach out for your father and . . ."

"And he takes my hand," Tara says through her sobs. Her body shakes so hard she feels sure she is going to fall to pieces, like a thrown doll. "He takes my hand, and I say, 'Let's go, Dad.' And he looks at me—a weird, piercing look that shatters me. And he says, 'I'm not going anywhere. And neither are you.' I don't understand what he is saying, and yet I pull away, or anyway I try to. But he's too strong. He holds on to me, even drags me toward him.

"'What are you doing?' I say in a dazed kind of way. And with the fire roaring all around us, he says, 'We're staying right here, you and me. Right here in her kitchen.' By now I can barely breathe. My mouth and throat feel scorched. I suppose I swallow smoke. 'You're crazy,' I say. And he shakes his head. He seems oblivious to the flames. 'Don't you understand? Don't you get it? Otherwise, we'll never be free of her. You

399

said it yourself when we stood over her coffin. This is the only way to beat her, the only way to be done with her forever.'

"The flames are running down his arm, onto my hand. I can't look at him a second longer. I feel Sophie rising, then, but I fight her down. Somehow I find the strength inside me to break away. I stumble back. My hand is on fire. Then powerful arms are around me. I'm so out of it I think they are my father's arms, so I fight them. Then I'm picked bodily off the floor and carried backward out of the kitchen, down the hallway, out the front door."

Palmer continues to hold her, reminding her of everything she has lost, and now she is crying for Christie as well as for herself. She holds on to Palmer all the tighter, as she wishes her mother once—just once—had held her, had murmured, *It's going to be all right. The night will end; the whippoorwill will grow still; the owl will return to its nest to feed its young and to keep watch over them.*

But none of that happened, none of that can ever have happened. Not in her household, not with her family. And now her tears come for them—all three of them. Her mother and father locked in their own private hells of abandonment, abuse, masochism, and a sadistic pleasure that is closer to pain than anything else.

But at last, somehow, as with all things human, the storm passes, and with it, the spell is broken. The glass bottle she held in highest esteem broken to bits, its shards glittering, sending bolts of light to pierce the dark glamour that has for years held her captive.

———

"Next week?" Tara says. It is far past her allotted hour, but Palmer hasn't moved, hasn't let her out of her embrace until she is ready.

"I think it might be helpful for us to schedule a session twice a week," Palmer says, datebook in hand. "We need to piece together not only the events you have written but how you felt during those years.

I think this is vital for your understanding of what was done to you." Her pen is poised to write. "What do you think?"

Tara is put in mind of a quote from Omar Khayyam she liked so much she memorized during her studies in Chicago: "The Moving Finger writes; and, having writ / Moves on: nor all thy Piety nor Wit / Shall lure it back to cancel half a Line / Nor all thy Tears wash out a Word of it."

That's what she wants now, more than almost anything. She tries out a smile. It flickers wanly, then brightens. She feels shattered but curiously calm, as if she is a sea creature sloughing off an old, worn-out shell. She takes one more look at the swimmer, for the first time understands her strength, her stamina in the face of the unknown.

"I think that would suit me best," she says.

ACKNOWLEDGMENTS

Thank you to my tireless and brilliant team at Lake Union and, especially, to my editor, friend, and sidekick, Danielle Marshall, who has believed in me from the get-go. Long may she wave.

Words cannot adequately express my love and appreciation for the dearest person in the world to me, my everything, without whom this novel would not have seen the light of day.

ABOUT THE AUTHOR

Leslie Archer is the nom de plume of a *New York Times* bestselling author of more than twenty-five novels.